THE STOLEN CHILDREN
OF WAR

JINA BACARR

Boldwood

First published in Great Britain in 2025 by Boldwood Books Ltd.

Copyright © Jina Bacarr, 2025

Cover Design by Colin Thomas

Cover Images: Colin Thomas and iStock

The moral right of Jina Bacarr to be identified as the author of this work has been asserted in accordance with the Copyright, Designs and Patents Act 1988.

Every effort has been made to obtain the necessary permissions with reference to copyright material, both illustrative and quoted. We apologise for any omissions in this respect and will be pleased to make the appropriate acknowledgements in any future edition.

A CIP catalogue record for this book is available from the British Library.

Paperback ISBN 978-1-83656-867-4

Large Print ISBN 978-1-83656-868-1

Hardback ISBN 978-1-83656-866-7

Trade Paperback ISBN 978-1-80656-054-7

Ebook ISBN 978-1-83656-869-8

Kindle ISBN 978-1-83656-870-4

Audio CD ISBN 978-1-83656-861-2

MP3 CD ISBN 978-1-83656-862-9

Digital audio download ISBN 978-1-83656-864-3

This book is printed on certified sustainable paper. Boldwood Books is dedicated to putting sustainability at the heart of our business. For more information please visit https://www.boldwoodbooks.com/about-us/sustainability/

Boldwood Books Ltd, 23 Bowerdean Street, London, SW6 3TN

www.boldwoodbooks.com

To every brave Resistance fighter who fought the Nazis and for freedom under the big top

PROLOGUE

ROUBAIX, FRANCE, NEAR THE FRENCH-BELGIAN BORDER—MARCH 1943

Circus Richter
Lia

The fat Gestapo man is chasing her. The beautiful circus queen with the white-blonde siren hair. Silver spangled costume.

She trips over her heavy satin cape and falls to her knees, ripping her leotard and hitting the ground hard. Her face scrunches up with pain. She struggles to pull herself up. She can't. She tries again, stumbles forward with a look of desperation on her face, as if she knows her fate but she won't give in even though the Gestapo agent is in fast pursuit...

'Damn it, this isn't happening to me,' she whispers. 'I'm the Queen of the Air.' She struggles to breathe but the secret policeman grabs her, planks his corpulent bulk astride her, his rough hand pushing her face into the moist earth.

'*Argh*...' She gags, choking when he wraps a leather strap tight around her neck. Her eyes widen with horror and she can't breathe. Sawdust and bits of straw from bales of hay swirl around her, flying up her nostrils, getting in her eyes, her hair.

'Where is she, Fräulein?' the Gestapo agent demands.

'Get off me... you beast.'

'You French whore... You're no match for me.'

'You disgust me.' She barely coughs out the words, pulling at the strap cutting off her air. Fear tightens the skin around her eyes, squinting to see her attacker, but she can't.

He yanks on her hair, lifting up her face. She's gasping for air and there's no mistaking his intentions. She has seconds left before she passes out and ends up cuffed and helpless, but she won't give up.

'Tell me where the Jew is *now*, Fräulein, or I shall pull the strap so tight your eyes will explode in your skull.'

'I don't know... what... you're talking about.' She spits out the words, her cheeks wet with a light drizzle, her eyelashes soaked, forcing her eyes shut. She puts her hand to her face. She can't see. She gasps with fear.

'Stop lying. You're a member of the Underground, and you know what we do to your kind.'

'Me? I risk my life for no one, monsieur,' she sputters when he loosens the strap around her neck, hoping she'll talk.

'You can't escape the Gestapo. I shall ask you again and this time you *will* answer.' He reaches underneath her cape and squeezes her breast, making her yell out with pain.

'You *pervert*,' she sputters. 'I saw you watching me coming down the rope after my trapeze act. You couldn't take your beady eyes off me.'

'You're a beautiful woman, Fräulein, but you made a big mistake when you took on the Gestapo with your silly games, swinging your cape in my face.'

He touches his cheek, a red welt appearing on his ruddy skin.

'How did I know you weren't a lion when you jumped me?' She finds her voice, the strap around her neck loose... for the moment.

'I will arrest you if you don't give me what I want.'

The Gestapo agent keeps his hold on the girl. He makes guttural noises in a raspy voice. Grunts. His black trench coat is pulled too tight with a thick belt. Big buttons. Fedora.

'You're from Berlin, monsieur, *n'est-ce pas*?' the girl blurts out, trying to stall.

He smirks, curious. 'How did you know?'

'Your accent. Clipped, harsh.' She spits on the ground to clear the dirt out of her throat. 'Like you.'

Her attitude angers him. 'You're trying my patience, Fräulein.' He huffs and puffs and pulls on the strap around her throat, making her eyes bug out, and then loosens it, not enough to let her go, enjoying his game of torture. She grabs her throat and takes advantage of the moment, twisting her head around and staring him down.

'What are you doing here?' she blurts out. 'Hunting for rabbits?'

'No... Jews.'

'You won't find any Jews here, monsieur. They escaped over the French-Belgian border.'

'You mean what "used to be" the border, Fräulein. We own everything now... including you.'

'You and your Nazi thugs will *never* own me.'

'We'll see how brave you are when you're deported to a labor camp and dumped into the lap of a depraved SS guard, hungry for female company.'

'You can't deport me, I'm the star of the show. Besides, what would the Führer say?' she dares him. 'He loves circuses.'

'He hates Jews more. You're a fool, Fräulein. Esther Fehler is an enemy of the Reich, aiding Jews with forged papers. Unfortunately for you, an informant gave you up, that you're hiding her... *and* her children.'

'Who?' she asks, looking for a rock, *something* to strike back at him with.

'That's my concern. Now, shall we continue our little game at police head-quarters... or end it here?'

'It's got to be Nadia... That bitch is jealous of me because I'm the headliner on the trapeze. And you fell for her lies, monsieur. *You're* the fool.'

He slaps the girl. Hard. She cries out, puts her hand on her hot cheek. 'Coward,' she whispers under her breath.

'Why are you protecting this Jewish woman? She can't mean anything to you.'

'I'm not. I don't care what happens to her *or* her children.'

'I don't believe you. You're not the first member of the Resistance I've tortured who's skilled in deception. You're all the same... protesting you know nothing while enduring excruciating manipulation of the human spine or broken bones or searing fire on your skin.'

'You know nothing about circus people, monsieur; that we endure intense, grueling pain every day under the big top, working our bodies to the maximum to perform our act.' She lifts her head, her cheeks wet with drizzling rain. 'You can't kill us, monsieur, we're too tough.'

'No? Watch me, Fräulein.' The Gestapo man pulls the rope tighter. Numbness overcomes her; painful gasps erupt from her throat. She can't speak, but you can see it in her eyes; she knows she's going to die.

He laughs. Raucous, insane laughter that makes her shiver uncontrollably.

She claws at the cold, hard ground. Her nails crack, her spangled costume rips. She struggles, strains to keep alive. Her breasts heaving up and down, her lips turning blue under her clown-red lipstick. She won't give up.

'For the last time, Fräulein, where is Esther Fehler?'

'*Damn you* and your Reich. Whatever you do to me, I can't... I *won't* tell you anything.'

The Gestapo man curses, then pulls on the leather strap around her neck and squeezes it tight.

'Then go to hell.'

PART I

ONCE UPON A CIRCUS...

1

PARIS, FRANCE—2007

Le Cirque Casini
Lia

'I am appalled the director put that scene in the film. No one could escape from the Gestapo squeezing a leather strap around their neck... and wearing silver spangles yet,' I quip when the lights go on under the big top. I cringe when the technician freezes that moment on the big screen rising twenty meters high behind me. Alas, there I am, albeit a younger version of me played by a wonderful British actress, splayed out on the ground like a nearsighted goose with her feathers plucked, the Nazi strangling me.

I clear my throat. I can't let this pass.

'I *did* escape from the worst excuse for a man God ever created on that drizzly, ugly night in 1943,' I explain. 'But it wasn't that dramatic. And Lord knows I didn't give myself away, clamming up and boasting I'd say nothing more. I was at a turning point back then, working in the downtrodden Circus Richter, camped out on the field of an abandoned mill in Roubaix in northern France, more than two-hundred kilometers from Paris, when I was accused of being a member of the Resistance when I wasn't. But my maternal instinct was so strong to save those children, I acted first without thinking about what insanity I was getting myself into. *Why?* I have secrets, *mes amis*, which shall be revealed in time. But for this scene, it's what they call drama.' I smirk. 'There was plenty of that in my life. The scriptwriter didn't need to make up this *merde*, but that's Hollywood for you.'

What propaganda, but the audience is eating it up. Cheers. Whistles. Foot stomping. *For me?* Incredible. I'm an *artiste*, an aerialist, not a cinema star, though I doubled for Sylvie Martone on the trapeze in 1929. Since I know something about the art of filmmaking, I wasn't surprised when the Tinseltown producers pushed me into promoting the film. Which brings me here today. I'm seated in the middle of the sawdust ring, speaking to the crowd gathered here for a special evening to celebrate my life in the circus. The film is titled *Queen of the Flying Trapeze*. Yes, I know it's cheesy and I cringe every time I hear it, but I have no say over what they call it. It's in my contract. The producers insist they know what sells tickets. Why I ever agreed to this overblown spectacle of a hyped-up soap opera on the silver screen about something that happened over sixty-four years ago, I don't know, but here I am, so let's get on with it.

'I feel like a rock star with all this fanfare,' I tell the crowd with a chuckle. 'Of course, I can't sing, I dance a little, but oh, I can fly. Soar and dip like an angel without wings, float in mid-air... pirouette without my feet touching the earth.'

'At your age?' someone yells out. Guffaws, nervous laughter follows.

I shade my eyes from the harsh lights to seek out the impervious heckler. There he is. Smug little twerp in the front row press box with what the Americans call a 'buzz cut'. A reporter no less. I'll show him.

'I see that skeptical look on your face and that squint in your eye, monsieur. You don't believe me, yet you're curious. You read the press kit and that enticed you to come here today. *Get a look at the old broad,* I hear you saying to your colleagues. *See how she's held up.*' I grin. 'I assure you what I said is true. My memory is exceptional, nourished by a lifetime of keeping my moving parts moving, allowing me to tell you a story I never told, all of us gathered here under the big top, not to just celebrate my one hundredth birthday, but my clandestine life in the circus during the war. Yes, *that* war. Black and white and Nazi red all over. I still marvel at how we circus folk survived the years of insanity after the damn Boches strapped on their jackboots and marched across Europe, clawing and grabbing up countries and destroying lives. Circus lives, if you were Jewish. We must never forget, so I'm tossing it out there. Ask me anything. I'm here for you.'

'They had circuses during the war?' someone asks, in a decent manner, thank you.

'Yes. When the Nazis Aryanized businesses after Hitler came to power in 1933, we circus folk performing in Germany went about earning our daily *brot*. "It doesn't involve us," we said and shrugged. We were golden, untouchable, because Hitler loved the circus. Even Goebbels gave us his stamp of approval. We had carte blanche to travel from town to town, cross borders with hard-to-get transit permits signed by snickering Nazi officials. We thought we were out of the reach of the long arm of the Third Reich. We weren't. And that's why I'm here today, seated on a royal-blue velvet chair on a varnished black platform decorated with fancy chinoiserie that we used for a magic act, speaking before a full house. What we call a straw house because there's nowhere left to sit but on bales of hay.' I point to the reporter with the attitude. 'Stick that up your—'

I catch myself before I go completely off script. The truth is, I'm amazed at the reception I've received when news went out about a special screening of the film. Cameras. Microphone clipped to my bosom. A queue around the main show tent all day, everyone waiting to get in, then sitting still in their seats. Anxious for me to speak. I suppose you're going to get a few heckling reporters eager to stand out. They don't bother me. If I can put up with disgusting, porcupine Nazi officers gawking at me and yelling lewd comments, I can take on baby-faced reporters. I let out a sigh. Whoever would have thought that skinny little girl doing tricks on galloping ponies would end up here in the famous Cirque Casini in Paris? A traveling circus that traces its roots back to the first equestrian show during the time of Louis XV and the court of Versailles. A first class operation in every way from the high caliber of the performers to the stalls swept clean after every show. I wasn't always so fortunate to work under the big top in such a prestigious venue. My work for the Resistance began far away from Paris near the French-Belgian border in that fleabag operation you saw in the scene from the film known as Circus Richter and, as I mentioned, where I encountered the Gestapo man. Though my circus life started way before that.

'I first came to the circus in 1920 during the glory years,' I continue. 'I was thirteen. Vaulting onto a pony, racing around the ring in a circle and doing tricks.'

I lean forward, a twinkle in my eye, alerting the audience I'm about to reveal a secret. Well, kind of. But I love the anticipation it creates. Like when they shine the spotlight on me when I ascend the rope ladder and 'miss a step and save myself' from falling. 'Do you know *why* we ride around in a circle?'

'So you don't get lost?' comes another sarcastic remark from that reporter.

Trying to take my spotlight? I'll show you.

'So we can take potshots at smart-aleck reporters,' I say, losing my patience. I muster up my courage and mimic a slingshot going off in his direction. 'I never miss.'

The audience loves it. More cheers, laughter. Not what I call professional on my part, but he had it coming. I calm down and explain to the audience the science behind trick riding and pray it's not too boring, how the centrifugal force generated going around in circles in a ring thirteen meters in diameter helped me keep my balance on the back of a horse at full gallop. I loved riding bareback, standing tall even at that young age, jumping through a hoop and doing somersaults. I felt like somebody, that I belonged and people liked me. Something I lost when my mother left us. Papa and me. That's not in the film, but it should be.

I take a moment to enjoy my reverie after putting the reporter in the hot seat. Not bad for 'this old broad', but it's easy for me to be brave when you know the only punishment you'll receive is a bad review and not a trip to a transit camp outside Paris like Drancy... and then the worst possible horror a human being can endure, in a camp like Auschwitz or Ravensbrück. Not just certain death, but the inhumane conditions and disgusting medical experiments the Nazis performed on women.

'How did I make it through those times? Why did I survive? *Why me?* I often ask myself. I'm just a circus queen... an old circus queen, I admit, but maybe that's what makes me strong. I never admitted I couldn't do something. I believed in myself and the brave Resistance fighters I teamed up with.

'And we did it. We saved those children.

'After the war, we—me along with the British and American war departments—came up with a confirmed list of sixty-seven children I saved from the Nazis. There could be more since many survivors chose never to speak about the war. Children stolen from their families, their parents sent to their deaths. I know there are other great humanitarians who did much more than I did to save the children, but they say God gives us only what we can handle. I believe that, because I wasn't perfect and I made mistakes. I was brave on the trapeze, sure—it was my life since I was a young girl—but I kept my head down when the Germans first came, just trying to survive. I had such upheaval in my life growing up, a poor excuse, but I lived in fear of being discarded like a broken wheel since I was a small child if I couldn't prove my worth. I came up the hard way with a drunk for a father, a mother who left me, trying anything I could to find my place in the circus. My papa was Roma and a horse trader. I get my blonde hair—*toujours* blonde, no snickering, please—from my mother, an English beauty I knew for too short of a time. I remember her riding a shiny bay mare and smiling at me. I adored her. Then one day she was gone. I was eight.'

I pause. Enough said. That part of my life isn't important here.

'All you need to know is I ended up in the circus, thanks to my papa's strong affinity for liquor,' I say in a firm voice. '*Odd*, you say. Not when you know the facts. He paid no attention to me after Maman was gone, leaving me free to find my playground in the horse corral, riding ponies bareback in the ring under the guidance of an ex-circus man with a Russian accent and stories about the Romanov girls and their ponies that made my head spin and my passion soar to ride like a princess. I found a loving home here in the circus, a place of refuge for people—not just unloved little girls, but people who'd been persecuted because of their religion, race, or disabilities. I learned how to survive in a world that didn't want us by putting my talent to work on the trapeze. By the time I was sixteen, I was an experienced aerialist performing double somer-saults, then the double with the half-twist and pirouettes back to the bar.

'I did my act on the trapeze twice a day, *anywhere* I could. I performed with circuses from Lyon to Marseilles to Berne to Rome and then back up the boot to Berlin.'

I take a beat, wondering if they're ready for my scandalous story about the time I performed for Hitler. Why not?

'I had my share of run-ins with the Nazis, including meeting the Führer.'

I hear the whispers, the 'shocked' mutterings. I chuckle. 'I knew that would get your attention and I shan't disappoint. Come back with me to 1936 when I was working in the Swope Circus, a "racially *pure*" circus appearing at the Wintergarten theatre in Berlin. I was a seasoned performer and excited to be the featured act on the Roman rings and the trapeze. I was quite the stunner back then, standing taller than most aerialists on the platform affixed to the ceiling of the big top, which made me appear like an Amazon high up on the perch, arching my left foot and pointing my toe. I had gold-blonde hair, slim body, strong arms and green eyes. I've been told by one admirer, who had a way with words, that they shone like "two emeralds, wet with dew under the lights".

'I shall never forget the evening performance when I caught Hitler's eye in my form-fitting costume covered with red spangles and gold sequins. When I ascended the rope up to the platform, the perverted little man couldn't take his eyes off me. Nobody loved the circus more than Hitler. He was often seen in the front row cheering what he deemed "regular folk" risking their lives to prove their superior athletic abilities. A trait he admired. He loved acts that featured a danger element and I fit the bill high up on the trapeze. With my light hair and green eyes, I passed for an Aryan, so it was no surprise I was *invited* to give a performance for our "special guests".

'I protested, of course, but the ringmaster grabbed me by the arm and spit harsh words into my ear. "You have no choice, Fräulein di Montieri, or there will be consequences. Now get up there and give our leader what he wants."

'I didn't like the sound of that, but the show must go on, even for that madman. I did my act on the rings with as much aplomb as a girl could with this monster staring at my butt as I twirled and twisted, hung upside down, my legs spread wide in a split, breasts heaving, not that he could see much that high up in the big top. But I felt his stare and it chilled me, knowing he held my fate in his hands. If he wasn't pleased with my skills as an *artiste*, or he discovered I'm half Roma, I'd be arrested. Then deported. That hit me hard. The unfairness, the quirk of fate that determines our journey in life and how damned hard it is to make your way in the world, even harder to achieve your bliss if you're a woman. For me, it's flying. How dare he or anyone judge me by my birth father, even if Papa *was* a mean bastard? Strange I can still say this without hating him, but the man is a talented horse-breaker and trainer. I hadn't seen him for years and the last I'd heard he was corralling horses, working at Longchamp racetrack in Paris.

'Something changed in me then. I swore I'd do whatever I could to help anyone caught in that madman's snare, to take a stand against the National Socialist Party. We'd already seen what they were capable of with the Vatican. After Hitler forced the Holy Father to recognize the Reich, the Nazis closed Catholic schools and imprisoned priests; public book burnings followed and, in 1935, they introduced the Nuremburg race laws that reduced anyone with a specific defined Jewish ancestry to noncitizen status.

'None of this was on my mind while I did my act. All I wanted was to get it over with, go back to my quarters, strip off my costume and wash the dried-up sweat off my skin. Pick off the loose spangles stuck in my armpits. You can't be an *artiste* and not wear spangles. Annoying, glowy slivers of silver and gold dripping from my costume that tickle me and end up in the oddest places.

'Then it all went wrong. I descended the rope quicker than usual, the coarse fibers burning my fingers, my palms. I was determined to make my exit without a bow, but my brave resolve disappeared in an instant. I'm embarrassed to say I froze when an official Nazi photographer from the German magazine for girls, *Das Deutsche Mädel*, snapped a picture of me standing in the sawdust ring flanked by the Führer and Goebbels on either side. Later I found out he also shot photos of me on the rings. I was scared. Really scared.

'What could I do? What would you do? Think about it.'

I let that thought sink into their heads, then I lay this on them. 'I remember how angry I got when a hard squeeze on my buttocks made my eyes pop open wide as the photographer snapped the photo. I don't know who pinched me; I shudder to think it was the little man himself, but it shocked me back to reality. I choked up and fumbled words of protest until Goebbels whispered in my ear, "Be careful, Fräulein, or you shall be the new attraction at Salon Kitty." I shut up damn quick. No way was I going to be fodder for the Berlin brothel catering to high-ranking Party members and SS officers.'

I smile now, but for a long time afterward I groveled with my cowardice, convincing myself the only way to redeem my actions was to work behind the scenes. Rally with others against a political party that pushed women out of the workforce and reduced them to baby-making factories. I didn't find the courage until years later when I met a remarkable Jewish woman and mother I will never forget.

'Was that the end to my adventure with the Führer?' I tease, shaking my head. 'It got worse. Margit Swope, whose family owned the circus for more than seventy years, wanted to score points with the Führer after her new husband admitted he had a distant Jewish relative. She used me and a too-playful lion to spice up the evening with a grand finale.'

Oohs and aahs.

'Hitler had no taste for the lion act, but Frau Swope knew he had a weakness for a "woman in danger" in the circus so I—'

'You put your head between the lion's jaws?' someone asks with a smirk.

'Would you?' I shoot back.

Laughter.

'I was scared, yes, but I was also determined not to show weakness in front of the Nazi leaders. I entered the big cage in the center of the ring, put one foot on the lion tamer's chair, and struck a pose while the trainer arranged the lion's paw on my left shoulder. I held still for as long as it took for the photographer to poke his head through the bars and snap the picture. Then Hitler jumped up and applauded my "bravery" while the crowd yelled "Heil Hitler" and angered the lion. He—the lion, that is—roared so loud my ears hurt, but when the flash-bulb went off, the big cat lurched forward and struck out toward me with its big paw and ripped my skin...'

I lower my eyes.

I hear heavy breathing... mine. But not another sound under the big tent. Not even a kernel of popcorn popping. They're waiting, guessing what happened, but I'm milking the moment to keep them interested. Then—

'The black and white glossy caught up with me weeks later along with a copy of the magazine. I was shocked to see myself on the cover of *Das Deutsche Mädel* as an "inspiring example of young Aryan womanhood and athletic female prowess". *Me*, Lia di Montieri, posing in the animal cage with the big cat's paw laying on my shoulder. God knows what other phony propaganda they perpetrated with that photo. All I know is that I got three long scratches from the lion on my shoulder that day. The wound was superficial, no muscle or tendon damage. You can barely see the scars on my upper left arm, but I cover them with spangled epaulets.'

I've never revealed *that* in public before. I *am* getting old.

'When I ran across the glossy picture after the war, I decided not to tear it up. I kept it to remind myself that in the end we destroyed him and his Reich. That I'm still here and so are the Jewish and Roma peoples, along with the gay and disabled performers he tried so hard to eradicate. And the children of the circus. It was a strange state of affairs for Jews in Berlin that summer of 1936 with the Nazi Party fooling us into believing things weren't as bad as we'd heard. All the anti-Semitic posters and signs forbidding entrance to Jews were removed from public places because of the Olympic Games. No wonder we didn't see the horror coming. I dismissed their goose-stepping and saluting as a bunch of hooligans. *It wouldn't last.* Foolish of me, *n'est-ce pas?*'

Anguished sighs. Coughs.

'I left the Swope Circus to let my shoulder heal and moved on, much to the displeasure of Frau Swope, but it was getting "too Aryanized" for me. And I didn't like what I was seeing in Germany. The persecution of Jews and Roma was escalating and it frightened me. Afterwards I worked in circuses across Europe, moving about, searching for a place to hang my heart, a place where it wouldn't get banged about like a balloon, blown up and away to the top of the tent. Stuck there all by itself. Alone.

'I rolled along like a Ferris wheel—during the war, we called it the Russian Wheel—reaching great heights in circuses in the Netherlands and Sweden, then spinning downward when jealousy and clashing personalities blindsided me. It was all about survival. My life had its ups and downs—more downs. And romance? Over the years, I had my share of love affairs, but in the end I was left with a lonely heart. I almost got married, but I never met a man I could trust. I had a longing for my own brood, but I accepted the fact I'd never have children. As the war dragged on, I didn't allow myself to get close to my fellow performers. Too dangerous. There could be an informant among them. I kept my distance, but I missed bonding with them. I pushed down any emotions to concentrate on just surviving. I had no real family, no support.'

I let my shoulders slump. I'm tired. It's not easy sitting up straight under the lights. I dare to take a moment to let my age show, closing my eyes as if I'm dozing off. I'm not. I just need to breathe. *In... out... in... out.* I'm fine now.

I continue.

'Enough of my sentimental flashbacks. We're not here to hear the regrets of an old circus queen who wore too many spangles. I've invited you here today into my world of circus *because* of the children we saved during the war and how I found myself caught up in the Resistance. How a trapeze artist used the spotlight to keep alive and fool the Nazis, as well as the odd twist of fate that gave me back a mother's greatest gift.

'I reacted to the Nazi Occupation by keeping my head down. It wasn't until 1943 I faced my fears and joined the Resistance, thanks to a very brave Jewish woman... and her son and daughter. I will always have a special place in my heart for Esther Fehler's children referenced in the movie clip you saw. You'll understand why as I continue with my story.'

Then again, how I got here is a tale both sad and intriguing, but what's important to me is setting the record straight about what happened during the war even if I have to put up with all this nonsense.

Still, it's been a homecoming I never thought I'd see. A chance to revisit those times at Le Cirque Casini, a place of fantasy and magic filled with heart, especially for a child who had nothing but her loneliness for company and a talent for trick riding. We circus people live in a dreamworld of the impossible, the glow and glitter of the spotlight, perfect timing and bigger than life spectacle. Where did the years go? But the minute I smell the greasy popcorn and dip my toe into the loose sawdust, dusting my soft ballet slippers, my mind leaves my body and I land back in 1943.

The crowd settles. I continue.

'I shall begin with that unforgettable springtime in 1943 when I was performing on the trapeze at Circus Richter, a traveling tent circus set up as I mentioned along the French-Belgian border. Nothing like Le Cirque Casini, which was far more of a glamorous sort of super-circus. That was a tumultuous time when I had that famous run-in with the Gestapo officer you saw on the big screen and I ended up back here in Paris.' I calm down, speaking to the crowd in a low husky voice. 'Le Cirque Casini was the last place I wanted to be. I swore never to return here after enduring a long, heartbreaking journey when I left Paris in 1925. For those of you who can't do the math'—I glare at the impertinent reporter—'I was a heartbroken girl of eighteen back then, in a torn spangled costume, with no future and a scandal riding on my back that left me childless.'

I leave out the part about the man who changed the course of my life, an extraordinary circus performer who captured my soul high up under the big top when he stole my heart then broke it, leaving me no choice but to run away from the pain on that rainy night. Alone. We had words; he said he loved me, but I could see there was no future for us. Life had dealt me a winning hand when I met him, a glorious romance with a bittersweet ending neither of us could control. I had to leave or both our careers would have been ruined. It was the last time I let a man make me cry. I choke back the emotion that hits me. I haven't spoken about him in years, pushed that time so far to the back of my mind, I thought I was done with it. I guess I'm not. The worst part is, I shall have to face it here with these folks, strangers, because I meet up with him again in my story.

All of a sudden, my emotions take over and I'm close to tears, remembering that grueling part of my youth when I ran as far away as I could from the Paris circus after I lost my baby, but I go on with as much bravado as I can muster seeing how promoting a film and speaking about myself is new to me.

'Over the next few years, I worked on the continent in one circus after another, making a name for myself with the only thing I had left... my skills as a bareback rider and an aerialist. I worked hard for years to combat the idea that a girl in a trapeze act was there merely to help the male aerialist, a pretty ribbon to tie up the act and give it glamor. I did that all right, used whatever feminine allure I had to grab the spotlight, to prove I'm just as good as the men. I played the Wintergarten in Berlin and La Scala where I performed death-defying trick riding—something which came in handy later—Circus Krone in Munich, and the famed Swope Circus.

'It wasn't all glamorous. By 1941, life as we'd known it became dangerous and frightening. A creeping horror known as the National Socialist Party swept over the small towns in Eastern Europe where we set up our tents. Then a funny-looking man proclaimed himself the Führer. I saw what that madman did to Jewish people and Roma, the heart of circus people. We learned real fast to keep our heads down, change our names, to dye our hair, and we got fake passports. And it worked. We became a refuge for the unwanted. The hunted. The Nazis became so bedazzled by the shows we put on night after night in town after town, they had no idea we were working against them behind their backs. Hiding Jews. Helping downed airmen get back home. Saving children.'

I pause to get my breath. Not a sound from the crowd. 'I came in contact with a small Resistance cell. I did what I could to help them, like keeping Jewish performers from discovery by the Nazis. My cover was my act in a traveling circus. We each did our part. Dutch, Belgian, even German. And French.

'Each time I took more and more risks high up under the big top, thrilling the audience with dangerous tricks. Then one day, I found myself back in Paris. It was 1943 when the skies darkened overhead with Allied bombers, the drone of their engines giving us hope that freedom from Nazi rule was imminent and my work in the Underground became more important than ever. When I wasn't flying through the air, I fought hard against the Nazis.'

'C'mon, you fought the Nazis?' that same reporter tosses out.

'Yes, *me*.' I hear that irritation in my voice again. I've kept my story to myself for so long, I don't know how to answer these questions. Most come from young reporters too green to know any better. I huff out a breath, remember I'm a pro and continue. 'I wasn't an under-the-cover-of-darkness saboteur blowing up trains, or a courier stuffing secret messages in my garters. Quite the opposite. I fought the Boches by being *in* the spotlight. Risking my life more than eighteen meters high up under the big top, twice a day, my costume dripping with hand-sewn sequins sparkling like tiny stars under the lights. Inviting every eye to watch me swing from bar to bar... and then let go. *Whoosh*.'

I make the sound of flying and they laugh. *Bon*. No sarcastic remarks, giving me the courage to keep talking.

'I flew across the big top at breakneck speed, as fast as a hundred kilometers an hour with the wind in my face before the catcher grabbed me around the forearms, then slid down to my wrists to get a firm grip on me.'

'Your wrists, madame?'

'Yes, *wrists*.'

'Why is that?' someone asks, sincerity in their voice.

I smile. 'If he seized me by the fingers, he couldn't hold on to me. A faulty grip spelled more than a mishap for me; it could mean death. My timing had to be perfect. And not too early. If my timing was bad or my swing across the big top too short, the catcher would miss grabbing me and I'd plunge straight down toward the ground so fast I'd leave a trail of sequin stardust behind me. If I *did* fall, I'd fall backward, crashing into the safety net, the metal framework rattling and creaking, my body bouncing up and down like a sparkly rubber ball. If I landed wrong, I could break my back.'

Gasps. Whispers.

'I saw it happen in 1934 in a circus in Munich when a trapeze artist got seriously injured when the flybar broke and he fell into the net. He fractured his left arm, suffered broken ribs and deep body bruises. I saw it again in 1941. That time, the girl died.'

'What does this have to do with fighting Nazis?' that snippy reporter calls out, digging his hand into a large paper cone of hot popcorn embossed with the Cirque Casini logo: a pretty blonde aerialist on a swing and a bald, old clown in whiteface. Seeing it again after all these years makes me smile. That girl is me and the clown with the deep wrinkles framing his smile like roads taken is Socks, a funny gentleman so close to my heart, even now I hear him laughing.

So get your spangles on, Lia, and let's tell these people the story you never told.

It's good to have you back in my life, old friend, even if you're only in my mind.

My pretty Lia, we had it all, n'est-ce pas? Socks loved to say. *The stars to make a stairway to the moon where no one could touch us. Until* they *came.*

God, he hated the Nazis... but that's a story for another day. For now, he'd encourage me to keep going and "leave nothing out, Lia, no matter how much it hurts. The world must know what happened here".

A slight dizziness threatens to derail me. I wish my circus family was here with me. Socks. Ugo and Pat. Zera, Wanda. Monsieur Rémon. Elsa. And of course, Josephine and Bébé—*maman* elephant and her calf. God, I miss them. Then, as if there's still magic in the old prop piece I'm sitting on—a pretty girl would disappear then reappear in the big box next to me—I feel a tremor zing through me, like I'm not alone sitting up here on the platform. I have the feeling others will appear, too. I'd give anything to see my love again... feel his arms around me. His voice low and gravelly, telling me he'd protect me, and then me shooting back I was doing fine on my own. I wasn't, and it took me a long time to trust him... He wasn't part of the circus family, but we're not there in the story so it will have to wait.

I fidget with the red sequins on my high-collared, white satin cape. I pray the audience stays with me. What worries me is, I'm talking about an era that doesn't exist anymore. No cellphones. Television, computers. We used good old-fashioned legwork to get out our message of resistance. We printed out political tracts on Roneo machines, left the stacks of news sheets on park benches in the nearby village, and hid them in the folds of the circus program to fight the occupiers.

'Le Cirque Casini was set up here in 1943 in the suburbs of Paris and remained here until the Liberation under order of the Reich. There were some rough years after that recovering from the Nazi Occupation and the turmoil, which you'll see later. The good thing that came out of it was that Le Cirque Casini had gained an audience and people came to see us from the city even though we operated out of a threadbare tent with holes in it. So the decision was made to set up here permanently. Of course, we weren't so fortunate back then to have this modernized tent with all its gizmos, strobe lighting, climate control temperature, and fancy seats. We had little heating, no air conditioning —the temperature high up in the tent on the trapeze was stifling on hot days— and outhouses for the performers and circus goers that smelled like animal cages.'

Groans. Gasps. Oh, my. What worries me is, will this group and their texting thumbs embrace such a different time? I must figure out how to bring them in closer to me, like a *maman* lion folding her big paws around her cubs, playful and cuddling them close to her heart where it's warm and secure.

I'm about to find out. Here I go.

* **

'I loved the cheers, the adulation. My name high up on the bill. I thought the ride would never end. Foolish, of course, but I worked hard and before I was twenty, I was a headliner doing two-and-a-half somersaults.'

Showing off, are you?

A little.

Bien, *Lia, but aren't you forgetting you're not the only drawing card here? The film is called Queen of the Flying Trapeze, but there's another side to this story, remember?*

I sigh. The producers will have my hide if I don't talk about what sells tickets. Murder. Jealousy. Intrigue. 'True Crime', I think they call it. I heave out a big gulp of air. I can't ignore the ugly part of my story, not with the movie trailer teasing it with the line: *When a serial killer targets circus queens in Nazi-occupied Paris, it's up to a beautiful aerialist to stop him before she becomes his next victim.* I know they're waiting for it.

So, get it over with.

I clear my throat. 'My story takes a strange turn in 1943 when a devious, calculating pervert who operated behind the scenes began murdering young women. At the time, I didn't realize I'd crossed paths with him before the war, this madman who targeted circus performers. But I met up with him again in Paris, a man dubbed "The Magician" by the press because he eluded the police, disappearing without a trace until 1944 when...'

I stop talking, grab my chest. Do I really want to go through with this? Expose my deepest secrets to these strangers? Face my past, a past I never intended revisiting because it hurt too much? Granted, I can't see their faces, but what if they judge me? I did what I had to... to survive.

Silence. They're waiting. I can't, I just can't. Then—

'Please, Mademoiselle di Montieri, go on with your story,' I hear a soft, feminine voice say somewhere in the upper bleachers. 'We want to hear it.'

Something in her voice gives me courage, a friendliness about her that makes me think I know her, but that's impossible. Other voices chime in like a choir of angels, and who am I to turn down a request like that?

'Ah, bon, you shall have it. I will tell you everything I remember about this monster. You'll meet him in this next clip from the film,' I begin in a strong voice. 'We first became aware of The Magician and his reign of terror during that spring of 1943 after the murder of Henriette de la Blanche.

'Henriette was a seasoned high-wire walker who performed in several circuses for more than a decade. She was famous for her evocative dance and elaborate Spanish costumes with rows and rows of ruffles hanging down from the wire.'

I close my eyes tight, but I can't block out the scene they're about to show. I heard what happened to her, but I wasn't *there*. But when we made the film, I wanted to be on set to pay homage to this brave circus queen.

So here we go.

'Sit tight. And please, be aware what you're about to see is horrifying, not just the physical depravity this monster perpetrated on this girl. But the mental torture. Her story still makes my thinning hair curl.'

2

CLIP FROM THE FILM QUEEN OF THE FLYING TRAPEZE

Paris, France—March 1943
The Magician

'Hold the girl tight, Yann, so I may secure her to the chair and go about my business.' The big man grunts his understanding as his boss, a forty-something physician, runs his fingers through his dark, straight-back hair in frustration, the poetic lift of his dark brow arched. Garbed in black like a dashing cavalier, he eyes the girl with disdain as his manservant squeezes her arms with his large hands. 'She must pay for her folly.'

'Let me explain, Monsieur le Docteur,' she blurts out, panicked. '*Please.*'

He slaps her face. She groans. 'I'm past listening to excuses, Mademoiselle de la Blanche. You knew the rules when you came to me for help, *begged* me to make you beautiful again, freeing you of ugly scar tissue and uglier memories, and yet you disobeyed them.' The physician grips the leather strips he holds in his hand, making a fist, his anger on display as he paces up and down the polished marble floors in his *grande maison* in a fashionable arrondisement in Paris. Hidden off the boulevard. Quiet. Safe. No disruptions. 'If you did as the Gestapo ordered as you claim, mademoiselle, I wouldn't have to drag Yann out of the cabaret without finishing his cognac.' He sighs heavily. '*And* pay my manservant extra.'

Yann, a big and burly man, clean-shaven, grunts his approval.

The doctor continues. 'But betraying the Gestapo... I will not tolerate that. My reputation with the secret police is at stake because of your stubbornness as well as my standard of living. Do you know what a good brandy goes for these days? Far more than a poor physician makes laboring in a Nazi hospital. Fortunately, I have filled my coffers to the hilt fulfilling the requests of impudent, vain Nazi officers eager to perpetuate their Aryan myth. Perfect cheekbones. Jutting chins. Straight noses. One SS captain insisted I etch out a dueling scar on his left cheek as a badge of Prussian honor to impress pretty Parisians. Poured wine into the crevice himself when I wasn't looking to make it more "realistic looking" after criticizing my skills as a plastic surgeon. And then *you* failed me, getting yourself on the Gestapo blacklist, mademoiselle, leaving me no choice but to bring you here. For I cannot allow you to fall into the hands of the secret police. They have no finesse, no respect for a man's talent, and will destroy your beauty I worked so hard to restore to further their own stupid medical experiments. I cannot allow that to happen. *Cannot*, do you hear?'

The girl leans forward. 'What you asked of me is unholy, monsieur, sending innocents to their death.'

'Jews are not innocent, mademoiselle. But that's not my problem. *You* are.'

He circles the girl to get a better view. She, in turn, regards him. The paleness of his skin belies the fiery dynamic of his persona, his padded, square shoulders, strong jaw. But it's his eyes that hold the woman in a trance. She stares into his black pools of perpetual movement, nearly paralyzing her when the manservant holds her down in the sturdy cane chair. Outside, a storm rages and heavy rain beats on the windowpane, clearly pleasing the doctor by the grin on his face.

'Ah, we have the elements in our favor, Yann, adding drama to today's episode in our circus queen adventures.'

Again, the man grunts.

The doctor rubs his fingertips together as he observes his victim with an eagerness that surprises the unfortunate mademoiselle as Yann keeps her arms pinned to her sides. She struggles in Yann's strong grasp, while the doctor relishes her futile attempts to free herself. She resists, but to no avail when the manservant leans down and sniffs the back of her neck, making her shudder uncontrollably.

She screams.

'Cry out if you will,' says the doctor, 'no one can hear you.'

'Keep this creep away from me.'

The doctor pinches her cheeks. 'You must excuse Yann. He's the curious type, sniffing the mesdemoiselles like a hound. But he's harmless.'

'I'm not a piece of meat, monsieur.'

The physician laughs. 'Oh, but you are, mademoiselle... a lovely addition to the ongoing display of my work of beauty that can't be destroyed by the SS.' He giggles. 'However, if you don't quiet down...' He brandishes a scalpel in his hand.

'*No, please!*' the girl cries out, her eyes wild with a fervor that unnerves him, his eyelids fluttering, but only briefly. While he readies his instruments, he hums a tune as the girl squirms in the chair, rocking back and forth. He drops the scalpel, curses.

'Don't fidget, mademoiselle, or I shall be forced to slice open your cheek and that shan't be pleasant for either of us.'

He nods to his manservant.

Without a word, Yann forces her hands, palms down, onto the armrests of the chair so the doctor can tie her to the side arms. The girl arches her back, digging her palms into the armrests, crying out, '*Stop, please!*'

Waiting.

Trembling.

She struggles in Yann's strong grasp, while the doctor relishes her futile attempts to free herself. When he attempts to gag her, she tries to bite him.

He yanks his hand away, shock making his eyes widen, and then anger. He snarls. 'You'll pay for that, mademoiselle.'

He's quick to notice a fine wetness sliding down her cheeks, onto her neck when Yann holds her head up and the doctor gags her with muslin strips, then leans over her, his fingers stroking her skin.

'I regret I must put you through this awkward phase before I kill you, mademoiselle, since I was so proud of my work, renewing your burned skin with pink perfection, but you leave me no choice but to add you to my display of "angel dolls".'

3

PARIS, FRANCE—2007

Le Cirque Casini
Lia

'Oh, God, that scene gives me the creeps.' I shiver. I hear sighs and coughing, heated whispers coming from the audience. I'm not the only one disgusted with the doctor's unnatural obsession to destroy what he created, how it guts out your psyche like nails raked across a blackboard. I clear my throat. Again. It's becoming a habit. 'We were at war in 1943 and not just with the Nazis,' I continue. 'But with this serial killer roaming loose in Paris, murdering beautiful young women in the circus world. We presumed The Magician was a man since women mass murderers numbered few. *Who will be next?* we asked.'

I go silent, curling my fingers up tight, let the audience digest what they saw. I hope I didn't sour their enthusiasm to stay and hear my story. It was the producers' idea to show clips of the film with The Magician, *unleash the beast*, in their words, *grab them by the throat*. I protested against it, insisting the serial killer is but a part of my story. I pray no one walks out, complaining they didn't come here today to see a horror film. Then again, what could be more 'horror-filled' than what happened in Paris and Poland and everywhere else during the war? I lift my chin, determined not to be put back in the box now that I'm here. So if they're too weak-bellied to take it, they can walk out and best be done with them.

I wait for the verdict. Whispers, coughing. Shuffling, but no one leaves. I heave out a sigh of relief. Thank God, but it's not the first time I find myself the object of overzealous promoters. How can I forget I appeared on the playbill cover for the renowned Swope Circus in Berlin in a scanty, see-through costume that wouldn't last two seconds while I did my act? Flying high on the trapeze above a hungry lion, his mouth open wide, waiting for me to 'drop in'.

A moment of mirth, but I have no light moments about the terror I experienced back then with a lion. I'm not ready to tell them *that* part of the story. Meanwhile, I hear someone call out: 'Tell us more about this killer, Mademoiselle di Montieri.'

'Yes, who was he? A Nazi?'

I shake my head. 'I can't, not yet.'

'Okay, but you're gonna have to spill the beans sometime.' That same reporter with the short haircut waves his notebook at me. He reminds me of a tall, skinny toothbrush. He infuriates me, but I won't lose my temper. I simmer, scowl, and fuss with my white satin cape, high collar, red sequins sparkling under the lights—the producers' idea to recreate the 'younger me'—but I say nothing. Someone else does it for me and it's not what I expected.

'Let her be. She's pushing a hundred. That's more than you'll ever get to.'

'You're right,' the reporter says, still munching on his popcorn. 'She can't help it if she's slow.'

'Slow? *Me*, the Queen of the Air?'

That did it. I jump up and walk with pride over to the rude reporter. Déjà vu hits me, reminding me of the Wehrmacht officers who coveted those seats during the war, leering at me and making crude gestures. Why do the dregs of the earth always get the best seats?

'Is that what you think of me?' I grab his popcorn cone and dump it on his head. 'Now be quiet. And no more protesting or I'll feed you to the lions.'

To my surprise, I hear a round of applause, everyone begging me to continue. The audience is enjoying my bit of humor, not knowing I have a history with big cats. I grab the sleeve on my left arm, making sure the three long scars are covered. I still carry that souvenir from a lion when I became a pawn in a Nazi publicity scheme.

I turn and walk back to my seat, sit down, smile big. 'Thank you for your confidence, *mes amis*. Next, allow me to set the scene for you, what we endured under the Nazi regime. Films with a lovely musical score and actresses with pretty, curly hair can never tell the real story. The hunger, the constant fear and hopelessness of this dark world we lived in during the war years and how it worked on our minds... how in 1943, the Germans intensified the suffering and pain they inflicted upon us. The deportations, the killing, the death squads, not to mention the horrific circus queen murders. We were in danger from the killer's evil presence everywhere in the City of Light. We were so vulnerable back then. Life under the Nazis was intolerable and some Parisians were tempted to collaborate, and others... well, they paid the price when they fought against the Nazis. We went about our lives, but with this macabre undercurrent that ran parallel to the everyday peril we faced dealing with the occupiers.

'Then one day it collided with my life and set off a hellfire I almost didn't survive and put in immediate danger those closest to me. My circus family. I had no idea how deeply I'd become involved with solving the mystery of these murders. And the amazing man who risked *his* life to help me. A man so strong of faith in the legal system he lost everything in 1940 and nearly his soul when the occupiers tried to silence him. I also met a beautiful, young aerialist I took under my wing when she lost her ability to fly. And the clowns. One in partic- ular I shall introduce to you very soon.'

I hear your laughter, Socks. You always told me long after the clowns left the ring, their laughter stayed and wrapped around your heart. As yours did around mine, my friend.

I choke up, let the memories rip through me as they do often. For I shall never forget Socks and the tent-man, with the strength of ten, who opened his heart to the pretty girl on the trapeze, a girl who touched me deeply. Changed the course of my life. And the man I loved. Not only did he possess a brilliant mind, but he was so brave he risked it all to save me.

4

PARIS, FRANCE—2007

Le Cirque Casini
Lia

'I will never understand the twisted mind of The Magician. *Never.*' I wipe my face, wet with perspiration, with a tissue. 'He was quite mad, you know, his younger years scarred by trauma and he was a murderer even before he went to university, the sordid details coming out after the war due to good reporting, but that doesn't excuse what he did.'

I'm greeted by silence, then loud whisperings from the audience, as if they're holding back their emotions. Anger, fear? Disgust. Again I question the logic of putting that degenerate in the film. I feel I have to explain *why* I allowed it.

'I only agreed to include The Magician in my story because I believe he's a lost chord in the history of wartime Paris that needs to be played, that these young women who stood up to the occupiers *must* be recognized for their bravery. They were victims of this man, yes, but they were also victims of Nazi tyranny. *Why* they were murdered was a crime against womanhood. You'll also discover what happened to The Magician when the Allies closed in. In great detail, I might add, which includes the exploits of a very brave and honest Resistance fighter who nearly lost his life unmasking the murderer. You shall meet him soon, I promise.' I pause. The audience leans forward, interested. I heave out a sigh. *Bon*. I keep going. 'It pains me to talk about this darker side of the Occupation when so many good people were lost, but I'm proud to say in the end we completed our mission. We saved the lives of many children in the circus.'

Oohs and *aahs* spread over the crowd like a healing wave. I see heads nodding, smiles. Wiping away tears. *This* is what they came for. 'So, you ask, who *is* this woman who lays claim to saving these children? Who *is* Lia di Montieri really? It's easy for me to say I was damned good on the trapeze. That I worked hard, blisters on my hands, every bone in my body aching, my arms hurting so bad I couldn't lift my spoon to eat my soup. Did you know I learned to tuck and somersault three times while swinging from the flybar before I was twenty-one? I did the triple blindfolded before thirty. I imagine you've seen the old photos of me online decked out in spangles—some colorized, God help me —and you think you know me. But pixels don't define me. I will show you something far better than digital dots dancing across the screen. I will prove to you I *earned* the moniker Queen of the Air.'

I reach down into the faded brown leather satchel sitting next to me and pull out... *Voilà!* Newspaper and magazine press clippings. I hold them up high, then flip through them. 'These are circus stories about me that appeared in newspapers in every language across Europe starting from my early days in the 1920s,' I begin, the yellowing and folded creases adding to their preciousness to me. Paper I can touch, hold up to my nostrils and smell the passage of time... and remember those I lost still close to my heart. 'Press clippings I've carried with me for years, wrapped in silk and folded into a circus playbill and hidden in this satchel... even when I was on the run from the Gestapo. *Oh, finally*, you say, *the juicy part*. Have faith, I will get there, but first I want to breathe in the smells of white clown paint and the collective sweat both human and animal clinging to the newspaper fibers. A cacophony of scent you never forget. My life *was* and *is* the circus. During the war years, that included the children. Not just the youngsters whooping it up in the stalls, cheerful, happy. But children in danger. Jewish. Roma. Sinti. The Germans discovered many circuses were run by these talented groups,' I continue. 'I orchestrated the journey to a better life for our most vulnerable. I helped children of circus folk escape, and any child that needed me. A dangerous vocation, but one, I assure you, I became very good at though not at first. Up until then, I'd kept my nose clean but I couldn't ignore what was happening around me. Jewish passports no longer served their owners, having been declared "invalid" that fall, even those performing in the circus.

'I made it my mission to save the children from the Nazis and give them shelter. Nourishment. And a warm hug.

'Here's how it all began. And almost ended when everything went wrong.'

* * *

'I failed in my first attempt to save the children,' I have to admit. My voice cracks, my hand shakes. My pain reaches a threshold when I remember those times, one I keep a lid on, letting it steam and pop, but I never open it. Today I have to. This audience *must* understand luck cuts both ways. Good and bad.

Chattering from the audience... They're getting restless. I raise my hand for silence. 'There were missteps along the way, including one I regret most deeply.' This is hard for me, a sobering moment I have to face, even if my heart is beating so fast I feel lightheaded. 'I was traveling through Poland in 1940 when a sympathetic social worker helped me get Jewish twin sisters out of the Warsaw ghetto. I smuggled the twelve-year-olds into the circus, hid them in my tent, but they wandered away during my act. The SS found them in the menagerie tent running after a mischievous monkey scampering around with one of the twin's sweaters with the yellow star still attached. The SS scooped the girls up. I don't know their fate, but I can guess. Dachau. I never forgave myself... *never*. I learned a valuable lesson that day. Hide the children in plain sight.' I feel nauseous. I try to conceal my bout of indigestion behind my hands, desperate to keep from throwing up what I ate earlier. 'You must excuse me, I need a moment. Remembering the Nazis dragging away the twins in braids and green corduroy jumpers that day killed my soul. I still haven't forgiven myself.'

I frown... No, it's more of a grimace like a clown makes when he's sad and paints teardrops on his cheeks with a pointy brush. I want to stop right here, go home to my little cottage near Marly le Roi nestled in the forest, cozy up before the fire in warm slippers and drink lemon tea and eat raspberry tartes, but I feel compelled to help these lovely people understand how I found the courage not to give up after such a devastating experience.

'I never thought I could ever make a difference in the war, but someone else did.' I force a smile, and it becomes easier to let go as I speak. 'A Swiss-German ex-sailor. A big man with a beard and a hearty laugh, Gunther Hein was a man of the world who somehow found his way onto land and into the circus. An ex-navy cook that I salute from the platform in my heart before every performance. He saw something in me I didn't.'

I pause.

'I shied away from trying any more "rescues", believing I was a failure, but Gunther—I called him "Gunty"—tried to convince me otherwise. I'd wander into the cookhouse, gathering potato peelings and scraps to feed the animals when I'd sit down, grab a paring knife, and help him with the spuds. He talked, I listened, how he lost shipmates and the guilt he suffered afterward, how he knew I was suffering, too. I trusted him so I told him I'd lost faith in myself. It took hours of talking, but I was so heartbroken losing the twins, I went even deeper into myself. Later I realized he saw in me what I didn't see in myself: that I had the markings of a good Resistance fighter, like how I observe the slightest thing about a performer, know when they're off, when they're hiding something, that I'm willing to try anything on the trapeze or the rings, even if it's dangerous to make the act better, stronger. He called me his "angel without wings". And how I care deeply about the animals, and everyone in the troupe, from the lion trainer with the flashing teeth to the saddest clown trapped behind a big smile. I didn't know it then, but he gave me back my courage when I needed it.

'I will never forget him. I will also never forget a young Nazi lieutenant, Lieutenant Horst von Ernst, who didn't fit the mode of a Party member, still a boy when he moved up the ranks in the Wehrmacht, but he taught me on a train ride where innocent lives were lost that human emotion to keep family close to us burns hot on both sides.'

I lean back in the wingback blue velvet chair, holding my chest. It hurts. Panic, but I can't help it. I swear I shall burst into tears if I don't move on. That's what I told myself then and I shall do so now. That doesn't make it easier. Finally, I say, 'I will continue with the story I never tell... Yes, the facts are up there on the screen, but these are the behind-the-scene moments you *won't* see in the film.'

* * *

'I was at a crossroads, when Hitler advanced his plan for world domination in September 1939 and started gobbling up large chunks of continental Europe.

Life in a traveling circus under Nazi control presented new challenges because I had to curtail any help I gave to saving children, keep my head down. We were dealing with a new reality. Everyone was suffering... Hunger, cold winters with no coal, and if you were Jewish or in the fight to oust the Boches, the dread of waiting for that "knock on the door" at 4 a.m. never left you. Arrest. Then held at Drancy or another transit camp. Finally, deportation to a concentration camp. So we hid those at high risk among us. Jewish circus performers, Roma and Sinti too, giving them new names, sorting them with false passports. A small victory, so even if the Boches *thought* they'd won, thought they controlled us, they didn't. We never gave up. Me and every performer under the big top.

'When the Germans took Czechoslovakia and then marched into Poland, we intensified our fight, even more so after they forced the French to sign the armistice in the Forest of Compiègne in June 1940. We circus people were determined to run the Nazis out of France. Belgium. Poland. Everywhere they hung that infernal red and black swastika flag. God help me, it pains me to think about what a state of turmoil we lived in. I thought life was hard growing up in a caravan wagon with a papa drowning his sorrows in whiskey, a man too quick to use the crop, not just on the stallions he trained but on me. It started soon after Maman left us. My childhood taken from me. Left alone shivering under a dirty, old horse blanket and crying from the pain, not just the welts on my back but the emptiness in my heart. It still hurts today, so when I saw what was happening to circus children whose parents were Jewish or Roma, I couldn't stand by and *not* help them.

'Young, innocent children. Scared. Alone. Their *mères* depending on me to keep them safe. But then you knew that.

'That's why you're here. To find out how a trapeze *artiste* got involved with the Resistance. I shall begin my story on the day when my life took an amazing turn. It was March 1943, the beginning of the season for Circus Richter, as I've said before, a traveling tent circus based in the Netherlands. I was a headliner and a member of The Flying Zollos. Two men, two women. Brought together by circumstance. And war. Two Jews, a Swede, and me. Jean-Pierre and his sister Aima were French Jews with forged passports and new names, our catcher Sven hailed from neutral Sweden, but hated the Nazis as much as we did. He was in love with Aima and worried about her being deported. We all had our reasons for joining Circus Richter. Herr Richter didn't ask questions. And he didn't look too closely at our papers. Especially when The Flying Zollos claimed to be of

Mediterranean origin; we said we were cousins, and we barely spoke Italian. I called myself "Gaia Zollo", dyed my hair a white siren blonde and with my natural green eyes, I worked in the circus as an Aryan.

'Mesdames and messieurs.' I push myself up from the blue velvet chair to stand tall, my arms still strong though not as muscular as the old days, and in the big voice of the ringmaster, I shout, 'Step right up, ladies and gents, members of the press. It's showtime! Hold on to your seats for you're about to witness a day in the life of a circus queen back in 1943 when I outwitted the Gestapo... and that photo of Hitler and me saved my life.'

PART II

THE GREAT ESCAPE

5

ROUBAIX, FRANCE—MARCH 1943

Circus Richter

Lia

I've been had. That good-looking Nazi officer in the front row hasn't taken his eyes off me since I entered the ring and made my way up the rope to the platform. He showed up at the matinee yesterday and now he's back. Filming the acts with his camera. Not the first German soldier I've seen in full tourist mode. But he's the first one who's wasted more film on me than the whole circus. What does he want? I smirk. What do they all want? I'm used to it, but I don't like it. The Nazis always have an agenda and it usually involves a dirty deed where someone gets hurt. I'll keep my eye on him.

I return to the perch after executing a double somersault and wipe the sweat off my face. I'm breathing hard and the chalk covering my hands is caked in the creases of my palms. I'm a mess and I don't need one of Hitler's boys undressing me with his eyes. I need a hot bath and flaxseed oil to quell the pain in my shoulder, a remedy I picked up from a Persian fire eater. That last trick was agonizing, my left shoulder aching like I'd torn the flesh off the bone. I'm sore from attempting to do the one-arm *plange* at practice, flipping my body over in a one-arm swing-over several times. I'm not adding it to my act, even if Herr Richter begs me. I'm not built to withstand dislocating my shoulder numerous times at each performance. Spinning in mid-air like a propeller going round and round on an RAF bomber. An amusing thought that makes me smile, a visual cue I would enjoy showing off to our 'guests' seated in the front row. Two Nazi Wehrmacht officers, including the one with the swivel head and the camera. Four tiny swastika flags—like the ones flying in the breeze on their Mercedes touring cars—stand up in a bale of hay sitting at the edge of the ring, marking the area reserved for the Boches.

We've had more than our share of battle-weary officers returning from the Eastern Front causing havoc, boasting about how they're going to take Paris by her panties—their words, not mine—and show the pretty French girls a good time. The lieutenant has already started.

With me.

I wave to the crowd, bracing myself for the crude gestures from the boys in the front row. Even from up here on the perch, I can smell the Nazis. Beer, sweat, and sweet popcorn like they eat in Germany. Herr Richter's idea to entice the German officers to come back and bring their friends, like schoolboys reliving their childhood circus memories. Instead they remind me of bugs in beetle-green uniforms stuck in a glass jar like dried-up honey, their eyes glued on every female performer. Glances up and down my body like I'm wearing nothing but a sheer leotard, his officer's baton rubbing against his thigh. Curling, wet lips.

I'm not impressed. I've watched these Teutonic warriors evolve since the early days of Hitler's brownshirts. It's like they're all carved from the same piece of wood. The lieutenant can't be more than in his early twenties with that noble but arrogant walk these German officers execute so well. Toy soldier stiffness. Privileged. Spoiled. Staring at me with clear blue eyes. I swear he's eyeing me like I'm a carnival prize. It's well known the Germans enjoy flaunting their victory over innocents, but I'm not a vulnerable young girl. I'm a grown woman and I'm not stupid enough to be swept off my feet by his good looks. I assume he's fallen under the siren spell of the circus-queen myth and thinks me uneducated and ready to succumb his Aryan charm.

Surprise, *mein lieber Freund*, my dear friend, I know your game and I'm in no mood to play. I'm in too much pain with a busted shoulder. I wave and blow kisses to them. I'm not pleased with this kind of attention. With more deportations every day, I can't let them suspect I'm anything but an *artiste*. No one here knows I'm half Roma, but that wouldn't stop an informant accusing me of something I didn't do. With the Gestapo, you're guilty first, then you have to prove you're not, especially now that the Resistance is organizing; everyone is suspect. Rumors circulating through the circus grapevine... the clowns... say that my old friend Gunty is in these parts working for a cell. Which is why I turned around sharply when I heard a muffled grunt and a familiar voice call me out yesterday when I was rushing through clown alley. When I spun around, no one was there, but it was him. I know why he's here. Seeking me out to join the fight. I can't. That would jeopardize my work under the big top and the performers I work with. It's taken me years to make my way into a low-budget circus and find the right flyers to work with. They trust me, and *I* trust them. Give this up? What if I fail? I can never make that fatal mistake again that cost two young Jewish twin girls from the Warsaw ghetto their lives.

Will God ever forgive me?

I haven't. A rush of heartbreaking memories hits me hard. Neatly plaited braids. Green jumpers. Screaming, terror in their eyes. I carry the guilt with me every day, at every performance. The peculiar thing is, an offhand conversation I overheard between two clowns makes me feel more guilty... What I *should* have done, but didn't.

God damn Boche pushed me to the ground.

He didn't bother you none?

No, he stepped right over me. We're clowns... we're invisible.

And that is the key. If only I'd hidden the twins in plain sight.

I try not to wince from the pain in my shoulder during my descent down the rope, but keep my eye trained on the Nazi lieutenant, even if I think he's harmless. I can't be too careful. I'd like to think of him as a bungling idiot, but he serves in the Wehrmacht, which I've heard means executing criminal orders that kill, including mass shootings of Jews. I toss my head, ignoring him. I don't need a soppy-eyed young soldier trying to assert his manhood on me. I'm no collabo. *Leave me alone*, I want to shout. What worries me is I'm not the only girl in the troupe who noticed his cool, Aryan looks. I saw Nadia, the lead ballet dancer, flirting with him, but he brushed her off. I smiled, hoping that was the end of it.

Still, I don't trust her. She joined our circus in Brussels, just showed up one day and begged Herr Richter for a job. When he asked her about her circus experience, she was evasive, explaining she was a chorus girl at the Bal Tabarin cabaret in Paris, but had left to find a job better suited for her 'talents' and steady eats. She's a pretty girl with cheeks as smooth as rare silk, but she's rough around the edges. She flirts with every male she sees, including German soldiers and the tent-men (unacceptable in Herr Richter's eyes—how long she'll last is debatable) and is always complaining the clowns get in her way. She considers them beneath her. She doesn't like me, always sniffing around me, asking questions and telling me I'm too old to show off my 'sagging bosom in sequins'. *Really?* Swinging on a flybar for years builds a strong ribcage and uplifted breasts. Again, that funny feeling hits me. She has a wicked grin on her face that sends chills through me. She could be a decoy or an informant. The Gestapo pay hard cash for information about anyone suspect. If Gunty *is* hanging around here, it could be dangerous for both of us. I'll have to warn him if he shows himself. I don't trust her. She tried to bait me, saying she heard my partners, Jean-Pierre and Aima, speaking Yiddish. I didn't bite.

I told her it was Swedish.

6

PARIS, FRANCE—MARCH 1943

The Magician

'I do not kill pretty girls for pleasure, Mademoiselle de la Blanche. Quite the contrary. I find the entire ordeal déclassé, beneath me as a medical professional, nor do I enjoy putting you through an earthly purgatory, wondering where you shall end up when the deed is done.' I smile. 'I imagine you're counting your sins, your heart beating as madly as a butterfly caught in a net, wondering if you'll go to heaven or hell. I dare say your fate is a by-product of your own actions and none of my concern. Now be still while I go about my work.'

I lean down with a sharp scalpel and slit open the blue velvet sleeve on her costume without touching her skin. Precise cutting. My specialty. I perfected my technique years ago in making skin grafts, separating the top layer from the flesh—preparing it in a proper manner so it doesn't wither and become lifeless —to use in repair elsewhere on the body. Now it serves a different purpose. To prepare this lovely for her final breath.

'There, you see? You felt nothing. It would be a shame to mar your lovely skin after I went to so much trouble to make you beautiful. Do you remember that day here in my surgery? Was it barely a year ago? Certainly not longer than that. I remember how you scoffed when Berthile prepped you, fawning over you with her apple-red cheeks and sniffling nose, the scent of fresh pink roses in a Daum glass vase mixing with the odiferous smell of antiseptic, your nostrils wiggling with distaste. You gushed and sighed. Admiring yourself in the long mirror. I remember it well. But I regret, mademoiselle, the vase fell and cracked.

'Since the Occupation began I have sent several mesdemoiselles on their way since I agreed to assist the secret police in their work. Four up to now... I believe you're number five. They look the other way since I'm doing them a service, saving them the trouble of deporting you. Fortunately, no one has complained I'm also depriving them of females for their experiments, but there are plenty of undesirables for that. Jews, mostly.'

Flash!

I nearly drop the scalpel when a lightning bolt as bright as glassy ice shoots through the exposed window. A fierce storm rages outside these medieval stone walls. I hunch my shoulders, my fingers crunched up into fists when an extraordinary light blinds me as it strikes me in the eye. '*Mon Dieu!* I can't see...' I blink away the silver bursts blurring my vision when—

Crash! The walls tremble. *That was close.* Gunfire? Are the SS Jew hunting again? I pray not. I loathe their distasteful crudeness in such matters. Blood everywhere. They never clean up after themselves. Swine. I peer outside. No, thunder rattled my focus. A celestial warning to hurry up and finish the deed.

I regain my composure. Not even a muscle twitches under my eyes, a trait I developed cruising the clubs of Weimar Berlin as a young man where a careless look or gesture provoked a strong fist to break your jaw, or caused a jackboot kicked into your groin. Most unpleasant.

'May I call you Henriette, since we find ourselves in this rather intimate situation?' I ask, returning to the young woman tied up and helpless. I ignore her shaking her head, but prattle on as I'm wont to do when I'm involved in a medical procedure. 'If the thunder rattling the leaden-framed windowpanes is any indication of your past sins, you're in for a long drop into the abyss. I see you agree and squirm about in your chair like a furry caterpillar. I've struck a nerve. *Bon.* It makes it more interesting. I shall carry on with a jaunty tune on my lips to set the rhythm. *La... la, la...* I have perfect pitch, mademoiselle, humming as I pinch your flesh to pull up a vein. Plump, ready for me to administer the syringe with efficacy so you feel no pain. I assure you, I've thought of everything to make you as pliable as possible so I can do the deed without making an error. Note if you will, you can't move about freely in the chair with its sturdy cane back, a classic from the Napoleonic period. You're gagged with a muslin cloth, your throat is dry and tight, your eyelids drooping, your wrists tied to the side arms with taut leather strips, your ankles fastened to its curved mahogany legs.

'Your bare toes curling. Pink, lucent nails.'

My pulse beats faster, my mouth waters. 'Dainty feet that once thrilled me when you walked on the high wire in the elite Paris circus. Oh, the fanfare in the big tent when you performed your act. More than fifteen meters high off the ground, wasn't it? The band playing a melodic Spanish tune. The audience twisting their necks to get a better look at you. Their mouths open wide, watching you holding the balancing pole in your hands, then feeling for the rope with your feet and taking small, graceful steps. Then jumping, turning. I shall never forget your performance on the swaying rope. You made my heart flutter.

'Don't look so shocked. I do have one, you know, inducing me now to stroke your cheek with tenderness. I shall miss your talented presence in the circus. But your star is fading, mademoiselle, like the glimmer of a firefly caught in the glow of intense moonlight. We both know how this ends. Like the tiny bug, your light will dim and you shall embrace the darkness.'

I chuckle. 'You didn't see this coming, did you? They never do. I agree that my smile, the gleam in my eye that you observed earlier when I seduced you to come with me is most deceiving, though this whole ordeal for me is rather trying even with Yann's assistance. Tying you up. Gagging you. Numbing your senses. I float outside my sense of reason when I'm in this state, doing what I must even if I find it distasteful.

'You see, I have a calling. A most demanding need that usurps everything in my life, a grand passion to allow the beauty I created to fade like that elusive firefly but in a civilized way rather than allow the Gestapo and the pompous SS to destroy it. Once they move in on a subject, I cannot control them nor their crude methods. They are trained to torture. Make the victim suffer. So because of your failure to carry out your orders—and to save myself the embarrassment of being called out by the SS—you now find yourself in my purview and at my mercy.'

I flinch when the pretty girl belches and vomit oozes from the side of her mouth. My little wire walker has lost her *petit déjeuner*.

'Aargh... Your lack of self-control is most unfortunate, mademoiselle. *Ta*. I shall be sick. Pardon while I turn away. I have no issue with the flow of fresh red blood, but human waste of the gastric kind is so *unpleasant*.'

I grab a dry gauze dressing to clean her up and try to hold my breath. She must be clean and tidy when I display this new 'angel doll'. It's an art, keeping the body fresh-looking when the heart ceases to beat.

'Don't wiggle. It will only draw out the inevitable.' She scrunches up her face, trying to speak, but can't. 'I fear you're in distress, but I regret I can't loosen the gag. Then you'll scream and I can't stand a woman screaming when I'm working.'

I shudder when her eyes roll upward and her chest starts heaving. More regurgitation appears. This is not good. I hate messes. I pinch my nose with a metal clip to defray the smell. 'I shall have to move this along quickly, mademoiselle,' I say in a frog-like voice, 'before you choke to death on your own vomit. No, I'm *not* a mad fool, unlike the debauched souls who kill and then find beauty in death. I restore a woman's beauty, then I save her from the ugliness of death... for a little while. Put her on display like the grand dolls of Russia behind beveled glass, so she may have the adoration of those who appreciate it, not destroy it with torture and ugly experiments. Damn Nazis.'

I pause a moment, ready the hypodermic while I make my case. 'Fortunately, I'm blessed with a natural charm women are drawn to, which makes my work easier. Yet I also blend in when I queue up for bread on Thursdays and meat on Saturdays. I avoid the elegant structure at 84 Avenue Foch housing the Gestapo "kitchen" when I take my daily constitution—I abhor their harsh methods to glean intelligence from detainees, the poor souls heard emitting tortured cries. I keep my ration book up to date and neatly clipped, and only when absolutely necessary do I buy supplies from the black market. That's cheating and I do not cheat. I pride myself on that. Surprised? You shouldn't be. I'm successful in my facial and body work *because* of my excellent work ethics. I don't skip steps, otherwise I would not achieve the perfection I seek.

'*Why do you try to improve upon what God created?* your eyes ask. I must emphasize, I do *not* improve. I merely restore what evil men have taken away.

'Second point: I do not go about ending lives because something is missing in my life. I was a well-adjusted little boy, good at mathematics and drawing, my favorite being delicate flowers, each petal perfect. I loved my parents, both claiming to be Prussian aristocrats in exile even after the German government disbanded that class, and I adored my little sister Noemi. I repaired the cracked faces on her porcelain dolls when she threw them against the walls in a tantrum—a psychological disorder we never talked about. I grew up privileged in a fourteenth-century castle in Alsace, I speak French and German equally well, and I possess intelligence and style.

'I do what I do because of injustice. Not to me. To women. Young, old... women with scarred faces, hands, body. I feel an obligation to restore their beauty with my scalpel. I traveled to Paris to study medicine as a young man, inspired by the years of abuse I suffered trying to make my sister happy by fixing up her dolls. That stirred my passion for facial reconstruction, that I could do the same with real victims. But it was in Berlin in 1923 when I first witnessed how cruel men could be when I saw a pretty girl burned by her jealous father. I endeavored to save her, restore her beauty as I had my sister's dolls, but she went into severe shock. Then infection set in. I vowed then I would render lovely again what was destroyed by men's anger. I'd found my *raison d'être*.'

I put down the scalpel. Wash my hands. Why *not* explain the process to her I've labored so hard to perfect? A confession of sorts. No harm, since mademoiselle will not live to tell anyone.

'I find a thrilling fulfillment in the process of reshaping a nose, cheekbones, assessing the cell damage, reimaging the facial structure, grafting skin... All are delightful tasks for me. I'm as giddy as a schoolboy when I set about using my medical skills and amazing eye for detail and precision and symmetry, all coming into play to recreate beauty destroyed. A woman's face, her neck, delicate shoulders, long, slim legs. For years, I deemed my work successful and it overfilled my coffers, but I now find myself caught up in a world dominated by a cruel man more obsessed with purity than I. A situation I didn't see coming when I learned my trade in the wily days of 1920s Weimar Berlin from the best minds in plastic surgery including Jacques Joseph. I also studied women's faces while attending the Hirschfeld Institute known for delving into the secrets of sexuality before the Nazis shut it down. I can't bear to see the beauty I've created mauled and slobbered over by these evil men with no concept how to treat a beautiful woman. Even if she did sin.

'And you *did* sin, mademoiselle. *Tsk... tsk*, don't deny it. You were only too happy to take what I offered but not give back as you promised. Come now, being an informant for the Nazis couldn't have been *that* difficult for you, in spite of what you say. A name here and there... Are those tears I see forming in your eyes? Sparkling like champagne from Maxim's. Your lips turned a vinaceous hue. I regret, I've made you cry, mademoiselle. 'Twas not my intention, not after I worked so hard to erase the ugly, scarred skin on your neck and the backs of your legs from the burns you received. You garnered a full column in the *Paris-soir* when your ruffled costume caught on fire in the sawdust ring. Did I not sculpt the skin on your shoulders until they were once again pink and pale? No more jagged, red gnarled flesh on the nape of your neck. You're lucky I was in the audience... but then again, I've haunted circuses since I was a little boy. Even at that young age, I think I knew the circus would become my hunting ground. A venue with spangles and glamour. I never get enough of the sparkles and the derring-do. The circus is also quite lucrative and allows me to maintain respectability and keep up my practice under the noses of the Nazis, repairing the faces, hands, skin on performers in need of a perfect body. I recruit circus performers for the secret police. The Gestapo indulges me, looking the other way when I partake in my dalliances with these once-lovely women who need my help. Why? Because I'm very good at what I do. I proved that after the Great War when my work in the facial reconstruction of injured soldiers came to the notice of a vain general left with a shattered cheekbone and gnarled flesh. In the end, my reconstructive work led to fixing up Hitler's officers in need of an Aryan "refreshing"—whether it's puffy eyes or crow's feet or a broken nose or a nose not Prussian-looking enough—and keeps me in black velvet morning coats. Gold cufflinks. Emerald-studded stickpin emboldened with my family crest.

'But we shan't talk anymore about me even if I am doing the talking.' I chuckle. 'Come now, I know you feel all jiggly inside, waiting for the syringe, what I call the *prick of death*. First comes the drop of blood, red and shiny, popping up on your skin. I imagine you're aching to ask me *why* you must die. Oh, you can't speak? *Pardon*, so silly of me since I'm responsible for your forced silence. Don't fret so. I shall tell you.

'It's quite simple. I fulfilled my part of the bargain, mademoiselle. You didn't. I restored your beauty as we agreed, but you disobeyed your orders to inform on your fellow performers averse to the occupying forces of the Reich or Jews in hiding, forcing me to destroy what I created rather than allow these pigs to take their pleasure with you. For that is the punishment designed by those in charge at 84 Avenue Foch for not obeying orders. The scratch you made upon the contract I offered you is binding, even if you didn't sign it in blood. 'Tis a pity. You're such an exquisite creature, but you didn't fulfill your mission as you agreed, not giving up the name of one Jew, but flitted and flirted like a circus

Liberty horse, independent and haughty. How do I know? *They* were watching you, the secret police—the Gestapo remind me of corpulent trained seals—to see if you were loyal to the Party. They spied on you everywhere you sat your arse or walked in the Italian shoes you conned the Germans out of, waiting for you to make contact with enemies of the Reich. Don't look so surprised. Everyone is a suspect these days.

'We were watching you, too. My man Yann is excellent at disappearing into a crowd, yet missing nothing with eyes as sharp as a predatory bird. Plucking you from the hands of the Gestapo before they could grab you. Mean, bull-headed dodos in their leather trench coats... though I doubt they ever take them off. And the smell... *ugh*, it makes my eyes water.

'Enough. We must move on. Next, I fill the syringe. Your eyes widen so big your lashes disappear. Don't look at me like that. I carry out this mission with the same professionalism as I do my healing. And stop squirming. No one's coming to rescue you. I demand utmost privacy in my work and here I have it. Not like the Rothschild Hospital—now under Nazi control—where I previously performed surgeries with the constant antiseptic smell that offends my nostrils day and night. Here we have luxury. Oak paneling. Immaculately clean white marble floors. Bronze statuettes of mythical Greek gods. Quite commanding, *n'est-ce pas*? The centuries-old *maison* is a grand structure once owned by a lascivious American oil magnate. It's ideal for my practice, hidden off the boule-vard behind an ivy-covered courtyard far away from curious eyes.

'Oh, stop wiggling, *please*. Trying to scream through the gag. Come now, pull yourself together. Your gurgling pleas will get you nowhere. The Gestapo has a list. Meticulous notes on you, the names of your relatives, addresses. They will come knocking on their doors because of your betrayal. Such is the drama of the secret police. I shan't cause you more distress by reminding you.

'You're shaking all over. Don't send me an accusing look. 'Tis not my pres-ence that elicits your shivers, but this cold room. I apologize. Coal is hard to come by this Paris winter and unfortunately, my German sources failed to provide me with a sufficient amount to heat *ma maison* much less dispose of damaged flesh removed during surgery... No matter. I must be flexible, adapt. With Yann's assistance. A degenerate but strongly built man known for his ties to a notorious Apache gang. I pulled him from the dark alleys of Montmartre years ago with slash marks across his neck, no sound coming from his throat. Alas, I was unable to restore his speech, but he's invaluable to me, a man adept in making my task doable, displaying my "angel dolls" as I wish... except when he's drinking, or worse, using drugs. Then he resorts to his old ways. Bagging the bones and dumping them into the Seine. I shall not trouble you with the details. Worry not, I shall send you on your way with decorum and you shall make a most charming display. The drug is absorbed quickly into your limbs, your chest, arms. And I assure you I use only fresh solution. *Alors*, it's time. I allow myself the luxury of a deep breath to reset my internal clock. *Pardon*, while I check the hypodermic—

'*Stop fidgeting, mademoiselle*, or I shall miss the vein and poke you in the abdomen. The result can be quite disastrous. Convulsions. Seizures. Pink foaming about the mouth. Try to relax... *No?* You can't? Then I shall tighten your bindings to hold you still. There, that's better. Next I prick your pale, flawless skin with the sharp steel point. Ah, yes... perfect, so smooth. Allow the drug to flow through your vein. Morphine. Two hundred milligrams. Enough to cause a fatal overdose.

'I push in the needle. Your pretty face tightens. Am I not gentle enough? I promise I shall do better with the next girl. For knowing circus queens as I do, there will be another mademoiselle under the big top who will lose her way and pay the price for having failed the Reich. But you needn't worry. Death is near. Yes, very soon. Your breathing slows, your wine-colored lips turning blue as you fall into a deep, endless sleep from which you shall not awake.

'Adieu, my lovely.

'Heil Hitler.'

7

ROUBAIX, FRANCE—MARCH 1943

Circus Richter

Lia

My soft ballet slippers hit the sawdust and I'm about to take my bow after I finish my act when I hear squeals and a big ruckus. I smile. The clowns. Bouncing into the ring from clown alley. Their refuge is located near the rear entrance and covered with a canopy. It runs parallel to the big tent and is reserved for the clowns so they can jump into the ring numerous times during the show. Half a dozen funnymen in red and orange polka dots and white cone hats, torn tuxedo tails and flattened top hats grab the Nazis' attention, giving me time to adjust the rows of spangles covering my upper arm. The left one with three long, jagged scars.

Faint, but I know they're there.

I draw back to the edge of the ring. The clowns always make me feel better with a laugh, and do I need that now. I never tire of watching the clown run-around. Pushing, shoving each other, cutting up. Tumbling and doing somersaults, slapping each other with rubber chickens. Last week, they started chewing on the rubber fowls since we hadn't seen a *real* chicken in weeks. Making the crowd forget the war, the rationing, the fear we face every day.

I strike a pose, curious to see if the Nazi officer watches me or the clowns.

I lose.

He's watching *me*. And filming me with his damn camera.

The clowns continue their antics, blowing their horns and grabbing patrons by the arm and pretending to kiss the ladies. Most likely Herr Richter ordered the funnymen to hurry the audience along to the *egress*, as he loves to call the exit. I'm thinking it's because there was a 'moment' earlier during the high-wire act when the four-brother wire walkers indicated a problem with the rope and didn't complete their final trick, a pyramid. Herr Richter is a stickler about the rigging, and those of us who work 'up there' are grateful for that. I grin. He's also a businessman and hangs a large poster near the entrance with one side showing clowns, bareback riders, tumblers, and a lion trainer... while the other side boasts a picture of Hitler. No surprise he turns it over to the Führer when the Nazis show up.

The Flying Zollos is the last act at tonight's performance—the lions get that privilege at the matinee and open for the evening show so the prop men don't have to change the set—so I don't expect any shenanigans. Everyone is exhausted and ready to roll up for the night. After the clowns hustle everybody out, they hang out in clown alley, grabbing whatever popcorn is left over and beer if it's to be had.

Then again, when two drunken Nazis occupy the front row, something awful is bound to happen. Tonight is that night.

Two Wehrmacht officers. One stern and mean-looking captain. The other, that same good-looking Nazi lieutenant, is craning his neck to keep his eye and his camera trained on me, but Félix the Clown keeps blocking his view, waving his clown gun in the air, laughing and twirling the top hat on his head. Félix doesn't mean anything by it; he's a gentle soul who found refuge in the circus when his family wouldn't accept his different lifestyle. It's his job to create havoc, keep the energy level high between the acts, but the Nazi isn't laughing. He keeps filming me like it's as important to him as Hitler's birthday parade.

I walk with purpose under the spotlight so the Wehrmacht officer can see me hoping to diffuse the situation, but I only make it worse. The lieutenant's pal, shorter and wearing a tight-fitting uniform, wants in the game, too. He leans over and grabs the clown's long tuxedo coattails and yanks on them. Hard. *Ooh*, he makes me so mad. Typical Nazi thug, executing a superiority move to show who's in charge. I've seen them push townsfolk out of their seats or grab a pretty girl and demand she sit with them. I'll never forget what happened when a woman called a German soldier 'a drunken sod' and the snotnose Nazi infantryman smacked her in the eye.

Oh, God, and now this.

Thinking it's a fellow clown pulling on his black coattails, Félix gets his bauble-shaped red nose in a twist and with his left hand on his hip, he spins around and trips over his big, floppy shoes, pointing his prop pistol at the audience like he's done a hundred times before. A funny, innocent act every clown has in his bag of tricks, but this time, there's an arrogant Nazi in his crosshairs. His brows go up and his big, red mouth drops in awe when he realizes what he's done, but it's too late—

His clown gun goes off with a loud *bang*.

His pants fall down, revealing green-and-white striped socks, garters, and shorts with red hearts. I can't help but laugh (me and everyone in the audience, including the good-looking German officer with the camera) as poor Félix backs away and lands on a tiny swastika flag on top of a bale of hay, squashing it. He laughs, awkward and embarrassed, but it isn't funny to the mean-looking German officer. Shoulders hunched, jaw set, his eyes go dark and cold. Like an angry bear standing on its hind paws, he's ready to attack, and it scares me. The Nazi's hand goes straight to his holster... *Empty*. All side arms are checked with a ballet girl—tonight it's Nadia—at the ticket booth. Since the Nazi Occupation began, it's mandatory at hotels, restaurants, even brothels. Nadia is, of course, flirting with the armed German sentry. This is the new 'normal', having a guard stationed here to curtail civil unrest under orders from the Nazi general in charge at nearby Lille. He's a mean old general from what I've heard, and doesn't take orders from Paris but straight from Berlin. What sends every performer at Circus Richter into a panic is this Nazi general's reputation. He takes hostages every time a German soldier is ambushed, wounded, or kicked in their Aryan arse. What Félix did is enough to qualify as political dissidence and attracts the attention of the sentry poking his head into the tent for a look. He's decked out in a metal helmet, ammo belt, and rifle with a bayonet fixed to it, ready for action.

Meanwhile, the pudgy Wehrmacht officer fumes, his pale face turning red. He shouts in German, 'You stupid clown! You insulted the Führer. You'll pay for this.'

What happens next takes me and the audience by surprise. The good-looking German with the camera grabs the clown by the collar, slaps him about in a playful manner and tells him to find a new job, but he doesn't arrest him. A distraction, perhaps? I get the feeling he's enjoying being a part of the show— I'd almost believe he was a clown dressed up as a Nazi, he's that good. He's smiling and taking bows when the sentry runs into the ring and, paying no attention to the lieutenant's demand to stand down, the *sentry* arrests Félix the Clown on orders from the senior officer, forcing him to march out of the big tent with his hands above his head, the bayonet of the guard's rifle prodding him along. I can't grasp what I'm seeing. Yes, he arrested a clown.

A clown.

Even the young Wehrmacht officer looks surprised and protests, reminding the other officer in German, 'It's the circus, we're here to have fun, not cause problems with the locals,' but he outranks him and the lieutenant is overruled. Two more German soldiers appear, giving the Hitler salute. The Boches leave quickly, amid booing from the audience.

I'm tempted to join in, but I have to play along, pretend I have no allegiance to anything but the circus. As if I am a marionette on strings. In that moment, I realize the young Nazi officer and I have that in common. We both do what our puppet masters tell us.

I grab my long, satin cape from the ballet girl standing outside the ring and make a quick exit. Where does it read in God's playbook the Nazis can march away a man of laughter for doing what he does best? A beloved character in our show whose only goal in life is to make the belly jiggle with a joke, or tap the brain with a witticism that bears truth even if it hurts. Isn't all comedy based on tragedy? And the human condition? Oh, yes, I forgot. We can't laugh like we used to. We're under the rule of a madman who doesn't know *how* to laugh. A man who thrives on the distasteful ideals of being a demigod and then proceeds to carry them out no matter who he hurts.

And tonight he hurt everyone here under the big top.

Because we learned not even a funnyman is immune to their fragile and bloated egos. Perhaps in the end, that's what will do the Party in. I hope so. For now, I add more guilt to my soul. Because German officers came here tonight to ogle me and other female performers like the ballerina sister act bouncing up and down on horseback, going around in a circle, giving them a perfect view of their backsides from any angle. Because of us, we've lost Félix.

What is it about men and pretty girls in a circus?

8

PARIS, FRANCE—APRIL 1943

Le Cirque Casini
The Magician

I need a new girl for my stable, a girl desperate for my services as a plastic surgeon who will agree to be an informant to keep my Gestapo benefactor fat and happy. The pig. He rarely washes and wears the same smelly trench coat for days on end. I, on the other hand, keep to a most dedicated regime when I'm trolling for my next mademoiselle 'to save' from the Nazi whore machine. I maintain a high degree of decorum so as not to scare them off. I dress with style, but I take issue with appearing too well off in these times of rationing. I don't wish to be taken for a collaborator like certain high-profile French aristocrats and cinema stars—what I do is *not* collaboration, but saving these girls from a horrible death under the Nazis. The Gestapo is very unforgiving to these female informants if they don't report back to Avenue Foch with useful information. In the eyes of the secret police, that means the arrests of Jews and political dissidents... and Resistance fighters. The girl will then be deported to a concentration camp called Ravensbrück, where she won't go through the art of selection by the SS when she arrives in a filthy boxcar smelling of her own excrement as in Auschwitz, but destined for the camp brothel or medical experiments that even make *me* cringe: breaking their bones, cutting open flesh and letting it fester, taking off limbs, experimenting with dangerous sulfa drugs.

I would *never* enact such crude methods on *my* girls, including the mesdemoiselles taking part in my ever-changing display of 'angel dolls'. So pretty in pink or blue or whatever color strikes me, artfully arranged and handled with care as if they slumber so when the police find them, they're not hastily buried in an unmarked grave. Rather, a picture is taken, the photo then appears in the *Paris-soir* and my work as a plastic surgeon is immortalized. What happens after that I can't control. Sadly, it's like a cream tarte. Once the sweet, milky cream is licked clean, the soggy crust finds its way into a pail. Tossed away. Like my 'angel dolls' who then end up in a pauper's plot. Still, it's vital I keep good hygiene whether they're dead or still breathing. Make certain my nails are clean and clipped. Very important since my routine examination of an injured girl needing 'restoration' involves inspecting the dead skin on her face, breasts, or thighs. I pride myself on being sympathetic and gentle. And, of course, I seek out my prey in her natural habitat.

The circus.

Which brings me here on an early morning to this traveling tent circus on the outskirts of Paris. Le Cirque Casini. A very old circus with roots going back to the equestrian talents of its founder in the late eighteenth century—an Englishman schooled in the art of horsemanship. I'm told the Casini name then came from his fiery consort, an Italian beauty from the hills of Tuscany with a streak of wildness that made her a skilled trick rider. Still, I'm not fond of circuses on the move with their transient flock of half-talented performers and sloppy clown fanfare, but Le Cirque Casini is a cut above the others and on par with the revered Cirque d'Hiver in Paris. According to my source at Avenue Foch, they're not going on the road, under orders from Goebbels. Interesting... I've heard their trapeze act of two men and a girl is a combination of dazzling youth and beauty combined with years of experience under the big top. I haven't seen The Flying Jouberts perform for years and I'd enjoy catching their new act, but I'm here on business. My gossip squirrels tell me a girl performing here recently had an accident... A fire. Burned nose, cheek, and hands. A performer gifted with skill and grace. The Gestapo is keen on recruiting her as an informant, a *collaborator horizontale*. Of course, champagne and a meal to fill their bellies is often all that's required to entice a pretty girl to work with the secret police. But women whose beauty is destroyed, or their body so unattractive men turn away in disgust, are the best candidates. Yes, most agreeable.

And making her even more agreeable, I've heard she has a child. I imagine the baby has the cutest tiny feet. I rarely work on feet. Perhaps that's why they intrigue me. But I know nothing about offspring. I have none, nor do I wish to impregnate the women I seek to beautify. They are merely vessels for my genius. Not receptacles for my sperm.

I go over my mental notes. I rarely keep written notes anymore. I learned they're too easily used against me as I discovered in late 1939 when I came up against a certain what I term *inspecteur* in the Paris criminal brigade, a detective with spit and grit who believes in fighting for justice with the vigor of a herd of elephants on the rampage. He used a notebook I'd written to bring a case against me for a botched surgery on a city official's wife. Her rhinoplasty was doomed before I started because of her impossible demands and I never should have taken the case, but I allowed my ego to take over and documented my disgust for her in the notebook. Then the vain female ripped off the bandages too soon and blamed *me* for her red, raw skin. The odds were stacked against me when the corrupt official brought charges, but then fate opened a portal when the Nazis occupied the city. I saw a way out and I took it. After a very productive meeting with Herr Avicus Geller of the Gestapo, the case was dropped. *If* I played their game. Of course I said *yes*. And here I am today, happily going about my work with the Party's blessing.

Today's mark is Mademoiselle Zera Bovier. I didn't glean much information about her, but I speculate my target was warming precious milk on an open gas burner for her baby when it spilled, scalding her hands and her cheek. No eye injuries, I'm told, though I've treated eye burns resulting from acid—a favorite of jealous lovers—by irrigating the eye with a boric acid solution and applying castor oil drops. Unfortunately, it must be done quickly for any effect and I'm rarely called in time.

Anyway, I'm here and up for the challenge. I remove my black leather gloves so the young woman can connect with me as a flesh and blood man, not an overworked physician with no knowledge of the sensitivity it takes to heal a woman's face. It goes deeper than the skin. It goes to her soul. Deep down to erase the scarred, ugly image she sees every time she looks into the mirror. Even after I've performed my magic, that image will remain stuck in her mind if I don't use human kindness to peel away the scar only *her* eyes can see. Gain her trust.

What strikes me is, if they don't fulfill their mission afterwards for the Gestapo, then I must use that trust to take them on their final journey.

I pray this girl doesn't disappoint me, like Mademoiselle de la Blanche. A difficult case. Against my wishes, I had to administer additional morphine to send her on her way and even then it wasn't smooth. She started having a seizure and died with her eyes and mouth rigid and open. Most ungainly and difficult to fix, making it impossible to present her as an 'angel doll' with her contorted face. I was devastated and, in a moment of despair, told my man Yann to dispose of her. But he got drunk and sloppy and tossed the body into the Seine and she ended up on a slab in a makeshift morgue behind Nŏtre Dame. Of course, I'm too good at what I do for her demise to be traced back to me. Still, the ordeal was traumatic and hard on my nerves. My hand shook for a week. I'm better now. I breathe in then out, eager for a new challenge.

I enter the main tent, poke around the perimeter with a gentle walk, kicking up sawdust in my polished black leather shoes, my laces tied with neat circle eights. I hold up my handkerchief to my nose to lessen the pungent circus animal smells and waste diffused with large amounts of ammonia giving me a headache, along with the aroma of a caffeine stimulant. I'll never get used to the strong chicory used these days. I scurry past the clowns wearing their white face makeup—I shudder to think what their skin looks like underneath studded with pockmarks, red and irritated—tank undershirts, trousers and suspenders, gathered in a circle and tossing the die. I see three ballet girls huddled in a corner, looking embarrassed when I catch them puffing on cigarette butts. I avoid making a comment, though I shake my head. This is one time I concur with Nazi policy that cigarette smoking is detrimental to one's health and German women are prohibited from smoking in public. Women in the Occupied Zone, it seems, are exempt. Which shows me the low opinion the Nazis have of Frenchwomen. Another reason for me to save them from their fate at the hands of the SS death squads.

'*Pardon*, mesdemoiselles, where may I find Zera Bovier and her baby?' I ask them in what I perceive to be a pleasant manner.

'Monsieur?' A dark-haired girl in a white tutu crosses her brow. 'Are you sure you want Zera?'

'Yes, I believe she had an accident and I may be able to help her.' I grin and smooth down my starched collar. 'And her child.'

They giggle, blow smoke at each other, whispering among themselves. Impolite, but I never judge. I never know where I'll find a new recruit.

'Cleopatra's in the dressing tent, monsieur, *with* her baby'—she turns to her friends with a smirk—'*n'est-ce pas, mes amies?*'

More giggles.

'*Pardon?*' I ask, not understanding.

'She plays Cleopatra in the parade.'

'*Merci.*' I nod, smile, then crossing the sawdust ring, I head toward the tent indicated by the precocious brunette when—

I see *her*.

Not Zera. But a blonde around eighteen, I'd wager. I'm an excellent judge of the formation of a woman's facial structure and how it ages. Exquisite cheekbones still forming. Tight skin at the jawline. Big blue eyes like crystal. High forehead. She's tall, slender, and wears a plain nude leotard with a wisp of silk wrapped around her waist, lace-up ballet slippers, the plainness of her costume making her beauty stand out. I'm dazzled by her profile, patrician nose, strong chin, long, curly lashes, then she turns toward me and oh, if I could but give every woman I take under my wing such a sweet pretty face, I'd be God. I can't help but stare at her. She pings a buried need in me with her perfection, an adoration I can't resist, her presence mesmerizing me as she walks with dainty steps toward the ring. Stretching and rolling her head from side to side to loosen up, the silk billowing out from her body like a butterfly's wings floating on a breeze. The blonde climbs the rope up to the perch and begins swinging on the flybar higher and higher.

Then she—

Rips off the pink silk around her waist and lets it go.

I'm in awe, my mouth wide open as the silk flies through the air, light and airy, like petals from a pink rose. Before it lands in the sawdust, I rescue the silk and put it to my nose, her scent lavender, light, airy. Her presence is so inspiring I can't look away, her moves so beautiful, her presence dangerous to a man catching up on a life filled with loneliness. She reminds me of an ancient water maiden filled with seduction. Her aerial ballet consists of dips and curls, sliding into one position then another until she's hanging by her knees on the swing, making graceful gestures with her arms, then pulling herself up and returning to the perch, arching her left foot and pointing her toe. She blows kisses to her one-man audience.

Me. I send her a kiss back and she laughs. An enchanting melody that rips through me with a familiarity you can't quite put your finger on, like you should know the words but you don't. A funny thought wiggles through me. I swear I've seen that face before... in my dreams, I imagine. It matters not. She's here now. I lose myself in this lovely epiphany that Divine art *can* exist on a scale equal to mine.

How long I stand here not moving, I don't know... until a handsome, muscular man brushes by me, muttering under his breath, 'When will she ever grow up? She's no longer a child even if she acts like one,' while the girl swings higher and higher under the big top. 'Come down here now, Jeanne,' the man shouts up to her.

'Watch me, Papa, while I swing with one hand—'

'*Now, Jeanne!* We have things to discuss... about the act.'

'But Papa—'

'You'll never be ready for your birthday performance if you don't take your work seriously.'

'*Bon.*' A pretty pout erupts on her face, but he's hit a nerve, something that means a lot to her. And I realize in that moment, this girl is Jeanne Joubert. And the man is her papa, Philippe Joubert, co-owner of Le Cirque Casini since he married Gisèle Casini years ago. I make it a point to know the players in my little dramas to avoid detection, deceit, and disaster. I also discovered Le Cirque Casini is high on Herr Geller's list of 'targeted' circuses. Targeted for what I don't know since he didn't share that with me before he left Paris for a sojourn up north near the Belgian border.

'I shall be back in Paris before you can belch, monsieur,' he insisted, his lack of decorum never ceasing to turn my stomach. 'I've had wind of a Resistance cell operating in the area from one of "our" informants. Nadia.' A poke in the ribs followed. I smiled weakly at his attempt to draw me into his nefarious dealings by mentioning one of my "girls". 'I shall return before you know it.'

Which leaves me in want if I need to speak to him about the behavior of Mademoiselle Jeanne's papa. I can't dismiss the man's chilling words. How dare he act so cruel to the pretty girl? Monsieur Joubert is fortunate I don't report his actions to the Gestapo agent when he returns. I've a mind to set him straight, but I know my place. I can't—*won't*—jeopardize my position and lose my freedom to return here. To see *her*.

All I can do is stare at her perfect face.

I pull back into the shadows, watch her descend the rope with such grace, and I sigh. I swear she winks at me when her arched feet touch the ground and she runs after her papa, looping her arm through his. She scowls at something he says, tosses her head back and breaks away from her father and heads toward the entrance alone. Such pride, such independence she shows. She's *incroyable*. I stuff the silk into my jacket pocket. Insurance for another day. For now, I accept the fact I'm gone from her mind, forgotten. But the damage is done. A heated emotion burns through me like my veins are on fire, bursting with hot blood. I can't move from this spot. It's sacred. Holy.

I'm in love.

* * *

'*Bonjour...* Mademoiselle Bovier?' I pull back the flap on the dressing tent and see a woman in her twenties sitting in the dimly lit corner on top of a large trunk with what appears to be a long scarf wrapped around her neck. She wears a full skirt fashioned in black taffeta with four rows of ruffles, a white blouse and a shiny purple vest caught in the light, a dim old-fashioned gas lantern that flickers. *Not very safe*, I'm tempted to blurt out, since I'm skittish about anything that could catch a spark, knowing as I do the horror and disfigurement fire and flames can bring. The tent overflows with clown suits, ballerina tutus, and leotards in all sizes hanging on racks. Feathers, silk wraps, capes. A small suitcase sits on the floor. Closed up tight.

'Who's asking, monsieur?'

She turns her back to me and I swear I hear her whispering to someone, '*We'll get by... I promise.*' Her child? I don't see a baby or toddler, and that milky-sick, urchin smell isn't present. Instead, I inhale a strong perfume of jasmine and violets. Or is it the sweet scent of the lovely aerialist still living in my nostrils? I will it away. I'm working now and my frivolous encounter with the young female must be put on a shelf. For now.

'I'm a physician,' I announce as I always do with a bow and my business card proffered to the girl. I never say my name, Dr Thaddeus Rose. I changed it years ago, for this line of work, to give it flair. I prefer they look at the card with the words I live by printed in raised black ink: *A rose never dies... she merely blooms again under my hand.*

She doesn't turn around. 'Go away.'

I huff out a breath and return the card to the breast pocket in my morning coat. I don't like being rebuffed like I'm a tent-man swinging a hammer. If I wasn't in such a good mood, I'd turn and leave and forgo my pre-determined lofty sum from the Gestapo for recruiting female informants easily swayed by a man of my talents. I use finesse in my recruiting, something the SS lacks along with body hygiene. I shouldn't judge their personal habits since they're wrapped in wool uniforms, but that doesn't excuse what they do to these women who have so much to lose if they fail to produce results. Their lives, one way or another. Deported to a camp... or me. However, what must be done shall be done.

I try another approach. 'I assure you, mademoiselle, I have your best interests in mind... and your child's.'

She laughs. 'I find that quite amusing, monsieur.'

'I'm not in the habit of making frivolous statements, mademoiselle.'

I let my words sink in as I run my fingers over a pink satin cape hanging on the rack. So lovely, each thread perfectly woven with a thousand others, smooth like a rosy cheek. I pride myself on achieving the same effort when I reconstruct a woman's face. It's an itch I have that I can't explain, my fingers aching to grab my cutting tools.

I rub the soft satin in my palm while I peek at the girl out of the corner of my eye. I can't see her clearly but I admit to a curiosity about the extent of her injury that gathers momentum with each moment she hides her face from me... until I can't stand it anymore, my psyche begging for a new challenge, a new face to fix.

I grab the lantern and shove it in her face and—

The devil she is... She covers her bandaged cheeks and mouth with the long, long tail of a... A *what?*

A huge snake that curls around the girl's shoulders, what I believe is a yellow python that hisses and slithers and causes the bile to rise in the back of my throat. I strive to keep control, but the creature is as surprised as I am and feels threatened by my swift movement. The impertinent reptile releases a foul odor in my direction. Musk. Makes me gag and my eyes turn watery.

It feels threatened? What about me? *I* feel quite nauseous. I put my hand up to my nose, hold my breath. I have an aversion to snakes. Slimy, sneaky creatures with scaly, dry skin. I prefer to work with soft, creamy skin, but the curious little boy in me can't resist the urge to see if this elusive apparition before me is real.

I reach out with my forefinger to give it a little tap when—

'Don't... *t-t-touch my b-b-baby!*' Mademoiselle Bovier hisses at me, slurring her words.

I choke on my own saliva. '*This* is your baby?'

'Yes.'

'Oh.' I wasn't expecting an unduly long reptile to raise the mademoiselle's maternal instinct; then again, it appears snuggled and warm, wrapped around her body as if it's in its natural habitat. I straighten my shoulders, regain my composure. In my business, I have to be ready for anything and proceed with caution. And courtesy. 'Does the baby have a name?'

'Violetta.'

A calm voice when she answers me. She pets her companion. Good. She's opening up to me.

I smile. 'I'm here to offer my services to you... and Violetta.'

Her eyes widen. 'Who *are* you, monsieur?'

I decide against presenting my card a second time. I sense she'll respond better to a personal, fanciful touch, a dreamlike wave of my hands in a circle around her head, as if I'm casting a healing spell over her and erasing what *she* doesn't want to see.

'I'm a purveyor of magic, mademoiselle... but truly, I am a physician, a surgeon of a specific manner. I can ease the pain you feel every time you look in a mirror. I can make your injuries disappear.'

'You can take away *this*?' She rips off the bandages covering her cheeks and nose, but her smile is weak when she leans forward into the light, unafraid now to show me her ugly wounds, her eyes searching mine. I know that look. Deep. Haunting, her eyes not blinking, pupils big and black. She wants more than anything to believe me.

I dare to touch her right cheek, puckered up and taut with jagged, ugly red streaks. 'How did this happen to you, mademoiselle?'

'Violetta loves to play hide and seek, don't you, baby?' she coos to the snake who, if I didn't know better, responds in the affirmative. The girl continues talking to the reptile, assuring it 'the nice man won't hurt us' before she turns back toward me. 'I was curling my black wig with a hot iron, testing the temperature with an old newspaper and getting ready for the spec before the matinee, when I realized Violetta was gone. I panicked and... Oh, it was awful, monsieur. I looked everywhere, but my baby was lost! We're a team. Violetta and me. She's everything to me.'

'How did you acquire this remarkable creature?' I'm curious to know. *Keep her talking.*

'She's a Burmese python brought to Paris from Singapore by an animal trainer. He abandoned her when she got too close to his trained piglets.'

I gulp. Why does that conjure up belly-rumbling thoughts that border on nausea with a bout of indigestion I don't want to pursue? Instead I ask, 'You *both* ride in the circus parade?' I refer to the spec or spectacle the ballet girl mentioned.

'Yes, on a float decorated to look like an Egyptian barge, a fancy wagon with big wheels and drawn by a show pony with me as Cleopatra, with Violetta looped around my shoulders.' She giggles. 'She plays the asp.'

I want to ask, *Isn't Violetta rather large for the part?* But I'm a gentleman so I listen.

'I was so consumed with worry Violetta would get trampled by an elephant or eaten by a tiger...'

Unless she eats the tiger first.

'...I left the hot iron on the portable gas stove,' Zera says. 'Then I searched everywhere for my baby, going from tent to tent, until I found Violetta curled up under my cot.' She lowers her eyes, repentant. 'When I raced back to the cook-house, I found the hair on the long black wig singed and charred by the iron and the heating paper black and crumbly and giving off hot sparks. I was afraid the gas would explode, so I grabbed the iron but I tripped over the wig, landing on the hard ground, my wrist sprained and the red-hot prong burning my left cheek.' She looks at me, her eyes pleading. 'Who wants a Cleopatra looking like a monster?'

'You got sacked, mademoiselle?'

She nods. 'I lost my job, but I still have my sweet Violetta. The boss man gave me twenty-four hours to pack my things and leave.'

I have no comeback, no words of solace. True, it was an accident, but she should have known hot irons are forbidden in the circus. Animal trainers have been known to use the irons to 'tame' a big cat. It's disgusting. It leaves scars on the skins of these beautiful creatures. It makes my stomach turn. So, what am I to do with this forlorn mademoiselle and her companion? I should walk away, look for another mark, but when I see how Zera hugs her snake with such affection, I can't help but feel empathy for her... and the snake. Am I going daft?

She sighs. 'Although now Violetta and I have no place to go, monsieur.'

'What if I could make you pretty again, mademoiselle?' There I go, getting soft with this girl. It will do me in someday. 'Then you wouldn't have to leave the circus, *n'est-ce pas?*'

'Could you?'

I smile so wide my face hurts. 'I'm sure you'll be pleased with the results,' I say with pride.

'I can't pay you.'

I raise my hand in protest. 'I have a patron in high places who loves the circus and will provide financial assistance for a talented performer such as yourself.'

'Monsieur?' She raises a brow.

'All he asks for is your loyalty to him... and the Party.' I grin. 'A simple request, *n'est-ce pas?*'

'Oh, I see.'

Her eyes open wide and as she starts to protest, the python slithers off her shoulders. I back away. The damned thing must be more than three meters long. I'm not amused when the reptile hisses at me, its slimy tongue dangerously close to my nose. She hugs the snake tight to her bosom. 'This place where you can help me, does it have rats?'

'Aren't they everywhere?' I smile, a rather loose smile. Since the war, Paris is infested with the rodents. I rely on Yann to take care of the nasty little creatures for me, but I'm getting a nagging signal the python just perked up, interested in what I said.

'Hold Violetta for me.' She hangs the python over my shoulders. My jaw drops. I can't believe I'm standing here with a bright yellow Burmese python looped around my neck. I shiver... then shiver again when the snake slithers down my back.

Oh, dear.

I remain still. I should be delighted. I've never had a young woman so agreeable to my request, but the creature is advancing too close to my groin. I keep telling myself it's my duty to befriend this girl and her unique companion, no matter the personal discomfort, as Herr Geller likes to remind me. Then again, I doubt if the dubious secret policeman ever had a python wrapping its tail around his legs.

Oh, what I do for the Party.

I clear my throat, give her my formal speech about what to expect, the hours-long surgery, clean white bandages—*don't touch them*, I emphasize. Then recovery time in my special 'patient accommodations'—the basement of *ma grande maison*—then she'll transfer to a medical facility in the south run by the Nazis for follow-up and rest. What they call a sanitarium. There she will also be schooled in the trade of gathering information. And, I imagine, the consequences of failure.

I will be here for her, if necessary, to pick up the pieces if she doesn't perform up to the standards set down by the secret police and gather names, addresses of anyone speaking or acting against the Reich. And Jews, too, of course, with false papers. *If* such an indiscretion is discovered, I shall be the conduit to help her avoid the heinous torture promised by the Gestapo for not being the perfect little informant they desire.

It's my duty to my profession.

'You shall accompany me to my surgery immediately, mademoiselle, where my assistant Berthile can prep you for the procedure.' I pray the woman isn't out hat-shopping again, the only thing in Paris not rationed. Last week, she turned up with a chapeau from the House of Péroline with hanging purple wax grapes. I say nothing about her extravagant purchases, even contribute to her purse to keep her quiet. She's been with me for years and doesn't approve of my work for the Nazis, but she has no recourse since I know her little secret. She hides it well, but—

Berthile is a Jew.

Zera pushes her hair away from her scarred cheek, a new radiance shining in her eyes. That makes me happy. For a moment, I put aside the tight feeling in my groin as the snake winds down my leg. I believe it's not venomous, *n'est-ce pas?* I enjoy seeing the confidence I bring to these girls. I have the feeling Mademoiselle Bovier will be an attribute and prime example of the success of my work... and a good informant for the Gestapo, though it will take weeks for the effects of the skin grafts to adhere properly once I remove the puckered scars. The face heals faster than the rest of the body, allowing her a quicker recovery time so she will be a soldier in my corps of beautiful informants by late spring if infection doesn't set in.

She grabs the small suitcase. '*Allons,* Monsieur le Docteur. Let's go.'

'Then you agree to the terms?' Like I said, a woman with a 'baby'—any baby —has a greater incentive to cooperate with the secret police.

'What choice do I have, monsieur?' Her eyes widen. 'You have rats. And Violetta hasn't eaten for more than a month.'

9

ROUBAIX, FRANCE—APRIL 1943

Circus Richter
Lia

I can't push the arrest of Félix the Clown out of my mind. It's an image of injustice I won't forget. A week later and no word of his fate, but I can still see the funnyman's shoulders hunched, his big floppy shoes kicking up sawdust on the Nazi officer's trousers. A final act of defiance from a man who's lost his freedom. For doing his job, to make people laugh? A dangerous move when a Nazi soldier is involved since an off-the-cuff gesture or remark that challenges the authority of the Wehrmacht is not tolerated by the Party. Not the first time I've heard this story. We hired a tent rigger last season who joined the circus in Aachen to escape the Gestapo after his wife told a neighbor she hated Hitler. That was enough to send her to a concentration camp. Now it's happening in our own backyard and it puts us all in jeopardy. We live with fear, knowing the Gestapo visits circuses whenever they have no one else to torment. Circus Richter is now suspected of employing political dissidents. Terrible news, setting us all on edge. It's more important than ever I don't bring attention to myself or I'll be shipped off to a labor camp if they find out I'm not pure Aryan. Thank goodness tonight is our last performance in Roubaix, a town north of Lille, where lace was made for decades before the Germans came, catching the locals in the Nazi noose. They're Frenchmen, but under the Nazi government in

Brussels. Why? Simple. It's easier to keep an eye on the coast so close to the English Channel... and fortify the Nazi war machine with the area's industrial power, including here in Roubaix where textile mills run day and night. It's also a favorite spot for the Richter Circus to put up its big tent and put on a show. People come from nearby towns and farms to see us. Which is why I shouldn't have been surprised when the strange woman showed up, but I'm getting ahead of myself.

We're moving out tomorrow, which isn't too soon for me. We had to cancel the matinee because the ticket seller—Nadia, of course—took off for a picnic with a German soldier and left the box holding the tickets where the monkeys could get to them. The impish creatures tore them up before any could be sold, meaning tickets for the evening performance were snapped up in minutes, making Herr Richter happy. He'd rather leave a town with a 'bang' than two lukewarm performances.

I'm anxious to get on to the next town. This place makes me nervous with so many Boche soldiers in their beetle-green uniforms racing around the country-side in trucks and on motorcycles. Poking their noses everywhere. I pray the prickly lieutenant doesn't show up tonight and cause more problems. After the incident with the Boche, my takeoffs from the perch aren't as smooth as I like. I have to work on getting my nerves calmed down. Let my mind refocus, reset that ticking clock in my head that keeps me on a steady track with the rest of my body when I'm swinging high on the flybar so I'm in sync with the catcher. We have to meet up at *exactly* the right moment. I can't do it alone. I need him. More important, I need to trust him. Her, maybe? I smile. Why can't a woman be a catcher? My arms are strong, muscular. Interesting thought, but it won't happen in a world dominated by the Nazis.

I let that thought linger in my mind when I go about doing what circus folks do on the road. Clean out our tents. Check our supplies. Wash our costumes wrinkled up and stiff with dried sweat. The smell can be as bad as the animal cages. I spent the early hours after dawn scrubbing my garments in hot water I heated on the gas stove in the cookhouse with precious soap we procured from the local black market. (The cookhouse is the first tent to go up... and the last to come down.) A traveling circus gets its supplies wherever we can, knowing the vicissitudes of our daily life depend on the weather, the mood of the locals, and, God help us, the Nazis.

It's a hard life. Grueling hours, practice every day, traveling, aching muscles.

Late nights are the worst when you crave a man's strong arms around you so you can close your eyes and pray the nightmare doesn't begin again. But I wouldn't change anything. It's freedom I find in the circus, to walk away on my own terms and never let a man hurt me again. I'm on my own and I know how to take care of myself. I don't need a man to make me feel like a woman.

Still, that doesn't mean I don't get lonely. Especially today. It was exactly eighteen years ago on a cool spring morning in a convent outside Paris, a holy place where the pink lilacs always seemed to be in bloom, when my baby was born. A little girl. My heart still cries... She didn't live long enough to bathe in the warmth of the noon sun.

I try not to dwell on it.

I'll never forget the brief joy of motherhood I had. Deep inside, I know that's why I fear getting involved in the Resistance. I can't promise another mother they won't go through the horror of losing their child. Does that make me a coward?

I make my way over the field where we've put up our tents. I don't want to answer that question. Instead, I focus on the lovely piece of earth filled with yellow buttercups dotting the green grass, the winding, worn paths of dirt and gravel pinpointing where we've trudged over the land in our caravans for years and other circuses before us. On this early spring day, my mind wanders, thinking about how our roots are different than other folks. How even when the war seems unbearable, I find peace within myself wandering over these fields of buttercups from town to town but always under a blue sky.

Even when it rains.

That's the way of circus people. We see sunshine where others don't. But we're human, too, and away from the lights and music and colorful satin costumes, we're plain folks. Doing what plain folks do in this war. Scrounging for food, bellowing over the awful barley brew that passes for coffee, queuing up in the local village to buy necessities like tooth powder—shampoo is impossible to get. And washing the grime off our duds.

I'm hustling a big basket of wet wash on my right hip when I see Nadia sitting on the steps of her caravan smoking what I recognize as a German cigarette from the rolling papers and pack sitting next to her. *Efka*. Not the usual homegrown cigarettes I see around the circus fashioned from old coffee grounds and dried lettuce. She's studying her face in a hand mirror. She puts down the mirror and smirks when she sees me with hair rag curlers sprouting all over my blonde head like cauliflower, then blows smoke in my face when I walk by. I ignore her. I'm in no mood to deal with a jealous female. I'm shivering in my teal silk kimono and blame it on the cold morning, but I can't shake the feeling she's hiding something. No doubt she got that pack of cigarettes from a Nazi soldier. What is she up to?

I'm careful where I walk in my marabou backless slippers to avoid patches of mud as I head over to the backlot away from the big top. I use this downtime to do my chores before the evening show. It's quiet here away from the bustle of morning practice in the big tent and clown alley. I start hanging up the wet costume pieces on a sagging clothesline including my nude-colored leotards with water dripping onto the soft earth and white and red sequin two-piece costume with blue and gold spangles. I've had it for years and it's become a trademark of sorts, even if the seams are loosening up and half the sequins have fallen off, but I can't toss it away. I've worn it under the big top from Berlin to Brussels. It's like an old friend, which makes me think of Gunty. If the rumor is true, what's he doing here?

I put that thought aside, go back to my wash. Underwear, brassieres, white blouses, and the men's trousers I favor when we're traveling. I pay little attention to a strange woman watching me. She makes no attempt to hide herself, and is that a young boy about ten and a little girl no more than seven hanging on to her long skirts? We often get curious villagers sneaking onto the grounds, mostly little boys trying to pet the animals. These two *enfants* don't laugh or smile. Instead they cling to the woman's coat like their fingers are sticky with gum.

I try to shoo the woman away, but she doesn't move. Neither do the children. So now my curiosity is piqued and I *have* to take a closer look. She's in her early thirties, a navy wool head scarf covering her hair, plain linen coat, gray housedress with a round white collar falling down to her ankles, and laced-up brown shoes with cardboard stuffed in the soles. She's not circus. She strikes me as too conventional in her clothing and serious expression, unlike so many circus people with their outgoing, friendly personalities. She ignores the elephants scuffling their big feet and munching up grass, the lions lazing around in their cages with full bellies, horses munching on alfalfa or drinking at the trough after a workout in the ring. She's even immune to the stilt walker feeding a carrot to a giraffe and two acrobats walking on their hands having a casual chat. Most townsfolk gawk at the unusual novelties displayed in the *parade de cirque* or sideshow like the giraffe or stilt walker, even a knife thrower. Not her. She keeps her eyes on me.

I keep to my task. I tend to shy away when civilians break the fourth wall and see me without my makeup and spangles. It takes away the mystery. I've found the public would rather see me as a mythical creature who can do magical things.

Not a washerwoman.

Why won't she go away? I have my answer when she opens up her arms wide to hug her children. Jakob and Anna, she calls them. The little boy wears a dark jacket, short pants, and white shirt. I see 'strings' from his traditional undershirt came loose and hang down the side of his shorts. Fear strikes the woman when she sees me staring at the child, and she moves quickly to stuff the strings into his waistband. The little girl is clothed like her *maman* in a dress coming down below her knees, covering her elbows, head scarf, dark opaque tights. I should have guessed. She's Jewish, Orthodox. Her modest clothes and head covering are a dead giveaway; so are the children's, though the little boy isn't wearing a skullcap... and no yellow star. On her or the little girl either. Dangerous move if they *are* Jewish. The woman must be desperate to take that risk. That funny itch slithers up my spine, that feeling I can't ignore. This young woman with skin as pale as milk mixed with rainwater and crying eyes isn't a threat and needs my help. I don't ask how she found me, but there's only one reason she'd risk trespassing onto the circus grounds. She's in trouble.

'Mademoiselle... may I have a word?' she asks finally.

I keep hanging up my wet clothes, looking left then right, making sure no one can hear us. I want to spare her any more duress so I ask her straightaway, 'How long have you been in hiding, madame... you and your children?' I focus on clipping my brassieres to the clothesline, then I realize it's embarrassing to this young mother. She's blushing. I unclip them, toss them back into the basket. I sometimes forget that unlike most women of my age, I'm used to wearing a tight, revealing costume that outlines my curves. It's part of my persona, just like this young mother's conservative dress is to hers. I respect that and under ordinary circumstances, she'd never seek me out, let alone speak to me. Yet here she is, talking to me, not judging me. I like that about her.

'Almost six months, mademoiselle,' she admits, her voice shaking. 'We barely escaped the roundup last September.'

I nod, understanding. Word was that Jews were loaded onto trains in nearby Lille and sent to a transit camp in Belgium before being deported to a camp. Auschwitz. Railway workers rescued more than thirty unfortunate souls, but that didn't stop the Nazis. The arrests continued.

'We thought we were safe.' She clenches her fists. 'We're French Jews. Most of the deported were Polish. But they're coming for us next... I feel it.'

I remain quiet. I understand. There's a network of sly looks and whispers that get passed along in the Jewish community about upcoming arrests by the Nazis. Which means that difficult, heartbreaking decisions must be made. Quickly. I give this brave mother the stage because she needs to say it out loud to convince herself the threat is real... and that she's doing the right thing for her children, though we haven't yet rendezvoused on a meeting of the minds or forged a plan. I need more information from her first.

'You have family here in Roubaix?' I ask her. I need to know if anyone else is aware she came here. I've seen what happens in other villages when the Gestapo comes up with a list of undesirables to eradicate to 'keep the *Vaterland* safe' and line their pockets with Reichsmarks. The greedy bastards get paid by the body count.

A long pause. 'My husband was shipped off to Germany to work in a factory under the new mandatory labor law.' She fidgets with her thick, gold wedding band, twisting it as if it's a magic ring, willing it to bring him back.

'Was he working for the Underground?' I want to know who I'm dealing with. She doesn't answer me. I expected that. Still, I have to be careful.

'Please, mademoiselle, my children are in danger. Only you can help us.'

'I'm an aerialist, what can I do?' I play innocent. I have no way to help her even if I wanted to hide her children, especially with the secret police showing up for phony 'inspections' without warning.

She smiles wide. 'I heard you're an angel... without wings.'

I turn, face her head on. That's what Gunty used to call me. Our special code when I needed to talk to him. I wonder, *can* I trust her? I want to, but in the end it isn't the toughness on the woman's face or her pleas that corral my heart, but her little girl's youthful curiosity... and belief in a fairy-tale-like dream.

'Can you *really* fly like a dove, mademoiselle?' the child asks me, staring hard at my white satin costume drying on the clothesline, then waving her arms about and pretending to soar high. 'Can you save Jakob and me from the bad soldiers?'

Oh, the way my heart tugs at hearing her sad but hopeful words, this *petite jeune fille* so young but already aware of the 'bad soldiers'. Yet she believes I can fly and save her brother. *She's* the angel, not me.

The woman pulls her daughter close to her, embarrassed by the child's blatant honesty. 'Forgive Anna, mademoiselle, she worries so about us. She even refused to eat the orange we found lying on the ground and gave it to me.'

'She's a brave little girl.' I continue hanging up wet washing, knowing this could be a trap. I still have my suspicions so I hesitate, though I want to help her. Want to badly. Before I can get over my fears, I get the awful feeling we're being watched, the morning breeze scenting the air with more than the smell of elephant dung, but a strong perfume and cigarettes.

Nadia.

She sashays by me, wrinkling her nose. 'It smells over here. Must be that soap you used.' She sniffs the air. 'Or is it something else?'

'It's *you*, Nadia... No one else smokes *Nazi* cigarettes,' I pop off in a flippant manner, then hold my nose. She's just fishing but I shield the Jewish woman with my laundry basket when she pulls her jacket tight around her. She's not wearing a yellow star, but the damage is done. Nadia is suspicious and that's enough to raise the hair on the back of Herr Richter's neck. I convince myself she's merely jealous. Spying on me to see who I talk to, notably if it's male with strong shoulders. I see her shake her head, then puff on her cigarette and walk toward the cookhouse.

Bon. Good riddance.

The woman gathers her son and daughter into the folds of her long skirt. 'We'll be going, mademoiselle,' she says, her lower lip trembling. 'We don't want no trouble.'

She starts to head off toward the morning horizon, giving me the horrible feeling that she and the children will disappear in the Nazi death camps if I let them go. Because I'm worried about my own safety? Seeing Félix arrested put me on edge and, if I dare say, has shaken my confidence. This isn't me. I'm Queen of the Air. It's time I start believing my own press. I immediately regret my overly critical mind and stumble after them in my backless slippers.

'No, wait,' I call out, sloshing through the wet grass. 'I need to know... Who sent you?'

The Jewish woman swings around, her eyes hopeful. I admire her dramatic pause, and as one who knows that a pause can be most effective with a dash of poise, she lifts her chin and says, 'Henri.'

I don't know any Henri.

'Sorry, I never heard of him.' I grimace, then turn away and go back to my own little world.

'He said that he misses the old days... the two of you peeling potatoes together.' She pauses. 'And the sea. He said you'd know what that means.'

Of course. Gunty. I draw in my breath and hold it for what seems like minutes while I mull this whole thing over. 'Is he a rugged, brawny man with a hearty laugh?'

She nods.

'This Henri... Where did you meet him?'

'He came to my father's button-and-thread shop in Lille to acquire new identity papers, but my father disappeared six months ago. I've been carrying on his work,' she finishes without missing a beat.

'*You* forged the papers?' I admit surprise gives my voice a funny squeak. This delicate woman defied the Nazis?

'I'm under no illusion, mademoiselle,' she says, 'that I will escape the wrath of the Third Reich. I will soon be arrested because I printed false papers and ration cards in the basement of our shop.'

'It takes great skill to forge papers. Where did you—'

'I was a watercolorist before the war,' she cuts me off, no doubt eager to get her business done. 'I came to the circus when it was in town to draw the clowns. My specialty.'

She pulls out a program for a circus with a clown along with the original artwork of that same clown shimmering with bright colors and attitude, happy, funny. Yes, she's brilliant. I have great faith she's able to execute passports, travel visas, ration books, and other papers needed to escape.

'You've done the hard work, madame.' I ask, 'Why do you need me?'

'I can trust you.'

'How can you be so sure?' I have to ask.

'Henri said you've helped others escape.'

And failed. Why would I try it again? Unless—

The woman is desperate and 'Henri' needs someone he can trust to hide the children.

She lowers her eyes, her words honest and sincere when she says, 'I have nowhere else to go.'

'Your family... your religious circle?' I ask, probing her.

She shakes her head. 'We're often betrayed by our own.'

I nod. The Nazis call a Jewish person who informs a *catcher*.

'I fear discovery by the secret police,' she continues. 'A fat Gestapo man from Paris is asking questions.'

'But Roubaix is under the jurisdiction of a general based in Brussels,' I insist, 'not the German High Command in Paris.'

She shakes her head. 'That means nothing to the Gestapo. They're everywhere.'

'Hiding under rocks or in my clothes basket, I imagine.' I attempt *une plaisanterie*, then I see two children watching me, their eyes big with fear, their mouths open. I've scared the bejeebers out of them. What came over me? Fear. I learned from the clowns to use humor in a sticky situation, but it doesn't work these days. I want to grab them and hold them tight. Tell them I can keep them safe, but can I?

I make up my mind.

'Come back tomorrow early, before we leave,' I say finally. 'I need time to talk to my contact.' I can hide them in the caravan I share with Aima. She's Jewish, she'll understand.

'Tomorrow will be too late, mademoiselle. Please, I beg you. I don't care about me, but Henri said you can get my children out of Roubaix to shelter tonight where they won't be found.'

Did he mean here, the circus? No, it won't work. It's too risky for long term. But what about... No, could I? Why not help him get them away from here where they'll be safe? I don't even know if the convent is still there, or if it's occupied by the Germans. I'm thinking about the Convent of Saint Daria in Ville Canfort-Terre where I had my baby. It's located about an hour outside Paris in a medieval château run by the Order of the Sisters of Benevolent Mercy. That's where I ran to back in 1925 when I was a scared girl, my heart broken, my body readying itself for motherhood. I shall never forget the Mother Superior who shut me out of God's house because of my pregnant condition, but I hold deep love in my heart for Sister Vincent, the kind-hearted nun who saw only a frightened, heartbroken girl and hid me from her superior's wrath. How she pressed a medal of Saint Daria into my palm when I was in labor to protect me. I wouldn't be surprised if the convent dungeon houses refugees, even weapons and ammunition since the Nazis confiscated all rifles and pistols at the beginning of the war. It would also make a wonderful hiding place for the children.

My pulse is racing and I can't move. Do I have the right to do this? Ask around? I know Gunty is here. It *was* his voice I heard calling out to me. This woman is in danger, but helping her will put everyone in the circus in jeopardy. Do I dare come out of my self-imposed exile? Defy God's will? Why else would He send them to me?

If I fail, they're doomed. I can't do that to this good mother. Especially today. My baby's birthday. I know the pain of having a child taken from you, then finding out they're lying still and cold. Never again to fill your arms. And there is nothing you can do to warm them. I swear I will *not* let that happen to her and her children.

'I will help you, madame, but you must not return here or all our lives will be lost.' I turn back toward her, noticing for the first time her cheeks are wet with tears. 'Are you certain this is what you want? To send your children away?'

'I have no choice, mademoiselle, I must protect them.' She pulls off her thick gold wedding band. 'Take this and use whatever you can get for it to keep my babies safe.'

She puts the plain ring into the palm of my hand and closes my fingers around it. It's heavy, pure gold. 'I can't take this, madame, it's your wedding ring.'

She throws her head back and looks upward. 'As God is witness to my prayer, like so many women of my faith before me, if you don't take it the Nazis will... and my children will have nothing.'

'They can't be that cruel... taking your wedding ring, a sacred link to your husband.'

'I've heard the stories dripping from the lips of captured Nazi informants how they strip a woman's dignity from her, taking her clothes, watch, spectacles, even her hair and do things too horrible to mention.'

I've also heard 'stories' too horrible to believe, but I didn't want to accept the fact things were as inhumane as the woman says they are. She explained that Orthodox Jews were even more subject to humiliation because in her words, 'We are the most Jewish'.

What can I say? I place her wedding ring on my left forefinger so as not to engage God's wrath for wanting to soak up the love I know goes with it, but instead I seek His blessing. What I must do is never easy. Today is no exception except that more than my life is at stake. If I fail, the children will die. It weighs heavily upon my mind. I take extra care to make sure the Jewish mother has her privacy (behind the clothes drying on the line) to say goodbye to her babies and squeeze a lifetime into every moment, my heart wrenching along with hers. While they hug, I pull out my old blue-and-gold spangled costume with the red stars from the bottom of the basket and hang it on the washing. If Gunty *is* lurking in the shadows, I'm praying he will recognize it and contact me. See it as a signal that I need his help. Then I hold the hands of the boy and girl tight when their *maman* makes a quick dash into the main tent and out the other end so they don't see her leaving them. I hug them close and their young bodies shake. Mine, too. Then I tell them how much their *maman* loves them and so do I. I know it's wrong to get emotionally involved with these children, more so with their beleaguered mother, but on this morning, with a sudden joy of heart I haven't felt in a long time, I do it anyway. I've been living with the reality I will never have another child for so long, that I lost my mother at a young age and my papa is a bastard, it feels good to let my feelings show and cry along with them until we can't cry anymore.

Then I take my charges in tow, dry their tears and make their mouths water with sweet popcorn. We take refuge in clown alley with Anna and Jakob holding on to me for dear life, but their faces shine with wonder being behind the scenes, the banter of clowns in street clothes with their painted faces cutting up with each other. Letting their topknots down without worrying about their act getting them arrested. They're always on edge, knowing they have to be more careful than ever in the ring and not insult the Germans in our audience. But they're also protective of children and suspect something's up. No one stops me when I gather up white paint, heavy tomato-red rouge, a thick barber's brush, black shoe polish, red nose rubber props, funny carrot-pink hair, and hats. I've been in the circus so long, I know the clown makeup routine by heart, how each clown's makeup is unique to that clown only. It's only fitting I dress up the Jewish woman's children as clowns to escape the Nazis. I hustle them back to my tent, careful not to pass Nadia's caravan or the cookhouse, our arms filled with funny costumes loaned to us by the generous Heurot dwarf family of Maman, Papa, and two boys protected from deportation because of their diminutive size (I suspect Reichsmarks cross the palms of the local police), making them laugh and for a while forget they will never see their mother again. Of course, I don't tell them that. Hope for a brighter day is what we live for in the circus. I promise them they will not just see the clowns in full costume later... but they will *be* clowns.

To save them from the Nazis, I must hide them in plain sight.

10

PARIS, FRANCE—APRIL 1943

The Magician

In a city where petrol is as hard to get as a good meal without a ration book, I revel in the fact I have a motorcar at my disposal. An old Peugeot with a big, black belly and headlights that pop out like ghoul's eyes. I sense curious passers-by asking themselves *Why him? Why does he have a motorcar?* I can answer that very well, thank you. As a physician, I'm considered 'essential' to the Reich and received a permit to operate this esteemed vehicle courtesy of the office of the German High Command (Wehrmacht) located at the Hôtel Majestic. Though I removed the miniature swastika flag from the hood—it looks rather bourgeois in my opinion.

Most Parisians take me for Gestapo or plainclothes French police when I speed down the grand boulevards weaving in and out of the light traffic with the windows down, avoiding bicycle riders, the wind blowing in my face. I like it that way. Gives me a certain cachet when I step out onto the curb, brush off my gloves, adjust my black Fedora. I intend to use that privilege this afternoon to further my acquaintance with the lovely Jeanne Joubert.

Rambling down the country road like a favorite uncle on holiday, I heave out a sigh, then burp loudly. (I think of Herr Geller now every time I expel gas through my mouth, damn him.) Undigested cheese. So difficult these days to get the aged goats' variety I'm used to, but one does what one has to. Still, it's unlike me to suffer an upset stomach over a woman, what the uninitiated refer to as *butterflies*. Most days, I spend my time with the fairer sex under less than pleasant circumstances, whether I'm cutting away layers of damaged skin or injecting morphine to slow their pulse until they turn blue, but I can't stop thinking about Jeanne's perfect face. It fascinates me how nature used her skill to recreate the beauty reserved for an exquisite flower onto the face of a young female.

Not surprising. Her papa is a most handsome man, but is the girl's mother as beautiful as her daughter? I haven't seen Gisèle Casini Joubert for years... I think back, but I don't remember her face striking me as extraordinary. She stopped performing after an accident years ago on the rings and is confined to a wheelchair. Unfortunately, I can do nothing for spinal injuries.

Humming, as I often do in the surgery, I'm in a delightful mood when I come to a fork in the road and maneuver the motorcar over the open field. I've been driving north from the city to the outskirts of Paris not far from Argenteuil where the circus tents and colorful caravans brush up against each other like a small, mythical village. I've looked forward to this visit since I completed my reconstructive work on Zera Bovier—a very successful operation, I might add. After giving the young woman a smooth new face and her python Violetta a full belly—my assistant Berthile is thrilled to have a rodent-free abode—I came up with a plan. Since Mademoiselle Jeanne doesn't require my services—*merci* to the heavens for that—giving me no venue as an entrée to get closer to her, I intend to offer my services as an on-call physician to her papa, the circus owner Monsieur Philippe Joubert. God knows, they need medical assistance. According to Mademoiselle Bovier, the small circus boasts only a tiny medical tent stocked with clean, white gauze bandages, antiseptic, a jar of oil salve, and is staffed by a... clown.

A clown. It's absurd. How this happened, I can't imagine, but no one knows much about this funnyman-doctor with a mysterious past except he came to the circus twenty years ago from England and he can bandage a sprained ankle or wrist with trained skill, treat food poisoning with amazing accuracy, and set broken bones. I believe the clown goes by the name of Socrates or Socks... An uncanny moniker, but then again, clowns are social misfits, *n'est-ce pas*? Yet I respect how he treated Mademoiselle Bovier's wounds albeit in the most rudimentary manner, tending to the burns with cool water, then applying petroleum jelly and covering them with a sterile bandage. Then, making a sad clown face, she told me, he urged her to seek further medical attention because her burns were serious and he had no skill with skin grafts and facial reconstruction. I imagine it was he who put the word out on the circuit the girl needed help and I answered the call.

I chuckle. I wonder what he'd say if he knew the price the girl must pay for my services. I received a report from Herr Geller that she's already balking at her first assignment for Hitler's minions at 84 Avenue Foch after she's healed— she'll return to Le Cirque Casini and spy on Philippe Joubert, who had no choice but to agree to rehire her... and Violetta. The python is a big hit with the children, rather slimy creatures themselves with runny noses and the like. *Why return to that circus?* I asked Herr Geller. It seems Berlin has some changes in store for Le Cirque Casini, and Monsieur Joubert isn't cooperating. I have confidence Mademoiselle Bovier will come around to fulfilling her mission or... well, I have my duty.

C'est la vie.

I have to say, I'm surprised when I squeal the big, black motorcar to a halt alongside the unpaved road near the main tent and no one rushes out to gawk at the stranger invading their midst.

Then I see why.

A huge pachyderm is stampeding across the road chasing after a baby elephant heading for the nearby forest. Then comes a balding gentleman in outrageous blue silk pantaloons with a white clown face chasing after them. Behind him is a motley crew of clowns, tent-men, acrobats, jugglers, followed by a man in jodhpurs, white shirt, and knee-high black boots yelling commands. *'Josephine... Bébé! Home... now!'* The animal trainer, I presume.

I chuckle. Morning exercise at the circus. The scene is like a comic opera without the music and a very short libretto.

I admit I'm curious to see how this scenario plays out when a beautiful blonde races past me on a bicycle, grabbing my attention. She's riding astride the seat dressed in those damned split skirts or trousers women have taken to wearing these days—culottes—along with a white blouse and flimsy blue felt hat tied under her chin with a pink ribbon. Platforms with the toes cut out. She looks as fresh and delicious as country milk. She's headed in the opposite direction on the road back to Paris, her bottom bouncing up and down on the seat. Of note is a square straw box tied securely to the bicycle. It takes me but a moment to recognize Jeanne Joubert. Where is she going in such a hurry? To rendezvous with her lover? My heart pings, my face flushes, cheeks bulge, lips pursed tight together. I won't have it. She belongs to *me*. I grab the steering wheel so hard I nearly rip off the leather cover, twist and pull until I turn this behemoth of a motorcar around so I can follow her—

Past fields of flowers, pink roses, peonies, and violets. The scent in the air is as pure as a young girl's heart. I can guess why. I believe there's a perfume factory nearby run by the House of Doujan, a posh perfume shop on Rue Saint-Honoré in Paris. A thought crosses my mind... Perhaps I should purchase scent for my surgery. Seducing the mesdemoiselles into a dreamlike state with alluring perfume is an interesting concept I shall consider. For now, I can't let Mademoiselle Joubert out of my sight.

I pull up alongside her and call out the window, 'May I give you a ride, mademoiselle?'

She keeps pedaling, eyes straight ahead. 'You're following me, monsieur, why?'

'I'm a friend of Mademoiselle Zera Bovier... and Violetta.' Why I added the reptile I don't know, but it seemed a normal thing to say. Making me wonder if I *have* gone daft. No, desperate fits better.

'Zera?' She turns her face toward me and it's not the sincere curiosity in her eyes that makes my heart flutter, but it's her beauty that breaks down my defenses. I shan't give up.

'I wish to speak to you.' I attempt to turn on the charm with a bigger smile than I usually entice my facial muscles to execute because I've been told it shows off a remarkable dimple in my left cheek that pleases the mesde-moiselles.

It works. Her eyelids flutter, and is she pedaling slower?

'Pardon, monsieur, but I'm late.' She hesitates, then, 'I'm meeting a friend in Montmartre, perhaps later—'

That hellhole. Only deviants of society dwell there. I must stop her, not with accusations. With sugar. The only kind we have left in these times. Flattery.

'He's a lucky man to catch the eye of a pretty girl like you.' I slow the motorcar down to a crawl.

She laughs and it's a lovely sound that makes my skin tingle. '*Mais non*, monsieur, Papa would lock me up in the lion cages.' She stops her bicycle and shades her eyes, staring at me. 'But Zera Bovier told me what you did for her before she left for the sanitarium. I'm very grateful to you. She's a good soul.'

'Then you *do* remember me?' I ask, a joyful tug at my heart.

'Of course. You were watching me on the trapeze. It's always delightful when *someone* appreciates my work.' She frowns. 'Unlike some people I know.'

Her papa?

'*Pardon,* monsieur.' She leans over and whispers, 'I must be on my way. I can't be late or she'll leave.' She looks around, making certain no one can hear us. Why, I don't know. I'm parked in the middle of the road surrounded by trees and flowers. Not a human or grazing bovine in sight. Her obsession with privacy tells me her trip to Paris is very important to her.

'Where are you meeting "this friend"?' I ask.

'At a bistro in the Place du Tertre. I'm on a secret mission.'

'*You,* mademoiselle?' This frightens me. Has the Gestapo somehow wound its influence around her, lured her into their trap? I must find out. I couldn't bear it if I had to... well, you know. I get out of the motorcar, bow low, and extend a hand to her. 'Pray, let me assist you.'

'It won't be a secret if I tell you, monsieur,' she teases.

I have to convince her to let me in. Whatever she's hiding, it must be in that straw basket.

'Then let me guess. You're bringing hot soup to your sick friend.' Riding her bicycle, it will take her around an hour to get there.

She laughs. 'Don't be silly, monsieur. The soup would get cold by the time I got to Paris.'

My eyes widen with feigned surprise. 'Of course, why didn't I think of that?'

'If you *must* know, monsieur'—she turns serious—'I'm bartering eggs and carrots and butter for something special that I need for my birthday performance.'

'Your birthday?'

She nods. 'I turn eighteen in two weeks. I can't wait.'

'Then you *must* allow me to drive you to the city.'

She lets go with a deep sigh, giving in. '*Bien*, I shall, but only because Zera speaks highly of you, *Docteur Rose*,' she says, grinning, 'and Violetta likes you, too.'

I raise a brow, horrified. That damned snake had its head pushed into my groin. What would have happened if it *didn't* like me?

I put my reptile experience into a box and push it to the back of my mind. It's best left there. I have a new mission. Life is beautiful. I can't believe my good fortune when Jeanne Joubert jumps into the passenger seat of my motorcar, smooths down her 'culottes' and crosses her ankles, then rambles on about this secret surprise she's picking up for her birthday show. She's so enthusiastic, I have to ask myself, *Is this really happening?* Girl talk in a black Peugeot that doubles for a Nazi vehicle while the world is at war. Somewhere, bombs are falling. Women are being sent to Ravensbrück for no other reason than they're Jewish. And the Führer is orchestrating more mayhem.

And here I am with this beautiful girl planning her birthday, as if everything in the world revolves around her. Was *I* ever that naïve? I'd forgotten how joyful it feels to be untainted by life's tragedies. To know nothing about the scars one acquires over the years on one's soul. Yes, I'm a scarred man, forced to carry out my duty in the name of Gestapo justice and recruit those unfortunates robbed of their feminine beauty either by accident, a jealous lover, or, these days, the sadistic games of the SS. Not Mademoiselle Jeanne. She's such an innocent, this girl with the perfect face, so young and unschooled in the ways of life, believing in the goodness of others. Even me.

A man whose obsession with beauty—restoring faces, healing them, then sending them into the darkness with dignity when they fail to pay the price demanded of them—drives me to obsession, an obsession I can't control.

Murder.

I pray I won't be her downfall.

* * *

We tie her bicycle to the trunk of my motorcar—I always carry spare rope, should I need it to restrain the mesdemoiselles I take on from escaping their fate—and stow away the straw basket of food in the rear seat, then I carry on a lively conversation with Mademoiselle Jeanne while we head toward Paris in my motorcar. Over the next hour, we talk about her act in the circus and the dangerous tricks she performs on the trapeze. I try to keep my eye on the road, attempting to read the confusing signs now in German script, but I can't help but sneak a peek at her sock-covered toes protruding through white anklets. I brace myself for the jubilant squeeze I get in my groin when I eye a pair of pretty feet, then let it go. *Ahh...* I keep my face masklike to maintain my self-control, just barely, making small talk and rambling on with an amused smirk about the two elephants I saw chased by the clowns.

'You mean Josephine and Bébé. The baby elephant loves to play hide and seek with the clowns, but Maman Josephine doesn't approve and chases after her.' She says their names in a soft, gentle tone as a mother hen might gush about her baby chicks. With care and with heart. Makes me lonely for my childhood when my *maman* would praise my flower drawings in the same gentle voice and have the cook bake a sweet bread with lots of cinnamon sugar, but then leave the room in tears when my little sister Noemi threw a tantrum and yanked the arm off her doll, then the leg. I would sit calmly licking the cinnamon sugar off my fingers. I learned to ignore her outbursts and went on with my business, but our dear mother assuaged her head pain with laudanum. A way of coping with what she conceived as failed motherhood. Until everything got to be too much for her wistful soul. It was I who found her. My first experience with the deadly effects of the opium tincture. I would later use it for my own purposes, but at that moment I was a naïve but curious sixteen-year-old. Trying to understand why she was so still. Lips blue. Not moving. Never again did I hear that voice. It delights me now to hear such a gentle tone again.

'The elephants have *names*?' I ask, surprised, though I shouldn't be, having had the pleasure of making the acquaintance of an overly friendly reptile named Violetta.

'Of course, monsieur.' She turns her pretty face to me, a look of concern making a frown line between her eyes. It's all I can do not to lean over and smooth it out with my thumb. Habit, of course. 'The elephants are part of our circus family and are most dear to me.'

Her kindness touches my soul like warm vanilla sauce. For the first time in years, I feel a rapport with a woman I'm not involved with on a professional level.

'You invite them for tea, I suppose?' I tease. Oh, it's lovely being with a young woman I'm not about to draw the last breath out of.

'Every afternoon at four.' She grins. 'Bébé loves apricot jam biscuits.'

'As do I.' I laugh without embarrassment. *Bon.* She's watching me, seeing how I react to her girlish attempts at humor. She's testing me. Why? An awkward silence falls between us. I, pondering my thoughts. *What do I do next?* Give her back her wisp of silk? No, I'll keep it. I so enjoy sniffing her scent, it's like when I imbibe a glass of brandy. And her, well, I don't know. I rarely entertain amusing conversation with the mesdemoiselles since I must maintain a professional demeanor as a physician, but Jeanne is different. I *want* her to flirt with me and me with her. I glance at her out of the corner of my eye and see Mademoiselle Jeanne looking out the passenger window at the elegant buildings, grand boulevards, then at me while running her fingers over the bare skin on her neck, as if she's trying to make up her mind about something.

Finally, she finds the courage to speak what's on her mind and it's the last thing I expect to hear. 'I may have a job for you, monsieur.'

'A job for *me*?' I slam on the brakes on a steep narrow street, startled by her words. We're not far from Sacré-Coeur and but a few minutes from the bistro of her rendezvous on Place du Tertre. I turn, study her eyes. Filled with a blue, thick like ganache, a deep, rich color one sees only in a cloudless blue sky. Bright, pure. Honest. I feel compelled to answer her with the truth. 'I'm not in competition with God, mademoiselle. He has given you His greatest gift. Your skin is perfect, as if it were spun from liquid gold.'

She laughs. 'How kind of you, monsieur. But you haven't seen me without face powder.' She blushes. 'I have freckles.'

I'm at a loss for an answer. I have to come up with something to appease her *and* myself... Ah, yes. I have it.

'Dots of a deep, golden sunset then.' I grin. Not bad for a dodgy old doctor without a poet's bone in his body. I continue maneuvering the motorcar through the narrow streets of Montmartre in the artists' quarter where windmills once stood. I'm nearly twenty years her senior, but I shall never admit it. And she'll never guess. I've been blessed with a marvelous epidermis. The pores around my eyes and cheeks are so tiny they disappear even under a microscope.

'It's for my friend Sandrine.'

'Sandrine,' I repeat. 'An unusual name. Let me guess. You're meeting with her today.'

'Yes. She's a dancer at the Bal Tabarin, not far from here.' She lowers her eyes as women do when they've uttered a faux pas.

'Mademoiselle... you have something to add?'

'Well, she's not really a friend, monsieur, Papa would never approve. I met her when she starting coming to the circus on the arm of Nazi officers. I was shocked to see a Frenchwoman fawning over the Boches, but she whispered to me the cabaret manager *makes* her go out with them. That if she doesn't, things won't go well for her.' A pause. 'I get it. We *have* to let them into the show; we even have to give them free seats. An edict from the Führer. I don't dare tell

Papa the SS officers want me to dine with them. He'd make me go. He says we must be agreeable with the Occupiers, keep our noses clean, but don't act obstinate or argue with them. I don't understand Papa, why he doesn't fight back.'

Because he's protecting you, my lovely, and knows the consequences if he opposes them.

'I want to fight them, but every time I find the political tracts opposing the Reich someone left in the main tent, he makes me tear them up and throw them away.'

He sounds like a wise man doing his best to keep the circus going, but for how long? In my position I hear things... things that will upset you, mademoiselle... A change is coming... as you shall see.

'I *hate* the Nazis, monsieur,' she continues, 'and I don't care who knows it.' She's breathing hard, relieved to say what she thinks.

'You're an intelligent girl, mademoiselle, but may I offer a word of caution?' I say slowly, parking the motorcar on the cobblestone street at a rather awkward angle. Not my choice for an afternoon tea. The young hooligans smoking on the corner with their caps pulled down over their eyes are not the welcoming committee I'd hope for. I huff out a breath. I should have left that damn swastika flag attached to the hood so no one disturbs the vehicle; then again, the pretty mademoiselle would never have allowed me to drive her to Paris in a car so adorned. 'Your papa knows best. Do what he says.'

She makes a face. 'Not you, too, monsieur?'

I panic at the thought of losing her and come back quickly with: 'I meant for your safety, mademoiselle. I would be heartbroken if anything happened to you.'

Her lips part in surprise. 'You really mean that, don't you?'

I nod.

'*Alors*, I'm flattered. Nobody cares about me, only that I can do double somersaults.' She lifts up her chin. 'I'm going to change that when I turn eighteen. I'm going to run away and—'

'Join the circus?' I quip.

She laughs. 'Oh, monsieur, you're too funny. But you're right, where am I to go? Le Cirque Casini is my home, my family... I can't abandon them in these difficult times. No, I must stay and fight the Boches *my* way.'

'How?'

'By helping Sandrine so she doesn't have to do... you know, unpleasant things to survive.'

I say in a quiet tone, 'Admirable, mademoiselle, but how well do you know this girl?'

Jeanne gets her dander up. 'When she comes to the circus, we talk and talk forever after the show. She's so... so sophisticated and independent. I want to be just like her.'

'Is that wise?' I say with caution. 'This Sandrine you speak of... your papa would not approve, *n'est-ce-pas?*'

'I don't care. Papa lives in his own little world. All he cares about is increasing house attendance, getting enough meat for the lions, hiring tent-men before the Germans deport them. He doesn't understand. You don't either, monsieur. You're a physician and sheltered from how life *is* now in Paris. How the Nazis hurt good people, *circus* people, making me afraid for them. I can't forget the awful, disgusting things I've seen, like how they treated the Jewish performers in our circus when we played Warsaw. I was only fourteen, but I shall never forget when they grabbed the woman's baby and...' She doesn't elaborate, *to spare me*? Oh, the dear girl. 'Anyway, like I said, I may have a job for you.' She smiles, adroitly changing the subject as smoothly as any sophisticate. 'Zera said you have the most skilled hands.'

'Did she?'

'And seeing how Sandrine had a bit of bad luck recently with the SS...'

'Most unfortunate, mademoiselle.' I smile, then wait. Of course I'm curious, but I've learned to assess a situation in a most cautious manner. That such a leading statement is often the beginning of a confession that will become apparent without further coaxing. Mademoiselle Jeanne has been holding in her emotions for so long, she can't wait to tell me.

'This horrible SS officer hurt her and I think you can help her.'

'Really?' I feign innocence and keep my composure, but my fingers tingle. I sense this is going to be interesting. This is also the opportune moment to present my credentials and, with a swift movement inside my breast pocket. I hand her my card.

Jeanne scans it, touching the raised printing with her fingertips, the fancy script. 'Docteur Thaddeus Rose... you *are* a class act.'

I make my pitch. 'Mademoiselle Bovier told me you're in need of a physician at Le Cirque Casini, *n'est-ce pas?*'

'Well, yes. Socks does his best...'

'You mean the clown Mademoiselle Bovier told me about?' I need to move this conversation along while I have her in my pocket. 'I would like to offer my services on an "as needed" basis.'

'Oh, I see. Socks is a dear, but he's not a real doctor.' She stuffs my card into her trousers. 'I'm sure Papa would approve. So many times our performers get hurt and there's no room for them at the American Hospital of Paris. Papa sends them to the Nazi-run hospitals instead, but I always fear they'll never return.'

'Good. Then it's settled.' Of course, it isn't. I must speak to Monsieur Joubert but with his daughter's enthusiasm, I don't foresee any problem. 'First, I shall assist to the needs of Mademoiselle Sandrine.'

'Don't say anything to her yet, monsieur, please. I'll do the talking. I don't want to embarrass her,' Jeanne says, grabbing the straw basket of food from the rear seat, then taking my hand as I help her out of the motorcar. A spark... or so it feels to me when I make contact with her smooth skin, then she pulls away, confusion clouding her eyes. Did she feel it as well? My, this *is* an interesting turn of events. A connection outside my usual quick brush in a woman's company before I administer the anesthesia or prick her skin with a sharp syringe. What *did* she feel when she touched me? I want to know, but I refrain from asking, allowing the seed to grow. 'Let *me* introduce you,' Jeanne continues, her eyelids fluttering, 'Sandrine is very shy.'

11

ROUBAIX, FRANCE—APRIL 1943

Circus Richter
Lia

Gunther Hein could peel a potato in twenty seconds flat, whip it up into a fried wonder with onions on a portable stove as if it were food from the gods. But today, his hands are slow with arthritis and I imagine painful when he grabs me and hugs me.

'Lia, my angel without wings, you were never prettier.'

'Gunty, you old seadog, how'd you find me?' I laugh when he grabs me around the waist. It feels good to have this dear man hold me, giving me strength when I need it. He was the big brother I never had. When I see tears in his eyes, I get warm and flustered, my cheeks tinting. He looks older, tired, dressed in a long overcoat, scarf. He's clean-shaven, surprising me. The beard is gone. He's as overjoyed as I am at this reunion. But it won't last. We both know why he's here. I finish taking down my laundry off the clothesline as the late afternoon sun cast a golden glow on his weathered face.

'When I heard about the amazing aerialist who could do a two and half somersault and reputed to do a triple... I knew it had to be you.'

I smile. 'I don't do the triple much these days, Gunty, it puts too much unwanted attention on me in these difficult times.' I start to pick up my laundry basket, but he takes it for me. I smile. 'What are you doing here in France?'

'I found a hungry bunch of Resistance fighters who needed a cook.' He grins. 'Not to mention, I hate Nazis.' A pause, deep heavy breath. 'When I saw how they treated the Jewish circus family where I worked, beating them, then shooting the oldest boy in the back when he tried to protect his mother, I couldn't stand by and not join the fight.'

The horror of his words grabs me with a terror I haven't felt since I failed saving the twins. I sigh, 'So that's why you sent that poor woman to me.'

'Esther.' He turns serious, his eyes glowing with respect. 'She forged my papers for me. Or should I say for "Henri".' He grins. 'She's an amazing artist, Lia.'

'And she adores her children, as do I.' I explain how I'm dressing them as clowns during the show to keep them hidden from any curious eyes. 'You knew I couldn't say no.'

He hugs me again. 'Esther can't believe how lucky she is to find you.'

'I'm in, Gunty, but what more can I do? Keep them in the show for a day or two, then what?' I tell him about the convent in Ville Canfort-Terre, and he agrees that it's a better place for him to hide them than a loft in a barn. 'Ask for Sister Vincent.' I clench my fists. 'But be careful, Gunty, we have an informant in the troupe.'

'That girl at the ticket booth?'

'Yes. Nadia.'

'I suspected as much, the way she cavorts with German soldiers, flirting and promising "favors".' He smirks, but doesn't say what kind. Then it hits me.

'*You*, Gunty?' I ask, curious.

'How do you think I got here?' He opens his overcoat and I see a German soldier's uniform underneath. 'Don't worry, I'll keep an eye on her and get those children to safety.' He hugs me tight and then whispers in my ear. 'Here's the plan...'

12

PARIS, FRANCE—APRIL 1943

The Magician

Did Mademoiselle Jeanne say her friend is *shy*? I roll my eyes, then take a sip of wine while trying to keep the smirk off my lips. Sandrine Aubert is a redheaded mamselle, poured into a tight, low-cut satin green dress with her bosom pushed up and falling out of the bodice like two ripe melons. She's anything but shy. Loud, boisterous, smoking strong-smelling German cigarettes, adjusting the angle on her smart cloche hat to accent her upswept eyes and, with words dripping off her tongue I've never heard even from the Gestapo, she exhibits every bit the behavior you'd expect from a cabaret dancer, as she swishes a purple silk scarf over her shoulder.

'So I says to the lieutenant,' she spouts, finishing her glass of wine. Her second. 'I ain't playing your games, monsieur. I'm respectable. And I got talent.'

She waves her glass in the air, looking for the waiter. We're seated at one of two tables outside the ancient bistro. It's a quiet morning with few passers-by. An old man sits at the other table, beret pulled down over his eyes, the *Paris-soir* laid out before him, but I believe he's asleep. I hear gentle snoring. I'm still on my first glass and Jeanne hasn't touched hers. She keeps fussing with the clasp on the straw basket sitting on her lap, unaware of what's she doing. She barely takes a breath, her eyes fixed on the dancer. She's in awe of this mademoiselle, hanging on to her every word. The woman is as cheap as faux pearls, but Mademoiselle Sandrine represents what Jeanne wants. Desperately. Freedom to lead her own life, *but at what cost?* I wonder.

Jeanne adds with a smile, 'Sandrine is the lead dancer at Bal Tabarin.'

The older girl's eyes soften, enjoying the adulation from this innocent child. She puts a hand on Jeanne's arm. '*Was*, Mademoiselle Joubert, till I got canned because of what that SS bastard did to me.'

I take the bait, eager to move this encounter along since I tend to get impatient with the games females play. I'm used to being in control of *every* situation. 'I find it difficult to believe an esteemed officer of the Reich would—'

She cuts me off with: 'See for yourself, monsieur.'

Before I can blink, she yanks off her flimsy scarf and exposes several deep, round cigarette burns on her neck. Deep layers of skin destroyed with small circular burns arranged in such a way to resemble a swastika. It turns my stomach. However low class Mademoiselle Aubert is, she's still a beautiful woman; and to see her scarred with second-degree burns and oozing blisters, dark and moist, is enough to set me on edge and my fingers itching to get to work. Her smug look defined by outrageously blood-red lipstick tells me she expects me to be shocked, but as we know, nothing shocks me. I am the epitome of reserve and decorum. It's my job. If I were to react to such horrors with disdain or pity, I would lose the trust and respect of my patients.

'Most unfortunate, mademoiselle, that you underwent a popular pastime employed by the Nazis at the "kitchen" on Avenue Foch.' I refer to the Gestapo torture room where arrested persons are 'encouraged' to turn in their family, friends. 'Why were you summoned there?'

'I didn't get these burns in no kitchen, monsieur,' she insists. 'I got drunk and hooked up with an SS major, who hurt me just because he said he don't like how the French smell.'

'And you would like revenge, *n'est-ce pas?*' I tap my fingers on the wine glass. The challenge here is not healing her burns—child's play for me—but it will take some talking to convince her to work for the Gestapo.

'Yes. Not that it will get me my job back.'

'Docteur Rose can heal you, Sandrine.' Jeanne is eager to chime in, nodding in my direction, hope lighting up her eyes, eyes that hold me captive *whatever* I read in their depths. Ah, this is the 'job' she has for me.

'And I'm Marie Antoinette.' Sandrine puffs on her cigarette with the disdain of a woman past believing in miracles.

Jeanne won't give up. 'He can make you forget you ever had scars.'

'But can he pay the wine bill?' Sandrine challenges me, giving me a hard stare. I take my time, sipping my classic red. She's quite a handful and needs taming before I take her on, so I let her rant. 'Where is that waiter?' she says in a loud voice. '*Garçon*, I need more wine.'

'*Chère* Sandrine, please listen,' Jeanne laments, 'you mustn't be so stubborn.'

'I don't trust any man to put his hands on me. Ever. Again.'

'He's a doctor, Sandrine. I've seen what he can do to heal a woman's face.'

She smiles. 'So I look as pretty as you? *Alors*, Jeanne, no doctor, no matter how good he is, can do that.'

'Me?' Jeanne asks.

'Youth. It's Mother Nature's trick on us girls. By the time we realize what we have, it's gone. Like a peach falling from the tree. Pretty to look at for spring picking until it gets tossed around and ends up bruised with puckered skin.'

I raise a brow. I'm impressed. The woman is no scatterbrain and one I'd find interesting to explore further, but as I said, female games make me impatient. Time for me to step in.

'Mademoiselle Aubert is in need of more wine, Mademoiselle Jeanne,' I say, then name an expensive vintage. 'Can you go and ask the waiter for her?' I send her a knowing look, signaling I will take over.

She nods, understanding. 'Of course, monsieur.'

Jeanne sets the straw basket down on the table, then scurries inside the small bistro, leaving us alone. I notice a battered, round pink hatbox *under* the table from the House of Péroline. Oh, dear, not another hat. Is that what this afternoon is about? Female frippery? I shall vomit, and we know how distasteful I find that.

I point to the hatbox. 'For Mademoiselle Joubert?'

'Yes, for her birthday show.' She leans over and in a whisper she says with a warmth I find surprising, 'I like her. She's a very sweet girl, never looks down on me, but I don't believe you can do anything for me.' She straightens her shoulders, her voice stern and hard. 'The SS mark their victims well, monsieur.'

'I *can* work miracles.' I pull out my card. As is my preferred form, I let it speak for itself.

Dr Thaddeus Rose, purveyor of perfection in the field of plastic surgery.

'A rose never dies… she merely blooms again under my hand.'

She gasps. 'I've heard about skills such as yours, but I never thought they'd be for the likes of me.' She stutters, words choking in her throat, and do I detect tears in her eyes? She stares at my card as if fearing the words will wash away if the wetness on her cheeks falls upon the pristine white linen stock. '*Will* you help me, monsieur?'

'Yes.'

'I can't pay you until I get my job back.'

'Don't worry about that. There *is*, however, one stipulation…'

She scowls then wraps the scarf around her neck. Tight. '*No*, monsieur, you cannot seduce me with your promises. I'd rather scrub floors than—'

'*No, no, no*,' I protest, my brow perspiring. Her mere suggestion of a sexual encounter sets off a reverse reaction in me physically. This is wrong, all wrong. I am not like *them* and so she must see me for the healer I am. 'You don't understand, mademoiselle, I wish only to help you.' Wiping my brow with my squared handkerchief, I lay out an alternative plan rather than the usual spiel I give. So I tell the mademoiselle that she will work for the secret police, but only informing on SS proclivities that upset the normal order of the local population. That is, telling them about Nazi offenses against girls like her. I feel confident in making my promise since I happen to know the Gestapo has jurisdiction over criminal activities, including the SS, so it will seem reasonable to her if she starts asking questions.

Sandrine smiles wide. I hit the right nerve. Her passion for revenge against the SS runs deep. 'I look forward to seeing that bastard pay for what he did to me… and others.'

I urge her to keep our arrangement quiet, that she'll be working on a mission known only to us and the Gestapo. I shall also convince her to keep an eye on Jeanne and her Papa under the guise of her concern for the girl.

'Don't worry about me, monsieur, I can keep me mouth shut.' She taps her fingers on the closed basket. She's dying to open it. 'But I'm worried about Jeanne.'

'Oh?' I ask.

'She's too trusting, monsieur. When I went back to the circus, I acted real nice to her because I needed a job. I could see she was starved for attention, so I played her. She said she'd get me work in the circus as a ballet girl, but when the ringmaster saw the swastika burns on my neck, he threw me out like I was no better than *merde* and said he'd have me arrested if I showed my face there again. I never even had the chance to meet with the circus owner. Her father. From what I hear, Monsieur Joubert is a decent sort, but nobody wants a girl branded by the SS. I had nowhere to go, nothing to eat, so I told her my old *maman* is gravely ill, so she's been bringing me food.' She opens the straw basket Jeanne laid down on the table and her mouth begins watering. 'Eggs... oh, she's an angel...' Then a worried frown appears deep between her eyes. She snaps the straw lid closed. 'I feel guilty, I can't accept this... not after how I tricked her.'

I can't let her change her mind. 'Jeanne will feel hurt, mademoiselle, she wants to help you,' I say, acting more defensive than I should. What's come over me? I never show my hand, yet here I am expressing emotion. No, this is unheard of... I must remain professional.

'You don't get it, monsieur. *Ma mère* died years ago in Saint-Lazare Prison, but Jeanne is so damn naïve she believed my story, even when I told her I studied art at the Sorbonne. I can't pay her for the food, my money's gone, so when she told me she envied the pretty outfits I used to wear at the cabaret, I "borrowed" an old costume for her from the wardrobe.'

'And that's what is in the hatbox?'

'*Mais oui.*' She grins. 'The costume needs an alteration or two, but when Jeanne puts it on, she'll shine like a beautiful circus queen.'

I cringe, hearing her refer to my lovely Jeanne with the same phrase I use regarding the mesdemoiselles I 'save' from the hands of the SS. It's unnerving, even for an old veteran of the syringe like me.

'You wouldn't take that away from her, *n'est-ce pas*?' I say with a grim smile, hoping I haven't given myself away with a sour look.

'No, monsieur, I wouldn't.'

'Then we have an arrangement?' I ask, eager to close the deal. I don't like getting too chummy with my patients. It leads to emotional attachment neither of us can afford. I twiddle my fingers. Of course, I feel differently about Jeanne. She doesn't need my services, but I need her. Purely professional of course. I want to study her facial structure. Who knows? The day may come when I encounter a mademoiselle who needs a new face and I want to be prepared to orchestrate such a transformation using the exquisite lines of Mademoiselle Jeanne. Which is why I must keep my personal feelings in check. If I move too quickly, she'll reject me. And unfortunately, I don't adjust well to rejection. I get quite angry.

'Yes, we have a deal, Docteur Rose.' Sandrine touches my arm. No spark. I'm not surprised.

'*Bon*. I shall prepare the surgery—'

'*Shhh*, monsieur... here she comes.'

I stand up, bow from the waist and pull out the chair for this lovely girl I adore as she goes on about the waiter and how she's sorry but they don't have the wine that monsieur requested, and am I going to help Mademoiselle Aubert?

I smile. 'Of course, anything for you, Mademoiselle Jeanne. *C'est vrai*, Mademoiselle Sandrine?'

She nods and with a grand smile, Sandrine wraps her scarf around her neck, though not tightly. 'I have to go, Jeanne,' she says, handing her the hatbox. 'The costume is in here.'

'The blue one with the sequins?' she asks, eyes shining.

She nods.

'*Merci*, I can't wait to wear it.'

'It was pretty once. Now the rows of sequins are loose or gone. The buttons, too.' Sandrine tosses off her comment, eager to be on her way before she's caught in a lie. No harm in me keeping quiet about how she 'borrowed' the costume. Anything for Mademoiselle Jeanne.

Jeanne takes the two-piece costume out of the box and my brows shoot up like two arrows. It's so small, barely any cloth at all. My God, I never expected this. Perhaps I can talk her out of wearing it... Then I see her blue eyes explode like shooting stars hitting the circus spotlight. No, perhaps not.

'Oh, I love it!' she says with so much enthusiasm, I knock over my empty wine glass when my body jerks, an unexpected reaction to this jubilant young mademoiselle. 'Elsa can make the alterations—she's a genius with fixing up costumes. Wait and see!'

'Why is this blue sequin costume so important to you?' I ask, intrigued by how a piece of silk and cheap sequins defines this beautiful young woman.

'I want to show the audience I've grown up... I want *everyone* to see me as a woman, not a little girl to be ignored, that I have feelings, too, and I can be a circus queen my way, *not* theirs. I want to make the audience say, "Wow, look at her. Look at Jeanne Joubert!"'

What can I say?

We bid the pretty dancer adieu with hugs and kisses from both girls, and I see tears in the cabaret dancer's eyes. I tell her to drop by the address I write on the back of the card tomorrow morning, any time. (I never expose my precise location until I'm certain I have engaged the mademoiselle.) Since we were forced to switch to German timekeeping, one hour ahead of us before the Occupation, I never get it straight.

'I shall be there, monsieur, I promise.' Then she scurries off with the straw basket filled with eggs, carrots, and butter, her long silk scarf flying around her like a victory flag. I smile. My victory, too, having secured her promise to work for the Gestapo.

No, I don't feel a bit of guilt for my deception, as she didn't for her fib about the origins of the scanty costume so brief I blush just thinking about Mademoiselle Jeanne exposing herself in it. Still, how can I tamper with the girl's excitement? She'd classify me as an old sod and I won't have that. She doesn't stop talking all the way back to the circus grounds. I find this afternoon so amusing. I never have time to talk to my mesdemoiselles. They're either under anesthesia or gagged. A most charming afternoon with these two. I listened, about hairstyles and sequins and spangles and girlish dreams. All the while I watched Mademoiselle Jeanne so animated. She's so perfect that I can't help but inspect every inch of her.

'You will come to my birthday performance, monsieur?' she asks as we near the circus grounds.

'I wouldn't miss it for anything, mademoiselle.'

'*Bon*. I'll leave a ticket for you at the entrance... a front row seat for my friend's savior.'

'I shall look forward to it.'

Then we're here. Back at Le Cirque Casini. My time with her is over. I look over my shoulder as I park the motorcar on the side of the road. I pray they have the elephants contained by now. Yes. All clear. With a whistle on my lips, I remove her bicycle and Mademoiselle Jeanne kisses me on the cheek and rides away, the precious hatbox attached to her *bicyclette*. I dream of the day I can see her from every angle, study her, and one day, see her dip her bare, pretty toes into the Saint-James Pond in the Bois de Boulogne in Paris. Then my life will be complete.

I lean back in my motorcar, close my eyes, and dream of her. Yes, without a doubt, it was a perfect day made in heaven. I make a mental list of the wonderful things I accomplished. I acquired a new client for my friends in the Gestapo, I enjoyed repartee with a lovely companion on the drive, and this exquisite young woman allowed me to enter her life.

As the rush of excitement fills my ears and my fingers tingle, readying to perform a healing procedure to create beauty, I'm a happy man. I can't wait for the birthday of Mademoiselle Jeanne and watching her fly on the trapeze, the thrill of her spilling into me with each swing, like the colors of a rainbow filling the sky after a storm. Only one thing mars the joy in me... I uncovered very bad news from the Gestapo concerning the Le Cirque Casini. Yes, a change *is* coming, a new Nazi owner, but I shall keep it to myself.

Why spoil this perfect day?

13

ROUBAIX, FRANCE—APRIL 1943

Circus Richter

Lia

I put on my grandest smile to mask the turmoil roiling inside me when I enter the sawdust ring before tonight's show. Our last performance here in Roubaix. Earlier I packed my worn brown satchel with my press clippings, identity papers, ration card—one can't breathe without it these days. My kimono and favorite marabou backless slippers. My good luck charm. And the Jewish woman's gold wedding ring hidden in the kimono pocket. For now. I don't wear jewelry when I fly. The rest of my clothes and costumes are in two big, navy leather trunks. Then, after a busy afternoon making arrangements with 'Henri', my old friend Gunty now in the Underground, for the children's escape, I took a cleansing breath, praying tonight goes smoothly. It's time for the spectacle, the walk-around-the-ring with the other circus performers.

This includes two pint-sized clowns in big, ruffled white collars. Adorable in striped-and-polka-dot baggy costumes, white face makeup, black-rimmed eyes and blackened and rouged lips with carrot top wigs and red rubber noses. Anna and Jakob... racing around me, then under my long, white satin cape, squealing and laughing. I urged them to play tag to keep them moving and bouncing about, otherwise, they'll be too noticeable if they walk stiff and scared. Something out of the ordinary an informant or Gestapo agent would catch on to. These two children must escape... *tonight*.

I hear the trumpeter blow on his horn, announcing the parade featuring performers decked out in outrageous costumes. Hooped skirts. Plume head-dresses. Billowing capes. Ballet girls in Degas pink tutus riding ponies. Liberty horses going through their paces. And, of course, the animals. Monkeys, dogs. Giraffe. Zebra.

And a pair of lions. Sasha and his mate, Velma, in their cages on wheels.

Though Sasha has been looking poorly, roaring and bellowing at odd hours. I suspect the poor thing isn't getting enough to eat, or he has a hurt paw or even a toothache. I make a note to speak to Herr Richter, ask him to admonish the trainer for not taking care of his big cat. He's a hard taskmaster, but Herr Richter is also a businessman, as I've mentioned, and the lions are a big draw.

I pull back my shoulders, swish my long, white satin cape around me with a grand gesture and remember how lucky I am to have a place here at Circus Richter. I never tire of the magic and excitement of the circus. The smell is what I always notice first, pungent and garlicky, though I'm well used to it. I breathe in the intoxicating aroma of hay and sweet popcorn mixing together—and one can't forget the manure even if you try—and tune my ears into the upbeat marching song the band is playing. Look everywhere, sizing up the crowd. Will they laugh? Cheer? I revel in the anticipatory feeling in the audience that pops when we enter the tent. Acrobats, dancers, equestrians, wire walkers, animal trainer. Clowns. Horses, dogs, monkeys.

We strut and wave to the crowd, our costumes dazzling, intriguing. Setting the stage for what's to come. Thrills. Derring-do. If they only knew that underneath the dazzle lies secrets. Deep, horrible secrets. Collaboration with the enemy by some... fear and frustration abound... the acrobats never stop squabbling over a stolen ration book... the hidden tricolor of France the old clown wears over his heart in defiance. The animal trainer's assistant tossing barbs at him aimed to let him know she's quitting. Going to Berlin to join a bigger circus. He begs her to stay. The wire walker is nursing a sprained ankle, a flask of black-market whiskey in his pocket to kill the pain, while the clowns laugh it up and tease the crowd... including my two little clowns hiding their Jewish identity under white makeup and red rubber noses. Their innocence is weighing upon me to get this right, since to reveal who they are means their deportation to a concentration camp. We can no longer hide our heads and pretend they're 'work camps'. After a miraculous escape from Auschwitz by two prisoners, word soon spread of the horrors that go on there, the murders, starvation, cruel beatings. Their account of the inhumane conditions stunned everyone, then we picked up news of what the Nazis are calling *killing camps*.

But for now, it's circus time.

The ringmaster in his red coat and tails, tight black trousers, and shiny black top hat blows his whistle twice and cracks his whip. That's the signal for us to make another tour around the ring, giving the illusion we're a bigger circus than we are. Every performer is whooping it up, smiling and waving, the clowns blowing their horns and revving up the audience with excitement. We have to work harder these days to give the crowd their money's worth since we're a lean troupe... fewer than twenty. We lost four members to Jewish roundups at the last town but tonight we have two new little clowns. I pray the Gestapo isn't keeping count. I will not lose these little angels to their cruelty.

Yes, the war has hit us hard.

But the show must go on. And it will.

* * *

'And now, mesdames and messieurs, the sensational act you've been waiting for, renowned throughout the Reich for their daring and athletic feats, those legendary daredevils of the air who will take your breath away. The Flying Zollos!'

Cheers. Applause. German soldiers stomping their feet when I enter the ring with my partners, Sven, Aima and her brother Jean-Pierre. Aerialists usually work in threes, but we defy that rule and watch each other's back. The four of us keep our secrets. We have to. The less the other members of the circus know about us, the better. Safer for them. And us. Informants are everywhere. I'm not ruling out Nadia—there she is, eyeing me. She's riding bareback on Misty, a bay show horse with a braided mane I rode last season in the ring filling in for a sick performer, a fiery mount unless you know how to handle her, and Nadia doesn't. She's not watching where she's going, and *oops!* Misty tosses her long mane in an uppity manner and Nadia slides off the running show horse and onto her backside.

I'd snicker, but I know how much that hurts.

It saddens me I'd even consider the fact we have an informant. I've always believed a circus family is a tightly knit group, but we've become unraveled since this war started. Arrests, performers fleeing to Spain. It's not like the old days when you shared the washing or borrowed lipsticks. Or brought hot soup to a sick clown. Now I don't know my fellow performers like I did. I *do* know others also do their part, carrying messages from one town to another. I'd bet my stash of sequins the Bernaz Brothers are couriers, jugglers hiding coded messages in their juggling pins. I saw one burst open when the Czech acrobat dropped it during practice and a paper fell out. He gave me 'that look' and I quickly turned away. Later I saw several *cracked* empty pins in a trash bin that disappeared before nightfall. The three-piece band finishes tuning up; even the lions in their cages quiet down. It's showtime. The flying trapeze is the last act and the audience is pumped up. For the past hour, the crowd thrilled to daring balancing acts on the high wire. Trick riders jumping through hoops and doing somersaults on the backs of galloping ponies. Elephants doing headstands, tails waving in the air, or balancing on all fours on large round drums. The big cats perched on pedestals in the animal cage, the brave trainer putting his head into a lion's mouth. And everybody laughing hard at the clowns racing around in their 'clown car' and blasting the horn.

For me, the best part is my two little charges in full clown makeup chasing after a rabbit and rushing into my waiting arms. The audience loves it when they mimic me while I pose for the crowd, chin up, and smile big. Blow kisses. I look over the audience to judge the crowd. I'm pleased to see the townspeople showed up and outnumber the German soldiers. Four Boches in the front stall whistling, boorish prigs, and that same young lieutenant with the camera. Doesn't he have anyone else to torment? The tall officer stands up and starts filming us. I can't have him filming my little clowns in case someone catches onto my trick. Their lives are at stake.

With Félix the Clown on my mind, I unclasp the hook on the high collar of my cape and pray I don't end up like him. Then, making a sweeping gesture with my long cape like a toreador, I toss it in the lieutenant's direction. It lands at his feet and not on his head, thank God, sparing him embarrassment and me arrest. He picks it up, but puts his camera down. I breathe out when he indicates he'll return my cape after my act.

The perfect alibi.

If the Gestapo happen to show up on one of their 'surprise inspections'—more likely because of Félix's arrest—the agent will see me with the Wehrmacht officer and leave me alone. Then after a few sultry looks and a promise I'll never keep, I'll head for clown alley and grab my precious cargo then we'll head out to the rendezvous point right after my act.

I send them off with the other clowns, who know better than to question who they are. As I said, the circus is filled with secrets. I imagine the children are exhausted and will soon be napping in the corner on a bed of straw.

With a nod to the Nazi lieutenant, I ascend up the rope ladder to the trapeze platform.

A hush comes over the audience as I take one slow, provocative step at a time. I demand every eye under the big top watch me, including the German officer and his pals in Nazi uniforms sitting in the front row of the stalls, ogling my rear. *I hate it, but I have to put up with it.* I never did like Nazis, not since I performed my act on the Roman rings at the Swope Circus at the Wintergarten in Berlin back in 1936.

The night the Führer was in the audience.

The night I got the jagged scars on my upper arm that run from my shoulder to my elbow. The idea of me performing for that madman was ridiculous, but in the end, I showed them. I didn't fall for their promises. *We'll make you a star, Fräulein, all you have to do is become a member of the Party.* I smirk. The laugh was on them. They didn't know that not only am I half Roma, but also that I'd never betray France. If there's anything I hate above all else, it's traitors and collaborators.

Every performance, I cover up the scar with dangling rows of spangles on my costume and my long white satin cape. High pointy collar. Red sequins dancing on the shoulders. Not tonight. I don't want any distractions. I rip off the spangled ribbons, toss them into the air. They drift down to the sawdust like moon bursts. The scars remind me never to give up, that my strength on the trapeze gives me a freedom not many have these days, that if I keep my wits about me and not get caught, I can do my part to oust the Occupiers. Like tonight. Save two children from certain death after my performance. Wrap them up in my arms and whisk them away under my cape, like it's a cloak of invisibility, before the Gestapo can claim them.

I take another step up the ladder, then two, three.

I must not fail. I promised their *maman.*

* * *

I reach the platform, blow more kisses to the crowd. I'm on a mission tonight which makes my stomach queasy and my nerves jumpy. There are lives at stake, young innocent lives. After my act, I'll shed my spangles and sequins for a farmer's wife blue kerchief on my head, plain dress and soiled apron and hand them over to 'Henri', though he'll always be Gunty to me. He will secure them safe passage to the Convent of Saint Daria run by the Sisters of Benevolent Mercy outside Paris, and when the weather is clear, he'll hand them over to a *passeur*, a guide, who will get them to England.

This man from my past I never thought I'd see again has faith in me to do the right thing. Somehow that gives me the courage and strength I need to pull this off.

The spotlight hits Aima and Jean-Pierre as they swing out on the flybar to Sven who catches Aima, then she returns to the flybar and next it's Jean-Pierre. Perfect execution. Now it's my turn... I perform a double somersault, then return to the perch. Applause fills my ears when I see my old pal Gunty as 'Henri' enter the ring and sit down next to the German officer acting as cool as an autumn day. He's right on time. Dressed in plainclothes. I'm to hand over the children to him after my act. I look down from the perch and see him offering the Nazi sweetcorn from a paper cone. The German grabs a handful then does his 'be polite to locals' smile 'because we have to', then another man sits down between them. Black trench coat with a newspaper sticking out of his big pocket. Wide lapels, tight belt around his fat middle. Dark Fedora.

Gestapo.

I'm not surprised to see him, but why is he sitting *there*? I get terrible butter-flies in my stomach. Big ones with flappy wings. I can't breathe. I assume Henri was cozying up to the German officer to gather intelligence, but did he know the secret police were about to show up?

The Gestapo agent chats easily with Henri, then says something to the German officer, his stoic expression never changing. Like he's in a dead zone, not a circus. What a heartless thug. Doesn't he ever smile? And what's he writing on the newspaper? Notes on the circus... or is he so bored he's doing the crossword puzzle? That must be it. He's pointing to the paper and asking the officer to help him. Wait, there's more going on here. Is this one of their impromptu inspections? What if the Gestapo man gets antsy and finds the children hiding in clown alley before my act is over?

Ten minutes I'm up here. *Ten long minutes.*

I can't let him leave. I have to do something to keep him from wandering off while my act is on and poking his nose where he's not wanted. Ever since the incident at the train station last September when the locals risked their lives to save Jews from being loaded onto the railcars, the Gestapo turns up everywhere at the oddest times looking for 'strays'. I have the feeling the children's mother was followed here and then picked up. How? Nadia, of course. She saw me with the woman and later she talked. *Damn collabo.* I'll deal with her later.

I *swear* I will make her pay.

How? Brave, angry words, but exposing Nadia means exposing me... Henri. No, I shall have to find another way, yet I can't help but question, why is it the guilty like Nadia, who destroy a sensitive, good woman like Esther Fehler and reduce her life to a bare mention in this war, continue to breathe and walk on God's earth? Where is the justice in that? I swear someday I will make certain this brave mother is not forgotten.

For now, I have to reason the Gestapo man is here to round up anyone hiding in the circus while the show is on. I have to keep him from leaving and finding the children. I need something spectacular that will grab his attention, his curiosity. Because even if he has no heart, the Gestapo are curious bastards. I look around. They travel in pairs... There. Another man in a trench coat standing off to the side. I use hand gestures to alert Sven that we have a problem. He nods. Then I give the signal to the ringmaster to make an announcement.

I put up three fingers.

The triple.

He looks surprised, but grabs his mic. I need a diversion to create excitement, and my man Henri catches on something interesting is in the wind. He doesn't let me down. He beats his hand upon his chest, stomping his feet, jumping up and down and blocking the Gestapo man, but the secret policeman is getting anxious and rises from the wooden bench. Henri, bless the man's audacious courage, jumps up and spills his sweet popcorn all over the Gestapo agent. He bellows, Henri shushes him, pointing to me posing up on the platform as the ringmaster speaks—

'And now, mesdames and messieurs, hold on to your seats. You're about to witness a trick so dangerous I must ask for complete silence.'

A hush comes over the audience.

Even the Gestapo man.

'And now the beautiful, the dazzling Gaia of The Flying Zollos, a circus queen renowned throughout the Reich for her daring and danger will now attempt what few flyers have ever achieved on the trapeze.' The audience leans forward as he clears his throat. '*The triple somersault!*'

The audience gasps.

I hold in my breath, waiting, praying. Will my ploy work? Keep the Gestapo from taking off and nosing about like a pudgy bulldog, looking for meat scraps? I let out the breath I've been holding when the portly Nazi sits back down. He looks up at me. Even from up here, I can see his dark beady eyes blazing... His curiosity won out over his duty.

Got him.

Everyone holds their breath, waiting for the *triple*. I don't do the dangerous stunt at every show, though I practice the triple nearly every day, swinging from bar to bar with help from my partners pushing the bar toward me at the precise moment so I can grab onto it. If I miss, I have the safety net. God knows, I come out of the third somersault like a bullet... blind, and with only a split second for the catcher to grab me and for me to grab him. It's an aerial *pas de deux*. I can't make a mistake, which means to complete the triple, I can't rely only on instinct, guts. Training is tantamount. I worked for years with the best catchers in Berlin, Berne, Brussels... and once upon a time in Paris. At Le Cirque Casini. A time in my life I don't talk about, but I've never had so much riding on doing the triple as tonight.

I can't fail.

I chalk my hands, nod to my fellow *artistes* standing on the platform next to me, then call out '*hup*' and take off from the perch. I do a wide swing back and forth, holding on to the bar but not too tight, kicking my legs up to the ceiling. A hush comes over the audience and I admit this is my greatest pleasure. The extraordinary moment when I take their minds off the war, the rationing, the pain of losing loved ones... make them forget the enemy is sitting among them, planning God knows what next. But for these ten minutes when I do my act, the world is a beautiful place for them. For me.

Twenty meters up high in the tent, speeding through the air at nearly a hundred kilometers an hour, I let go of the flybar, tuck my head to my knees and—

One, two... three!

I complete the triple. Return to the flybar, then the perch. I feel pumped, ready to take on the whole damn Nazi regime to save those children. I wave to the crowd with the biggest smile on my face though my heart is pumping madly, so fast the blood is filling my ears and I feel giddy. It's wonderful.

Like I said, I can fly.

14

ROUBAIX, FRANCE—APRIL, 1943

Circus Richter
Lia

'Don't be afraid of the lion, *mes enfants*,' I whisper, holding on to the children's small, cold hands. Anna squeezes my fingers so tight, I wince. Poor child is terrified. Damn Nazis doing this to an innocent little girl in pigtails is unforgivable. 'Sasha is nothing but a big ole scaredy-cat.'

'Are you sure, mademoiselle?' I hear a squeaky little boy's voice ask. Jakob.

I turn, smile. 'Of course I am.'

I don't tell this curious little boy I have experience with big cats like Sasha, and even if I did help deliver his mate Velma's cub several months ago, they're still wild animals and can act unpredictably, though I've never lost my sentiment for the animals in the circuses where I perform, going back to my childhood when my papa put me on the back of a horse when I was five. Still, we have to be careful since I observed earlier Sasha is acting moody and could be in pain.

On cue, the lion growls and puts his paw through the bars on his cage, catching my cape in its grip and ripping it. I stiffen, pull in my gut. The move is as startling to me as that night in Berlin when the lion attacked me. My cape falls open and reveals my bare left arm. And the three long jagged scars.

The little boy points to my arm, curious. 'Did you get hurt, mademoiselle?'

I smile. A chilly smile because there are some things you don't forget. 'A long time ago. It's all healed now.'

'Who hurt you?' Anna wants to know.

'A big bad wolf with a funny moustache,' I joke. 'Come, children.'

A nursery rhyme of my own making, but we'll leave it at that. I want to get these babes to safety so they'll have a chance at life. What sets my mood spiraling downward is that their mother may pay for their freedom with her own life. And her wedding ring. I can't forget that. I know she wants me to pawn it, and I shall, and send the money to her children through the Red Cross, but what if I could return it to her after the war? Silly me, *that's* a fairy tale but the ending isn't written yet. What this war has taught me is that no matter if it's two adorable children or a lion cub struggling to be born; the power of a mother's love can do anything.

I only wish I'd learned that years ago... but I was so young and vulnerable and had no guidance, thought I was invincible and I could continue to fly on the trapeze, even when I was several months pregnant, that I didn't deserve to have my own child to give my love to. But I'm also conscious that my up-close moment with the Nazi regime in Berlin also put the fire in my belly, to fight them, right from the moment Hitler went on the march in 1939. Now the smelly lion cages provide good cover for our escape. I grabbed my two little clowns after my act and we zigzagged around the big tent and through the line of caravans, back again, ending up here near the animal cages. We're safe here. Even when the Gestapo invades the circus grounds for their inspections, they never venture here. The smell keeps them away, though they should be used to it.

It's the company they keep, *n'est-ce pas*?

This is the last place the Gestapo will look for anyone they deem politically undesirable. Even these sweet babes just because they're Jewish. I once dared to ask a local French official, *What do the Nazis want with the children? Surely they're innocent and do no one harm.* He laughed. *The children grow up, mademoiselle, and they breed more Jews. A mortal sin in the eyes of the Reich.* I never forgot that. How these miserable creatures who call themselves a master race destroy such purity with their cruelness, sending children to their death in what we've learned are concentration camps. It keeps me on my toes, knowing the secret police make no bones about 'inspecting' our tents and wagons without notice.

'Listen to mademoiselle, Jakob,' his little sister says, her teeth chattering. 'She'll protect us.'

'Of course, my darlings,' I assure them, walking faster. No telling when that Gestapo agent will catch on something's up when I disappeared after my act, descending the rope quicker than I should, resulting in rope burns. Not serious, but my hands sting. I did have enough presence to establish my alibi with Lieutenant Horst von Ernst; he informed me with a bow and click of his heels when he wrapped my satin cape around my shoulders how much he enjoyed my act, sniffing me and touching the nape of my neck with his gloved fingers. I broke my personal credo and flirted with him. Insurance. He likes me and if I convince him there's an opportunity for him to know me better, I can use that as leverage with the Gestapo, make it clear I have a special relationship with the Wehrmacht. And the Gestapo agent will have nothing to show for his efforts but a dumb crossword puzzle in a Paris newspaper.

To seal the deal, I invited the German officer to come see me perform on the trapeze at the next town where Circus Richter sets up camp so we can 'talk'. Near Ghent on the way to Brussels.

'I regret, mademoiselle,' the young lieutenant said with a voice tinged with a genuine sadness that left me confident my subterfuge worked, 'I'm on my way to Paris.'

'Oh?' As if I didn't know. He mentioned it previously with a vulgar comment. 'I shall miss your presence in the front stall, Lieutenant, you and your... camera.' I hoped he'd lost it, but he pulled it out of his pocket. He grinned. I grimaced, praying it would end up somewhere in the catacombs of Paris, lost for centuries among the dead.

'And I shall miss admiring your beautiful...' His eyes took a road trip over my curves outlined in the tight leotard and jeweled design. I could feel the spangles melting. 'Costume.'

Now I *do* feel exposed, him staring at me, like this is the midnight show at the Moulin Rouge and not a family circus. '*Pardon*, Lieutenant, I must pack. Until we meet again.' I swish my cape around me and blow him a kiss, then dash off.

And so it went. Me flirting with a Nazi officer *years* younger than I am, and feeling like I was an aging diva running after a boy soldier. Was I crazy? Inviting a future liaison with the Wehrmacht? I've avoided getting too chummy with the enemy, but Lieutenant von Ernst left me no choice if I'm to get the children to Henri. Of course, the chances of seeing the lieutenant again are remote, since I have no intention of returning to Paris. Bad memories. A man, of course. My first love. I avoid saying his name because if I do, warm thoughts of him linger in my head like a melody you can't forget. Which is why my love affairs never last. I'm still in love with him.

I check the perimeter. Clear. I cross my fingers Sasha will keep his growls low and grumbling so as not to create anymore fear in these two little angels. They have a winding road ahead of them without anyone to turn to. I should go with them, but if I disappear, my cover will be blown. I'll be on the run, nowhere to hide. 'We're almost to the meeting place. I won't let anything happen to you.' I hug them close to my chest. 'I promise.'

'Maman says the only thing we have to be afraid of are the soldiers.'

'*Nazis*, Anna.' The boy clenches his fists. Tightens his lips. I swear he's about to cry, but won't, not in front of me. Then this brave little boy looks me square in the eye. 'They took Papa, mademoiselle.'

I hug him closer and I swear he's shivering. 'That's why your *maman* hid you with me. You liked being clowns in the circus tonight, *n'est-ce pas*?'

'Oh, yes!' they say together.

'*Bon*. Now it's time for you to escape like the rabbit. Do exactly as I say.'

* * *

My heart flutters madly, praying we get through this night. Me and two little clowns with runny noses, sniffling as much from the cold as from the sweat on their faces, perspiration oozing through their white makeup. I pop off their red rubber noses and smear cold cream on their cheeks, finding the children under the greasepaint. We've set up a makeshift waiting area behind the menagerie tent, the squawking monkeys getting on my nerves. I stuff their clown costumes under a pile of hay and now we wait.

They're trying so hard to be brave, but they've been crying, though neither will admit it. I talk to them in hushed tones, telling them how wonderful they were in the ring, but I have to keep us moving. Our timing for the pickup must be perfect. After the last show, the circus goes into a deep hundred-years-like sleep until dawn. Everyone is exhausted, their adrenaline shot from the tension, the near-misses on the high wire, the jugglers arguing again, the ringmaster barking orders. The deep quiet lasts long enough for me to get the job of escape done... *if* I don't make a mistake. When I was a young woman filled with hungry needs and desires, I found this time to be the most romantic for a quick affair.

Sighing and kissing and... things I'm not proud of, but I've outgrown my girlish escapades after I slipped more than once from fatigue on the rope going up to the platform and skipped sleep. My flirtatious adventures were hurting my act and Frau Swope, co-owner of Swope Circus in Berlin, gave me a hard talking to... I wasn't indispensable or invincible, she said, especially in these difficult times. I listened. I changed my name, and I've stayed low key ever since.

Until now.

Thanks to 'Henri', I'm in the game.

I have the feeling he operates like a hand shadow on the wall; you think you know what you see but when you turn your head, it's gone. He knows what has to be done and executes his moves like a crafty tiger planning a rear attack. I don't have to look for him; he'll find me. Us.

I wipe the children's faces with a discarded towel I find lying on a bale of hay, still damp with the sweat of its user. It's brisk out here and cold enough for me to wrap my long, heavy satin cape tight around me. I'm shivering in my thin leotard costume. Glass beads jingling in time to my racing pulse, I debate if I should take the children inside the menagerie tent now that the monkeys have quieted down. No, I don't want to start them up again.

'There, now I can see you, *mon enfant.*' I rub the white makeup off Anna's cheeks.

'I'm sleepy, mademoiselle, may I lie down?'

'Oh, my sweet, soon you'll have a lovely bed at the convent with a big, soft goose feather pillow.' I try to remember *if* the convent ever had such pillows; it's been years since I've been there.

'Me, too, mademoiselle?' Jakob asks, my little warrior slowing down in spite of his resolve to lead the charge against Sasha.

'Yes, Jakob, both of you.'

I look around, anxious. The truth is, I'm getting nervous. That Gestapo agent could be lingering around here; he could have talked to the lieutenant, asked about me... He could be watching us.

Waiting.

So *now* we wait, and I have to do something to keep up their spirits... and mine. Their fate depends on me. So we play a game.

'A game, mademoiselle?' Anna's thin body perks up. She even smiles.

'Yes, look at my beautiful cape.' I twirl the heavy satin around in an arc. 'You tell me why it's a magic cape.'

'Aw, that's for girls, mademoiselle,' Jakob insists.

'Have you heard of the Knights of the Round Table?'

He nods. 'Yeah...'

'They wore capes, too, *n'est-ce pas?*'

He grins. 'Well... I suppose so.'

'And if you hold on to my cape and say the magic word, you'll disappear.'

Anna claps her hands and grabs onto the hem of my cape. 'I want to play!'

'Me, too!' Jakob says, now into the game. 'What's the magic word, mademoiselle?'

'Yes, tell us please,' Anna begs.

'*Papillon.* Butterfly.'

* * *

'Are the children ready, mademoiselle?'

The raspy, disguised voice comes from inside the menagerie tent as the canvas flap flies open. Henri. He keeps to his new persona, not calling me 'Lia' and changing his voice. More like a stealth moth than a butterfly, he swoops down on us, hugs me, the salty smell of peanuts on his dark navy pea coat, his beret pulled down to cover his eyes. I know now why the monkeys quieted down. How long was he watching us? And why did he wait to reveal himself? Was he waiting to make sure we weren't compromised before showing himself?

'Yes, their names are Anna and Jakob, and this, too.' I try to slide the thick gold band off my finger, but it fits tight and won't budge. My hands are swollen. 'The children's mother asked me to sell her wedding ring... You take it. It will help the nuns take care of them.'

'Keep it, mademoiselle. I'm certain their *maman* would want you to have it.'

'I can't do that... I'll sell it on the black market and get the money back to her.'

He shakes his head. 'She was a wise woman, mademoiselle. She knew the Nazis would rip it off her finger when—'

'*Oh, God, no!*' I hug the two children closer to me, attempting to put my hands over their ears. 'They arrested her?' I pull him aside and whisper so low he can barely hear me, but he can read my lips.

He takes off his beret, holds it in his hand, whispering back so the children can't hear. 'I'm so sorry, Lia. I tried to intervene but she was hiding in the basement and the building was filled with German soldiers... French police... Everyone was pushing and shoving each other in the narrow stairwell to see what was happening. Then a fat man in the black trench coat showed up with another man and they beat her upon the shoulders with clubs, pulled off her head scarf, and dragged her away by her hair.' His ruddy cheeks sag more than the last time I saw him. 'It killed me to do nothing to help her.'

'You *are* doing something, *mon cher ami*. You're *here*. Giving her children what she couldn't. A new life without fear.'

I see the pain in his eyes turn dark like the storm that follows the Gestapo everywhere. I know what he's thinking. He's shown himself to the secret police. And Nadia in a soldier's uniform. They don't forget. He'll have to move on. I'm more determined than ever to save the children. I've half a mind to run off with them myself, but they stand a better chance to escape with Gunty... I mean, Henri. After all, what can I do? I don't have the resources, the connections with the French Resistance he has. With me it's always been hit or miss. Sometimes I get lucky and hook up with the right people willing to help, to trust me. But I'm not known to the Underground; I don't have a code name, a handler. No, it won't work. Me on the run with two children? I'm no hero. I've done everything I can to stay hidden; why risk it all now?

Because Esther reminds you of yourself... and how your baby was taken from you before you had a chance to say goodbye... and you never want another woman to go through that grief. It's your little one's birthday today and you want to honor her.

My friend takes my hand. His is cold. 'I regret I can't do more, but if you get into a jam, there's a pawnshop in Paris on Rue Saint-Jacques... Ask for Jarnak. He will help you.'

I shake my head. 'I'll be fine. The circus is heading out tomorrow toward Ghent.'

Coward. Taking the easy way out. Right, stay with the circus, let others take the risk. Some circus queen you are. These are babies who need you, mademoiselle.

I push that irritating voice out of my head that comes from my heart. *I'm no fighter.*

'I'd head in the opposite direction, mademoiselle, before the Gestapo sink their teeth into you.' He puts on his beret, pulls it down over his eyes. It's then I see a motorcycle and sidecar hidden in the tent when he pulls open the flap wide. 'We must go before the fat Gestapo man follows his nose and finds us.'

Why can't I be brave like this wonderful man?

I lay my hand upon his arm. It's the kind of gesture one does without thinking and yet I know this is the last time we'll meet, and I want to grab the moment and keep it safe in my heart. 'I shall miss you, Henri... Gunty. You're a true hero in this war.'

'I do what I must, mademoiselle.' He stands taller in an 'at-attention' military manner because he doesn't know what else to do, I gather, by the awkwardness of the situation. The implied intimacy of my words, that we've shared secrets, confided our beliefs to each other, our joys, our fears. We haven't done *this* before. Resistance business, which reduces human emotions to pinpricks on a map. Pickup spots, rendezvous points. Our paths have aligned again in this war because of a mutual passion to save these children.

I feel my cheeks tint. And now our strange relationship is ending and I can't let him go without him knowing how I feel. No, my emotions don't run toward the romantic, never have, more like family and a partnership in a once-in-a-lifetime experience we both feel privileged to be part of, and now it's ending. It seems he's of the same mind, and that means more to me than I let on. Opens up one of the tragic little holes in my heart that have never healed. Losing someone in my life I trust.

'I shall you miss you, too, Lia. You're an extraordinary woman and the best aerialist I've come across in the circus in the last thirty years. You make me proud to know you.' He's speaking from the heart and for a moment we connect in a different way, with him saying the words I wished my father had said to me the day he left me riding a pony in the ring. I did a back somersault, jumped through a hoop, then dismounted. I looked around to get his approval, but he was gone. I haven't seen him since.

I was thirteen.

With a kiss on each cheek, I entrust the safety of these two Jewish children into Gunty's weathered but capable hands. He takes on the part of *grand-père*, a role I imagine he's played on previous missions and one I sense he never tires of. Then, under the cover of a lingering darkness, he jumps on the German motorcycle, telling the children to duck down low in the sidecar and get ready to cover themselves with the canvas.

Don't let them go. What about the Nazi patrols? It's more dangerous now that Gunty is compromised.

I shrug off my fears. *What am I worried about? He has everything under control,* I force my mind to accept. *I have no choice.*

'Time to disappear, *mes enfants*,' I call out in a loud whisper, and I toss my cape so they catch it and hug it tight to gain strength from its power. I smile, but I'm crying inside, knowing if they're stopped by German soldiers, they'll poke their rifles and bayonets into the canvas and find the children. And then... Gunty won't let that happen, I convince myself, noting the pistol stuffed into his trousers. 'What's the magic word?'

'*Papillon!*'

I cover them with the canvas, my dumb smile still pasted on my face. Now I know how the clowns feel when they're crying inside. With his back to me, Gunty fires up the motorcycle and revs the engine, ready to take off. It's then I see their pinched faces pop up from under the canvas, their cheeks wet, even Jakob's. I feel so ashamed for thinking of myself. It feels wrong, so intolerably wrong, to let them go out all alone into a world that hates them. *They need me.* No, I'm not their mother, but I *was* a mother. Once. Briefly. I birthed a child; instinct will tell me what to do. I can be a good mother. So I act without thinking, push my cape over my shoulders and raise up my hands. '*Gunty, wait!*'

But I'm too late.

The littlest of God's angels race off before I can catch them, my heavy cape dragging me down. *Poof!* Lost to me in a cloud of white smoke. I sink down into the mud and cry. I can't stop the numbing fear gripping me.

That somehow I failed Esther.

15

ROUBAIX, FRANCE—APRIL, 1943

Circus Richter
Lia

My two little clowns sped away in the Nazi sidecar minutes ago and I miss them already. I fiddled with the idea of allowing a moment of joy in seeing my mission accomplished, but I harbored too much guilt inside me for letting them go. I take a cleansing breath but I feel empty, and a little joy would help. Two more little ones ripped from the horror of the Nazis? God, I pray so. If only we could have saved their *maman*. A hard knot in my stomach makes it difficult for me to lean over and pick up my satin cape with a long tear in the sumptuous fabric. Sasha's signature. I'll be up till dawn sewing it so I don't have to explain the tear to Herr Richter. Luckily I'm a damned good seamstress, having taken up the needle at eight to embroider Papa's cambric shirts. The man loved his 'gypsy' attire, as he liked to call it, delighting in using the pejorative word to watch me cover my mouth in horror. My *maman* taught me that 'gypsy' was a word we never said, even in front of Papa.

Funny I should bring up Papa now. I hated him for years, not understanding what I did to make him abandon me. Yet now, I feel maudlin, even regretful I didn't look harder for him. My guess is because tonight I saw the beauty of a mother's love for her children and how she sacrificed herself for them. And I'm jealous.

I never had that kind of love from my father.

And I lost my one chance to give it to my baby daughter. A stab in my heart... I have never said those words. Ever. God, what's happening to me?

I push everything soft and sweet and heartfelt to the back of my brain. I have to keep up my cover. Forget whatever grandiose ideas that fly around in my head about *really* joining the Resistance. It's not for me. I'd flub up the mission. I fly, thrill audiences twice a day. I'm an *artiste*, proud, strong... I have to show that to Herr Richter and that damn Gestapo man if he comes calling at my tent. I need to fetch white thread from the costume tent without waking up the old monsieur whose sole job is to keep thieves away from our spangles. Clothes are severely rationed and our flesh-colored leotards are in demand during the cold months when coal comes around in dribbles. I hug the cape to my chest so its satiny shine doesn't catch the moonlight. Night sounds from the animals rise and ebb with roars, rumbles. I remember how I wanted to speak to Herr Richter about Sasha. It will reinforce my alibi if Nadia comes up with a story that puts me in jeopardy about where I was tonight.

I approach Herr Richter's tent set apart from the main area when I hear—

'Fräulein Zollo is Italian?' The voice is gruff, speaking heavily accented French.

'That's what her passport says... Gaia Zollo from Firenze,' I hear Herr Richter answer. 'She's a star here in the Circus Richter. You saw her do the triple somersault. No other woman I've had in my circus comes close to her skills on the trapeze.'

'Yes. She's an amazing woman... but that won't stop me from arresting her.'

I can't see his face. Is he the Gestapo man I saw earlier?

'Good grief, *Mein Herr*, what has the woman done?'

'She's a spy.'

I shudder when I peek inside the tent and see Herr Richter laugh, his belly jiggling like jellied consommé in a teacup. 'And I'm Herman Goering.'

Yes, it *is* the Gestapo man. He doesn't find that remark amusing and pulls out his Luger. Herr Richter mumbles and fumbles like an august clown, wiping his brow with the sleeve of his red ringmaster's coat. 'Just kidding, The Reichsmarschall is welcome at Circus Richter, in any city where we perform.'

'Fool, you shall find yourself shipped off to Drancy for your brashness. Our Führer ordered free circus tickets for all German officers. You have no bargaining chip here.' The Gestapo agent circles him like an angry tiger. 'Fräulein Zollo was seen this morning by a reliable source...'

Nadia.

'...meeting up with a known enemy of the Reich. We believe the Jewish woman passed anti-Aryan missives on to her to distribute among the local factory workers.'

Not true. But I can't bust in there and defend myself. I keep listening.

'You have proof of this?' Herr Richter dares to question the secret policeman.

'I don't need proof. I'm Gestapo.'

'But she's my star attraction,' Herr Richter spouts, gripping his chest like his heart is about to burst through and explode into bits. 'My God, man, she did the triple tonight and brought the house down.'

'Yes, she is quite impressive.' He taps his foot, his gloved hand on the table in a syncopation, thinking. 'A most unfortunate situation; however, since you advised the authorities of the Jewish acrobats hiding in your troupe when you played in Brussels, you have shown yourself to be a loyal Party member.'

The pit of my stomach drops like I'm falling from the flybar with no net below. I feel sick. I accept the fact Herr Richter is a hard taskmaster, rides us performers to do better, but I always thought it was because he cared about us and loves the circus. Now I find out he's also a damned informant? That he'd sell out anybody for a pat on the head by the Führer? Dearest God, that thought crushes my spirit and leaves another hole in my heart I hadn't expected.

'I shall give you two, maybe three days,' the Gestapo agent continues, 'to add a different act at the top of the playbill before I apprehend her.'

'Very generous of you, Herr Geller.'

Geller. I clench my fists. I will *never* forget that name.

'I'd take her in for questioning tonight, but I think arresting the beautiful aerialist will tip off her partisan friends. I shall wait, watch her, and see who she talks to, before making the arrest.'

He lights a cigarette with a sulfur match, tosses it, and it lands near the tent flap. Herr Richter dives for the match. Makes sure it's out. Fire is a great enemy of a traveling tent circus, something every circus performer fears. I learned that early in my career when a clown left a burning cigarette on top of a bale of hay in the wardrobe tent. It smoldered for a while then the whole tent went up along with costumes collected for more than a decade. I never forgot watching the sparkly and satiny capes, baggy pants, leotards, top hats and fancy plume headdresses reduced to what looked like crisp, blackened paper. I was around fifteen and working in a circus in Paris... and as young girls do when their emotions rise high on the tide, I cried to see such pretty things destroyed. Then a very strange thing happened I'd forgotten about until now. A debonair-looking man came out of the shadows and said, 'I pray you never see what fire can do to a woman's face, *ma jeune fille*. It can be quite ugly.' He cupped my chin, his fingers smooth, too smooth for a circus performer, running them along my jawline, nose, and forehead. He was fascinating to listen to, with his stories about the Bohemian and vagabond clubs in Berlin and the search for pleasure and youth. He told me how lucky I was to have such perfect skin. Like roses... I was still innocent, but instinct told me to get away, that in spite of his charm and dapper appearance, something tainted his words with a devilish satire that seemed 'off', more so when he said, 'I would fix your pretty face just for the joy of it.'

Why I remember that now baffles me. Yet not surprising, considering the frame of mind I'm in. Revisiting that moment near the lion cages with the children, knowing I'm about to be arrested by the Gestapo and I have no plan, that my world is shifting again and my life is passing before me. I still have bad dreams about the time I performed for the Führer, but then who wouldn't with the leader of the National Socialist Party standing so close you could see the popcorn kernels stuck in his teeth when he laughed at the clowns?

A memory best forgotten.

'May I remind you that you have little time to add a new performer at the top of the bill, Herr Richter?' the Gestapo agent bellows. 'I suggest an elephant. They don't forget who they work for.'

'And neither do I, Herr Geller.' Herr Richter takes a decanter of liquor off a small table and nods to his unwelcome visitor. 'One for the road? French brandy.'

The secret policeman smacks his lips. 'Well...' He rubs his chin. Why is he hesitating? I've never seen a Nazi who didn't enjoy imbibing stolen French liquor. A sharp pain jabs my brain, sparking the words Henri said earlier, his warning never more true than now, *I'd head in the opposite direction, mademoiselle, before the Gestapo sink their teeth into you.*

Of course. Herr Geller has no intention of waiting two days to arrest me. Even if the Nazis have no proof, 'suspects' are routinely tortured with their heads pushed into cold buckets of ice water and held down until they'll agree to anything. I can't let him take me. I'd rather die than give up my old friend Gunty and his partisan friends in the Resistance. Which means I can't continue on with the troupe to Ghent. That's what he was trying to tell me. I have to escape from Circus Richter.

Tonight.

I tiptoe away from the tent, dragging my satin cape through the wet, dewy grass. I need a plan and no more stalling. If I run into this Herr Geller, I don't stand a chance against him. I need a diversion so I can escape behind their backs. Would a loud roar do? I know where the lion trainer keeps the key. It's in a box over the door to the cage. A naughty chuckle escapes my lips. I'd enjoy seeing the fat Gestapo man lose his trousers *and* his dignity. No one deserves it more. And if the big cat takes a piece out of his behind, I don't think anyone would object.

I head toward the lion cages.

I'm not a fool; this isn't a show of bravado. I'm stalling. I need to keep the Gestapo from arresting me while I grab my satchel and get the hell out of here. Make my way to Lille, get on a train. Go somewhere, anywhere I can disappear for a while. And a grumpy lion is going to help me. First I locate the feeding pail the groom always leaves outside the cage. With luck, there are a few scraps left-over... My nose leads me to where I want to go—

A deep stench shoots up my nostrils. While I struggle to keep my gagging reflex intact and my stomach rolls over numerous times, I pull out measly scraps of rotting meat. Bartered from the Nazis, I'd bet, now that I know where Herr Richter's loyalties lie. Then I unlock Sasha's cage and I hear him snoring in a steady but loud rhythm in a dark corner. Velma and her cub share another cage, but the king has earned his privacy and a snooze. I've interrupted his beauty sleep and I don't want to bring up his ire and for him to lunge at me, so I let him smell me, a familiar human he lets get close to his lioness... That memory is what I'm banking on so he doesn't swallow me up before I can blink. Curious, he plants his big, dirty paws one in front of the other and lets go with a big yawn as I talk to him in a low, calm voice. 'You want to have some fun, Sasha? Play tag with a bad Gestapo man?' Another growl. 'You do? Then follow me.'

Sasha lets out a loud roar that sends shudders through me. I jump out of the way when the big cat leaps from the cage to the ground, its tail wagging, its tongue shooting out of its mouth like it's a separate creature on the hunt for food. My eyes remain on him, not showing fear, then I back up slowly, whispering sweet words. 'Good boy, Sasha... Let's take a walk, shall we?'

He lets out a low growl.

I wrap my satin cape around me and play a game of Hansel and Gretel, dropping pieces of rotting, raw meat in a zigzag path, and the lion follows me, taking time to gobble up the meat scraps with each step leading back to Herr Richter's tent and his brandy-sniffing cohort.

Or so I thought. I underestimated the obsession of the German secret policeman to catch his prey.

'Halt or I'll shoot.'

I slide to a stop in my soft ballet slippers on the wet ground. Already that voice is familiar to me. My world just turned upside down like I'm hanging from a flybar from my heels. One wrong move and I'm going straight down.

'I'm unarmed.'

'*Sei still.* Be quiet, Mademoiselle Zollo. Turn around and step into the moonlight so I can see you.'

I pivot slowly. He's pointing a Luger straight at me. I forego any grand gesture with my cape that will get me shot.

'Didn't get enough of me on the trapeze, monsieur?' I grin.

'You insolent little—'

What follows next is a disgusting pejorative in German I'd rather not hear as Herr Geller throws a disapproving glance at me, then drops another command, expecting me to give up.

Really? I may not have a chance against him and his Luger, but my secret weapon is right behind him, its big paws silent on the wet earth as he follows the path of 'breadcrumbs' I dropped. The timing is perfect.

'*Now, Sasha!*' I yell.

I shiver when I hear a loud roar that makes me giddy, then a flash of lion's teeth that greet the Gestapo agent when he spins around, and I swear I see a look I never thought possible. Surprise, shock. He gets off one, then two panicked shots that go wild, dirt flying up into the air, getting into my eyes, my throat, but one thing I *can* see clear. The fleeing Nazi doesn't wait to see what happens next and runs in the opposite direction away from the big cat while Sasha roars loudly and lets Herr Geller know he's one lucky bastard his belly is too full to chase after him.

Or so I imagine.

I race back to my caravan, shaking madly, keeping my head down in the melee that follows the loud roars and gunshots when the clowns descend upon the scene in white tank undershirts and trousers *sans* makeup followed by Sasha's trainer in shorts and knee-high boots, cracking his whip, but the lion takes his time heading back to his cage. I keep my smirk to myself. I remember what I told the children earlier: that Sasha is a big scaredy-cat. No, it's not the lion with the coward's stripe running down his spine.

It's the fat Gestapo man.

16

ROUBAIX, FRANCE—APRIL, 1943

Circus Richter
Lia

I have no illusions regarding my chances to escape Herr Geller's clutches when he spreads his Gestapo net. I have about as much chance as me doing a quadruple—four somersaults—on the trapeze. What I need is a really good, infallible circus trick, like the magician's disappearing 'girl in the box'. But that requires skill, patience, practice, and fast moves. I have none of the first three, but I *do* have the last one. And she's fast, *very* fast.

Misty, the sure-footed pony with a persnickety attitude. The bay that sent Nadia flying into the sawdust.

I find the pony at the trough, drinking water. Alone. She's that way. Stand-offish. Knows she's the star of the show ponies. Fast, sure-footed, but not easy to ride unless she likes you. I got to know her when I filled in as a trick rider, how she takes the corners with a little jump, how she likes to be patted down with a soft chenille blanket after the act, and her favorite oats.

'It's a beautiful night for a midnight ride, Misty, *n'est-ce pas*?' I rub her back. 'The wind at your neck, fresh air, and what you like best. Freedom. For you. For me. What do you say?'

She wheezes. Shakes her braided, gray-dove mane.

I'm in.

I put a bridle on the pony—I'll ride her bareback—then pat her with the resin trick riders use for their feet and lead her over to the caravan I share with Aima. It's empty. She's with Sven, thank God. I don't want to drag her into this fiasco. She's a kind, sweet girl and she adores Sven. It's better for her if they believe I've abandoned them. Keeps them both safe. I shall miss Sven, Aima, and Jean-Pierre, but the less they know about me, where I've gone, the better it is for them. They'll be under enough scrutiny when Herr Geller demands to see their papers. They'll pass. Made by the best forgers in the Underground in Brussels. Mine, too. I've crossed from Belgium to France many times since I left Paris in 1925, but tonight I shall say adieu to Gaia Zollo. She's wanted by the Gestapo for questioning. The borders will be watched and the French police can ask to see your papers at any time, but since I also have a passport and papers under Lia di Montieri, I shall welcome back my true identity.

Only one problem.

Lia is a dark, ash blonde.

I wrap my white-blonde hair in a dark, filmy scarf with gold threads sparkling through it I use when I perform on the rings. It's not unusual to see a woman's hair covered with a turban since shampoo is nearly impossible to get, so I know this won't be questioned. Then I grab my worn, brown satchel with my precious press clippings inside, passports, and papers, along with a long black wool cloak with a hood I've had since my cold winter days in Berlin. It's served me well on clandestine rendezvouses and also because it has a hidden pocket. I stuff what little francs I have into the pocket since Herr Richter hasn't paid the troupe for two weeks. We don't complain, just happy to have a tent or wagon to sleep in and hot food. Unfortunately, I put my earnings in German banks during the thirties since I worked often in Berlin and when the war started, my account was confiscated by the Nazis. Whatever money I have, it's got to be enough. Who am I kidding? The Swiss border is nearly seven hundred kilometers from here. I'll be lucky if I can escape to Italy and find work in a circus in Rome, so I can eat, bypass whatever political hubbub is brewing with Mussolini and his Fascists cohorts. Word is they'll be out if the Allies land in Sicily. Then maybe I can make my way to the Knie Circus, traveling solely in Switzerland due to Nazi restrictions.

I shall be safe there.

I twist the Jewish woman's gold ring on my finger. I could pawn it, as Gunty suggested, then I decide against it. I'll wait. I have high hopes I can get it to her children to help *them* survive. I still carry around the deep guilt that somehow, my mother's leaving us was my fault and my father wouldn't have beat me and left me afterward to fend for myself. I don't want her children to carry that same guilt and feeling abandoned. I want them to know how much she loved them. I *will* find them and return her wedding ring.

No time to change, so I don trousers over my gold sequin costume, then I pack my ballet slippers and slip into the knee-high, black leather boots I wear on muddy days. Before I jump onto Misty. I also loop an old belt through the handle on my satchel, making sure the snaps and leather straps are secure, then attach it around my waist.

Then, before I take off into the drizzly night—

'Mademoiselle, *mademoiselle,* help us please!'

Jakob? I blink, shake my head. I can't believe what I'm seeing. Jakob and Anna run into my arms, shaking, their faces cold, their eyes wide with fear.

'My God, Jakob, what happened? Where's Henri?'

'Monsieur Henri pulled us out of the sidecar and told me to grab Anna and run back to you... back to the circus... We hid behind a big tree... then we heard guns firing... We saw Monsieur Henri grab his pistol, then he yelled out... He fell, then Nazi soldiers shouting... then... then...'

A burst of gunfire shatters the air from somewhere nearby and the young boy puts his hands over his ears and squeezes his eyes tight and gasps for air, while Anna just stares into the darkness. Her eyes widen, her lips part, but no sound comes out when I hug her and ask her if she's hurt.

She turns up her small face and stares at me. She moves her mouth, but again no sound comes out.

Jakob, still shaking, recovers and grabs my hand. 'She can't speak, mademoiselle, not after she saw.'

I can guess what the little girl experienced, and her mind, not to mention her heart, can't process it. A very brave man gave up his life for her... for Jakob. And her brain is stuck in that moment. A German patrol must have spotted them, cornered them, and the worst happened.

Gunty is either dead or a prisoner of the Nazis.

Take care of him, God, please. He's a good man.

It's up to me now to save these children.

'I won't let anything happen to them, Esther, I promise,' I whisper. Somehow I knew in my gut I was destined to help these babies. I just didn't know a dear, honest, good man would pay the price for his part in my ongoing drama. Still, I can't tamp down the anguish I feel that if I'd made up my mind sooner to take them, I would have intercepted the children before they left and Gunty wouldn't have been caught in a firefight. Again, guilt rakes my soul.

It surprises me how, in spite of my fears, I got us this far. But do I have what it takes to finish the job?

Do it for her... your own little angel. For her.

Yes, my little girl. It spurs something in me I've kept dormant for a long time. It's what I needed to give me confidence, to finally come out of the shadows and fight the Nazis with everything I have. Without wasting another moment, I unhook my satchel from my waist, then help Jakob to mount Misty, lift Anna up to him, hand him my satchel then the reins, vault onto the pony from the rear so I'm standing behind the children. A trick I've done since I was five. Seconds later, I'm sitting astride the pony, reins in hand, satchel back around my waist. I kick my heels into the mare's flanks and slap her haunches, and the pony tosses her head and mouths the bit. I bend down, telling the children to do the same, riding low over her neck and again kick my heels into the horse's sides, encouraging the mare to dash into the darkness of the woodland then onto the main road lit by moonlight. I feel confident I can do this guided by Madame Moon, having traveled this road with the circus numerous times. Even after all these years, I still have a good seat and hand and can ride any mount, aside or astride. Since I added resin to her hide, it's easier for the children to remain seated on the horse, and for Misty, well, she's used to having more than one rider bouncing on her back. I pray we make it to freedom.

The Gestapo will be expecting me to head for the Roubaix railway station to blend in with the locals—it isn't a main pickup point for trains taking Jewish prisoners to the Mechelen transit camp in Belgium then Auschwitz. So I'll go to the main station at Lille, fifteen kilometers away, though it's heavily patrolled since the brave actions of the locals who saved Jewish prisoners last September. I have no choice. Where we go from there depends on the first train going south and from there we'll make our way to Italy then Switzerland, where the children will be safe.

Working the bay mare with a light rein, I coax her over what remains of an old Roman road overgrown by vegetation, the narrow pathway barely visible through the overhanging trees thick with the smell of pine, the cold ground rocky and uneven, the mare's breath strong and rhythmic. We pound through the dense labyrinth of brush and bramble, my heart racing as we escape to freedom, praying to God I don't let the children down. I ride astride the mare, preferring the easy freedom of soft trousers, my sequined costume hidden under a long black woolen cloak hugging my shoulders to keep out the chill, my body heat keeping Jakob warm while he hugs his little sister, keeping her close.

Running, running. Horse and riders, we're ripping through the gauzy gray-blue mist hovering over the horizon. The sun will be up in a few hours with a secret smile, urging us to hurry before we're seen. Going at around six, seven kilometers an hour, we should get to Lille in two hours. I don't want to ride her too hard; after all, the little lady did two shows today, but she senses the urgency and takes off for me, thundering down the empty road through the night. We're gifted a shaft of moonlight, and I feel her hooves pounding into the earth, my obsession to escape from the Gestapo now hers too. I pray that path ends here and doesn't follow me.

* * *

Two hours, fifteen minutes later.

I'm exhausted, my eyes tired and burning from straining to see the road ahead, Misty snorting and throwing off sweat that sprinkles the air like dew and hits my cheeks, my nose. 'We're here, children.' Jakob mutters what I think is a prayer in Hebrew and Anna shudders. I lean over and whisper to Misty, 'We made it, girl.'

I slow my pace when I get a glimpse of the Lille railway station ahead with its big, round clock outlined in celestial light from its stylish arched windows like a beacon, bringing everything back into focus, no longer a blur, my shoulders relaxed, neither tensed nor pushing. I pray no Nazi sentry sees us cutting across the field not in a trot, more like a canter. I dismount, but remain cautious, moving with the wind, not against it, my head high, guiding Misty without appearing suspicious, my stride confident. I instruct the children to remain on the pony, though I have no idea where we go from here. An unmarried woman with two children is suspect. Then I get an idea. With a few words, I explain to the children we're all in danger and I'm wearing their mother's magic ring to keep us safe. Jakob nods, Anna smiles. I want them to understand *why* I'm wearing the ring.

A *married* woman with two children is a different story.

I stroke the mare's mane the color of sown wheat, trying to calm her. Jakob and Anna remain good little soldiers. Helping them dismount, I tell them their mother would be so proud.

Perspiring hard, I toss the heavy cloak over my shoulders. My costume reeks of my sweat, my trousers sticking to my thighs like a second skin. I press forward through the tangled bramble, my black leather boots treading through the fine dirt without a sound. I crouch down behind an overgrown bush and check out the train station. Anna and Jakob join me. All quiet. No trains sitting on the tracks. No truckload of Jews waiting to be thrust aboard an incoming train. A good day.

My two little charges are all tuckered out; me, too. And Misty. Anna has cuddled up close to me, her eyes closed, her soft breathing telling me she feels safe. Jakob is trying to stay awake, but I encourage him to close his eyes and hold my hand while the three of us take a nap. Misty grazes nearby... no doubt sleeping, too.

When I wake up, it's nearly dawn.

I pray I have enough francs for tickets for the three of us to head south, but what to do with Misty? If I let her loose, send back down the road with a slap on her haunches, there's a good chance the Nazis will pick her up and conscript her for an SS horse cavalry unit. I can't do that to this pony. She got us here; now it's my turn to take care of her.

With the two children at my side and a rising sun at our backs, I approach the train station, holding the reins in my hand, my head on a swivel, when I see a farmer unloading his wares, the answer to our prayers.

17

LILLE, FRANCE—APRIL, 1943

Railway station
Lia

I run into Lille railway station with a grand smile on my lips, clutching my old brown satchel to my chest and holding Anna's hand tight, Jakob behind us, after finding a new owner for Misty. I also run straight into the arms of the one person I never thought I'd see again.

The camera-toting, young Wehrmacht officer. Lieutenant Horst von Ernst.

'Mademoiselle Zollo,' he greets me, kissing me on both cheeks like we're old friends. 'What a charming coincidence running into you.'

'Do we know each other, monsieur?' I feign innocence, batting my eyes. *Oh, mamselle, you're so obvious...* but the Nazi eats it up. I sense he enjoys a challenge, especially when it comes to the female sex.

'You're the circus queen every boy dreams of meeting.' He takes a long look at the children. 'Though I had no idea you were the maternal type. Charming *kinder*... children. Yours, I suppose?'

I find that an odd thing to say, then he smacks his lips, lowering his eyes, trying to see under my cloak half-open. I go into an uncomfortable mode, my pulse racing madly and my cheeks flushed like I'm standing in a ring of fire. Nazi officers rarely travel alone. Is the Gestapo waiting in a dark corner? His hands itching to wrap them around my neck?

I didn't see any sign of the wretched black Citroëns the Gestapo use parked anywhere near the station when I approached an old farmer toiling to bring vegetables to the city with a horse and wagon. I let Misty smell him, sniff around his wagon and give him a knowing shake of her head that she was a far superior breed than the poor old mare attached to the wagon. I was right to appeal to the taste of freedom she enjoyed on the ride. The farmer looked her over with a wise eye, checking her teeth, her hooves, and to my surprise, she let him. He reached into his vest pocket and pulled out a handful of oats and started talking to the mare. He was only too happy to take Misty, rub her down, and feed her until I return... *Is that agreeable, madame?* I smiled. He didn't question my status that I'm married and that the children hiding behind me are mine. The look in his eye and the nod he gave me told me he knew I wasn't coming back so there was no need for further conversation between us. I handed him the reins and with a few soft words to the mare, I watched as he led her away. Neither of us wanted to arouse suspicion from the sentries posted in front of the railway station. A smooth, uneventful transition that made my heart lighter. He seemed kind, good. I have no guilt that Herr Richter's pony act has one less pony. The man is a Nazi informant and Misty will have a better life with the farmer.

I breathed a sigh of relief only to choke on the dust in my throat when I pushed into the railway station holding on to Anna and Jakob's hands and saw the lieutenant pacing up and down in the waiting room. He's the only Nazi officer hanging around inside the station for the next train. A trio of German soldiers loiter in the far corner, smoking. I look for the schedule, but the timetable chalkboard hanging on the wall is empty... Is the clerk sleeping? A smattering of civilians eye us with curiosity, hugging their suitcases and tied-up cloth bundles close to them. They look forlorn but not in distress. Not a yellow star among them.

Still...

The children huddle together, waiting, unsure what to think of this new development... Their mademoiselle is *speaking to a Nazi*, they must be thinking, *He's going to hurt us*. I must reassure them they're safe because in spite of the uniform he wears, I don't believe the lieutenant wants to harm us. 'Leave the officer to me, my angels, he likes circuses like we do.'

'He took away our papa and...' He can't finish his thought. I haven't told them yet their mother was arrested. Anna buries her face in her hands; Jakob hugs her. She still refuses to speak. This will build her fear to even higher heights. I sink to my knees, hug them both tight. Now the news will have to wait. I can't destroy their world until I find them a safe place with good people to love them.

'We must be brave, my darlings, not let the Nazis see us weak, *n'est-ce pas?*' They nod, barely agreeing. But it's done. For now. I have to get them out of here on the first train.

I stand up, tall, look the Nazi in the eye. 'You've mistaken me for someone else, monsieur,' I answer in French, making it clear to the curiosity seekers clustered around us at varying listening posts I'm no collaborator.

'Why are you avoiding me, mademoiselle?' He smirks. 'I mean, madame?'

'Am I?' I should turn and walk away, but a girl doesn't turn her back on a Nazi officer. Who can forget what happened to Félix the Clown?

He grins. 'You're clearly running away from that lion trainer who never took his eyes off you.'

I hadn't noticed, but I doubt he had romantic notions about me when all I did was complain about how he treated the animals.

The lieutenant continues. 'What's his name?'

'The Great Hasso, and no, I'm not. I— I need to catch a train to Lyon... to see my sister,' I lie. 'She's ill.'

'You're out of luck, madame... You and your "children".' He lights a cigarette. He doesn't offer me one, not that I'd take it, but it shows his lack of manners. Worse yet, he blows the smoke in my face, making me cough. Or is he jealous of my brood taking the attention away from him? Then he delivers the punchline with another puff of smelly smoke. 'There are no civilian trains on the morning schedule.'

Why aren't I surprised? These days Lille station must be busy with troop transport trains racing through the station moving German troops and supplies —leather goods like shoes, grain, even coal and petrol—to Germany.

I smile. 'Sabotage?'

'That's a dangerous statement, madame,' he says, accompanied by a smile. 'You're not very subtle, are you?'

'If I was, you never would have noticed me, *n'est-ce pas?*'

'You have a beautiful face and... a figure hard to forget.' He enjoys making me uncomfortable, his eyes watching me. There's purpose behind those Aryan blue orbs. What is he after?

'I should slap your smug face for your insolence,' I dare to say.

'But you won't.'

'No, I won't.'

'Especially in front of your children.'

He bought it. Me and the children, even if there is no family resemblance. Fortunately for me, Anna keeps her head down and Jakob won't look at the Nazi. Not that I blame him.

'Besides,' I continue, 'I saw what happened to poor Félix the Clown.'

The officer sighs. 'I regret the funnyman was collateral damage. I found him quite amusing and filmed his act. I never intended to see him arrested, but my strait-laced colleague is a by-the-book officer who counts the unfortunates he detains instead of sheep at night. He boasted afterwards about the arrest to the secret police. Even I don't have the power to override the Gestapo.'

'Since when does the Gestapo care about a poor clown?' I don't understand what's going on here.

'Since an informant revealed he's a member of the Underground.'

'Nadia,' I whisper. *That bitch*. It's totally false, but if I insist Félix is innocent, the lieutenant will wonder why. No, let him have his flirty talk to keep him from looking too closely at me and the children, but I can't let Félix down. I have to try. 'Isn't there anything you can do for the clown?'

I don't know if it's the fatigue circling my eyes with deep blue shadows or the clumps of travel dust making my eyes tear up that move him, but his attitude shifts and for a moment I almost like him. Almost.

'I'll speak to the Kommandant about having him released. After all, we only have the word of the informant who isn't very reliable,' he says, and the shock of his willingness to help me leaves me without anything to add. Then he's back to being a Nazi, clicking his heels with a slight bow. 'I must insist you allow me to help you and your children with your travel plans to visit your ill sister. If the partisans *aren't* blowing up the train tracks, they're doing enough sabotage to upset the schedule, causing the cancellation of this morning's train to Paris and leaving me stranded.' He brushes up against me with his broad chest, backing me up against the wall, trapping me in his orbit. What is it about Nazi officers and their need to dominate? 'Now I'm glad they did.'

I wiggle away from him, show him I'm not easy to snare in his web. 'No direct train to Lyon either?' I probe. I'm taking a chance revealing my destination, but if I can get to Lyon, I have a good chance of sneaking the children over the border to Switzerland before anyone is the wiser. As in Gestapo.

He shakes his head, but looks pleased. 'No, not until late this afternoon. You're stuck here... with me.'

'And your camera,' I grumble.

'Unfortunately, I loaned it to Lieutenant Kieffer since I have urgent business in Paris and I'll have little time to record my favorite subject.'

'Me?' I offer, keeping up the game. I wonder, is he comfortable in his Aryan skin or is it for show? I get the feeling he's found himself in a position of importance and he doesn't know what to do with it. It's obvious he's still a boy in many ways and he's fumbling his way through this war. I can use that to my advantage. I take off my scarf and fluff out my blonde hair to up the stakes in our little drama.

'No,' he says with a wry smile. 'The circus.'

I back off, pretend to look offended. I am merely part of the circus to him. *Really?* I already feel the noose tightening around my neck. It's still very early morning but word will surely have spread by noon that the Gestapo is after me. I have no doubt the young lieutenant will do his duty and turn me in.

I hesitate, thinking. *Mais non...* they're after Gaia Zollo, *not* Lia di Montieri. All I have to do is wait for the next train, get a ticket with my real identity card, hope the clerk doesn't ask for the children's manila-colored identity cards and just hands me the tickets—I never thought to ask Gunty if he has papers for them—and leave the Nazi officer in the dust. Only one way to do that.

Get him drunk.

'I don't suppose you could rustle up a bottle of wine while we wait, Lieutenant von Ernst? And milk for the children?' I give him my best 'stage' smile, eyes big and sparkling like stars, lips moist and parted. *His* eyes widen then pop out, embarrassed by my overt play for him. An uncomfortable ache in my groin unsettles me, sickens me. I feel sinful flirting with a young officer with barely a shadow on his tanned face. My God, I can't do this.

Yes, you can... or it's a concentration camp for you. And worse for the children.

'Don't move, madame,' he says, blocking my path to the door. 'I'll be right back.'

'Is that an order?' I quip.

'Yes.'

One word, but it hits me in the gut like a stone. Hard, precise. His 'niceness' turning into Nazi protocol. What else did I expect? In his eyes, his command is law and I'm subservient to him, not his equal. The lieutenant has a way of making me go cold all over, so cold I can't stop shivering. He thinks I'm excited by his manliness and that embarrasses him, his pale Aryan blue eyes darkening with questions before he sweeps out of the train station on his 'mission'. The lieutenant promises to get the most expensive bottle of wine he can find—most likely confiscate it in the name of the Reich—and milk fresh from a cow—difficult even for a Nazi officer—then leaves me standing in the railway station feeling as if I have the cross of shame branded on my forehead after throwing myself at him. Especially since I'm supposed to be the children's mother. And here I was touting myself as being a good mother. So far, I'm not doing so great. I'm disgusted with my behavior. I've turned to the lowest trick in the saboteur's book of tradecraft and I have no recourse but to follow it through to save our arses.

I turn my face away and gaze out the station window with a view of the platform as the passengers—locals, I assume—stare and gloat and whisper among themselves. Pointing, shaking their heads. 'No, it's her. Like he said. She's that girl from the circus, the one on the trapeze... I saw her act last Saturday,' I hear. 'It can't be,' says another. 'Why is she talking to that Nazi?'

Another retorts, 'She's a blonde, ain't she? What'd you expect?'

I can't believe I'm hearing this. Twittering insults and judging me because of my hair color. I've never come up against anything like this. I've always been untouchable, protected by the fourth wall when I'm performing, then I'm off to a different town, village. I've been envied, even adored by the crowd. Now I'm hated for no good reason. Oh, my God, now I know what that Jewish mother felt, how Jews feel, and Roma when they're booed by the crowd. And me? Too many years I've passed for Aryan. Now I'm ashamed, terribly ashamed, fueling my resolve to save these children to redeem myself for assuaging the pain over my own loss by trying to save the twins and failing, but not fully understanding their plight.

I do now.

'Go back to the circus!'

'We don't want your kind here.'

'You're a disgrace, acting like this in front of your children.'

That last comment breaks my heart, cracks it wide open, spilling my emotions everywhere like milk, and I can't put them back. I'm not worthy of this task of even *pretending* to be a good mother.

Then I hear a young voice whisper to me, 'Don't listen to them, mademoiselle, we know you're just trying to keep us safe.' It's Jakob, grabbing my hand, then Anna nodding her head. Oh, my poor sweet babies, they understand, they do. I'm about to break down in tears, but I must stay strong. For them. They believe in me; why can't I believe in myself?

I keep mum rather than incite the restless passengers to surround me, put me at a disadvantage then attack me for what they perceive as collaboration with the enemy. I can't blame them, but I need to get ahead of the situation or we'll never get on a train—

A loud whistle.

A train whistle.

I race to the high arched window, pulling Anna and Jakob with me... The other passengers follow suit, their insults and sarcasm toward me forgotten at the sound of the huffing and puffing locomotive, pulling into the station with half a dozen brick-red railcars attached.

Boxcars.

'Forty and Eight' they call them because it's clearly printed on the side that it's big enough for eight horses and forty men. (Women? How many?) It's not a passenger train but a freight train, the locomotive hissing and squealing its brakes, coming to a stop, white smoke swirling around it like an Impressionist painting come to life. A collective sigh arises from the other passengers, their disappointment replacing their interest in me and Lieutenant von Ernst.

Then a different reality hits each of us like dominos falling, a familiar fear no doubt striking many of us in the heart. Are those boxcars filled with Jews?

18

LILLE, FRANCE—APRIL, 1943

Railway station
Lia

The boxcars are empty.

The train's conductor goes from car to car, sliding the doors open. We all watch, transfixed, scratching our heads like chickens pecking for food in an empty dish. Darkness is the only occupant in each one. What's going on here? From the gossip I pick up eavesdropping on the excited passengers chattering— I count at least twenty or more—Jews aren't loaded up here but on trains at Lille-Fives, located less than two kilometres away from the main station. Is this a maintenance stop for water for the locomotive before picking up its human cargo? I don't think so. This train is headed south, not east to Belgium.

So why did the empty freight train stop here?

Not for passengers. Civilians are warned to stay away from freight trains since they're considered targets by Allied Forces, but with the constant disrupting of passenger trains, it's not uncommon for both German soldiers and local townspeople to hitch a ride.

'Mesdames and messieurs, *faites attention, s'il vous plaît*,' shouts the bespectacled railway clerk, waving a clipboard in the air. *Where was he?* Hiding from the irate passengers, most likely. 'I regret to inform you there are no passenger trains leaving Lille this morning due to circumstances beyond our control...'

Moans from the passengers. Inconvenient for them, a death sentence for me. I think about making a run for it when—

'However, the freight train sitting on the tracks is on its way to pick up another cargo of flax'—he pauses—'having just returned from dropping off political dissidents at the transit camp in Mechelen.'

Code for Jews. God help those poor people... Then my stomach plummets and the worst thought hits me hard. I can't help but wonder... if Anna and Jakob's mother *was* picked up by the Gestapo, was she on that train? I feel a sudden chill hit me and for the first time since I embarked on my midnight ride, I can't help it. I slump down in the corner and turn my back to the wall, cry quiet tears where no one can see me, letting go feelings that still haunt me, emotions I buried and never allow back into my mind let alone my heart because they cut deep like a curved dagger, twisting in the wound. That wretched day when my papa abandoned me revisiting me now when I'm at my lowest point because that's when it hurts the most. I didn't feel sorry for myself then; why now? Simple. I was a young girl, not beaten up by life, bad love affairs, cruel ringmasters... Nazis. *Am I that old at thirty-six,* I ask myself, *that I can't pick myself up, find the courage to go on?* This is *me*, Lia, Queen of the Air, I really do fly.

So why can't I fly now? Am I that much of a coward?

Forget the warnings. You and *the children will end up in Gestapo hands if you don't. Get on that train, go wherever it goes—*

Damn, it's that's insistent little voice again.

The clerk continues. '...and will be leaving shortly for Paris.'

Cheers. Laughing. Hands clapping.

Paris. I jump up, but my hands shake so bad I drop my satchel. I lean over, but Jakob picks it up for me. Did he see me cry? Could be. I imagine he saw his mother cry and she tried to hide it, too. He's a brave little boy, and Anna is brave, too. They both sat quietly, waiting for me to finish. I wipe my face with the back of my hand, look at the satchel, see the straps are loose, but nothing else has changed. Paris and everything it was and wasn't makes me bleed. *God, no, I can't go back.*

And revisit heartbreak? I won't. I still suffer an emptiness in the core of my womanhood never filled. I swore when I left, I'd never lose my heart again. The devil ripped my soul out of me, but that's a story for another day. One I keep close to me because then I can believe what I want, that someday I *will* see him again and it will be just as it was between us. I've never revealed that story to anyone and I never shall.

'Are we getting on the train, mademoiselle?' Jakob asks in a hopeful voice. Anna, sitting with her chin in her hands, looks hopeful, too.

'I—I don't know, *mes enfants*... No, we're not going to Paris. We're going to Lyon, there we can—'

What am I going to say? *Sneak over the border* so everyone can hear?

'Please, mademoiselle... we're hungry and tired,' Jakob pleads. Next to him, Anna is shedding tiny tears down her cheeks. Of course they are. Who knows when they last ate or slept? I can't imagine what they've been through. Losing their home... and the unthinkable. Their *maman.* I'm used to the grueling training, long hours, skimping on meals to stay slim. They're not. I have to do something... *fast.* Get them some food, a blanket. There'll be another train. There has to be.

No time for you feeling sorry for yourself, Lia... Look outside.

I hear the roar of a Citroën before I see the ugly black motorcar screeching to a halt, its tires spinning and kicking up dust everywhere. Gestapo. I press my face against the glass, taking in the motorcar spewing nearly as much smoke as the locomotive sitting on the tracks. That's all I need to spur me into motion. There's something so horribly inhumane about the Gestapo and the SS, something so against the teachings of God, something so gut-wrenching and sick about the way they destroy mothers and innocent children in their grip, that I kickstart my life in a different direction. I won't let them beat me, but I have to be careful about not being taken in by my own emotions. It could prove deadly. First, I've got to get us on that train even if it is going to Paris, and take the children with me.

I check the contents of my satchel. Everything's here, including my precious press clippings. I'm wearing the gold wedding ring. Sure, I can go to Switzerland or Spain and join another circus, take Anna and Jakob with me. Keep them safe. Hell, I can work in the Resistance (after I get Anna and Jakob to safety—I won't jeopardize saving these children no matter what path I take), but the young girl named Lia di Montieri never had her day... never knew what really happened to her child, if the man she loved ever tried looking for her. A day where I stop wishing for a different outcome and do something about it. What if I return to Paris?

Face my demons. Face him.

No, I can't lose the memories I still keep close to my heart. If I see him and he turns me away, then I have nothing. I remember an old clown once told me that as long as you have one person who has your back, a heartmate, he called it, who cares about you, you'll survive anything. After my papa left me, I thought the man I loved was that person. Then we were torn apart by the greed of someone else and I left rather than see him hurt. I made my way alone and swore never to return.

I should wait for another train for the children's sake, get them to Lyon then Switzerland, but I don't know if it's Herr Geller behind the wheel of that monstrosity. If so, it's too much of a coincidence to take any chances. If I can do a damn triple with the secret police watching me, I can escape under their noses.

'After the train takes on water and the boxcars are swept clean,' the clerk continues, face sweaty, voice raspy, though I notice he makes no mention of disinfecting them, 'passengers can climb aboard the freight cars.' He pushes his glasses up on his nose and he waves the clipboard in the air. '*If* your name is on the list to prevent stowaways and dissidents from eluding the authorities.'

List?

My name isn't on any list. And of course, the children aren't. I didn't even know about it. Or is that by design? Does the lieutenant *know*? Is he leading me along with no intention of letting me on that train? Does he know the Gestapo is looking for me and he's toying with me to keep me here? Is that why he seems so embarrassed by my flirting?

I'm not waiting to find out. I'm getting on that train with my children. Strange, but I don't feel wrong saying that. I know Esther would want them taken care of by a woman who embraces them as her own. Once we get to Paris, I'll find work in another circus, any circus but the Le Cirque Casini. Keep the children safe.

Passengers line up, clutching their luggage and their hopes, the clerk checking off names. When he comes to me, he stops. Looks me up and down with that guilty pleasure men won't admit to when they see a curvy woman.

'Name, mademoiselle?' he asks. I hold up my left hand. 'I mean, madame.'

'Lia di Montieri.'

'A blonde Italian, huh?' His spectacles slide down his straight nose as he checks his clipboard. '*Hmm...* you're not on the list. Neither are your children.'

At least he didn't ask for their papers. 'Step aside for additional screening, *s'il vous plaît.*'

I can't. Won't.

I've traveled enough during this war to know that 'additional screening' means you're on your way to police headquarters.

I stand fast, poking my nose in his face. 'I've *got* to get to Paris, monsieur, please.' I strike a pose both provocative and endearing, my white-blonde hair curling over my cheekbones, then biting my lips to make them swell and appear fuller, blowing out my breath in a kittenish manner... entreating the overworked clerk to take a second look for a name we both know isn't there. He begins salivating, my seductive body language having the effect on him I prayed for. He's weakening, then for the second time today I feel shame in what I'm doing in front of the children. 'Your papers, please, madame?'

'Yes, of course.' I open my satchel and fumble through my press clippings, looking for my French identity card.

'Why are you going to Paris, madame?' he asks.

I can't say I'm running away from the Gestapo, but as I grab my *carte d'iden-tité*, my eye falls on that infamous photo of me with the Führer in the lion cage. My hair is a darker blonde, but it's still me. I grab on to an idea and blurt it out, no matter how crazy it sounds.

'I have orders.'

His brows shoot up. 'Orders, *you*?'

'Yes, me,' I say with an authority that surprises me since I'm shaking all over. 'I received a personal request from Goebbels' office in Paris to give a command performance at the Circus Medrano for Reichsmarschall Goering and his wife, Magda.' Having met the woman years ago and knowing her penchant for fashion and parties, she's probably in Berlin, but he doesn't know that.

'Let me see the orders, madame.'

Again, he ignores the children, as if they're luggage. Which works in our favor. Keeping the heat off these innocents. I pull out the newspaper clippings, pretend to thumb through them... Drop two, then three press clippings, hoping the clerk picks them up and is impressed enough to put aside protocol when I feel a breeze at my neck and the smell of—

Fresh bread up my nose. And milk and cheese. Suddenly, the lieutenant—the one who is missing his camera today—sweeps down on me with a burlap bag slung over his shoulder, grabs the clippings, including the one with me posing with Hitler and Goebbels. (Has he been imbibing wine to beef up his courage?) He then clicks his heels and gives the clerk the Hitler salute. 'Madame di Montieri and her children *must* get to Paris, monsieur. It's a matter of most urgency.'

The clerk's eyes bulge out. 'Yes, of course, madame. The lieutenant may escort you and your family aboard the train. Allow me to congratulate you on the great honor the Führer has bestowed upon you.'

'*Merci, monsieur,*' is all I say, my eyes riveted on Lieutenant Horst von Ernst, who hasn't yet looked me in the eye. I know when to keep my mouth shut. I'm eager to get out of here with Anna and Jakob in hand, and I can't believe the lieutenant came to our rescue. I misjudged him... Hold on, not so fast... At that moment, the fat Gestapo man barges into the station, his eagle eyes as sharp as the bird's beak, looking at every passenger with a creepy sixth sense as if he can read their minds. The lieutenant sees him, too, and what happens next surprises the hell out of me. The lieutenant grabs me and turns my face away from Herr Geller as if he's about to kiss me.

But he doesn't.

No, instead he holds me tight, shielding my face from the man's scrutiny, but there's nothing sexual in his embrace; more like protection.

Grumbling, the Gestapo agent leaves in a show of bluster that even if I can't see him, I know he's huffing and puffing like a mythical dragon with enough stored-up fire in his breath to burn us all. Yet I escaped. *We* escaped. This time. I pray I never see him again.

'No time to waste, madame...' insists the lieutenant with an urgency in his voice. '*Allons...* let's go!'

Before I can thank him, he grabs my arm, hoists Anna onto his shoulders, who surprisingly doesn't protest, with Jakob following, and hustles us toward the last boxcar, me fumbling with getting my press clippings back into my satchel because I'll need them more than ever if I'm to pull off my big return to Paris, and the lieutenant determined to avoid any further conversation with the clerk or the secret policeman. I swear, everything about the lieutenant goes against what you'd expect from a Party member, helping me and the children escape the eye of the Gestapo.

We move as one, me, the children and Lieutenant von Ernst, and there's even a moment when I wish the young officer and I were on the same side and were fighting for freedom together, but I quickly push that absurdity back into the envelope and remind myself I have a mission to save these precious children from the regime he serves, something he'll never understand.

God works in mysterious ways, but I'll keep that to myself.

I climb aboard the last car then the lieutenant hoists Anna up into the boxcar, then Jakob, then climbs in himself. The smell is reminiscent of the animal cages but worse and the locomotive spews white smoke that sets off an alarm bell in me. *Dangerous smoke,* that little voice reminds me, popping into my head now. Is it? After all I've done to escape, it's just now reminding me that cheap coal is something to look out for, but I push aside that little voice. I'm too focused on escaping the Gestapo.

19

EN ROUTE TO PARIS—APRIL, 1943

Lia

I am folding up my press clippings with shaky fingers when I look out the open door of the boxcar and glimpse the wing of a fighter plane circling the sky overhead.

'Is it one of yours?' I blurt out to Lieutenant von Ernst, a silly thing to say, but this is one time I'd relish seeing a Nazi plane since we're in occupied territory.

'No.'

Precise. Final. I feel a barrel of apprehension tumbling over and over in my head in that one word. The young officer lapses into a silence that makes me shudder. We know what that means, my fingers automatically slipping my old newspaper stories and photos inside the satchel and adjusting the straps as I've done many times before. This time it's different. I've escaped the wrath of the Gestapo only to fall into the dangerous path of an Allied aircraft. The liberators we've been praying for have no idea we're here. The skies are wide open spaces for bombers searching for German industrial targets, airfields, and troops on the move. To the pilot in the aircraft, he sees a freight train with no red cross painted on the roofs of the boxcars, but in his mind it could be carrying armaments to the front, making us a military target.

To us in the boxcar, a smattering of French civilians, German soldiers besides the lieutenant and me, and two very frightened Jewish children, we're conscious of the overworked steam locomotive pulling the freight train over the countryside on its way to the Paris Gare du Nord railway station. So far, the nearly three-hour trip to Paris from Lille has been normal, if you call riding in a boxcar normal. No derailment or bombs. Instead, low voices, snoring, soft crying. Empty milk bottles, breadcrumbs but nary a scrap of cheese. All consumed by hungry children now with their bellies full. I thank God Anna curled up in a fetal position with her head on my lap and is sleeping peacefully. She still hasn't uttered a word. Jakob, on the other hand, kept asking Lieutenant von Ernst if he's ever shot anybody while he gulped down the milk. I held my breath, but the Nazi said no, he was a desk clerk in the records department, not a foot soldier. Is he lying? I don't know, but Jakob seemed relieved and laid down next to his sister and fell asleep. Not much conversation between the lieutenant and me, neither of us wanting to say much about ourselves but we keep the dream going, pretend the bond that we'd forged would last, knowing it won't even if we want it to. Until he confirms my fears. 'The pilot is roaming the countryside, looking for targets.'

'Which makes us the perfect bullseye,' I say with no humor in my voice. I slump back against the cedar wood of the car, pulling my woolen cloak over my knees and covering my chest to keep out the cold.

We lapse back into an uneasy silence as the train barrels down the tracks like a metal monster pulling a heavy load, brakes squealing and tossing us from side to side. Jostled about, I end up in the lieutenant's arms and he doesn't let me go, though his words are far from comforting. 'Don't be afraid, he must have already dropped his bombs or we'd be dead.'

I give him a quick nod, then—

I stiffen and bury my head in horror when loud, sharp pinging hits the roof of the boxcar, then the plane circles back, flies lower and strafes us again. Bullets flying everywhere. Jakob jumps awake, throwing his body over his little sister's. Anna cries out and grabs her brother and clings to him. 'Hide in the corner, *now*!' I yell, but they're too scared to move, then I hear the dull thuds where the bullets land in the oak floor strewn with leftover flax. My God, that was close. The lieutenant picks up both children and deposits them in a dark corner, away from the open door. I grab the lieutenant by his uniform jacket, clutching the fine wool with my fingers. A natural response, I suppose, when a man and woman find themselves in a life or death situation, but it doesn't mean

I'm not embarrassed by my intimate reaction. The lieutenant gives me a shocked look, surprised in the heated moment, but he says nothing.

More strafing.

There are loud gasps from every corner of the railcar. Two women crying, the German soldiers drawing their weapons, but they can't get close to the opening without getting shot, the local men cursing and raising their fists since they're unarmed—the Boches confiscated guns early in the war—as the crazed train conductor puts on more and more cheap coal to outturn the fighter. 'A Thunderbolt,' someone yells out, getting a good look as the aircraft whizzes by then pulls up and out of sight. I have no idea what that is except it's trying to kill me. It's then I realize the lieutenant is shielding me and the children with his body, keeping us from catching a bullet. Oh, God, how strange to feel safe in the enemy's arms. I try to see his face, read his eyes, his thoughts, try to understand what's going on in that Aryan brain of his. How will he explain his actions to the German soldiers snickering and pointing to him, a superior officer, protecting French children from their own aircraft when we get out of this?

Hold on... *If* we get out of this.

In that moment, I feel death with its stealthy footsteps silent and sure, looking for a shoulder to lay its cold hand upon... and a queasiness so frightful and final hits me hard in the gut, and I'm scared, really scared. The idea of dying lurks in my mind every time I climb up to the platform, but there's something noble about it. Not here. Caught in the crossfire, my life ended and forgotten. The children's lives ended. My promise to their mother broken. I'd rather choke than cry out my fear... I swore never to let the enemy see me weak, but is the lieutenant still my enemy? Our enemy? It frightens the hell out of me if he finds out they're Jewish. Then what?

Fool. Once you arrive in Paris, he'll turn you in.

As sobering as that thought is, I don't want to believe it.

We're approaching the outskirts of the city when for some reason I don't understand, the conductor veers off the main track onto railroad tracks circling around Paris, that I never knew existed, to elude the Allied aircraft, perhaps. I feel like I'm in the sawdust ring, going around in a circle until finally the tracks lead us toward a deep tunnel. At first I believe it to be a makeshift structure like the tunnels the Nazis constructed to hide tanks and trucks. Then an old man chewing on a pipe with no tobacco calls out, 'She's taking the route for the old railway line around the city...' *She* meaning the locomotive. 'These tracks've been closed for nearly a decade.'

I smile. The perfect place to hide, *n'est-ce pas?*

But that little voice seeps back under my skin and gets under my craw when the train rushes into the dark tunnel covered with green overgrowth and tall weeds at the mouth of the opening big enough for the locomotive and the boxcars. We hear the fighter circle a few times then buzz off.

But we're going nowhere.

The locomotive hits something on the tracks with a big bang; something metal. We can hear the locomotive huffing and puffing up ahead, and I'm guessing it's the cheap coal the Nazis supplied making it sluggish and slow.

The train is stalled inside the dark tunnel. White smoke pushing out all around us. Me, Lieutenant von Ernst, and the children. Anna is pale, she's shaking, while Jakob keeps clenching his fists, like he wants to fight.

And we sit. Waiting. For several long minutes. I should rest, but I'm too amped up, too nervous, and too scared the plane will come back. I do my best to keep the children calm, whispering to them we're almost at our destination and then we'll be safe, but we're in the last boxcar sitting on the tracks, our rear exposed *outside* the tunnel.

The lieutenant heaves out a breath.

Groggy looking and lids drooping, he smiles at me. 'Time for a little shut-eye, madame, before I escort you and your children to your new circus...' he mumbles. Although now I'm headed back to Paris... where I'll end up, I don't know. I pray Gunty's contact at the pawnshop can assist me in finding a room for us, me and the children, until I figure out what to do. But something else is at play here. Anna has gone a bit peaky and Jakob is looking sleepy. Very sleepy. Then the lieutenant closes his eyes, his head slumps against his chest, and now I have a new problem. How to escape from *him* so we can make our way to the pawnshop on Rue Saint-Jacques, not to sell the wedding ring, but to inquire which traveling tent circuses have set up south of the city, so I can join up and hope to head for the Swiss border. Get the children to safety... and freedom. The advance agents leave posters and playbills everywhere to advertise 'the circus coming to town', so even if it's a hundred kilometers from Paris where they've set up camp, I'll be able to find them.

I ease the lieutenant off my shoulder and lay his head down on scattered flax, then wake up Jakob and motion for him and Anna to follow me while I crawl on my knees to the open sliding door. No one pays attention to us. The German soldiers jumped off before we stopped to relieve themselves; a local man already left for a smoke, two women holding each other and praying. I poke my head out of the boxcar and throw my satchel on the ground, then balance myself on the wooden plank that serves as a step, and jump. I turn and hold out my arms and grab Anna while Jakob jumps off the step and lands on the hard ground. I put my finger to my lips for them to remain silent while I pick up my satchel and hide it under my cloak. We don't get more than a few steps when I hear strange noises coming from the freight cars farther up ahead in the tunnel. That's odd. And that damn white smoke keeps drifting out from the tunnel. A sickening feeling rolls over and over in my stomach. The locomotive is burning that cheap coal. A nuisance, of course, the train chugging along as slow as a Sunday snail to the boiling pot on the stove, then the near miss by the aircraft, and what should now be a quiet respite for all involved has an eerie feel to it. I shrug it off. The train is stuck in the tunnel, going nowhere, but we've got to disappear before the lieutenant wakes up. I hold on to the children's hands, and we start off in the opposite direction toward the gray-blueness above the rooftops that is Paris, then stop. There's a fluttering in my stomach that won't go away, like when a bird flies into the tent and under the big top during a show.

It's a bad sign.

'Stay here, *mes enfants*,' I whisper to the children, leaving them in a clearing several meters from the boxcar, then creep closer back to the tunnel opening when I see several bodies sprawled beside the track and passengers gasping for air. Two, three people stumbling around. *How, why?*

Then it hits me. That cheap coal is poison.

And this train is stuck in an airless, dark tunnel surrounded by white smoke from the locomotive. I don't feel sleepy—the children were but the fresh air has revived them—and my adrenaline is kicking in with a big burst of energy, but I wasn't in a boxcar wholly in the tunnel. We still had air, though gas could have seeped in... I call on the German soldiers milling around, begging them to help me drag as many passengers as we can stumbling out of the tunnel. We can't go inside without gas masks, which means we can only save a few... There must be twenty, thirty souls in those boxcars. Oh, my God, these poor people are dying from carbon monoxide poisoning because the train is stalled on the tracks.

'*Danger, danger*,' I shout, cupping my hands on my mouth. '*Poison gas*.'

I pray I wake them up, but the damn low-grade coal burns at a reduced power and the people inside the tunnel don't know they're becoming asphyxiated. The horror is that it hits you so slowly, you get so sleepy you don't realize what's happening to you—

The lieutenant.

Our boxcar is *partially* in the tunnel. My God, the gas has affected him. I can't let him die.

I grab onto the sleeve of the young Frenchman I saw earlier in our boxcar, frantic. '*Please*, monsieur, help me save Lieutenant von Ernst.'

'Save a Nazi?' He spits on the ground. 'No way, mamselle.'

He walks away. I call after him. 'Then you're just like them, you bastard.'

I combat his harshness by reminding myself these people know the wrath of the enemy firsthand. They've suffered terribly, but this German saved my life. I can't and won't abandon him.

I swing around, make sure Anna and Jakob are nowhere near the train— they're holding hands, watching me race back to the last boxcar, where I throw down my satchel and jump aboard. The other passengers are gone. I race over to this dear young man who has touched my maternal soul. He's slumped on the floor... I fall to my knees, my mouth dangerously close to his, and yes, he's breathing.

He's still alive.

I have no doubt gas is seeping in here even if I can't smell it, the smoke dissipating, but the fresh air kept him from inhaling too much. I act quickly, finding the strength deep within me to drag the unconscious Nazi officer across the wooden floor, grateful I *am* a circus queen, that my upper body strength is equal to a man's and my arms are muscular and taut. My little stunt takes thirty, forty seconds, then with a loud grunt and a fast rolling action, I give him one final push onto the landing step, praying he doesn't hit his head.

I've got to get him to take deep and heavy breaths.

I get one better.

The lieutenant rolls off the step onto the hard ground and jolts awake. He sees me, curses in German, and then lets out a painful groan when he observes the dead bodies up ahead on the track. He pulls himself up from his crouched position, asking me if there are more victims, and we must save them—

Then he hits the ground and lapses into semi-consciousness.

I have only a vague idea of what's happening around me, the German soldiers trying to round up the passengers crying and praying at the same time. I don't react to anyone around me. I'm right where I should be, holding the lieutenant in my arms, close to me, rocking him back and forth. I'm reminded of Velma the lioness enfolding her new cub to her warm body. At this moment, I feel a kinship with the big cat that warms my heart like a hot, sweet lemongrass tea. A tear falls upon my cheek. I can't help it. I wish I didn't see something good in this young man. It would make my escape so much easier if I didn't.

* * *

'Why did you save me, madame?' The Nazi Wehrmacht officer has a raging headache, but he's smiling. We're sitting in the backseat of a Mercedes touring motorcar which mysteriously showed up away from the scene of the tragedy. Anna and Jakob keep their heads down, as I'm certain their mother taught them. The poor angels are holding each other tight. I've got to wait for the right moment to get them out of here, de-escalate the terror they must be feeling.

'You were only on that train because of me, Lieutenant.'

'How do you know that?'

'No Nazi Wehrmacht officer is going to ride with the riff raff in a boxcar. All you had to do was ask the clerk to call the local police and Nazi headquarters would send a motorcar to pick you up like this one... then I popped into the scene.'

'Still, you didn't have to warn me.'

'You saved me and my babies from the Gestapo, Lieutenant. Now we're even.'

'I had to. Herr Geller boasts a despicable reputation. I couldn't let you fall into his hands.' He shakes his head. 'However, I believe there's more to it why you saved me.'

'Don't read something into it that isn't there,' I insist.

'Why not? Because I'm your enemy?'

'Yes, but you did teach me something about myself.'

'Me?'

'You showed me there's honor among people who respect each other... even if they're schooled in hate.'

'I don't hate you, madame; in fact, I've been holding out on you.'

'Let me guess, you're joining the Resistance.'

'I could have you shot for that if I wasn't so fond of you.'

'But you won't?' I ask, flippant. His words chill me. I believe him. Still, I'm curious and hide my fear behind a smile. It's worked before, so I stay on the same beam.

'My mother is circus through and through and she's a lot like you. Strong, hotheaded, and gets things done.'

'*Your mother?*' I throw my head back and laugh. Now I get it why he brings out the maternal instinct in me. I remind him of his mother. That's why he has a need to protect me. This boy with the Hitler salute on the tip of his tongue refrains from saying it in front of me out of respect. Yes, he's acting nice, but I can never forget he's a Nazi, that he's hurt I don't know how many innocent Belgians, French, and Jews. Even Roma. I tell myself that before I start believing he's a good 'German'. How many times have I heard from a Resistance fighter who's been arrested and tortured by the Nazis that there are no good Germans?

I'm beginning to get a bad feeling. That he set me up. But why?

And who *is* his mother? Instead of asking him, I plan my escape. 'These people need someone in charge, Lieutenant... They need *you*.' I kiss him on the cheek like his *maman* would. 'I must be going. Adieu.'

He shakes his head. 'It's not adieu, madame, I *will* see you again.' He pats Jakob on the head. 'And your children, too.'

'You know where to find me, Lieutenant,' I tease him. 'Under the big top.' Before he can stop me, I open the door and nod toward the children. They can't wait to get out of the motorcar, which I'm certain represents 'bad' Nazis to them, though Anna gives the officer a faint smile and Jakob stands tall, imitating the German's straight posture. Oh, my, is this how it starts? With the children?

Yes.

And I'm to blame for exposing them to this Nazi officer. Lieutenant Horst von Ernst isn't the typical Wehrmacht officer and I can't for one minute allow the children to let down their guard around Nazis. I'll have to be careful, very careful. I can't trust him, even if I want to... especially when he points out the white greasepaint I missed on the back of Jakob's ear and remarks how much he enjoyed the clowns in Circus Richter... *all of them*. And how easy it is to hide in plain sight.

He knows. Knows they're not my babies. And suspects I ran away with them because they're Jewish.

Brave or dumb on my part? Letting him know where my head is. I duck down when I see the local French police descend upon the scene, then medical ambulances arrive along with the coroner, men in white uniforms unloading stretchers, making it easier for the three of us to disappear in the gathering crowd. I wish I could have saved more people, *God, do I.* Not just one heartbreak weighing me down but two as I lower my head and let my shoulders slump because I'm all done in.

I take the children by the hand and we start walking toward the pawnshop on Rue Saint-Jacques.

20

PARIS, FRANCE—APRIL, 1943

Montmartre
The Magician

When I was a young physician in 1931, tripping the light fantastic, and downing French champagne in the Himmel und Hölle Club (Heaven and Hell) in Weimar Berlin, I wondered what it would be like to lose a patient in the worst way. That is, when a girl dies and it has nothing to do with my skills and I get the blame.

Now I know.

I lost a beautiful girl during surgery two days ago. A trick rider named Ambroisine from a Dutch circus. I refrained from arranging her dead body in a lovely display like a beautiful 'angel doll' for the police to find as I usually do. I don't need my failure broadcast across the headlines of the *Paris-soir*, reminding me I'm not God, not even His disciple. I am distraught and crying in my cups since she turned blue, an overreach of emotion gone awry like my little sister Noemi when she smashed her doll's head against the wall. I, of course, came to her rescue and saved the doll until the next time... until her behavior dictated there was no next time. But I digress. I'm not at ease revealing more.

I'm still heartsick over this whole debacle. The circus girl was a victim of fire on the back of her legs, a miscalculated jump through a fiery hoop. I don't know how the medical procedure went wrong. Everything was going so well with the skin grafts I lifted from her torso until her pulse became faint after I attempted to remove the burned skin from the upper layers on her thigh. She went into shock. Berthile, my inglorious assistant, was no help with her winter cold that seems everlasting. She kept wiping her nose instead of stopping the bleeding, sneezing and coughing in my face. I sent her out of the room so I could grieve.

Not for the girl. She knew the risks. But for my professional pride.

I must elaborate. Seeing the exquisite work you perform on the patient shrivel up and die can do strange things to a physician's brain. You scrutinize every cut you made with a magnifying glass, convinced some pesky pathogen took up residence in the wound and is thwarting your efforts. And yes, you repeat to the four walls what's sticking in your craw numerous times. You hear every drip of the water faucet in the ancient surgery room as steady as your heartbeat. The sound is so acute, you can't turn it off. You're convinced your own heart would then stop. And damnation, you want the corpse off the table and out of your way. *Now.*

Why keep *reminding* yourself you're not God?

Losing the girl isn't the worst of it. My man Yann made a mess of disposing of the body. Again. I'm not pleased with his sloppy methods, tossing her into the Seine with the rest of the lowlife victims. He has about as much subtlety as a lion passing gas in its trainer's face.

Good help is so hard to get these days.

So I shut myself up in my second-floor parlor. And here I sit, alone. I don't get out much since this war imploded in my beloved Paris. I miss the glory days in Berlin at the Heaven and Hell Club when the worst that could happen was a week of gastric distress from eating too much bockwurst. To console myself, I drank a bottle of good brandy until I passed out. I even had a moment when temptation whispered in my ear morphine would make the pain go away, but I don't indulge in the needle. I'm not a fool. I've seen what addiction does to a man, the hold it has on you, and if there's anything I abhor it's not having control. Period. (I forgot to mention I pay Yann in morphine doses, so why am I surprised when the man fails at his job?)

So I slammed the door shut on my lovely *maison*, locked it up tight to thwart thieves—you can't trust anyone—and I'm off to the circus. To find my muse again.

Mademoiselle Jeanne.

I do my best to retain in my mind all the things about her I adore. I see her pretty face with her freckles barely hidden under pale powder, her upswept eyes always curious with their blue hue reminding me of blue topaz polished by a tiger's tail. She brings my entire world back to life.

I arrive at Le Cirque Casini, my psyche revved up and singing a new tune. Oh, how I love the glitter and gold of the circus, the distinctive smells, the roar of the lions, the spangles and cheap sequins. I rush into the main tent, restless, my face cold as ice, my hands shaking. My heart racing as I take a seat for the afternoon performance. I had to come. Regenerate my energy by seeing my beautiful mademoiselle flying under the big top on the trapeze. To make my life more than a smattering of bad luck.

To see *her*.

To speak to her.

My excuse? I have final word from Herr Geller about the big change coming to Le Cirque Casini and I shall warn her about the new Nazi owner to keep her safe. Then she will fall into my arms and she shall be mine to keep. No, not to touch her. I just want to look at her.

For now, I cheer and applaud with the rest of the audience when The Flying Jouberts take to the big top and do their act. Swinging, flying, too many somersaults in mid-air to count. She does her routine with beauty and grace, her body a glittery ball of gold spangles at the very top of the tent, then blowing kisses to the crowd on her graceful descent back to earth with a tent-man holding the rope steady for her.

Ah, the gods are good. She's coming back to me.

Meanwhile, I observe the two men flying with her. Her papa and his brother Édouard, I believe. Shorter, stockier, but a good flyer. I sense tension between the two men when they wave to the crowd, nudging each other as if they're about to come to blows, then taking off in opposite directions while Mademoiselle Jeanne is—

Where is she?

I take my eye off her for a moment and she's talking to that tent-man. How dare he take up her time when *I'm* here? I approach them, adjusting my shirt cuffs and black bow tie, smoothing down my fine wool jacket, avoiding two clowns, one blowing on a trumpet and the other hitting a metal triangle with a silver stick and a loud ping that hurts my ears. Oh, the injustices I have to suffer from these fools. I'm seconds from sweeping in front of her, then I stop when I see her look up into the big top, pointing.

'You're lying, monsieur,' Jeanne is saying to the tent-man, allowing the wardrobe girl to drape her long cape around her shoulders and fasten a chain with a medal around her neck. 'You didn't check the rigging.'

'I don't take well to being accused of something I didn't do, mademoiselle.' Oh, my. He clenches his hand into fists, making his arm muscles bulge. The man is a giant. 'Ask the boss man who he assigned to check your rigging. It wasn't me.'

Jeanne pretends not to notice his physical display of strength. 'You're new here, *n'est-ce pas*?'

'So?'

'So every tent-man who works on this show knows it's common knowledge the aerialist's rigging is checked every night, pulling and tugging to make sure everything is safe.'

'You *are* safe, mademoiselle, or you wouldn't be standing here. It's not my fault if your act isn't good enough and you have to make excuses for it.'

'You insolent, ungrateful—'

'Just stating what my eyes can see.' He grins, taking the win.

'You work for *me*, monsieur, don't forget that.' She swishes her cape around to mark her superior position to him.

'I work for your father... *You* remember that.'

Her cheeks redden, then her neck. Chin lifted, young, high breasts pointed, she's magnificent and doesn't let him go. 'The flybar was shaky when I grabbed it. Make sure it's fixed by tonight's performance.'

She turns to leave, her cape fluttering around her, but he's not finished. 'I heard you were a handful when I joined up here.'

'How dare you?'

'Don't worry. I'll do my job... Make sure you do yours.'

'Oh, and what's wrong with the act?' she stammers, clearly upset. She takes a step forward, tries to get in his face, except she only comes up to his chin. But oh, is she adorable. Like a pretty girl clown with big, blue painted eyes.

He grins. 'You can't do a triple.'

'Almost nobody can! I'll have you fired, monsieur... whatever your name is.' Even from where I stand, I see her eyes raking over him. Is it anger? Or is she taking in his manliness? That disturbs me.

'Mox.'

'Mox what?'

'Just Mox, mademoiselle.'

'I'd fire you myself,' she threatens, 'but we're short-handed. Of course you knew that.'

'I don't want any trouble, mademoiselle, but I won't stand here and not defend myself. Now, if you'll excuse me, I'll get to that rigging.'

He turns on his heel, leaving my beautiful Jeanne standing there with her mouth open. I echo her frustration dealing with this beast, though I'm bothered by the fiery light blazing in her eyes, the way she pushes out her breasts, lifts her chin in defiance, drinks in his bold stance and, like most women, she's impressed by his broad shoulders and hard chest exposed by his skimpy white tank top. He's as sure of himself as a barnyard rooster, believing he can hold back the dawn with his handsome smile.

The bastard.

I *loathe* his type.

* * *

'Have you spoken with Sandrine?' Jeanne asks me, wiping the perspiration off her face with the hem of her cape and acting as if nothing happened with the tent-man. I catch up with her as she walks toward her caravan wagon. 'I'm worried about her.' She keeps twisting a silver medal around her neck. Nerves.

'I assure you, mademoiselle, she's perfectly fine, healing better each day.'

But I actually have no idea if that's true. The cabaret dancer insisted on leaving the sanitarium where the Gestapo placed her. I heard rumors she balked at returning to the cabaret and spying on the dancers at Bal Tabarin. (The owner was 'encouraged' to take her back or face extra scrutiny regarding his black-market practices.) I'm not surprised. I mentioned to Herr Geller to go slowly with her—damned Gestapo agent returned to Paris sooner than I bargained for—humor her, discipline SS officers or pretend to, but the man has no common sense. All he thinks about is the Führer. His plans. His rules. Always his damn rules. Nothing else exists in the fat Gestapo man's life. Certainly not women. The man has no class. At times, I find these Nazis so tiresome, but they allow me to continue my work. Does that make me a collaborator? Of course not. I provide a service, a specialty I sell to the highest bidder. And if it's the National Socialist Party, so be it. Of course, I say nothing to Jeanne about my personal beliefs.

Instead, I placate the object of my obsession with: 'I sent a personal message to the concierge at the small apartment where Sandrine lives, but I've heard nothing.'

'Perhaps she's back at Bal Tabarin.'

'Perhaps.' I shall have 'the talk' with the dancer where I explain to her the consequences of her defiance, but no one has seen her for three days. I pray I'm not too late. I can't bear another failure upon my shoulders.

It will ruin my reputation.

We reach the performers' caravans and Jeanne looks over her shoulder at me with the biggest eyes, like a child who's never been denied a thing. 'You don't think she'd forget my birthday?'

'And miss seeing you perform on the trapeze in her costume, mademoiselle? I'm sure we shall both be here in the front row.'

She lowers her eyes, thinking, then. 'He's right, you know.'

'Pardon?'

'I can't do a triple and Papa won't train me.'

'Why not?' I ask, surprised.

'He says it's too dangerous for his little girl.' She grits her teeth. 'I'm not his little girl anymore, why won't anyone see that?'

'I see you as a beautiful young woman,' I dare to profess, trying to take her hand, but she turns away quickly. To avoid my touch? When will I learn a pretty woman needs to be coaxed to allow you in? *She's not one of your poor unfortunates who have no choice but to succumb to you.*

'You're too kind, monsieur,' she says, her smile warm, making me hopeful I've made some traction with her. 'I was hoping Uncle Édouard would train me, but he's not himself since the Occupation, fretting and arguing with Papa over everything. I'm so worried about him.'

So I wasn't wrong about the tension between the two men. Does it have anything to do with the news I have brought to share with her about Le Cirque Casini?

'Mademoiselle Jeanne, I must speak to you...'

'Can't it wait?' she begs off with a tired smile. As if she's averse to any more drama after her run-in with the tent-man. 'I'm late with Bébé's feeding.'

It takes a moment to register, then it hits me. That lovely day I drove her to Paris.

'The baby elephant?'

'Yes... you can come with me if you like.'

Well, if this isn't a breakthrough. An invitation to spend time alone with her. I huff out a breath, keep my news close to my chest—it can wait—and follow Jeanne to the elephant tent where the *maman* elephant Josephine is struggling with her calf trying to feed from her, its mouth suckling from her teat. Or trying to. I gather the calf with the big floppy ears isn't getting any milk.

I look away. I may be a physician, but I find this female display of mother-hood off-putting.

Jeanne believes she knows how to fix it. 'Josephine won't hurt you, monsieur. The poor dear is in a tither, suffering so with little milk to feed her baby, so I help her.' She settles down on a bale of hay and calls the baby elephant over to her.

'Bébé... *Bébé*, I have something for you.' She pulls out a glass bottle of milk from the metal box sitting nearby. I gather a worker from the cookhouse left it here earlier. The baby elephant starts squealing and jaunts over the straw-laden floor and nearly knocks over my beautiful Jeanne to get to the milk. She laughs. 'You poor baby, you must be so hungry after the show.' The calf nudges her with its round body. 'Yes, yes, I love you, my sweet baby.'

She loves the baby elephant? My heart skips a beat. What about me? I dare to hope when she turns to me with the biggest grin, but no, it's not for me. I'm crestfallen and barely listening when she says, 'Bébé can drink ten to twelve liters of milk a day, now that we can get it. Papa says we're lucky to have friends to help us.'

Friends? Does he mean Nazis?

Is this why he was feuding with his brother? Like most Parisians I come in contact with, they do not welcome or like the Germans. I feel in my gut Jeanne doesn't suspect her papa leans toward the occupiers. And I shan't tell her. Why spoil this moment with just the two of us?

And the elephants, of course.

With Josephine looping her trunk over Jeanne's shoulder, watching, observing as the beautiful girl holds the baby elephant close to her and Bébé drinks greedily from the glass bottle, spilling milk on herself, on Jeanne. And on me, for God's sake. But I'm enjoying this too much to get upset, watching this lovely creature twisting and turning her perfect body, and I just about faint when she kicks off her soft ballet shoes and wiggles her stockinged toes in the straw. Oh, damnation, I have to sit down. Compose myself. I'm sweating in my wool jacket and can't find my handkerchief. I loosen my tie. Oh, dear, I forgot it. And Bébé thinks I have milk and, squealing, knocks me on the ground.

'She wants to play.' Jeanne laughs. 'You should see her rolling around in the mud when it rains.'

'I look forward to it, mademoiselle... Seeing more of Bébé *and* you.'

She stares at me with a look I can't translate. 'Yes, of course, monsieur.'

She loses her smile, grabs another bottle of milk and continues the feeding session with the baby elephant. But the magic is gone. I've made her uncomfortable with my boldness. I must tread more carefully. I can't reveal my feelings to her. I will work my way into her life in such a way so I'm as familiar to her as an old ballet slipper. I smile to myself. A perfect metaphor, *n'est-ce pas?*

I should have known a girl as beautiful as Jeanne would have many admirers, men so bold they have no restraints on their behavior. One such man bursts into the elephant tent. Wearing camel jodhpurs, white shirt open to the waist— another ridiculous display of faux masculinity... The animal trainer. I've seen him abusing the lions with his training stick. He gives me a look a charging bull elephant would give an interloper in the herd... He wants to kill me. Not very pleasant, but I remain calm. I always carry a syringe filled with morphine in my jacket pocket should I need it to defend myself.

'What's *he* doing here?' he demands, pointing that stick at me.

Jeanne, bless her, juts out her chin, defiant. No wonder I adore her. 'He's helping me feed Bébé.' She grabs the last bottle of milk from the case.

'Get rid of him. I don't want him anywhere near my elephants. Or you.'

'Josephine doesn't have enough milk, Kaspar. Her baby will starve.' She stands up, holding up the empty bottles as proof. 'If you don't allow me to feed her, I'll tell my father.'

His eyes narrow.

'No need to be so hasty, Jeanne. You can feed her, but let's keep it between us. I don't want anyone getting between me and my animals. They're precious to me.' He grins. 'Like you.'

He puts his arm around her and hugs her, kisses her nose. Jeanne pushes him away, while I watch, my emotions simmering.

'You don't know when to stop, do you?' she accuses him.

'You'll come around, Jeanne,' he snickers. 'Girls like you always do.'

I'm not used to keeping quiet, so I blurt out, 'The mamselle requested you keep your hands to yourself.'

'Who *is* this clown?' Kaspar growls at me.

'A friend,' she says with a sweet smile in my direction. Suffering the humiliation thrust upon me by this hooligan just became worth it. 'Now let me finish feeding Bébé and leave us alone.'

'He looks harmless enough.' He turns to Jeanne. 'Keep your mouth shut. Both of you.'

He leaves in a huff. Josephine makes loud trumpeting noises and shoos him away with her trunk. Bébé hides between her mother's legs while Jeanne entices her with a fresh bottle of milk, and I sit on a bale of hay, thinking.

I'll not share my news with Jeanne just yet, but there is no doubt in my mind, the first thing I'm going to insist on from the new owner when the Nazis take over Le Cirque Casini is to have that animal trainer Kaspar fired.

PART III

THE LAST TIME I SAW PARIS

21

PARIS, FRANCE—APRIL, 1943

Pawnshop on Rue Saint-Jacques
Lia

'You and your children are not safe here in Paris, mademoiselle, with the recent roundups.'

'Jews?'

'And Roma.'

'How did you know?' I ask with a weak smile, surprised the shopkeeper guessed my secret in spite of my bleached white-blonde hair. We walked for what seemed like half a day, but it was only an hour or so from the tragic scene at the train. Time drags on when your body reaches its limit of endurance, like pulling taffy while it's still warm, and when you're hungry it seems you'll never feel right again. But we three made it. We're here in Paris at the pawnshop. I remember this place back in the twenties with the white enamel plaque claiming it has been here since 1779. It's where the circus band pawned their instruments. Now I'm here, throwing myself on the mercy of this man Jarnak. He didn't seem surprised when I told him my story, and how I will never forget the poor passengers suffocating from the poisonous gas, then sleeping like characters in a fairy tale but with no prince to wake them up. There was nothing I could do save shouting out the danger, and a few made it out. I keep quiet about how in the end I did save a life. A Nazi's life. A boy not yet a man. I don't want to explain something I don't understand myself. Still, it makes me wonder, if Hitler is sending young men with no life experience to fight, have we the right to hope the end of this horrible Occupation is near?

But I won't live to see it if the Gestapo catches up with us.

'I *didn't* know you were Roma, Mademoiselle di Montieri.' He smiles, looking at my identity card and from that curious look, I'd say he's admiring the forger's work.

'My mother was English, but to the Nazis I'm Roma.'

He nods. 'Anyone as desperate as you to seek me out by walking into my shop trying to hide shiny spangles under a long cloak and looking like she spent the night in a cattle car with straw clinging to her has something to hide...' He looks me in the eye. My green eyes. 'I took you for a friend of the Underground. And the children for Jewish refugees.'

'Me? I work in the circus. I'm Queen of the Air. And these two are my babies.'

Anna curtsies; Jakob bows from the waist. They're turning out to be good little troupers. Their *maman* would be so proud.

'*Bien*, I'm aware of many performers like you who claim as you do no knowledge of the Resistance, and I respect that. Still, I can't arrange for you and your'—he clears his throat—'*children* to make your way to Spain. It's far too dangerous.'

Is it money he wants?

'I can pay you...'

I'm heartsick. I don't want to sell the ring, but I can't stay in Paris.

I study the man with the kettle-black eyes with deep shadows, his balding head ringed with sooty-looking dark hair. Can I trust him? He's slow but methodical. He never looks over his shoulder like he's waiting for someone to back him up, though he does look toward the far wall frequently, and it's then I remember the rumors about the 'peepholes' in the shop they used to catch thieves. I suspect now they're used for something far different.

Like setting me up.

And catching me off guard.

'I don't want your money, mademoiselle,' he says, grinning. 'Unfortunately, the Nazis have compromised the escape line with arrests and even executions... We must wait until we establish a new route over the Pyrenees. Until then, may

I suggest you seek employment in a Paris circus? Hide them in plain sight?' He nods toward Anna and Jakob.

I have to smile. I like him. He's using my line for hiding the children.

'It's been a long time since I worked in Paris, monsieur. Few will remember me.'

'I do. You were with The Flying Jouberts before you mysteriously disappeared.' I hear the curiosity in his voice.

'I was just a girl—'

'But you were magnificent, mademoiselle.' A statement, not a compliment. 'Surely Le Cirque Casini will welcome you back... I recollect they're camped in their usual place, just outside the city. Though we'll have to do something about your hair.'

'I'm not going back there, monsieur, *ever*.'

'You'll be less suspicious if you're not a blonde,' he continues, ignoring me.

'No.'

'It's easier to hide in a circus outside the city.'

'*No*,' I say, adamant, 'I'm not going back to Le Cirque Casini. I hopped aboard a train when I was eighteen and never looked back. I'll find another circus. Cirque d'Hiver, Circus Houcke...'

'*Hmm...*' is all he says, looking through the mishmash of bottles and the like in a wooden box he pulls out from under the counter, half-listening or not listening to my protests, I'm not sure which, but I'm dead serious about my decision. I'd rather find any other circus than face *him*. Philippe Joubert. I can't do it. I'm used to the stares and strange looks I get whenever I join a new circus, unasked questions about how I could leave Paris and never return. I don't have an answer, but this is different. Opening old wounds. Leaving the city of my birth, where I fell in love, was my only option back then. Staying away from the man who was my heart *because* I loved him so much. I couldn't see him hurt because of me. I was pregnant. I found a new life. I admit I carry guilt in my heart because I lost my girlhood with him and then what every woman cherishes... her child. Over the years, I pushed aside those memories and replaced them with press clippings of my triumphs on the trapeze. It's how I survive and not let the travails of my past swallow me up. I've always believed if I go back, my meticulously planned life without him will come crashing down and destroy me. I don't tell the man Jarnak that. He'd never understand how deep love can hurt... or would he? What lies underneath the many layers of his soul? I have the feeling there's more to this pawnshop than I will ever know.

'I can ask for shelter at the Cirque d'Hiver,' I say. 'Circus people stick together.'

He shakes his head. 'They'll turn you away, mademoiselle. They might even report you to the Gestapo.'

'Why, monsieur?'

'The Nazis are cracking down on anyone hiding Jews and Roma and checking the papers and identity cards of circus performers. Cirque d'Hiver has given up many of their own. The same at the Medrano, but I hear Cirque Casini has remained untouched.'

'Still, it's not for me. For us.' I hug Anna, clinging to my cloak. 'So I have no place to go, monsieur.' I heave out a heavy sigh. I start to pull off the gold ring, ready to take what I can to rent a room somewhere. 'How much for this ring?'

He waves my hand away. 'You and the children can sleep here in the back room tonight.' He chuckles. 'You won't be the first refugees we've helped.'

'We?' I have to ask.

'The Count.' He raises his brows, his deep-set eyes warning me not to ask any more questions. He thinks a moment, checks a ledger, running up and down the written list of names. He stops, smiles. 'Ah, I was right. Le Cirque Casini is camped on the outskirts of Paris.'

'No.'

He doesn't listen to me, but places a bottle of hair dye on the counter. 'I remember a sly old clown coming in here last week to pawn a Luger and two Swiss watches.'

'*No*,' I repeat, louder.

He ignores me. 'I remember him because he tried to con me with a card trick to double his take.'

An old clown with sleight of hand. Card game. No, it couldn't be after all these years.

'What was his name?' I ask, my heart leaping, pulse racing, for if it *is* him, I have to make a hard decision. At a time when not only is my body exhausted, my strength depleted, every ounce of my being tortured with grief and guilt and wondering how I shall on fighting the Nazis, but my heart is so lonely it swells up and hurts so much I keel over, clasping my hands to my chest. I'm so bruised and battered, but God in His wisdom knows I need a friend.

Jarnak smiles. 'Socrates.'

Tears well up in my eyes and all my defenses drop because this is the one person in the world who ever cared for me, who watched me grow up riding show ponies then performing on the rings, who convinced the Great Gio di Montieri to train me on the trapeze... A man I thought of as a father and who held me tight, as my own papa should have done when I bared my soul to him that night before I left Paris, telling him my precious secret, a secret I never told anyone else in the circus.

I pick up the bottle of hair dye off the counter. I don't know the color; what does it matter? I've been conned into doing what I swore I never would.

I'm going home to Le Cirque Casini.

* * *

The name on his *carte d'identité* reads Sebastien 'Socrates' Dubois, but everybody calls him Socks. Always have since I can remember when he took me under his wing when I was thirteen and began performing as a trick rider with the Le Cirque Casini. He was also there on the night I packed my patched-up suitcase with my spangled costume and ballet slippers with a heavy heart and left Paris. Over the years, I've gone over that night again and again. Swinging on the trapeze under the big top, the wind in my face, sunning myself outside my wagon on a crisp, clear day... Lying alone at night under a heavy quilt and a full moon.

How I fell in love with a man everyone adored, the star of the circus and the trapeze. Philippe Joubert. Gio warned me about him when I was sixteen and perfecting my double somersault under his guidance. (I cried for days when I heard the maestro of the trapeze had passed on.) He said Philippe's handsome looks were like the spangles we wore. Shiny objects that had no substance and broke easily.

I didn't listen. I flirted and adored and loved that man ten years older than I, but in my girlish eyes, so much wiser. I believed he not only loved me as I did him, but he intended to marry me and make me an official 'Joubert' and we'd start our own little family of aerialists. His brother Édouard never approved of us, but then again he was jealous of his older brother's looks and prominent standing in the circus, although Édouard was the better flyer. I never knew what was going on in that man's head, and what young girl would? I was in love with his brother and nothing else mattered. Phillipe was a man who women ran after, including me, but I was an innocent girl and no match for a man of his experience, and what happened next lies buried within me. I didn't see the signs that Philippe's ambition surpassed everything else and his confidence that he was the star of the circus was so solid he didn't see the obvious. The circus is a business... and even he couldn't change that.

The owner wanted Philippe to marry his beautiful daughter, Gisèle, and threatened to fire him if he didn't. Philippe balked, said he was in love with me. He wanted us to run away, but I convinced him to stay, sure that if I showed Monsieur Casini I could wow the crowds, he'd change his mind.

I did.

But Monsieur Casini wouldn't budge. I was good, but I was a girl *and* a horse trader's daughter and not good enough for his star attraction.

Then everything fell apart like a juggling act when you miss a ball. I found out I was pregnant. I said nothing to Philippe, but even though I initially hid my emerging tummy under a tutu—pink with diamond-esque sequins that sparkled when I swung across the big top—eventually I started to show. Then I panicked. I begged Socks to help me... hoping that the good sisters at a nearby convent would take me in. Sister Vincent brought the orphans to the circus and when she noticed my condition during a matinee—nuns have a way of knowing these things; Divine intervention, perhaps?—she insisted I have my baby there. Socks wanted to tell Philippe about the child, but I begged him not to, convincing him this was best for everyone. The clown commandeered an old truck we use to haul hay, hid me underneath a big pile of prickly straw and drove me to the medieval château run by the Order of the Sisters of Benevolent Mercy in Ville Canfort-Terre about an hour outside Paris. I stayed there for nearly four months since I couldn't go to a hospital when my time came, and if Monsieur Casini found out I was with child, he'd fire Philippe.

But the baby died. A little girl lying cold in my arms in the convent of Saint Daria infirmary. I was young and scared, and the good sisters told me they would pray for me. Yes, I needed prayers, but I needed my baby more. I kept asking the Mother Superior—Sister Ursula—why my stillborn child was taken from me so quickly. I never had time to grieve for her, hold her tiny hands, count her little toes, blow the crown of wispy hair on her head, and kiss her cold cheeks.

All they let me do was wallow in my shame.

I protested, asked to hold her for a while longer, but the Mother Superior refused my wish with an angry, ugly scowl I'll never forget. I *hated* that woman. Terrible thoughts raged in my head like a rainstorm. I yelled at her that she was cruel and mean, and she shouted back that I would pay for my insolence in solitary, then left me in tears. I knew my emotional display was against God's teachings and waited for a heavenly hand to strike me down. I have the saintly Sister Vincent to thank for saving me, clasping her hands holding the rosary over my clenched fists and calming me down, praying the Mother Superior wouldn't carry out her threat of locking me in a closet. Sister Vincent let it slip a girl died in there. I have a deep fondness for this good soul. She had no love for Sister Ursula either and hugged me to comfort me when the Mother Superior returned and told me I had until morning to leave. Go back to the circus.

Go back to what? Hard stares, snickering. I was a bad girl in everyone's eyes because I fell in love with a man better than me.

I'll never forget what Socks said to me when I asked Sister Vincent to stop by the circus on the way to the train station. I sneaked into clown alley to say goodbye—I didn't dare look for Philippe; if he kissed me, I'd never leave—and somehow Socks got it out of me that I lost the baby. He held me, treating me with kindness and wiping away my tears. 'A circus queen never cries, my pretty Lia. She dazzles.'

'But I'm not a circus queen, Socks.'

He laughed. 'You will be, *ma belle*. You have a gift up there under the big top like I've never seen in all my years in the circus. Work hard. Someday I will see you again and be able to say I knew you back before you were famous.'

That someday is today.

I never thought I'd see him again and I wonder if he'll recognize me; after all, it's been eighteen years. No one but Socks knew why I ran away from the circus. The angst in his eyes sent shivers through me when I told him it was my choice to leave... Philippe wasn't to blame; this was best for everyone. I don't know if he believed me, but I'm about to find out.

I'm here.

I stand at the entrance to the main tent instead of barging into clown alley and knocking Socks for a loop in his big clown shoes. Especially with two children in tow. I'm Lia di Montieri again. Papers in order. Even a ration card in that name, thanks to Jarnak. And the children have papers, too. Anna is now Marie Deleon and Jakob is Luc Deleon—my 'late husband's' surname. We spent two nights at the pawnshop, holed up in a small room with a lumpy cot big enough for the children, a mattress on the floor for me, and an end table with a lamp with its fringed ivory shade, and a full-length mirror. We slept, ate the hot soup and brown bread the shopkeeper left for us, then with Jarnak's insistence I availed myself of trying on the dresses hanging in the dark oak garderobe, choosing a blue poplin dress with a white lace collar and peplum and long sleeves, cotton stockings, black lace-up shoes, and a black hat. He had the children's clothes washed and pressed and nodded knowingly when he saw Jakob's undershirt with the strings. He spoke a few words in Hebrew to the boy. Jakob smiled big. The older man's kindness warmed my heart.

I dyed my hair an amber red in the sink in the toilette and when I saw myself in the long mirror, I smiled. Anna laughed and clapped her hands with approval, though my poor little angel still refuses to speak. It makes me cry.

I looked quite respectable, thank you, not a fugitive on the run from the Gestapo. Then Jarnak arranged for a man dressed in black, from his low-brimmed hat to his black cloak and boots, to drive the children and me out to the circus grounds in an old green Peugeot, which I found rather curious, then dropped us off. The Count, I assume.

I breathe in the fresh country air, feeling free but not in my heart. It's tied with strings from what happened years ago that I've never broken, squeezing it tight. Today I have to cut those strings, be humble, beg for a job and assure Philippe I shall say nothing about the past. Our past. No, *my* past. Leave him out of it, for isn't that why I left, to protect him?

It's an early morning, dewy with dreams, as the circus comes alive. Everyone's up at dawn, rehearsing their acts, checking their costumes, gossiping before heading to the cookhouse for a good breakfast. Or that's how it was before the war. I imagine now they survive on barley coffee, an egg once a week if the local farmer is a circus fan, potatoes with scallions not fried in butter but lard, and coarse bread made from black-market wheat since the Nazis have a bad habit of sending our food to the *Vaterland*.

I'm taking a chance coming here, but this is the only tent circus on the outskirts of Paris, making it less likely the Nazis will trek out here for entertainment. Jarnak assured me he knew of no informants here and indicated Socks has been a regular for the past month at the pawnshop and mentioned they're not moving on for a while, but he didn't say why.

Yet I hesitate. Will they hire me? I need to work. I have two children to take care of, though it will be interesting to see how Philippe reacts when he sees 'Marie' and 'Luc'—we still use their Jewish names in private. From the playbill I see hung up near the ticket booth, they have a female aerialist along with Philippe and Édouard. I smile. Well, that's fine. I couldn't be that close to him again. But circuses always need accomplished bareback riders. I often used to fill in and ride the ponies when a rider quit or was sick, and I can still perform the trick riding I learned as a child. My body is more womanly yet slim, my makeup sophisticated, my voice silky... not a young girl's. I'm better than ever and I'll challenge anyone who thinks otherwise.

Still, I shall miss flying under the big top. Back in the twenties, I was called *la blonde* by everyone and with a sneer by the daughter of the owner, impresario Trevalino 'Val' Casini. Gisèle was a gorgeous raven-haired creature who excelled on the rings with exquisite form. Long neck, slender body, toes pointed. I often wondered why she didn't try the trapeze. I would have thought to see *her* on the playbill on the rings, not this blonde aerialist. Who trained her? Does she love the circus as much as I do? Is she any good up there? Then another thought hits me: did Philippe replace me with her? Maybe she's been here since I left? The artist's rendering depicts her as a fantasy female with flamboyant curves and long, long legs, but it's impossible to guess her age.

For now, I'd settle for a safe place to lay down my head and sleep. A place where the children can sleep without nightmares, where Anna can once again find her voice—a little girl should be able to sing a lullaby to her doll (I must find her a doll!)—tease her brother, and pray out loud to God for her mother. I'm so tired of us running, always looking over my shoulder, freezing up every time I hear the thumping of jackboots. Someday I shall fly again, but first I must survive. The children must survive. I will do anything for them. Wash clothes, peel potatoes, clean up after the animals, *anything* but give my heart away to a man. I did that once and paid the price. I shall never do it again.

I walk into the main tent. It's showtime.

22

PARIS OUTSKIRTS—APRIL, 1943

Le Cirque Casini
Lia

'It's me, Socks.' I take off my hat, smooth back my newly dyed red hair. 'Lia.'

'Oh, my God, it *is* you.' He laughs and I swear he cries real tears, making the painted-on ones on his cheeks drizzle down his face in long streaks. 'My wonderful, beautiful child.'

'I'm all grown up, Socks.'

He grins. 'So I see, and more beautiful than ever.' He runs his fingers through my hair, laughing. 'Really, Lia? Clown red? There must be a story here, *hmm*?'

I ignore his question. I can't tell him I'm helping the Jewish children I brought with me escape from the Gestapo, about my strange encounter with the Nazi lieutenant, then nearly dying from poison gas. Instead, I say, 'I see you're still wearing your painted-on smile and black eyebrows.'

'I'm a clown. I make people laugh.' He gives me a wide grin. 'People see my smile, a big, happy smile that says I'm on top of the world, and they smile too.'

Why don't I believe him?

Something's changed about Socks. Not just his appearance; yes, he's older, but the way he carries himself. I should say Socks always carried an aura of mystery with him, whether it was a mischievous glance at a pretty girl in the audience who smiled back, or a game of cards in clown alley when he won over and over, him in his baggy silk trousers and red-and-white striped suspenders, tank top undershirt, showing off his bare arms, insisting he had 'nothing up his sleeve'. But he's sadder, a defiant purpose in those hazel tiger-eyes that soften when he sees me. Suddenly he grabs me, swings me around like I'm as light as silk. His body is bulkier, his strength coming more from his core than his muscles starting to sag.

He must be close to fifty. His trousers fit him snugger, he sports a paunch in that tank undershirt, his clown horn hangs low on his belt cinched in at the last notch, and his signature makeup is expertly applied, even at this early hour.

I just accepted his quirky notions when I was a kid. Like he was a crazy uncle who let you eat too many chocolate macarons and treated you like an equal when the adults didn't. But now I wonder what he's hiding. I sense he's also reluctant to fill in the years we missed. Whatever it is, it could be far more dangerous with the Boches poking their noses everywhere. Whatever he's done, Socks is my friend.

Always.

'I see you're still keeping secrets from me, *mon ami*,' I say as we loop arms and take a walk around the sawdust ring for old times' sake.

'Seems you're the one keeping secrets, Lia.' He waves to my dear little angels chasing each other up and down the rows of seats for the circusgoers, laughing. I was hoping being here in a place of joy would help Anna find her voice, but she only nods or shakes her head when you talk to her, then lowers her eyes and shuts down.

I'll keep trying.

'My story is for another day, Socks. Fill me in on Cirque Casini.' I brush off his question. I don't want to trip myself up tossing out information I'll later regret. Like who is the children's father? Where is he? I don't have my story together yet.

'Well, Lia.' He gives in, seeing I'm not spilling my guts. 'Few of the old crowd is still here. The Jouberts, of course, but almost no one else.'

No wonder I don't see any familiar faces. Still, the Le Cirque Casini is like every traveling show. Noisy and moves on wheels. But that ring under the big top is filled with magic. Acrobats somersaulting and landing on their partner's shoulders, high-wire walkers climbing up the rope, ballet girls primping and vying for top position in the lineup, the big cats providing a cacophony of rumbling roars in the background, show ponies wheezing, getting ready to get into that magic circle. A chittering monkey hopping up and down on the ornate saddle of a pony.

No one pays attention to us.

Why should they? I don't recognize anyone. To them, I'm an unwanted interloper who burst into their world. To me, it's a day of reckoning and humbling, a day filled on one hand with the joy of seeing my old friend, and on the other, an intense ache in my gut, wondering, what will I say to Philippe? Will he even talk to me? Especially when he sees the children. Will I crumble at his feet, beg him to take me back into the circus?

God, no. I loved him, still do, but like I told Socks, I'm no child. I'm a survivor and I intend to act as such. And of course, I shall make no mention that a certain Gestapo agent has me in his crosshairs. With any luck, Herr Geller will continue his nefarious snooping near the Belgian border and never return to Paris.

'*You're* still here, old friend,' I say with a warmth in my voice I don't try to hide.

Socks comes back at me with a teasing smile: 'I have no choice. I have to stay.'

'You do?'

'Sure... I'm a famous bank robber hiding out in the circus and I've got a million francs stashed in my clown box.' He honks his funny horn. 'Where else can I hide from the police?'

I have to smile. I have an agenda on my mind, but I'm worried about Socks. He's trying so hard to make me laugh, bring back another time when all we did was laugh, but we both know that world is gone. He seems older... not just in years, but in heartbreak. I know this clown, know he's like a bull elephant charging through each show with amazing energy and a commanding presence, capturing the audience in a bubble that follows his every gesture, every funny joke, but that's gone. His shoulders slump and his chin droops. He's hurting inside. Bad. From what, I don't know, but I'll find out when he's ready to talk.

Until then, I act coy, telling him I've worked here and there with circuses in Belgium, Italy, Germany, but I never made it to the top of the bill. So I got married and I have two wonderful children that I adore. Otherwise he'll wonder why I'm here and not performing in a circus in Lyon or Brussels.

'Don't try to fool this old fox, Lia. I followed you over the years whenever I could... circus chatter when we were on the road. Clowns talk, you know.' He winks at me. 'You're a circus queen, just like I said you'd be.'

'Well, I had success in Berlin and Rome, then the war came...'

'And you disappeared.' He grabs me tight, buries his face in my hair. 'I was so afraid you'd been deported to a concentration camp, or worse. The Nazis have no appreciation for us, what we do in the circus. The danger. The hard work. All they care about is their damn Reich and bleeding us, depriving us of a decent life, and taking from us what we love the most.'

He doesn't let me go, clinging to me and whispering in my ear, *damn Nazis*, over and over, and my pulse jumps to a rapid pace because this is not the Socks I left behind; this is a man hurting so bad inside he finally let go with a torrent of emotions, and I'm the cause of it. Seeing me after all these years made him snap and he released his pain. His deep and loving hugs make me believe he never saw that photo of me with the Führer or 'my athletic pose' on the cover of the German girls' magazine. If he did, he's not mentioning it, so then neither shall I.

'Where's Philippe, Socks?' I ask, pulling away from him, searching his face with that smile that never fades. I can't read his pasted-on smile. He pops off his red rubber nose as if unmasking himself. For me.

'He's not here, Lia. He's in Paris meeting with bankers, which means the Boches, since they took over every business.'

'But surely Philippe is still an *artiste*?' I question, pointing toward the advertisement board, with the picture of the Flying Jouberts on it.

'Yes, but also he's been running the circus since old man Casini died.' He glances away, not waiting to see my reaction. I didn't know... Not surprising. Val Casini was a hard-drinking, womanizing businessman with a penchant for greasy fried duck and red wine. What surprises me more, and it shouldn't, is when Socks finishes with, 'A lot has changed since you left, Lia. Philippe married Gisèle, you know.'

I didn't. But I'm not surprised. Her father hated me, because Philippe made no secret of his love for me and not his daughter.

'So Val Casini got what he wanted after all.' I pause, saying what's on my mind, even if my lower lip is trembling. Finding out the truth hurts, so why wasn't I more prepared for it?

Because you're a romantic fool. Why did you come back? Why?

It's that voice again. Damn.

Because I still love him. And let's not forget that pesky detail. The Gestapo.

Agreed. But Philippe isn't here. Now what?

Honestly, I don't know.

'I'm happy for Philippe.' I blurt out the words. 'He's a magnificent flyer.'

'Not as good as you, Lia.'

I smile. 'Well, he's a damn good catcher, Socks; strong, powerful, perfect timing. I couldn't let him ruin his career because of me, especially when I...'

I leave that thought unfinished. That's my sorrow, and I don't intend to tell Philippe. He didn't know I was pregnant, and when I started gaining weight, I smiled prettily and told him I was putting on more muscle. I was so naïve; it never occurred to me he didn't believe me, but he never let on. So, in my mind, it made it easier for me to leave that night not to hide my shame, but to save the man I loved from scandal. Even if he did guess, he couldn't find me... I wouldn't be surprised if mean old Monsieur Casini threatened him with dismissal or worse if he *did* look for me. The circus world prides itself on presenting family entertainment, and anything like an affair can make or break your career if you lose bookings because you violated the 'morals clause' in your contract.

'I had no choice, Socks.'

'Philippe broke your heart, *n'est-ce pas?*'

'Yes... we loved each other, but—'

'Old man Casini had other plans for Philippe and they didn't include a half-Roma girl, *n'est-ce pas?*'

I take his hand in mine. It's warm; mine is cold. 'I can't stay, Socks. I have to get back to Paris. I'm opening next week at Cirque d'Hiver.'

He tilts his head, grinning at me in that warm, wonderful way he has with engaging an audience, especially the children. 'You're lying, Lia.'

Did you really think he'd believe you? This is Socks you're talking to.

'So what if I am?'

'So tell me why you're really here. It's not just to see old Socks.'

I recognize the fact my 'coming home' reunion needs to get honest. Real fast. My freedom—my life—is at stake.

'I need a job.'

'Are the French police after you?' he asks, dead serious.

'No.'

'Then it's the Gestapo—'

'*No*,' I say too quickly. I can't tell him I ran off with two Jewish children to save them from deportation and I have no idea what I'm doing. Though I trust him with my life, these *children's* lives are at stake.

He heaves out a heavy breath. 'I guessed you were on the run when I saw your red hair.' He knows my father was Roma and that's enough to get me deported to a transit camp. 'It's not safe for you here, Lia, what with German soldiers showing up at nearly every performance, and we can't turn them away. Chain-smoking pigs, leering at the pretty girls, making sport of tragedy, then doing nothing to help. I swear, someday I will tie their sorry asses to a team of horses, slap the ponies' behinds and...'

I squeeze his hand. 'Careful, Socks. The Nazis have spies everywhere.'

He laughs. 'I'm just a clown, Lia. Harmless.'

What about poor Félix? I want to warn him, but I feel the bones in his hand go rigid and hard when he squeezes me back. There's a hatred eating him up that scares me. I want to help him, so I kiss him on the cheek to bring down his temper.

'Don't worry about me, Socks,' I say, looking him straight in the eye. 'I've been passing for Aryan for years.'

'I'm not judging you, Lia. We do what we have to, to survive, but these damn Boches took from me what was closest to my heart and I shall never forget.'

'Do you want to talk about it?' I ask quietly.

'No.'

Fair enough. We both have our secrets. Discussion closed.

23

PARIS OUTSKIRTS—APRIL, 1943

Le Cirque Casini
Lia

'So do we ask Philippe to add another flyer to the act?' Socks got me a plate of morning grub: a grainy bread, a fried egg—my lucky day—and a cup of coffee that's decent. For the children, bread, porridge, and milk. We're sitting outside the cookhouse on a bale of hay, finishing up. Anna and Jakob found seats inside at the clowns' table and are loving every minute, giving us a chance to talk. I was starved and didn't turn down a second egg when Socks flipped his onto my tin plate.

'I doubt he'll agree when he finds out it's me.' I wipe my chin with the cloth serviette embroidered with an elegant letter 'C' for Casini provided with the knife and fork. The classy *serviette de table* is a nice touch. I imagine that's Gisèle's doing. She always was proper and precise about the particulars of Le Cirque Casini, from the hanging banners to the costumes to the decorative rugs for the elephants with their names hand-sewn on them in spangles.

Socks smiles. 'He will, when I tell him Lia di Montieri once gave a special performance for the Führer.'

'So you knew?' I raise a brow.

'Like I said, I don't judge. You had your reasons.'

'It's called "I like to eat".' I sip the hot coffee, smack my lips. 'And so do my children.'

'So I guessed.'

I reach out to touch his hand. 'There's more to it, Socks...'

'Not now, Lia. The time will come when we can talk, really talk. For now, let's keep you safe.' He cups my chin like I'm a child. Anybody else, I'd hate it. Not Socks. He makes me feel like I really *have* come home.

I grab the children and more coffee, then we walk back to the main tent in silence, each with our own thoughts. It's getting busy in the ring with different performers warming up, rehearsing, and craning their necks to see who the disheveled woman is who has captivated Socks' interest. Even if the faces are strange to me, the morning run-through isn't. I hear the crack of the lion train-er's whip and the roaring yawns that follow, dogs barking, girls giggling, horses snorting... and the heralding of a sole elephant trumpeting, and is that a calf I see wallowing in the sawdust with a pretty young woman? She's playing with the little elephant, showering it lightly with dirt to protect its baby sensitive skin, a ritual too often ignored by uncaring trainers. The kind gesture tugs at my heart. Why do I sense a bond here that brings a tear to my eye? Because I've taken under my wing two children without a mother to care for *their* needs and it won't be the last time as long as France is occupied by the Boches. When the little elephant nuzzles its head and trunk in the girl's lap, it makes me smile.

My God, the girl is lovely. Very tall. Blonde, her figure not yet mature, her laughter childlike, but not silly. She's wearing a plain, gray-pink leotard with a fabric belt and soft ballet slippers.

'Is she the elephant girl?' I ask, curious.

'No, the animal trainer Kaspar is a strict taskmaster and keeps his own girl Wanda busy cleaning out the lion cages.'

'He sounds horrible.'

'He is.'

'Where's the baby elephant's mother?' I ask.

'With her trainer. Which means there's no breakfast for her calf.'

His voice softens when he explains that after the bull Napoleon fell victim to a Nazi's rage and a shower of bullets, that girl helped the grieving mate Josephine care for her calf. He doesn't elaborate, but I can guess what happened. The Boches have no respect for life of any kind, even God's gentlest creatures.

I watch the girl blow a kiss to the baby elephant then make her way up the rope to the platform and start practicing her swings. She's got style and grace, rough around the edges, but a few dance classes will smooth those out.

'So who is she?' I ask.

'Jeanne Joubert. Philippe's daughter.' Socks eyes me warily, waiting for my reaction. I couldn't be more shocked. Around me, nothing's changed. The lions are roaring, monkeys chittering, but I'm shaking with a sensation I haven't felt since I lost my grip on the flybar during an air-raid and fell straight down into the net, my instinct saving me, but my ears rang for days. Now my ears ring with his words over and over again because I can't believe it.

'His *daughter*? She can't be more than sixteen.'

'She'll be eighteen tomorrow.'

Eighteen?

I drop my metal tin cup onto the soft ground spilling coffee onto the dirt. The cup doesn't make a sound. So what is that loud thudding in my ears? It's my heart pounding madly. I look at Socks like he just said the Allies have landed, disbelief slamming into me. That means Philippe was having an affair with Gisèle when he was professing his love for me. That can't be true. We spent every night together in each other's arms, and yes, I was aware Monsieur Casini wanted Philippe to marry his daughter and for me to be gone from the circus. He knew Philippe spent his time working with me on the trapeze. But Philippe fooled us both. He got what he wanted: the circus in his back pocket and a very young me—barely eighteen—in his bed.

What a fool you are, Lia di Montieri, carrying the torch for this two-timer for years.

My stomach sours and my joy at reclaiming a spot in the circus I loved gives me heartburn. I also feel overwhelmingly sad. This lovely child with the kind heart could have been my daughter.

My homecoming is over.

I stand up, turn to the clown. 'I shan't be needing a job after all, Socks. I was wrong to come back.'

'You were so young, Lia. You fell in love and got your heart broken—' I notice while he's talking to me, he keeps a watch on everything around him. Who's coming, who's going... especially a man hovering in the shadows in the back of the tent.

Gestapo? Every circus I've worked in has a code when the secret police show up. The ringmaster knocks on your wagon window or whispers into your tent something like: *Go see the elephants.* Socks would warn me, wouldn't he?

I'm still reeling over the newsflash about Philippe as Socks continues his pep talk. 'I thought you were tough, a real trooper. Guess I was wrong...'

I can see the challenge in his eyes, big and bold with those black rings painted around them. 'You don't know anything about me, Socks, what I've done—'

'Whatever it is, Lia, no one will find you here.' I see that poignant look on his face, and I should have known he'd come up with something to get me to stay. 'Why don't you hang around for Jeanne's birthday performance? She's going to debut a new trick. Two and a half somersaults.'

'Can she do it?' I ask him.

He's grinning, knowing I'd be intrigued. 'Stay around and find out.'

I admit it's tempting. I could give her a few tips; after all, she's Philippe's daughter, but the heartache of watching the child who could have been mine hurts too much. Socks must be reading my mind because he comes up with, 'He talked about you for the longest time, Lia, even after he married Gisèle. He still loved you. What happened?'

A baby happened. Stillborn. But Socks knows that. What he doesn't know is I convinced myself it was my fault because I didn't stop flying soon enough. Guilt rides me every day. I don't need him or this place to remind me.

'See you around, Socks.' I start toward exiting the main tent, calling out for Anna and Jakob—that is, Marie and Luc—to come along, time to go. It takes them a minute to realize I'm calling them by new names, then Anna grabs Jakob's hand and they run into my arms. I admit I enjoy my new role as their *maman*, their warm hugs helping me cope after finding out Philippe has a daughter. I ignore the spotted pony going through its paces around the ring with her trainer, when Socks goes into his old tricks. Tripping, stumbling over his own big feet, he tries to vault the horse and misses, falling flat on his arse in the sawdust. So now he has my attention, worried as I am about him—he's not a young clown anymore—then he turns to me and makes a sad face. Then to the children. They laugh, enjoying the attention. I shake my head, sighing. He tries again. Misses again. *More* concern from me. Finally he vaults onto the racing pony and rides around the ring before dismounting with a double somersault and a big grin on his face.

He reaches out his hand to me. 'C'mon, Lia, for old times' sake.'

'I—I can't...' I keep walking. 'We have to go, *mes enfants*—'

'Do we have to, mademoiselle?' Jakob pleads, and I freeze. I pray Socks didn't hear him call me 'mademoiselle'. If he did, he hides it well.

'Lost your touch?' he asks.

'You old devil!' I turn back, the fire in my belly bursting into a hot urge to show him, show everybody watching us, who I am. Ego? Of course, I just found out the man I loved was having an affair while telling me how much he wanted me, and that we'd be together forever.

So flaunt it, Lia!

'You asked for it, Socks.'

Am I crazy? Yes, I was a trick rider for years, doing bareback tricks with skill at high risk, standing on two horses and controlling the reins, racing around the ring at top speed, jumping through fire hoops, executing somersaults. Do I dare go for it? In the circus, you learn to trust your instincts, that inner self that knows every trick, files it away, and kicks it into gear when you need it, like a gun going off. You can't stop the bullet once it's left the chamber, but if you're a good shot, you know where it will land. So without thinking *why* the hell I'm doing this when I should be skedaddling my butt out of here but knowing I can, I peek out of the corner of my eye at the growing gathering of my peers including the pony's trainer on the side of the ring, whispering and chatting. What performer can resist appearing before *this* crowd? Show them I'm one of them. I unlace my shoes, kick them off, lose the cloak, unbutton the top buttons on my dress so I can move my arms freely, hitch up my dress, toss the hat and in my stockinged feet—

I vault the pony with the same charisma I had when I was twelve.

Not bad, *n'est-ce pas?*

Socks claps, his white clown paint glowing with sweat. The children are beside themselves, jumping up and down, but there's only mild applause from the others. I keep riding around the ring bareback. I feel confident sitting astride the pony who doesn't seem to mind my impromptu trick, fueling my confidence, but no one except Socks and 'my children' is impressed. *Seen that before, mademoiselle,* the others seem to say. *You ain't so hot... Is that all you've got?*

Think. What will impress this crowd?

I know. A trick I did in Berlin back in the thirties. I wasn't a headliner yet so I was still doing trick riding to get noticed by the circus owners. I learned this stunt from a famed horsewoman after I saw her swinging from the saddle horn as her horse reared up and spun on its hind feet.

I doubt this pony is trained in the art of trick riding, and the Liberty horses I observed earlier are so named because they perform with no riders. But I did learn from her how to do a wild horse ride that keeps the audience on the edge of their seats, a brave woman facing danger and coming out triumphant. A fantasy ride embracing the romance of sensationalism the audience can't get enough of, rooting for the rider lying against the side of her mount. Helpless. But in the end in control.

Me.

I close my eyes for a moment, praying I can do this, knowing the pony could get spooked, but the horse keeps up a steady canter around the ring as she's trained to do. I'm not going for the theatrical 'out-of-control' galloping horse I rode in Berlin albeit on a large stage, but something impressive enough to engage these skeptics. What we call a 'layback'.

I keep circling the ring, preparing mentally for the stunt, quieting my nerves, then sucking in a deep breath and maneuvering the reins in such a way my leg is caught in the leather straps. Done. Now, God willing, after a few attempts I slide down the side of the horse—the 'audience' gasps—and I get my other leg up in the air so I'm lying across the horse's back sideways with one hand holding the leather strap and the other hand dragging the ground, my fingertips picking up sawdust. Round and round the ring I go, one leg caught in the reins and another up in the air as if I'm about to fall off, tension mounting with each full circle I make in reckless abandon.

Or so it appears.

It's not.

I'm in control, knowing how many times I can circle the ring safely, instinct telling me how long I can sustain this upside-down position, my dress billowing, and God, are my garters showing?

How I'm getting out of it is another story.

24

PARIS OUTSKIRTS—APRIL, 1943

Le Cirque Casini
Lia

In the circus they talk about the act that makes your career. Shot out of a canon, the five-person pyramid on the high wire. Putting your head between a lion's jaws. Circus people are daredevils. Or at least we know how to make it appear we're amazing. And sometimes we are. We hit the consummate note and you wonder if you'll ever do it again. That's where I am at this moment, riding upside down around the sawdust ring on a galloping pony, barely hanging on. To think I spent my whole professional career perfecting the triple somersault and I find myself in this predicament. But I couldn't have foreseen that a trick I learned in Berlin could change the course of my life. What I didn't take into consideration is that my skinny eighteen-year-old body has changed. I'm still slender, but after years of performing my joints are starting to creak and pop... my feet are calloused, heels rough. Shoulder hurts when rain is coming, but I pray years of training on the rings won't let me down. I suck in my gut, tightening my middle core, and even if my arms ache for days afterward, I've got to finish what I started.

Ego again.

Funny, how we circus people torture ourselves to achieve that magic that borders on madness and has nothing to do with genius. It's called timing.

Around the ring I go... my 'audience' cheering, clapping... a ride that surpasses the acute danger... more than exhilarating with all the blood rushing to my brain, squeezing my cheeks so tight they feel like they're bursting, then loud *whooshing* sounds escaping from my parted lips until I panic. I feel myself slipping... If my head hits the ground or the pony kicks me, I could be killed. Or bruised badly. Jaw broken, eye sockets smashed.

What was I thinking?

I try to raise myself up... the leather strap gripped in my fist.

Can't.

Dammit, this isn't happening. The physics of what I'm doing is against me, the speed of the pony making it harder to fight gravity. I try again... Again, I fail. *Where's your grit? Or did you leave it behind when that Gestapo man nearly did you in?*

'Lia, Lia!' I hear, but it's like an echo far, far away. The sound is bouncing off the ground and even in my upside-down position, I see Socks with his worried-clown grin running alongside the pony. He's reaching out, trying to grab me. I shake my head from side to side, pushing him away with my hand. *I can do it!* I try to shout, but the words are only in my head. Socks falls back, leans over to catch his breath. I'm not the only one feeling the pain.

I try again to pull myself up and get a long, swishing tail coming at me that burns my right cheek like sharp bramble, but it's just what I need. I don't know if it's the shock of horsehair in my mouth that gives me the impetus to get this done or anger with myself for even trying this trick to prove something—which I don't know—but I find the 'oomph' to pull myself up so I can grab the reins wrapped around my ankle with both hands and hang on to it and, holding on to the reins, I shout commands to the pony to slow down until I can pull myself up onto its bare back.

God, I did it!

I untangle myself, sit astride the pony and take another lap around the ring, waving and blowing kisses to Anna and Jakob, their smiling faces making it worth every agonizing second, the crowd whistling, stomping their feet, clowns honking their horns, before I dismount right in front of—

Socks. Cheering the loudest and whistling through his teeth. Never was I so relieved to see his funny face doing his best to pump me up. Not an easy task. I recognize no one milling around the ring, eyeing me with curiosity. Envy. This is not how I imagined my return to Paris. I thought I'd find Philippe swinging on the trapeze, looking as young and handsome as he did when I was eighteen, then he slides down the rope with the energy of a lightning bolt, pulls me into his arms and professes he's never stopped loving me. And will I join him high up under the big top on the trapeze? Hugs and kisses, as if I never left.

Instead, I stand here like a freak. An interloper. A show-off, when all I want is to find that piece of myself I left here so long ago. And Philippe? He loved the excitement of applause. Surely he'd be curious to see who evoked such a response on this early morning? Where is he? I forgot. He's in Paris. I thank everyone, shaking hands. The hearts of circus people are warm, giving, but I feel like a fake.

I jump like a frog when Socks hugs me so tight my ribs hurt. 'You're better than ever, Lia, you crazy, beautiful girl.'

'I don't belong here anymore, Socks. What I had, or *thought* I had, is gone. It's time for me to go.'

His eyes bug out. '*Where*, Lia? You're safe here.'

Does he know the Gestapo is after me? You can't read a clown's face with its happy smile, but I see the answer in his eyes. Of course he does. Why else would I show up here?

I make my case. 'I can't put you in danger, Socks.'

'We're *all* in danger, Lia, as long as the Boches occupy France.'

'Thank you, old friend, but the past is done. Philippe isn't interested in seeing me again. I have my children to consider... I'm all they have.' True enough, but I can't tell him why.

'Lia, *wait*... there's something you should know—'

'Nothing you say, Socks, can change the past.' I pick up my shoes when—

'*You were magnificent, mademoiselle!*' It's Jeanne running up to me, then hugging me, kissing me on both cheeks. I wince, my forehead furrowing. It's been a long time since anyone broke down that wall I built around myself and got close enough so I smell the sweet lavender scent on her skin. The Nazi lieutenant encounter doesn't count. He's the enemy. This girl is... *what to me*? A younger version of myself, and that scares me. I hate to see her make the same mistakes I did. 'I've never seen *anyone* do that trick before,' she gushes. 'You must join our circus.'

'I can't.'

'I won't take no for an answer.'

'But will the circus boss approve—'

'Oh, you mean Papa? I'll handle him.' She hugs me again. I protest again, but she's not listening. 'I can't wait to see what you do next, mademoiselle. Welcome to Le Cirque Casini!'

I turn back to Socks for help, but he has the biggest grin on his face, a real grin, not the painted-on one, so big I can see his pink gums and yellowing teeth. His eyebrows shoot up and his smug look sends me a clear message.

She's got you, n'est-ce pas?

I hate to admit it, but he's right. I'm caught up in the girl's excitement and what I just accomplished on the pony after suffering through so much sadness and heartache, grabbing Anna and Jakob, knowing they'll never see their mother again.

At this moment, I live vicariously through the joy of this young girl racing off to the wardrobe tent to 'Tell Elsa to hustle up a costume for you... Lia, is it? You're Italian? How thrilling. I love Tuscany and the beautiful hills of flowers. We haven't performed in Italy since the Occupation and now we're stranded here outside Paris, but we're all circus people here. We're family.'

She's so eager to share the magic of my trick that she's willing to hire me, knowing nothing about me, seeing in me a kindred spirit who loves the circus as much as she does, embraces the danger, and lives in the moment by doing an impromptu trick that captured her heart.

I slump down on a bale of hay, thinking. I'm either braver than I thought or a damn fool to let her talk me into re-joining Le Cirque Casini. Or curious as hell. Jeanne doesn't know my past so I'll have to keep a low profile, but who is that handsome man in the long camel overcoat, running his fingers through his rich, dark hair, black Fedora in hand and giving me a more-than-curious look? Was he the man I saw in the shadows? I'd swear he's not Gestapo. He doesn't have that cold, executioner gleam in his dark eyes that's de rigueur for that type. More like a hungry tiger on the prowl. And why is Socks avoiding him? I ask him who he is and the clown mumbles he's a detective. Figures. I hear the man in the overcoat grilling the circus people milling around, then shaking their heads and walking away. He doesn't stop. Poking around, asking questions, making notes on a small pad and eyeing me with interest. Cop interest.

Why is he hanging around here?

Did that Gestapo agent, what's his name, Herr Geller, send out an alert? Is that why the policeman was watching me perform the death-defying ride?

By the smirk on his face, I'd say he saw more than my garters.

25

PARIS OUTSKIRTS—APRIL, 1943

Le Cirque Casini
Lia

I honestly don't know why I don't run when I see this messenger of what I'm certain is bad news sweep into my view and roar at me like a lion... and I'm dinner. But he intrigues me. It's so damn obvious he's police. A detective, according to Socks. The man has 'that look', his brows crossed, eyes intense like two spotlights zoning in every one, asking questions he doesn't have the answers to yet.

He's not secret police—he doesn't have the beady eyes of a sewer rat—he's a Frenchman, a charming, sophisticated, and I can tell by his dark, smoldering eyes, he's on a case that involves a woman. He's too interested in every pretty girl here. Surveying them like he's the worker bee and he's got his stinger out and looking for a queen.

Don't get too close or you'll *get stung.*

Is he Milice? I shiver. I've heard about these French police, a new unit worse than the Nazis. Nervous types, looking over their shoulder, fearing the Gestapo or SS will boot them in the arse to carry out orders that crush innocent lives into sawdust. Yes, he has something on his mind.

I catch him giving me another glance, but he doesn't make a move. I grin. He's not comfortable around the female sex. Women know these things. Men give themselves away by a little trait they don't know they have, but we do. It usually takes time to find out what that is, but not with this plainclothesman. He exhibits a flair not found in policemen when he puts on his black Fedora, gives it a hard twist to the right and pulls it down over his eyes. Dramatic, coy... and calculated. A silent vow that he *will* keep me in his sights. He intrigues me, but he also frightens me.

But I won't let him drive me away. Since Jeanne convinced me to stay, I need to ramp up my courage.

To see Philippe.

God help me.

'Quite an impressive trick on the pony, mademoiselle,' the detective throws at me in a voice neither threatening nor friendly. 'Where did you learn to ride like that?'

I lace up my shoes, keeping my head down. 'That's none of your business, monsieur.'

'But it is, mademoiselle. I'm here on a case.'

'*Really?* I never would have guessed.' I stand up to my full height—even then he's two heads taller than me in my shoes—and button my dress with defiance. Show him I kowtow to no man. 'Whatever you *thought* you saw, monsieur, the game is over.'

'Inspecteur Bérenger Varon of the Criminal Brigade.'

'*Pardon,* Inspecteur, but I'm not used to being questioned by the police after I nearly had my head bashed in by a horse's hooves.'

'Good try, mademoiselle, but you were in complete control. I've never seen a woman with such strength and...' A smirk. I was right. He *did* see more than my garters. 'An amazing stunt, which leads me to believe you're no country girl riding a pony. Do you carry papers?'

'Yes, of course.'

I raise a brow, looking miffed. If he expects me to fall apart or beg him for mercy, he's wrong. I evoke a lovely gesture with my hand, my fingertips dancing over my satchel when I unbuckle the straps and open the clasp, then hand him my *carte d'identité* with a grandeur usually intended for my work on the rings. '*Voilà,* Inspecteur, satisfied?'

He gives my papers a cursory look, just long enough to grab my name. 'Lia di Montieri. Phony, of course.'

'It is *not*,' I protest. 'My father was Giovanni di Montieri, the great aerialist,' I lie. I took my mentor's name when I was sixteen. He was more of a father to me than that alcoholic horse trader ever was. I can never forget that.

He's grinning big. He played me, knew he'd get a rise out of me, and I fell for it.

Score one for the inspector, but we're not done here yet.

'I believe you, mademoiselle, though I'm surprised you didn't follow in his footsteps.'

Is he baiting me again?

I ignore his statement. 'So what brings you and your police nose to the circus, Inspector? You love the smell of popcorn... or is it the elephant dung?'

'I've been canvasing this circus for two days after I received a tip about a girl's disappearance. I hear she got her start in this circus a few years ago. A high-wire walker famous for her Spanish dance on the tightrope. Mademoiselle Henriette de la Blanche, did you know her?'

'I just arrived from Berlin.' That should get him off the scent. Let him think what he wants. I don't like police. French or Gestapo.

'With that hair and figure, I took you for a ballet girl, not a trick rider.'

'Fresh, aren't you?' I accuse him.

'Pardon, mademoiselle, but in my line of work, pretty girls don't give me the time of day.'

'Smart girls.'

'Not smart, mademoiselle, dead.'

Why do his words make me shiver?

'And this Mademoiselle de la Blanche. Is she—?'

'Deader than a doornail. Fished her out of the Seine two days ago.'

'I see.'

'The reason I'm here is that she's not the first circus girl we've found bloated like a fish. Another body washed up... Preliminary identification indicates she's from a Dutch circus. I'd be careful if I were you, mademoiselle.' He leans closer, scrutinizing my face, my neck, as if he put me under a looking glass. What's he looking for? 'I assure you, I shall be watching you.'

That puts a different spin on my homecoming. The last thing I need is a detective following my every move.

'I'm a bareback rider who's just joined Le Cirque Casini, Inspector, so if you enjoy peering up a horse's arse, be my guest.'

He laughs and for a moment he smiles faintly, letting his stiff detective mode drop, and I notice a glimmer of interest in me that's not police business, like a switch turned from *Off* to *On*. Or is that wishful thinking on my part? I admit an odd attraction sparks in the air between us. He brings out the defiant female in me, the woman who tricked the Nazis to save these two children— who, by the way, have wandered off... Not good, I must find them—who believes no one has the right to take them from their mother... The woman who wants freedom for everyone to be who they are, not what the Nazis want. It's been a long time since a man affected me like this, so I take a closer look. I judge him to be in his early forties, broad shoulders you don't get walking a beat so I imagine he can take care of himself in a fight, and a handsome face, square jaw, eyes dark as a moonless night with an occasional star floating in their depths, giving them a sparkle. He's a man's man, unlike the young German lieutenant, who's still trying to figure out how to shave. I get a funny shiver looking at him, my woman's body betraying the young girl who left here so long ago who wants her youth back. An attraction I can't deny, even if he *is* dangerous to me.

Then he becomes a detective again, spoiling the moment.

'I saw you talking to that old clown—'

'That *old clown* is my friend, monsieur.'

'I'd be careful who I choose as friends, mademoiselle. I do think there is a mass murderer loose in Paris.'

'You mean the Gestapo?' I snap back before I think. Isn't that what the deportation of Jews and Roma is? A mass killing? I went too far, but to my surprise, this detective doesn't slap the bracelets on my wrists for my arrogance. No, he grins.

'You interest me, mademoiselle, but not enough to take you to Gestapo headquarters for your wry observations. I solve homicides, not runaways.'

'I'm not a runaway.'

'Then what are you?'

'A woman who needs a job. And whatever passes for coffee. Now, if you'll excuse me...'

I hesitate, forego any mention of my 'crew' seeing how he keeps calling me 'mademoiselle' and not 'madame', so I can get my bearings before I head off to... Where? I'm sweating, my heart racing. Exhaustion threatens to turn me into a lump of wet sand. An acute dizziness drills into my head. Damn, it's been a rough twenty-four hours. A midnight ride on a spirited pony with two young children, the trip to Paris with them in a freight car that almost killed us, then reinventing myself by performing a dangerous trick I haven't done in years. No wonder I'm about to keel over, but I refuse to show weakness in front of this man and in a strange way, he senses that and backs off. Why? What am I missing here?

'You'll be seeing me around, mademoiselle,' Inspector Varon says. 'Somebody here knows something and I'll be back until I find out what it is.'

I can't forget what he said when he turns and walks off, leaving me to mull over his words. Why do I get the feeling that *somebody* is Socks? What is my old friend hiding from me?

26

PARIS OUTSKIRTS—APRIL, 1943

Le Cirque Casini
Jeanne

You can't let your maman *rule your life.*

I tell myself over and over when I approach her tent, my fists clenched, lips tight, that it's time to stop being the 'little girl' she pats on the head and ignores like I'm not there. I'll be eighteen tomorrow and I can't keep pretending she loves me because, well, she doesn't. I don't know why I can't accept it. Get on with it. But no, I keep hoping she'll let me into her orbit of pretty costumes heavy with the scent of golden jasmine. A world of circus and glamor. Instead I must face the truth. That no matter how good I get on the trapeze, in her eyes, I'll never be as good a performer as she was.

Was.

That's the rub. My *maman*, Gisèle Casini Joubert, queen of the Roman Rings, daughter of the late circus impresario Trevalino 'Val' Casini, now spends her days in a wheelchair, her legs thin and weak hidden under a velvet navy blanket studded with white stars and musical notes, her white ballet slippers peeking from underneath. When I was a little girl, I often wondered if she ever wiggled her toes. Of course not. She can't.

How did this terrible thing happen?

Maman will tell anyone who will listen, how her papa sent her to New York in 1924 to study how they do circus under the big top over there, but that's not the whole truth. Elsa, the wardrobe girl, loves to gossip and *she* says the story is that Maman was getting too 'chummy' with the trapeze flyer fellow so her papa whisked her away. Seems Maman didn't know she was pregnant... and so she came home with me. Then she and Papa were married right away but when I was two, she fell when she was doing a 'heel hang' from the hoop and missed the safety net by several centimeters.

Since then, she lives her days in a wheelchair. *Dearest Maman, it hurts me to see you like this and I feel guilty for being angry with you.* But isn't it natural for a child to want the closeness of her mother's love, her approval? *Why doesn't she like me?* I've asked myself over and over, staring at the medal I wear. Papa told me it belonged to my mother, that it's a medal of Saint Daria and how she's special because God sent a lion to protect her when she was in danger back in old Roman days. That it will protect me. When I thanked Maman for the medal, she pretended it wasn't hers, then pooh-poohed it and told me not to mention it again.

I don't get it. *What can I do to make my* maman *love me?*

I saw that same yearning affect Bébé when Josephine became so sorrowful after the death of her mate Napoleon. The big elephant had a difficult time mothering, and Bébé got so lonely she made noises akin to a human cry. It broke my heart. I went up against Kaspar, her trainer, insisting on feeding the baby elephant with a bottle until Josephine gets out from under that dark cloud. I had to. Kaspar spends his time with the big cats and considers it a waste of time hunched over feeding the calf while the little elephant gobbles down the milk. Yet he's quick to use the stick to get the elephants to perform. *I don't like him,* I told Papa... How he treats the animals *and* Wanda. That poor girl is so smitten with him, swooning over him. How can a girl act like that around a man no matter how good-looking he is? But Papa is too busy with circus business to worry about an animal act, he told me. Something's in the wind, but I'm not worried. Since the Nazis took over, we've been lucky, traveling about the countryside in the Occupied Zone in our wagons and trucks—we have a petrol ration because the Führer loves circuses, can you believe? We're a traveling circus but we've been camped here for weeks on the northern outskirts of Paris, waiting for permission from Goebbels' office to move on to Belgium for the spring. We left our winter quarters early and put on shows here near Paris to make up for a slow season last year.

Does being stuck here have something to do with what Papa said? *Who knows how long we can keep the elephants, Jeanne.* Then he pulled on my long hair and reminded me to pin it back when we fly, something he does when he wants to change the subject. I let it pass. My father is always there for me, teasing me, helping me with my swing on the trapeze. He'll never let me down. Yet I can't forget it. I'll never let him sell the *maman* elephant and her calf. I adore them both. Bébé and I have so much in common. I also hunger for my *maman's* approval and I want to look special for my big day, but she's so picky about the costumes I didn't ask her ahead of time.

The truth is, I didn't want her to say no. I want so badly to wear the gorgeous costume Sandrine gave me. Elsa altered it for me and added rows and rows of blue sequins she was saving in her special ribbons and buttons box.

No more dawdling.

I hide the exquisite two-piece costume studded with blue sequins and rhinestones behind my back, working up my courage to approach Maman with my plea. What if she considers it too shocking? The costume reveals my midriff and cups my breasts. Bad enough, but if I tell her it belonged to a dancer at the Bal Tabarin, she'll throw a tantrum. To her, the circus is first-class entertainment but a cabaret is for scum. Not Sandrine. She studied art at the Sorbonne, she told me.

But where *is* Sandrine? She hasn't come to the circus since the doctor worked on fixing up her scars... she's still healing. She's so nice to me, a real friend. I pray she didn't flaunt her new look in front of the SS officers. I don't trust the Boches; they're such awful meanies and don't play fair. I worry about her. Then again, she'll show up; she always does. So why am I stalling? I want to be independent like her, *so let's do it.*

I pull in a deep breath, give myself two minutes more to gather my courage before making my big speech. I'm standing outside Maman's tent way in the back of the encampment. She and Papa don't share the same quarters, haven't for years. Gossip from Elsa is they didn't even before she fell from the rings. Now her accident is Maman's main excuse to keep their lives separate, though I find it strange she's friendly with Uncle Édouard. She insists he's better with keeping the books than Papa and is a great help to her. If she's not with my uncle, she's with her companion, Ondine, who is always busy picking up after her or getting her tea or the *Paris-soir*. Ondine is why I'm still hanging around outside her tent. I waited for the middle-aged spinster with the haughty scowl to leave. She doesn't like me. I'm not surprised. Maman talks about me and how I'm not like her—shameful, but I've eavesdropped on them—and how I tend to read novels when I'm not rehearsing instead of picking up my clothes. Or that I go to the pictures whenever we play a town where there's a cinema—I worship Sylvie Martone. I don't like Ondine either. She is prissy and so neat her face powder sticks to her skin like wax. And she gets appalled when I get stinky hanging out with Bébé. If that's not bad enough, Maman says I look like a skinny scarecrow standing on the perch and I should 'fatten up' in certain places to appeal to the male audience members. I can't help it if I don't have the figure she did when she was my age. Her companion just giggles when she says that and she and Maman tell me I'm too modern, talking to the children and the old folks waving at me from the stalls when we walk around the sawdust ring during the pre-show spectacle. They claim that a true circus queen keeps her distance from the audience.

Phooey, I say. They paid their four francs to see me and if I can make them smile and give them a special circus moment, then *that's* what a circus queen does. It's all I ever wanted since I was a little girl and Papa put me on a portable swing and I wouldn't get off. My mother laughs when I say that. She loves to torment me, says I'll never be as good a performer in the ring as her.

And that hurts.

Ever since I was a little girl, I've always been shut out. I've tried, really tried, to find a connection with her, but to no avail.

I inch closer and hear a jazzy tune playing on the phonograph with Maman humming along. I grin. *Bon.* She's in a good mood today. I tap my foot on the ground. Then what am I waiting for? I know. Every time I enter her tent, she intimidates me without saying a word. It's like I'm entering a religious shrine. Posters of her from years ago and photos showing her in various graceful poses on the hoops and the rings sit on her dressing tables. Her long, glorious black hair done up in braids and buns. Sassy, dark brows. Red lips. She still favors red lipstick and spends her days here, when she's not racing about in her wheel-chair, giving orders, poking her nose into everyone's business—though she avoids me—giving advice to the performers and reminding them that Le Cirque Casini has been around since the days of Versailles and we have a repu-tation to uphold.

In spite of the Nazis occupying Paris.

Strange, but Maman treads very carefully around that subject. Acting kind to them when we get soldiers in beetle-green popping in to see the show since Papa says we have to be nice to them. I've heard her complaining to Ondine the Nazis are ruining circuses with their race laws, which is why we can no longer hire Jews, Roma or Sinti. Though truthfully, although some left of their own accord, we didn't fire anyone... just changed the names of those who stayed.

That's one thing Maman and I agree on: how the Reich is unfair to so many good people. Honestly, when I was growing up, I never once heard Papa or Maman ask a juggler, or a high-wire walker, or a tent-man, who their parents are. Which reminds me. I checked on that new tent-man, Mox, after my run-in with him, when he told me I can't do a triple. Lucky for him his papers are in order, meaning he'll be staying. For a while. *Bon.* I'll show him *and* Maman there's no stopping me. He got under my skin in a funny way and, though I have no interest in men, since my career comes first, I can see how a girl could fall for his good looks and muscular body, that cavalier swagger and unbelievable strength in his upper body when he works on the rigging and swings from one bar to the next. How quick he is on his feet carrying a heavy load of rope and cables. That kind of strength and agility makes me think his so-called 'papers' don't tell the whole story, something that has become my job for every new hire. Which I neglected to do before I took on that sensational bareback rider. I haven't told Papa yet. Another 'tell him only when you have to' moment I'm hoping to avoid until he sees her do tricks on the ponies. Their trainer, Monsieur Rémon, couldn't wait to get her started.

Till then, I'm dealing with one thing at a time. My costume is high priority. This is the first time I'm the headliner of The Flying Jouberts and I want to look grown-up, but as I predicted, Maman has other ideas.

'That costume isn't practical for your act, Jeanne.'

'Why not?' I ask, holding the two-piece top and shorts up to my chest. I thought she'd be pleased I have a new outfit for the special performance instead of redoing what we call a 'pulled costume' from three seasons ago.

'It's so pretty, Maman, with the rhinestones and blue sequins.'

She grabs the brassiere top and shakes it. 'The rhinestones make it too heavy.'

'But they'll catch the light—'

'You want to perform or pose?' She cocks a brow.

'Papa says I'm ready for the two and a half somersault.'

'In this costume?' She scoffs at the idea. 'The material is flimsy. What if it rips apart or slips while you're swinging on the bar?'

'Elsa triple-stitched every seam. Look.'

Maman squints. 'The girl's good, but you're also too young for such a scanty costume. And look at the size of these brassiere cups.' She smirks. 'Too big for you, *mon enfant*.'

She tosses the top back to me and I catch it by the straps.

'I'm not twelve, Maman. I—I'll fill them out.'

She smirks. 'When you do, ask me again.'

My mother dismisses me, dabbing a perfumed hankie to her forehead, and the scent of jasmine wafts around me. It gives me a headache, but she doesn't care. She has a new audience waiting in the wings. Maman waves and blows kisses to the clowns peeking inside the tent, eager for her to bless them with her smile.

Ugo and Pat. The clowns love her. And she loves them.

They play to her ego, her narcissism, telling her how beautiful she is and pushing her around the ring in a tiny cart overflowing with fresh flowers during the spectacle before the show. She in return makes them feel like they're the most important act in the circus. Even if their act is stale, *who cares*? They've been anointed by the great Gisèle Casini Joubert and everyone knows it.

That's the root of her magic. Make everyone feel important. Everyone except me.

Odd, isn't it, there's not enough magic left over for her own daughter.

27

PARIS, FRANCE—MAY 1943

Montmartre
The Magician

Sandrine Aubert is missing.

And it's my fault.

I never should have agreed to meddle with the work of the SS, using my talent in the surgery on her scars to diminish the cigarette burns on her chest and throat in the form of a swastika. She's still in the healing process, but according to Herr Geller—*ugh*, interfering with my world again and insisting I meet with him later—what I did is akin to treason against the Reich. The only reason he grants me a pass is because he needs me. Not the same for Mademoiselle Aubert. What tipped the scales against the pretty dancer is, she didn't follow the rules and she flaunted my work in front of the Gestapo agent, then refused to inform on *anyone*.

Oh, dear. Oh, sweet misery rests upon my shoulders like a cat's claws digging into my neck.

But my beautiful Mademoiselle Jeanne will be angry with me and I can't bear that, so I must find this girl. Give her money, get her out of Paris to somewhere safe. Yes, yes, I know, this isn't my usual modus operandi, but I know this will help secure Jeanne's love, something I need, want badly.

The hunt to find Mademoiselle Aubert urges me on; the hunt keeps me looking.

Instinct makes me turn down a small alley, a light rain splattering the brim of my black Fedora, my long overcoat dragging on the rough cobblestones. I'm careful to keep my torch hidden in my coat pocket and use it sparingly. Paris is under a blackout, but that didn't stop me. I've been out and about for hours, searching, when raspy, high-pitched noises draw me deeper into the dark. Or is it my man Yann? I sent him on ahead of me on reconnaissance on this late-night journey into the underbelly of his hunting grounds. I shall need his help if...

I dare not surmise the worst, but the missing mademoiselle wears cheap spangles and dangling beads and doesn't understand the great gift I bestowed upon her. Yet she's resourceful, smart. Surely she can elude a fat Gestapo man. If she *did* return to Montmartre, she may have taken refuge in a local seedy café or bar. Yann is a familiar figure here and if anyone can find her, he can.

I hear the sounds again. My hearing is so acute, the sound of a beating heart echoes in my ears when I'm in the surgery. I often sense when a patient is in distress and recalculate the procedure. It's like a vapor exhaled from the girl's flesh, the heart's quick rhythm creating a wave of sound that grates on my ears.

Here, I'm not certain what I'm hearing.

I spin around, my long overcoat swirling in a black half-moon, searching the darkness. I listen. *Footsteps. Running. Nazis?* Of course, that's what I heard. Denizens of the Gestapo. SS men killed and mutilated this girl then ran off to wash down their dirty deed with warm beer. Their victim left behind, battered, skin pale and gray from fear, limbs broken, face beaten... and *bleeding*. Or so I imagine. What if I'm right? I flatten myself against a stark gray building reeking with odiferous black shadows. And wait. I'm in no haste to find myself on the wrong end of an SS baton.

Patience is as natural to me as death. I can't perform my surgery without it. A chill rises up in me like the cold blade of silver lancing flesh. I sniff. I smell blood. A mysterious allure in my profession, a red mist that delights me. Its rich, vibrant scent makes me tingle. I revel in the seduction of lifting the shadow of the scarred flesh while the patient slumbers in a state of bliss and warmth while I work, dreaming of the day they will once again dazzle on the high wire or the trapeze or in the lion's cage. This smell is more pungent. From the scent wafting in the air, I'd say this female recently indulged in sex.

The footsteps stop. I listen.

Nothing.

With long, purposeful strides, I turn the corner in the narrow winding street of buildings leaning inward. I dare to turn on my torch and through the dim lighting, the broken cobbles, the gentle hiss of light rain, I locate the Nazis' prey. A silky purple scarf covering her neck, her face. I know without looking it's *her*. Disbelieving, I bury the lower half of my face in the heavy folds of my overcoat as the stench from rotting garbage shoots up my nose and a fierce pain hits me in the gut. Because what I see offends me. Stark, maddening to my senses. Under my flickering torch, a misty patina makes her skin shine with the freshness of youth. She lies on the wet cobblestones, shivering uncontrollably. Breathing hard, bleeding from open wounds, her torn, pale pink silk chemise hiked up around her thighs, her feet bare. I avoid any further scrutiny. I can't tolerate the idea of finding pleasure staring at her toes. It seems sacrilegious somehow. My heart bleeds for the beautiful woman lying on the street in the rain. Near death.

Sandrine.

I had nothing to do with this. I only take the life of a young woman when I have to. Add her to my changing display of 'angel dolls' after death with dignity. This was a brutal act of terror performed by violent men who hide in dark shadows where the sins of the devil reside. I look closer, attempting to grasp what happened to the former dancer. Her facial muscles are pulled tight, her eyes bulging, her skin stark and bone white. The heaviness in the night air makes me gag, an involuntary response to what I'm seeing. One thing clear to me on this cool night: someone left Sandrine Aubert here to die. No doubt those were the footsteps I heard.

Leaning down over her, I can see she's in shock, most likely caused by the effects of the pain of her wounds and the damage to her nervous system brought on by fear. Her face and lips are pale, her skin clammy. A closer look reveals a gruesome act. The bitterness of an acrid aftertaste makes my mouth dry. Sandrine was beaten, then violently sexually assaulted.

Lustmord, the dailies called it back in Weimar Berlin. Lust murder.

I sputter, spittle catching in my throat. Only the SS could have done such a vile thing. Yes, I assist the mesdemoiselles on their final journey to endless sleep, but my work is to save them from the horror of the concentration camps. I never take a life like the SS with such depravity, such carelessness. I find it insulting the Paris newspapers barely give half a column to my girls after their bodies are found in the Seine, referring to them as suicide victims. Yet they give detailed descriptions of attacks where the victims' throats are punctured with jagged, ugly bite marks. The work of these sadistic Nazi amateurs. Although I did chuckle when *Paris-soir* quoted a local detective who believed the last two victims weren't suicides and the girls had significant but flawless plastic surgery before their demise. He referred to me as 'The Magician'. Finally, *someone* recognized the skill and expertise of a genius, a master of the art of restoring a woman's face. How it takes a deft hand to hold the girl's head in a perfect position, monitor her breathing, count the pulsating beats on the side of her throat throbbing... *One, two, three, four...* Then at the precise moment she makes a deep sigh, he can use the scalpel to forever heal her.

I aspire to reading more reports from this Inspecteur Varon.

'Help me, monsieur, *please*,' Sandrine begs, trying to raise up her arm. 'I'm so thirsty.'

Bracelets of wiry rope hug her thin wrists. I hold her hands in mine and see deep red marks on her skin, indicating she was tied up.

'Don't speak, mademoiselle.' I check her pulse. Quick, feeble. 'I shall help you, don't be afraid, it's me—'

I stop. What can I say? *I'm your physician? I can heal you.*

But can I? I must. It's my duty to Jeanne.

Where is Yann? I call out his name, praying he's nearby. Praying my hands haven't lost their magic. It happened to me years ago when I was called to a brothel in Berlin, to deal with a plague-like venereal disease. I froze. Couldn't work through the misery I saw there, so I left.

I won't torture myself any longer. I decide I must save this girl. I become once again the healer, not the killer. I wrap my long black overcoat around her and attempt to lift her...

I hear a loud grunt, then another.

It's Yann. I breathe out a sigh of intense relief. My man is here. He picks up the girl in his muscular arms and carries her into a doorway of a boarded-up building. Warm. Safe. I hand him my torch and with the light as my wary witness, I survey her wounds, cuts cruel and deep around her breasts, most likely internal bleeding from the lungs by the frothy, bright red blood she coughs up. Needle marks on her thigh as if more than one syringe found its way inside her firm flesh.

Crude. Sloppy... *very* sloppy.

I go about my work, but as I remove my black gloves, my hands shake, nervous. I retch at the sight of her torn flesh when I cut away her chemise with my Opinel, a useful pocket knife I still carry. Such degradation of a female disgusts me. I work on her for several long minutes, trying to stop the blood flow, making a bandage with her purple silken scarf. I can't leave this girl. Strange, this feeling of compassion that's possessed me. Seeing Sandrine helpless and afraid, the prudent counsel of my profession overcomes the dictates of my usual quick dismissal of these girls, a deep-seeded need to heal without consequence that still flickers within me. I knew her but that one afternoon when we sat at a café in the Place du Tertre, but I formed a subtle bond with her. Because she's Jeanne's *chère amie*, of course.

'Who did this to you?' I ask, desperately trying to close the wound around her breast with my bare fingers, the redness surrounding her flesh radiating like a halo. *Damn, I'm losing her.*

'It was—' she whispers, her eyes struggling to open, to see me. Her words are indistinguishable, but I lean closer to her lips and ask her again who did this horrible thing to her. This time I *do* hear her. 'SS.'

My heart squeezes for this girl. What they've done cannot be undone. A fatal and revolting violation of a human female that defies the bloodlust of even the most decadent of men. A flash hits my eyes, a moment of truth that sets my resolve. I *must* continue my work helping such unfortunates from falling into the hands of the SS, men who will never pay for their deeds. It's my duty as a practitioner to ease suffering, no matter what I have to do to bring them peace. Even if I have to induce death.

For Sandrine, I have but one recourse. The syringe of morphine I carry in my overcoat secret pocket.

Forgive me, Jeanne.

I speak to her in quiet tones, pulling out the hypodermic, trying to comfort her, and I believe she understands. She parts her lips, trying to speak, but it's too much for her. She goes into a seizure, her body racked with convulsions. Jagged schisms of pain travel through her body like tongues of fire slicing off her skin, causing unbelievable agony. Holding her in my arms as a lover would, I lean over the girl and do what I must to ease her suffering. I inject her with a fatal dose of morphine. Her head falls back. I search for a pulse. She's dead.

I hold her in my arms, cursing myself for not being able to save her. Damn, I couldn't even ease her pain. I sit with her for what seems like a long time until the faint fingertips of an anxious dawn stroke my cheek, reminding me there's little time left before the harsh reality of daylight invades my realm. A war rages within me. An inner voice penetrates my brain with cutting precision, the part of me that yet harbors emotion, a secret self I call it. But it does nothing to ease *my* pain. That Jeanne will blame me for the girl's death. I must somehow convince her otherwise.

I instruct Yann to leave her still body in the abandoned building where she'll be dry and warm until they find her. Not my preferred 'angel doll' display, but it can't be helped. At least she'll not be fodder for the fish or the rats. Then I send my man off with francs in his pocket to reward his good work. I care not where he goes. I want to be alone. A cry of anguish wrenches from my chest, anger with Herr Geller and his Nazi minions doing battle with the man I've become. A man without conscience, without remorse.

A killer. Mass murderer, if you will.

It has such an ugly sound to it, it makes me cringe. An intrusive thought I can't block. Partaking in this orgy of blood and sadism, albeit against my wishes, has weakened me. Damnation to hell, how did it come to this? I'm an intelligent gentleman, schooled in the mind science of psychology (you have to be when you're dealing with a woman's scarred face), so I'm aware of the root cause and why I avoid the phrase 'MM'. Because of the guilt I harbor regarding my little sister. So I avoid dealing with it. This unfortunate chink in my perfect armor came to be years ago when Noemi incessantly went off on violent tantrums, smashing and hitting her dolls' heads against the wall, stomping on their faces with her buckled shoe. She badgered me to fix the broken dolls and I did my best, but in her eyes it wasn't good enough and her torment of me continued. I was a young, skinny fourteen-year-old then, my skills in the surgery years away, but I did possess a natural healing talent with my hands and I had the eye and the gift of symmetry to correct what was broken using both nature and art. The sad part is, it was Noemi that was broken, and I couldn't fix *her*.

So I helped her find peace.

And eternal sleep. With laudanum.

I have an obsession, some might call a perversion, with my 'angel dolls'. Healing their scars, then saving them from the wrath of the Gestapo by turning them into beautiful works of art after death, like I saved the dolls from Noemi's anger and fixed *them*. My little sister was the first in a line of many I helped, releasing tortured souls like Noemi from the pain that squeezed their brains and made them go mad. Now I serve the Reich, I remind myself shivering in my motorcar. And I'm the one going mad. I can expect no relief from my fate. I have no time to mourn for a dead girl. Such is my loneliness, for I, too, am a victim in this war since I've had to resort to the use of lethal drugs to save these girls from the injustice that has taken over France. I feel as if I've been cast in a horror film. I flick on my torch and look in the rearview mirror. Deep purple circles ring my eyes; my cheeks exhibit deep shadows like the flesh underneath has melted. This is what the Nazis have done to me. I can't bear the ugliness of their world any longer. I need the beauty of Mademoiselle Jeanne to warm me so I may survive their treachery before my blood turns cold and loses its vigor. I crave to drink the nourishment that comes from seeing the girl's perfect face, lovely skin, soft red lips... the amazing sensation filling me with an orgiastic high that makes my life bearable.

So off I go into the heart of a desolate darkness. Driving into the night, risking the wrath of German patrols as I head down the boulevards, then heading north, but I don't care.

I *must* have her.

It's just after dawn when I park my motorcar on the grounds of Le Cirque Casini. I used up nearly all my petrol to drive out here, but it's worth it. My beautiful Jeanne doesn't see me when I sneak into the main tent to watch her practice on the trapeze. I observe her from my shadowy hiding place, but I can't stay. I leave as quietly as I came... I have a pressing appointment with Herr Geller, and you don't keep the Gestapo waiting. (I hate dealing with the man, but he supplies me with what I need, including petrol.) But I shall be back for tonight's performance.

Today is her big day, Jeanne's eighteenth birthday, and I shall be there in the front stall.

I shall.

But not Sandrine.

But wait... I can make this work for me. Since I'm unable to display Sandrine in an exquisite setting as I did the first three girls, 'angel dolls' that I assisted on their journey—with flowers and herbs and perfumed swaths of silk blowing in the breeze—I can regale Jeanne with the tale of how I tried to save her *chère amie*. Of course, my heroics must remain *our* secret. The police wouldn't understand.

They never do.

28

PARIS OUTSKIRTS—MAY 1943

Le Cirque Casini
Lia

With the grace of a lunging tiger, I jump out of the way when I'm nearly run down by a woman in a wheelchair. Gisèle Casini Joubert declared war on me the minute she found out I'd showed my face back up in *her* circus. Speeding through the main tent, she laughs, reveling in nearly missing me and marking me as trouble. She waited for this moment when the main tent is like a busy hive, everyone a witness to this drama playing out on a drizzly, cool spring morning. Rehearsing, working on the rigging, clowning around—where is Socks?—gossiping, I'm now the focus of everyone's morning routine, from the performers to the tent crew. I shudder; my teeth chatter. Even though I know my way around circuses, this is a first for me. After easing into the rhythm of Le Cirque Casini like soft butter spread on toast, reality sinks in when Gisèle whizzes through the open tent flap.

Here I'm not Queen of the Air.

Here I'm the new hire. A lowly performer in the circus queue.

And she's letting me know it. Which, in the eyes of the troupe, makes me appear suspicious, subject to heated whispers. Long looks. *Who is she? Where did she come from?* I dazzled them on the pony, but they don't trust me. And they shouldn't. Not in these times. Not until I prove myself not only in the ring, but also in keeping secrets. And there are many here to keep. The hushed words when I pass by the acrobats that have the ring of Yiddish. The humming of Roma folk songs I haven't heard since my papa sang them to me. The passing of folded-up political tracts. It's a motley group. I don't yet get a mention on the program, so no one knows me by anything but 'Lia'. Better that way. Too many questions if anyone finds out about my past on the trapeze—I pray that photo of me on the German girls' magazine stays buried. I make my debut tonight as a bareback rider in the sawdust ring before Jeanne's birthday performance, so I must prove my worth, that I'm not just a 'one-trick' horsewoman.

Then Gisèle makes her entrance with no breath to waste and tries to mow me down.

I won't let her spoil this homecoming. Barely a whisper in the main tent. No one is moving about under the big top, all waiting to see what happens next. I earned *some* credence in their eyes before Gisèle pulled this stunt, thanks to Jeanne. Introducing me, linking her arm through mine, Jeanne had helped me try on costumes smelling of mothballs while Elsa in wardrobe pushed toiletries on me—lemon soap so old it smells like dirty dishwater, caked tooth powder, and a comb with half the teeth missing—a cot, pillow, and blanket set up for me in the bareback riders' tent. Jeanne donated to me a leotard, pretty underwear and makeup, and later showed me the gorgeous blue-sequin costume she had altered for her birthday performance. She admitted her mother has forbidden her to wear it, but I gather she's not on good terms with her *mère*. She tells me that Gisèle ignores her, shoots down her confidence with cold looks of disapproval. Which is why Jeanne hides in novels. I noticed books and papers scattered around her wagon. That made me smile. I, too, devoured books when I was growing up. Like most circus children here, her schooling was probably just Socks serving as her tutor, like he taught me. She couldn't have had a better teacher. I never asked, but he let it slip he went to university in England where he learned to play chess and he once performed for the Royal Family.

I don't let on that Socks and I are old friends. Since I showed up at Le Cirque Casini, I stay in the shadows except for rehearsing my act with the jovial Monsieur Rémon. A lively horseman, he's a widower with three daughters under the age of sixteen, who are sweet girls still learning the art of trick riding, so he's grateful for an 'older girl'—his words, not mine—to join the act. They're Roma, of course, hiding here in the circus with forged papers. I play dumb, rolling my eyes when they paint moon symbols and stars and flowers on each other's arms and hands with henna paste, remembering I did the same thing when I was their age. Their mother was a fortune teller, I gather, and I have an uncomfortable feeling Monsieur Rémon is a lonely man with potentially roaming hands... so I keep to myself—not easy sharing a wagon with three giggling girls. They adore Anna and Jakob and, fortunately, the girls spend their time rehearsing and don't ask a lot of questions. Still, it's not easy for the children to deal with this new 'life', while I have my own loneliness to deal with, coupled with the trepidation we may not continue to have a place here once Philippe returns from the city. Then I never envisioned this exquisitely made-up woman in the wheelchair would descend upon me, like an avenging she-devil.

Gisèle spins her wheelchair around in a circle, then squeals to a stop mere centimeters from my vulnerable toes protected only by pliable ballet slippers. Jeanne's, of course. We're the same size.

'Lia di Montieri, I don't believe it. When Socks told me you were back in Paris, I popped the zipper on my girdle.' She looks me up and down with a smirk on her face. 'So now you're a redhead... covering up your roots?'

'No more than you.'

I note her dark hair folded into braids wrapped around her head like a tiara. A conversation with Gisèle always felt to me like I was the ugly stepsister. She had the prettier costumes, her floor-length cape fashioned from the richest satin, and a stretchy silk-like leotard woven by a secret sect of nuns along with a splatter of real gems sewn on the neckline to frame her face.

She scowls. 'You look good... for your age.'

Same old Gisèle, never a compliment without a snide undertone. But I'm not eighteen anymore and she can't hurt me, like when she'd remind me my papa was a horse trader and her father was the circus owner. Besides, I feel for her. I can't imagine not going up the rope and swinging on the trapeze.

'Gisèle—'

'No need to say you're sorry, Lia, you don't mean it.'

'I do, Gisèle, you were a marvel on the rings.'

She ignores me and pats her midriff, her eyes rolling upward. 'I hate this iron maiden. I feel like a pregnant pony, but it's a by-product of sitting in this damn chair for more than fifteen years.'

She laughs.

'What's so funny?'

'I never wanted children so I wouldn't spoil my figure. Now look at me.'

I find that a strange answer, but let it go. I don't want her asking me about *my* children, where they were born, who their father is… and why doesn't Anna speak? Fortunately, they magically spend all their time in clown alley. Filled with cigarette smoke and often bawdy talk, it's not the ideal place for them but I don't feel they're safe anywhere else. Socks looks in on them to help me out, and other clowns enjoy their youthful appreciation of every stunt the funnymen pull off. Which leaves me free to undertake this meeting which was inevitable. Gisèle and I were never close—both loving the same man, how could we be?—but my homecoming takes on a sad moment seeing her in that wheelchair, her once slender figure matronly, her face round and smooth in heavy theatrical makeup, brows deeply arched. She fiddles with the sparkly blanket covering her legs, catching her long pink nails in the threads. An uncomfortable silence settles between us. Anything I say, she'll twist it to make it mean something else, though I sense she wants to tell me something.

'Let's not quarrel, Gisèle. I need your help.'

'You ran away in the middle of the night and now you want my help?' She crunches the blanket up in her hands and tosses it aside. It lands in the sawdust. 'I wondered how long it would take for you to come back and cause trouble.'

'Since the war times are bad, Gisèle, the circus I was with in Lyon folded.' A lie, but I'm desperate. I stand my ground, throw a panicky glance in her direction. 'I needed a job so I came north.'

'Why here? Why not Circus Medrano?'

'I tried,' I lie again. I hate kowtowing to this woman, but my life is at stake along with the children's. I wonder how much longer the Rémon sisters and their Papa will be safe. 'Please, Gisèle—'

She cocks a brow, eager to show me she has the upper hand. 'Let's get one thing straight, Lia, I may be a cripple, but *I'm* in charge here.' She laughs again. 'Even in this chair.'

'Isn't that what you wanted? The circus…' I ask. 'And Philippe.'

'You mean what my father wanted,' she scoffs. 'That bastard ruined my life.'

A surprise statement, making this encounter more confusing. I move to pick up the blanket but she shoos me away, her eyes remaining on me as she bites her lip and makes her hands into fists. Her icy eyes tell me she hates me. *Why*?

'Leave it. Édouard will pick it up.'

'*Édouard?* He's under your thumb, too?' I ask, surprised. Philippe's younger brother, the third member of The Flying Jouberts. A damned good flyer. I would have thought he had a wife and a brood of children by now.

'Édouard is *my* affair, Lia. Keep your hands off him or you'll find yourself deported. And don't think I won't. No one will help you if I turn you in to the Gestapo.' A satisfied smirk appears on her lips. 'Everyone's terrified of me.'

'Even your own daughter.'

Her brows shoot up. 'You mean Jeanne? Oh, my God, Lia, you don't know, do you? And here I thought... But you have two children of your own now, so why would you care?'

Nothing gets by her. I don't answer, don't want to tangle myself up in lies I can't take back. She narrows her eyes and warns me, 'I'll keep you on, Lia, but only because we're short of good talent, what with the Nazis popping in without notice and arresting our best performers when we least expect it.' She huffs out a breath. 'I never thought I'd see the day when Le Cirque Casini was a bunch of misfits and refugees. And God knows what else we're in store for when Philippe returns from Paris.' She laughs and rolls her eyes. 'I'd pay a thousand francs to see his face when he finds out his precious Lia is back.'

'You needn't worry, Gisèle, I have no intention of causing you pain. You can count on me to do my job.'

'*Lia!*' I spin around and Édouard pops into the main tent, looking much older and, more surprising to me, there's no joy in his eyes. He always had a smile on his face, a lightness to his movements swinging on the trapeze. Like he was made of air. Now he looks like he's weighted down with a sandbag tied around his neck. Still, that doesn't stop him from hugging me tight. 'Socks said you were back. Where have you been all these years?'

I smile. It's good to see a friendly face.

'Berlin, Geneva, Brussels. It's not easy since the Nazis occupied France.'

He nods. 'Does Philippe know you're back?' His tone is serious.

'No. They tell me he's still in the city.'

'Meeting with those damn Nazi officials and giving away the store.'

I wait for him to explain, but he looks transfixed, his eyes glazed with what I can only describe as affection, even nostalgia, for this wonderful old circus. Then anger blazes in them as if everything he loves is about to disappear. The clowns, the lions, the trapeze. Then he switches moods as easily as he flies under the big top when he turns and picks up Gisèle's blanket, turns to her and sniffs it. 'Jasmine... with a mix of florals?'

Gisèle smiles widely. 'A new fragrance from the House of Doujan.' She giggles like a young girl when he tucks the blanket around her legs and tells him in a loud whisper, 'She doesn't know, Édouard.'

I don't know what?

'Some things are best left alone, Gisèle,' I hear him tell her.

What things? What's going on here?

'I can't, Édouard.'

'You *must*, Gisèle. What if she keeps asking questions about Jeanne?'

Gisèle grins. 'She won't. She has her own brats.'

'How can you be so sure?' he whispers.

'She's half Roma, *n'est-ce pas*?'

Now I get it. She looks straight at me. Her threat to turn me in to the Gestapo is real. And if she finds out Anna and Jakob are Jewish, there'll be no stopping her.

I step away when he kisses her on both cheeks, then brushes her lips. *Hold on, Gisèle is having an affair with Édouard?* Does Philippe know? More importantly, does Jeanne know about her mother's relationship with another man?

I'm about to find out. I frown when I see her race into the tent looking so young and innocent in a plain blue leotard and white ballet slippers. I stand there awkwardly asking myself, what just happened? Jeanne seems indifferent. She's talking to the tall tent-man, ignoring her *maman* and Édouard wheeling her *mère* away. Like her life consists of moments like this; no wonder she's hurting inside. A young girl needs to believe in her family, not see it torn apart. I didn't have that, but I did have Socks... and Gio. They were my family. We faced life together with all its difficulties and for a while I knew happiness... then I left. Why do I have the nagging feeling my run-in with the Gestapo in Circus Richter isn't what's keeping me here? I've contained that feeling in my heart since I saw Jeanne, an uncanny feeling we've met before. Ridiculous, of course, but it's still there.

I approach the young girl with so many questions. I'm curious to see her rehearse on the rings and observe her swing on the flybar, give her a few pointers without giving myself away, but I'll say nothing about her *maman*. I can't. This moment has so many layers, I can't grasp them all at once. I'm dizzy. What are they keeping from me? Baiting me to see what I know. Philippe will be back soon and God knows what that reunion will be like. Until then, I'm not going to back down. I said my piece to Gisèle and I stand by it. The other performers go back to what they were doing, but I see nods and grins aimed at me. My new circus family accepted me because I'm still here. I didn't let Gisèle scare me off. I breathe out a sigh of relief. Obviously, Gisèle isn't popular among the troupe, but Philippe will be the determining factor as to where I go from here.

I see Jeanne making her ascent up the rope to the platform, looking over her shoulder, smiling. That tent-man holding the rope is interested in her and, even if she doesn't know it, she likes him, too. I sigh. She reminds me so much of a younger 'me'. Is that what set Gisèle against me? That I came back to cause trouble... reveal I had an affair with her husband and bore his child? Édouard made me even more curious when he told her that some things are best left alone.

Or is something else at play here?

A crazy idea takes hold of me and won't let go.

Gisèle is worried about me asking questions about Jeanne. Why? Because—

An unbelievable tear in my heart rips open again and I can't stop thinking about the impossible. What if my little girl *wasn't* stillborn? I was so tired and groggy from the labor of childbirth, I was an easy girl to fool. The Mother Superior whisked the child away so quickly, I barely had time to fold the Saint Daria medal Sister Vincent gave me into her blanket to keep her company on her journey to heaven. Then I cried myself to sleep, not caring what happened to me. How could I? I had it all planned. My daughter and I would be together. She had no one but me, but I'd be the best mother ever. Then she was gone. Afterwards, I prayed because I didn't know what else to do, whether I should fight on or just give up. I left the convent when the Mother Superior ordered me to get out. Alone. Never questioning if anyone had lied to me.

Now I do.

What if Jeanne Joubert is my daughter?

I take a long look at her, the way she moves with a controlled grace, her muscles tight, shoulders swaying like a big cat on the prowl, how she arches her left foot and points her toe. Like I do. Why didn't I see it before? Because I spent so many years beating myself up for losing my baby, telling myself it was my fault, I never considered it wasn't true. I never doubted the Mother Superior's declaration my baby was dead, though she hustled Sister Vincent out of the room and wouldn't allow her to speak to me.

Gisèle's not-so-subtle innuendos opened up my mind to a new scenario. Or is she just playing me? That would be just like her, but the fear in her eyes that I'd upset her world was real. Something I didn't understand had drawn me to Jeanne from the minute we'd met. I see the way she jumps headfirst into everything, the way she swings across the big top on the flybar with such glorious enthusiasm. At first, I thought it was because I'm trying to recapture my youth, relive it through her. Now I'm questioning what happened to me, to my baby, eighteen years ago. But in the end, it isn't Gisèle who gives me the answer.

It's Saint Daria.

PART IV

THE DARING YOUNG GIRL ON THE FLYING TRAPEZE

29

PARIS OUTSKIRTS—MAY 1943

Le Cirque Casini
Jeanne

I turn eighteen today and I've never felt more miserable. I yank off my tiara sparkling with pink and blue rhinestones and plop down on a bale of hay. I hug my long cape around me, creating a safe place for a good cry. I need time to pull myself together before the spectacle, the walk-around-the-ring before the show. Bébé, wearing her cute red rug with sequins and Juliet cap, nudges against my leg and rubs her trunk against my thigh. She knows I'm feeling low. I plant a kiss on her trunk and she makes that special sound she does when she's 'cooing'. The spec starts in minutes and I'm panicking because on my special day, my mother has seen to it once again to ignore me. I went against her wishes and put on the blue sequin costume. I need a good cry, but I can't because deep down I knew this would happen. It always does. Maman enjoys hurting me.

'I can't find Maman anywhere, Bébé. She's not in her dressing tent or her caravan. Ondine disappeared, too.'

Bébé makes a trumpeting sound. Loud. She knows how much my mother upsets me. I fought with *ma mère* again and this time I went too far. I'm not surprised Maman is avoiding me. I sank to a new low in my battle to gain my independence. I insisted on wearing the blue sequin costume and she insisted I didn't have the figure. She couldn't have made me feel more like a child than by pointing that out. Now she's ignoring me completely.

Like I don't exist.

And the tears fall. I get a funny feeling she's no longer even trying to act like my *maman*, like she's washed her hands of me.

'Surely she'll come around,' I tell Bébé, still snuggling against me, 'and she'll be there for me when I do the double and a half somersault. I mean, she will be there, won't she?' Bébé wiggles her big ears. She always makes me smile, but tonight I'm worried. I've practiced and practiced and Papa says I'm ready, and yet I want my *maman*'s approval in the worst way.

'The truth is, Bébé, I'm afraid. Afraid I'll fall like Maman did. But if I become a true circus queen, then it will be like the both of us are up there under the big top and maybe, just maybe, she'll smile at me, and tell me she loves me. Papa never says he loves me, but he's a man and men don't say those things. But he shows his love by indulging me with more time with him on the trapeze and taking me to the pictures to see each new Sylvie Martone film. Thank God the Nazis only shut down filmmaking for a short while.'

Bébé has no idea what I'm talking about, but she listens. The adorable baby elephant followed me around the circus grounds earlier, kicking an empty can toward me and wanting to play, but now she's tuckered out and hunkers down for a quick nap. Nearby, Josephine abandons her pile of grass and saunters over to Bébé to check on her, then goes back to eating. She's never far away and is a good *maman* to her calf.

My mother could learn from her.

I dry my cheeks, then pick up my tiara and head for the sawdust ring in the main tent when I see Kaspar heading toward the elephant tent to get Josephine and Bébé ready for the spectacle. I'll give him a piece of my mind if he pushes them too far today. Wanda skips along behind him, grinning. I envy her girlish naiveté. Not me. I get upset over a silly thing like a costume, but I have to put out there how I feel. What will Sandrine think if I don't wear it? I wouldn't want to hurt her feelings.

Looking back on my run-in with Maman, maybe I shouldn't have acted like a spoiled two-year-old. I went too far, knowing she's fragile like a gazelle, highly strung and prone to flight. When she's all decked out for her ride in the parade, she uses her ostrich plume headpiece with silver beads and sequins as a prop, swishing her purple feathers around her like a fleeing bird. Not today. She's nowhere to be found. Pulling this disappearing stunt is her way of showing me she reigns supreme over me.

Today of all days.

I'm eighteen and grown up, but I'm scared. All my life I've lived in a world where trapeze artists swing through the air as if they'll never fall. Where clowns act out the human comedy and jugglers spin and twirl everything so fast all you see is a rainbow of color. Red, blue, yellow. I don't want to lose all that, no matter how hard circus life is, how we shiver through cold winters and sweat through hot summers on the road with flat tires and rain seeping into our tents and caravans. I'm amazed we can put on a show at all.

Today I'm drifting around the grounds like a turtle without her shell. Naked and alone in a cold world, hobbling over sharp pebbles, trying to make it to the pond, wondering if I ever will. Everything is turned upside down. Papa returned from Paris a short while ago and barely said two words to me. I don't know what to think. I should be floating on air, but I feel awful. My mother hates me. Papa wished me a happy birthday but he won't look me straight in the eye. What's on his mind making him act so distant? Uncle Édouard has a sour face and is grumpy and forgot it's my birthday; Socks and the other clowns whisper among themselves. Even their painted-on smiles look droopy. Something's up, but what? The only birthday hug I get is from the new bareback rider. Lia. A stranger. She's waiting for me at the entrance to the main tent, waving at me while the rest of the troupe scrambles to get into parade formation. Her two children are at her side, Marie and Luc. Dressed as clowns. They're so quiet and respectful and adore Bébé. I noticed Marie can't speak... I wonder what happened? I try to talk to her but she just smiles, though I swear I hear her whispering to Bébé when she thinks no one is looking. I plop my tiara on my head and my cape falls open. Lia stares at the medal I wear around my neck.

Then she starts shaking, her knees wobbling, like her balance is off... Strange for a rider with her skill. She lowers her eyes, then drops her head, her breathing ragged.

'Saint Daria, *n'est-ce pas?*' she asks. I nod, but she seems surprised when I mention it was a gift from my mother.

'I always wear it for the spectacle,' I tell her, but not when I fly—what if it came loose? 'It's my good luck charm.'

Her eyelids flutter, her cheeks flush, and she hugs me again so tight it's like she doesn't want to let me go. I'm taken aback—it's been so long since anyone hugged me with such feeling and warmth—it feels so nice to be wanted. I hug her back and I swear she has tears in her eyes. Which brings up a sticky point. Lia is about the same age as Maman, but right now she spends more time with me than my own mother, listening to me, like when I gush over my blue-sequin costume.

'My friend Sandrine gave it to me... Sandrine Aubert. She's a dancer. Maman says I shouldn't wear it.' I show off the glittery blue costume, posing. 'That it will tear. But I'm grown up now and make my own decisions.'

'Your costume is beautiful, Jeanne,' Lia says softly, 'but it must withstand the pulling and tugging when you're swinging on the flybar. I remember a night in Berlin when—'

She clams up, bites her lip. *Why? What is she keeping from me?*

She changes the subject, showing me how to apply my lipstick so my lips look fuller. How to walk and not to stoop over because I'm tall. She insists I have immense power over the audience because when I fly on the trapeze, I'm a star. I don't even mind that she agrees with Maman about the costume, but what she does next is a huge surprise to me. She charms a small dagger off the knife thrower and before I can protest, she cuts off the rhinestones and two rows of sequins on Sandrine's costume. *My* costume. 'That's better,' she says. 'Now you don't have the extra glitter weighing you down.'

I suppose I should be angry, but she's right. I *do* like it better. I twirl around in a circle, wave my arms about. Her children clap their hands, honk their clown horns. I feel like I can fly. She's wonderful!

'Happy Birthday, *ma petite*,' she whispers, then she adjusts my tiara. 'Now let's go out there and show them what a real circus queen can do.'

* * *

This damn tiara is giving me one big headache.

Who knew rhinestone teardrops were so sharp they could dig into my skull? It never hurt before, but I wasn't as agitated as I am now. My eyeballs feel like they're bulging out. I'm so confused. Papa whizzes right by us when he enters the main tent, waving his cape around like he's fighting a bull, not welcoming the crowd. Lia grabs my arm when she sees him, drawing in deep breaths, and I swear she's going to faint. Papa is a handsome man, yes, I agree, but he's not *that* fascinating, to make a grown woman swoon. Especially a married woman with two children. She loses her composure for a moment, lowering her head, disappointed Papa didn't see her. I could have told her, my papa never notices the girls in the circus no matter how pretty they are, and Lia is gorgeous... even at her age. Yet a strange stillness and uneasy quiet settles over her.

I'm worried.

'Lia, *Lia*, are you ill?' I ask, taking her arm. She worries constantly about her children, checking on them frequently, but Socks grabbed the two little clowns and hustled them over to clown alley where they'll join the others in the parade. 'If you're worried about Marie and Luc, they're with Socks.'

'Thank you, Jeanne.' She attempts a weak smile. 'I'm fine, thank you.' Then why is her hand shaking when she places it over mine?

'It's just so exciting to be a part of the circus.'

Strange.

'I thought you worked here in this circus, that's what Uncle Édouard told me.'

'I—I did... when I was your age.' A pained look crosses over her face, making her light eyes seem a deeper green. 'Is your papa always in such a hurry?'

I grin. 'Yes... always. He runs the circus with Maman...' Then it hits me. Did Lia know Papa when she was here? My birthday has gone from disappointing to strange and now unnerving. Why is Lia so interested in Papa? My God, an awful thought hits me between the eyes. Is she a Gestapo informant? Is that why she came back? If she is, why bring her children? Or are they hers? She keeps them close to her, allowing only Socks around them, and I swore I heard the little boy call her 'mademoiselle'. I keep my thoughts to myself. I'm determined to find out what Lia is really doing here.

The ringmaster blows his whistle.

The spectacle around the ring begins. I can't tear my eyes away from Lia as we walk together around the sawdust ring with the ponies, Liberty horses, monkeys, ballet girls, jugglers, acrobats, high-wire walkers, Kaspar walking alongside the lion cages on wheels, Wanda sitting high atop Josephine and Bébé following, the elephants now wearing their royal blue velvet robes and yellow beaded Juliet caps tied under their chins. They look so regal, but I worry Kaspar has been striking their sensitive feet too hard with his stick when I see Josephine starting to limp. That saddens me. This majestic creature is such an important part of the circus spectacle, but she pays dearly for that role. Abused toes, beatings.

Next comes Socks and the clowns, the two little ones I know to be Lia's brood, whooping it up—I catch Socks grinning at Lia and 'playing' up to her with his 'beating' heart—another mystery to solve—while the brass band plays a snappy tune. And what's Lia doing? The girl—make that woman—who told me she hasn't worked in a circus in years is waving to the crowd, blowing kisses. Dancing. Clapping her hands. Strutting and stopping to talk to the children in the stalls, clasping the weathered hand of a woman crying. She's so at ease with the audience, it's like *she's* the circus queen, not me.

I try to be like the beautiful redhead, talking to the crowd like I usually do, but today I'm a dunce. I stumble over my words like a panicked monkey. I can't keep my smile going because I have a sick feeling in my stomach. Maman didn't show... and neither did Sandrine. I search every face. I want to show her I'm wearing her costume, that I'm ready for my big moment on the trapeze. Two and a half somersaults.

But am I?

I'm shaking with nerves, my cheeks burn hot, and I don't feel like myself. Like my world shifted and I'm going in the wrong direction. I don't see Sandrine in the front row, the back row. I don't see her anywhere.

Why isn't she here?

30

PARIS OUTSKIRTS—MAY 1943

Le Cirque Casini
Lia

I'm still reeling from seeing the medal of Saint Daria hanging around Jeanne's neck. It can't be a coincidence. I tucked that medal into my baby's blanket over eighteen years ago. What puzzles me is Jeanne said it was a gift from her mother. Did Philippe tell her that? Of course, he didn't mention *I'm* her mother. The runaway girl on the trapeze who's now come back to claim her child. That's what Gisèle thinks. My baby was born a few weeks earlier, but evidently someone had the audacity to change the date. This is *not* my baby's birthday, but I'm desperately serious when I remind myself I didn't even know I had a daughter, so why the fuss? I will celebrate *this* day with her, the day I found her again.

I detect movement behind me, but it's the clowns scrambling out into the ring. Socks is among them.

'Good having you back, Lia,' he whispers in my ear, brushing by me. I smile, surprised he hasn't approached me about Jeanne, but maybe he doesn't know *I* know. *Don't be a fool.* Of course he does, but he's waiting to see what I'll do. For as long as I've known him, Socks is like a set of suspenders... holding us up so we don't fall down. Socks knows *everything* about this circus. Years ago, when I was at my lowest point when I realized my pregnancy would hurt Philippe, he told me, 'I make people laugh, Lia, but more important I pull them up from the darkest places and find something to make them smile, make them see there is always sunlight when the dawn comes.'

Dawn just arrived for me.

But I can't tell Jeanne who I am... not yet.

First, I *have* to see Philippe.

The evening performance is underway with its mayhem and madness, the clowns racing into the ring causing chaos, horns honking, my two children the loudest of all. It makes me smile to see them with happy faces, their young spirits healing somewhat from losing their mother. The Rémon Sisters' trick riding act with me as the fourth 'sister' just finished and it was playtime for me. Except I hate the costume we all wear. A leotard with a pink tutu. I vaulted onto a galloping pony, turned somersaults, jumped through a hoop, jumped off then back on the pony, but I left the forward somersaults to my 'younger' sisters.

The band strikes up a polka, while a clown wearing a big bustle and floppy hat cranks up a fake sausage machine, filling it with phony bratwurst. Twiddling his thumbs and tapping his big clown shoe, Socks waits at the other end until—

A bouncing dachshund jumps out and lands in his arms.

Whistles. Foot stomping. No custard pie-throwing. The Nazis banned it.

Socks gets on a tricycle and drives around the ring, holding up the wiggling dog for the children in the audience to see. He blasts his shrill whistle and several more clowns race into the ring on tricycles. Including Anna and Jakob. Before the war, they'd jam into the ring in a clown patrol wagon, siren blasting. Jump out, pull children out of the audience and take them for a ride.

Not anymore.

I guess it's too frightening to these children who often see friends and relatives taken away in a patrol wagon. A sudden dread comes over me. What if I'm discovered before I can settle this matter about Jeanne? What if Anna and Jakob are unmasked? I can't wait any longer. I have to confront Philippe.

I left Jeanne in clown alley, sitting in a quiet corner, appearing confused but happy with what I did to her costume. She needs to focus, I told her, take her mind off what's bothering her, do something for somebody else to lift her soul. I didn't bring up her papa, how Philippe didn't recognize me when he rushed past us. Or he didn't want to. I think she suspects I'm not who I said I was, but

I'll sort that out later. Philippe is a different matter. I'm getting to the bottom of this now.

I shuffle around the circus grounds from the cookhouse to the lion cages to the menagerie tent, then I hear men's voices coming from inside a fancy caravan. Philippe and Édouard. I crouch down behind the wagon with *Le Cirque Casini* painted on the side in blue and yellow. I'm not above eavesdropping to find out what they know.

'If you go through with this ridiculous plan,' Édouard is saying, 'you'll have to tell Jeanne the truth.'

'I can't, it will ruin her.'

'What if the Gestapo find out her mother is half Roma and arrest her?'

Me. He means me. No more guessing... it's true, Jeanne is the baby daughter I thought I'd lost. I'm one heartbeat away from crying out my joy before I grab onto myself and shake from head to toe. I squeeze my eyes tight and revel in this moment. I squeeze my eyes tighter and let the anger welling up in me settle at a simmer, not a boil. Whose insane idea was it to take my baby from me? Philippe's? Oh, God, I have to find out if he was behind it. The man I loved, adored, gave myself to without regret because I believed in him.

How could he betray me so?

I open my eyes and let the smell of fresh dew on the grass shoot up my nostrils and clear my head. Then I bury my head in my hands and cry softly. And I listen...

'They won't find out,' Philippe shoots back, 'unless you tell them.'

Édouard's voice cracks. 'My God, Philippe, I love Jeanne... she's the daughter I should have had—'

'With Gisèle?' Philippe sighs heavily. 'At least you have each other. I lost the only woman I ever loved.'

I choke. *Does he mean me?* Then he *did* love me. So why did he take my baby... our baby? And why is he ignoring me?

'You came between us, Philippe. Gisèle is still bitter.'

'I had no choice. Her old man was going to drop our act if I didn't marry her.' I hear a wistfulness in his voice I never expected. 'The Flying Jouberts were the top act on the trapeze back then. You, Lia, and me. Every week we got offers from circuses in Berlin, Sweden, even America, but Monsieur Casini didn't want to lose his biggest draw, so he threatened to blacklist us to other circuses on trumped-up charges of embezzlement. When the baby happened, it was the perfect way out. Gisèle didn't want children, but her father wanted to carry on his legacy. We got married... Instant family.'

'What you did to Lia was unforgiveable.'

'It was that Mother Superior who came up with the scheme when Lia's secret came out at the convent. She blackmailed Monsieur Casini that she'd reveal his 'star' performer's indiscretion if he didn't pay up and I went along with it. What else could I do, after she told me Lia ran off without our child?'

That's not true. They told me my baby was dead.

Philippe continues. 'But with Lia gone, we had no act. Marrying Gisèle kept us off the streets, little brother. I looked out for you then and I'm doing that now. The Nazis will crush us if I don't go along with their plan.'

'Lia's back.'

I hear Philippe draw in his breath. 'I know. She's more beautiful than ever.'

So he did see me.

'So what's holding you back?' Édouard says, smug.

'That Gestapo man... He's bringing the new owner from what was the Swope Circus in Berlin here tonight.'

I suck in my breath. *The Swope Circus.* I never thought I'd hear that name again. I haven't worked there for years, but it could be a problem if I'm recognized.

Édouard lets out a low whistle. 'I didn't think you'd stoop that low, collaborating with the Nazis.'

Philippe remains silent. All I hear is the two men breathing heavily... and the sound of heavy footsteps. Someone is coming. I pray they'll pass by me on the other side—

'Send Jeanne away,' Édouard pleads, 'to somewhere it's safe, before it's too late.'

'I can't.'

'Your ego, dear brother?'

'No,' is his curt reply. Then, 'Jeanne is part of the deal.'

'What?' Édouard raises his voice to a high pitch. 'You're selling your own daughter to the Boches?'

'You want us all deported to a concentration camp?' Philippe yells. 'I'm warning you, Édouard, keep your mouth shut or you'll have me to answer to.'

'I will. For now, but if Jeanne is in any danger—'

Footsteps louder.

I nearly die when the tall tent-man Jeanne is starry-eyed over walks briskly past me and pretends not to see me. That just made him a lot more interesting in my eyes. He has an agenda and it goes beyond being a tent-man, I'd swear it. He's waiting to see what I do... if I'm just a nosy eavesdropper or something more provocative, like a member of the Underground. I let out my breath. But I have to be careful. I could be wrong. I'll see what his next move is before I talk to him.

He knocks on the caravan. '*Pardon,* messieurs, I found a problem with the rigging for the trapeze.' The door opens and the tent-man explains he discovered a loose cable along with a powerful electric current connected to the trapeze. 'If that current was turned on during the performance, messieurs,' the tent-man says, his voice raw, 'anyone on the trapeze would be electrocuted.'

I hear the pain in his voice. He's thinking about Jeanne.

So am I. I slip away quietly. I've heard all I need to hear: that the Gestapo has targeted Le Cirque Casini and is taking it over, making it unwise for me to stay here?

Within minutes, I'm back in the main tent, looking for Jeanne. To warn her? No, that will put her off her game. The Flying Jouberts are the final act and will make the slow ascent up the rope to the platform soon. Besides, the tent-man fixed the problem with the cable and the trapeze. That doesn't mean Jeanne isn't in danger if an unexperienced tent-man sets up the rigging, seeing how difficult it is to find skilled workers. Which puts me in a dilemma.

If I stay, I can protect my daughter. Check her rigging myself. Keep an eye on her. If I run, I can save myself from the Gestapo.

It's a choice only I can make.

31

PARIS OUTSKIRTS—MAY 1943

Le Cirque Casini

Jeanne

'Get up on the stool, you stupid elephant!'

I flinch. It's that damn animal trainer. How dare he speak to her like that?

Bébé looks at me with an expression in her eyes so confused, so raw, I can't stand by and allow that man to hurt her. Now he is rapping her on her baby toes with a wooden stick. Hard. Kaspar is a monster and if I expect Wanda to do anything about it, I'm as silly as a rubber duck. But I can't stand here on the side of the ring and do nothing.

I couldn't sit by myself another minute, trying to focus on clearing my head. I can't. My mind is a mess, so I headed into the main tent to see the show. And look to see if Sandrine is here yet. She isn't, but I never expected *this*. Kaspar must have lost his mind putting the little elephant on display. Papa said he has no time to talk to him about how he treats his animals.

I do. I'll fix that.

Maman will kill me for meddling, but I strut into the ring, whipping my long satin cape around me, blowing kisses to the crowd like I saw Lia do. *Applause. Shouts.* 'We love you, Jeanne!' 'We can't wait for the trapeze!' I smile wide. Why not take advantage of what Lia calls my 'star power'? Something, anything, to distract Kaspar from his cruel game. I take another walk around the ring, point to the trapeze swing. More applause. It works. For a few seconds.

Then...

'On the stool. *Now!*' he yells and hits Bébé again. She cries out. Elephants have very sensitive feet and trainers use that to force them to do tricks. I stop breathing. It's cruel, unjust, and if I'm ever in control of this circus, I won't allow it. Ever. For now, all I can do is try to help the little pachyderm put her feet on the multi-striped stool in the middle of the ring.

'You can do it, Bébé,' I whisper in her ear, stroking her head.

Her feet slide off. She's not coordinated like an older elephant. She's still learning how to use her trunk to grab her milk bottle, while I've seen Josephine do the trick a million times, where the elephant puts her feet on the multi-striped stool, then raises her two front legs while Wanda waltzes around her and Kaspar cracks his whip.

It disgusts me.

Josephine isn't in the ring yet. Kaspar is smart enough to know the *maman* elephant would charge him and skew him with her ivory tusks if she saw him mistreat her calf.

'Stop interfering with my act,' Kaspar whispers in my ear.

'I will... when you stop abusing the elephants.'

'Your father won't always be around to protect you, Jeanne. Remember that.'

'Is that a threat?' I ask, anxious.

He grins. 'You'll see.'

I hate him, but I can't ignore him. The audience is unaware of our heated conversation. They can't hear us and see only big smiles on our faces so we appear to be a happy circus act. Strike that. Wanda is scowling at me.

Jealous, is she?

She's not the only one.

A loud, and I mean *loud*, trumpeting echoes in the main tent and before anyone knows what to expect, Josephine arrives with three keepers hot on her tail. She heard her baby's cries and broke free from her bindings. She goes right by Kaspar, ignores Wanda, and heads for Bébé waving her trunk around. The audience gasps, Kaspar cracks his whip, Wanda faints—or pretends to—and I watch the most beautiful moment I've ever seen in this circus unfold.

Josephine nudges her calf with her trunk toward the stool, puts her own front feet on top, then backs off and puts her trunk under the baby elephant and works with Bébé, guiding her, helping her place her two front feet awkwardly on the stool.

The audience cheers, Kaspar takes a bow—what a phony—Wanda also takes a bow—amazing how quickly she recovers—but they've all forgotten about me. Yet my heart is full, my confidence in myself restored. Lia was right. Take the focus off yourself, look for ways to help others. I slink off to the side, wiping away the tears. I've just been upstaged by a baby elephant and it's a wonderful feeling. Seeing the love and care Josephine has for Bébé is the nicest birthday present I could ever have.

32

PARIS—MAY 1943

Earlier at the Grand Hôtel du Midi
The Magician

I'm late arriving at Le Cirque Casini for Mademoiselle Jeanne's birthday performance and I'm so stressed I spilled greasy, sweet popcorn on my trousers. I rushed back to my abode to refresh my wardrobe after my distressful meeting earlier at the Grand Hôtel du Midi with two *filles* who I never would have approached under ordinary circumstances. I was ordered there by the secret police. *Ugh.* My nerves are ragged, my sensitivities defiled at the humiliation I had to endure at the hands of that Gestapo misfit, Herr Geller. He paid me a visit and presented to me an insoluble problem.

He needed me to procure fresh female flesh for his stable of informants. He has this obsession with recruiting girls who have something to lose. Not family or friends but their looks. Girls who represent a standard of beauty he finds enjoyable to gaze upon. I didn't understand his abruptness with me, not after I put into play two women with lovely new skin on their faces a week ago and they're happily supplying their handler with information. Not always the case. I wondered if he'd discovered that Mademoiselle Zera Bovier hasn't given up anything of importance; if anything, she's holding back. However, I have no intention of tackling her, especially not if that python of hers gets its dander up and wraps itself around my neck. A man of my sensibilities can only stand so much, so to keep in the good graces of the Gestapo, I smiled and didn't put up a fuss earlier when he insisted we had an appointment in the Sorbonne quarter.

'Get your overcoat on,' he snarled at me, then forced me into his monstrosity of a motorcar. The devil himself must have owned it. I've never seen such a mess with crumpled up newspapers and empty beer bottles and the smell of cheap cigars. I had to hold my handkerchief over my nose while he rambled down the boulevards before stopping at a dingy hotel on a small street in the 5th arrondisement. Unfortunately he then led me to a room on the third floor and pulled down the lever and opened the door, and the smell took me to a new level. Females. Unwashed.

Disgusting.

'Do your job, Docteur Floquet,' he ordered me then left, holding his nose. I rolled my eyes in horror when he used my given name. I *never* allow the women I take on as patients to know me intimately and there's nothing more intimate to me than my original family name which I discarded years ago. To my relief, the two nude women paid us no attention and were lost in scrapping with each other. A dirty-red velvet coverlet lay strewn across the bed, the women grabbing each other's hair, clawing, biting with as much vigor as two black cats scorched by a hot poker. It was as if they escaped from iron cages, eyeing each other with a depravity I found distasteful. Cursing, spitting, and rolling around on the dirty velvet with abandon. Herr Geller informed me he told the two women the 'winner' of the brawl would receive my services gratis. I suffered a nausea attack, observing the catfight. There's no limit to what he'll do to make others suffer.

Then I saw why the Gestapo agent brought me there.

The women boasted scars.

On their buttocks, their cheeks. Ugly, red marks.

I was to make them 'beautiful'? They never *were* beautiful and my magic can't make them. I leaned forward, groping for a reason to stay, observe, and keep the Gestapo man from taking me for a ride to Avenue Foch. The girls frolicking on the bed were dastardly young, the dim electric light spread over their nude bodies a thin layer of false glitter, adding a charm that *could* be cultivated with time. I'll leave that to Herr Geller. They run more to the appetite of the Gestapo agent than mine.

Knowing they'd inform on *me* if I didn't do my job, I laughed with wry amusement when the woman with hair streaked the color of a pomegranate yanked out a handful of dark roots from her opponent's head. The other girl screamed then fought back until I clapped my black-gloved hands together and yelled, 'Stop this nonsense, mesdemoiselles, or I will leave you to your games and do nothing to help you.'

'Don't go, monsieur.'

'Please, Monsieur Geller promised you'd fix us up. Get rid of our scars.'

'Yes, we'll be good.'

I struggled not to smile. Even if I find them distasteful, I'm under orders to give them every opportunity to prove their worthiness for transformation under my thumb. Remove the ugly scars from their bodies. Yet I damn the cold fever in me that has brought my existence to such low depths I find myself in a corner with nowhere to turn. Damn Nazis. I should have seen this coming when I frequented cabarets in Berlin, haunts catering to a depraved sense of eroticism. Spankings, slave auctions. But I was spreading my wings then, operating on women as if they were already corpses. For practice. I no longer need to perform such charity work. Look what happened with Mademoiselle Sandrine. A complete misuse of my talents. She threw it all away for revenge. I know Mademoiselle Jeanne will ask me about her. So I made subtle inquiries about the discovery of young women murdered and got no further than that damned Inspecteur Varon. I didn't speak to him, of course, but the young clerk out front in his office was the talkative type—when several francs crossed his palm. The girls' bodies have all been in the underground morgue behind Notre Dame, he informed me, but no, Inspecteur Varon had no leads. The man is a thorn in my side with his insistent following of the case, showing up and asking questions at Le Cirque Casini. If I can turn the tables on him and have the detective arrested on a phony charge, I'll do it.

Bon. A little good news for this evening when I was obligated to inspect these two whores lined up for my perusal. I insisted they put on under slips. Then, standing before me, I caressed each girl's neck slowly, then her scarred cheeks, my black-gloved fingertips trailing along their flesh. The work of a jealous lover, no doubt. Or client. They wouldn't say. Could be SS. I'm not asking. I'm happy for the work... and the recompense that comes with it.

I inhaled deeply, the beating pulse on the side of their throats striking me as warm and vulnerable, their blood rich in texture under their pale white skin, waiting patiently for me to give them hope I could help them so men wouldn't turn away with distaste. I did. I had to. Not my usual style, but what choice do I have?

Herr Geller isn't a man to be toyed with. I've seen his dirty work at Gestapo headquarters when they bring me in to clean up their messes and repair flesh only so they can have another go at the victim. The man is a beast, spilling blood like it's as plentiful as the ink used to sign deportation orders for Jews. The sincerity of my talk with them endeared me to the young *minettes* no doubt more accustomed to men pushing their tobacco-stained fingers between their legs, sniffing, probing.

'Fix me first, monsieur...' 'No, *me!*' they echoed in a chorus, their voices sweet like cooing pigeons vying for crumbs. I told them to come see me in a fortnight, then I will operate on them both at the same time. Of course I won't, but that satisfied them. Besides, I needed to be on my way.

It was getting late and nothing will keep me from attending Mademoiselle Jeanne's birthday performance. I rushed here in my motorcar after the secret policeman dropped me off at my *maison* and sped off, explaining he had a special visitor from Berlin to pick up from the airfield at Le Bourget. I didn't ask... I was too worried about missing Jeanne. I can't wait to see her swinging high on the trapeze under the big top, beautiful in flight, pale of skin but with half-closed eyes that seem to invite me, almost saint-like, never judging, only needing me, the promise of her beauty belonging to me, filling me. Years and years of seeking companionship with a woman as perfect as she is tries a man's patience and brings about a profound wandering that exhausts my soul, if I still have one, an unconscious response to a need in me that lays unfulfilled. Yes, she's becoming an addiction. But I can handle it.

I'm Docteur Thaddeus Rose.

The Magician.

And this is the most important night of my life. And Jeanne's. I rub my hands together with glee. Herr Geller was only too happy to reveal they will make the big announcement tonight.

33

PARIS OUTSKIRTS—MAY 1943

Le Cirque Casini
Lia

'Slumming, Inspecteur Varon?'

I don't pretend to be happy to see the plainclothes detective when I scour clown alley for Jeanne. I don't need him interrupting my mission, which is to find my daughter and prepare her for the journey ahead of her. I don't know what that is yet. I've just met her; I don't know her strengths, weaknesses. I will. I'm staying here; I'll get close to her. She likes children. Anna and Jakob can help and hopefully she can help them, too. It's not just her act tonight I'm worried about. She's in for a fight. If it's true Philippe is collaborating with the Nazis, she faces scorn, ridicule, even prosecution. When this war is over—and I do believe the Allies will free France—she'll be held accountable for her father's sins.

I won't abandon her. I can't, though I'm putting myself in danger. It's reckless, but isn't what I do every day a 'death-defying feat'? Helping my child survive this horrible war means more to me than anything. Besides, I've had my time in the spotlight; she hasn't. I want to give that to her. I was willing eighteen years ago to risk everything for her. I'm willing to do the same now.

'I like popcorn, mademoiselle.' The detective shoots me a grin that has 'I'm watching you' written all over it.

'I don't. It sticks in my teeth,' I snarl at him. I've got to get rid of him. The Flying Jouberts are up next after the big cats. I wince. I'd rather not watch. For years I've observed the lion trainers work the cats with a chair, a whip, and charm. Not Kaspar. This sweaty specimen of manhood who enjoys showing off his bare chest has but one of these tools to work with. A whip. It's loud and off-putting. I'd rather not be that close to him or the lions, a phobia of mine, so I keep walking and the detective follows me like a tiger. And like a tiger, I expect an attack from the rear.

He doesn't disappoint.

'I caught your pony act tonight, mademoiselle,' he says, sneaking up on me. His hot breath on the back of my neck makes me shiver in a pleasant sort of way. Not the response I expected. He continues. 'Where did you perform before? Your face looks familiar.'

'Yours doesn't. Now if you'll excuse me...' I toss back at him. Where is Jeanne? I left her here in clown alley and now she's gone. I'm alone with the detective. The clowns including Socks are out in the main tent, going up and down the aisles, mixing with the audience, making sure everyone feels safe during the lion act. Le Cirque Casini prides itself, to quote Jeanne, on presenting a safe, family environment.

Will that mantra hold up when the Nazis take over?

When I *do* find Jeanne, I'll say nothing about our relationship, that I'm her *maman*. I feel reasonably certain neither will Philippe. I take a moment to dwell in a warm, happy place when I whisper his name. '*Philippe.*' I wish I could have seen his face when he called me 'beautiful'. Did the light in his eyes burn brighter? Hotter? Is he as nervous as I am about seeing each other again? Will he kiss me? Or turn me away?

As I continue walking away from the detective, I start to cry. Soft tears I wipe away with the back of my hand. I have no guarantee Philippe will hold me in his arms and kiss my neck, nuzzle his face in my hair like he used to. It's not like the old days when we flew to heaven at every performance, joining up together in mid-air high under the big top. The Nazis have made that impossible, since I have to remain low profile, but I can dream, can't I? And then there's Jeanne to consider. After what I overheard earlier, I don't feel it's my place to tell her she's my daughter. What if she doesn't believe my story? That she was stolen from me? I *do* feel it's my duty to remain an enigma to her and everyone else in Le Cirque Casini *not* part of my story. I must remain undercover so I can operate freely without restraint. I can only keep her safe if I remain outside the purview of the Gestapo. And that includes this policeman.

He makes another attempt to engage me. 'I always wanted to run away and join the circus when I was a boy.'

'We could use a new popcorn vendor,' I offer. 'You can poke your nose into every corner and fire off questions to your heart's content—though I'd stay away from the lion cages.' I hold my nose. He laughs.

Then his eyes turn serious. 'I'm here on official business, mademoiselle.'

'And here I thought you made a special trip to see me.' I flutter my lashes like they do in the pictures. Wiggle my shoulders. I'm flirting to dissuade him. He strikes me as the type of man who picks his women carefully and is immune to such frivolous behavior. Flirting with him is my way of sending him running and leaving me alone. I can't allow the police to get too close to me and take a dive into my papers. He doesn't take the bait. His eyes are everywhere except on me. He's making notes in a small black book, including drawing the layout of the tent. Entrance, exit. Figuring out how many clowns hang out here by counting the number of makeup boxes. The man is dead serious about his work. I admire that, but that's not the only thing about him that unnerves me.

He's got a haunted look in his dark, smoldering eyes. I know that look. He's lost someone close to him. And that touches every bone in my body with a deep emotion I know so well. I respect his right to keep it private. I back off with the sarcasm.

'I could detain you. *If* you're withholding information.' He gives me that devilish smile again. Unnerving.

'Sorry, Inspector, but I can't help you.' I change it up, say what's on my mind. 'You don't think about anything but your job, *n'est-ce pas?*'

'It's my duty.'

'Is it your duty to harass me?' I challenge him. To my surprise, he takes off his Fedora slowly, holds it in his hand and looks me square in the eye, as if he has something important to say and I'm going to listen.

'I regret, mademoiselle, there's been another murder.'

'Oh, my God...' My hand goes to my throat.

'The victim was a young woman,' he continues. 'She was found beaten and drugged and left in a dark doorway in Montmartre wearing only a torn slip.'

'A girl from the circus?' I ask.

'Not this time.'

I breathe out, but my whole body is shaking and I suffer once again the terror of knowing an innocent girl faced a horrible death alone. 'Then why are you here?'

'To gather evidence about her habits, mademoiselle. I find there's no such thing as a random encounter, that there's a pattern to these murders. The victims share a history I'm not at liberty to discuss with you. All I can reveal is that from previous evidence, I'm convinced there's a mass murderer loose in Paris targeting circus queens and that someone lured her to that alley and attacked her in a violent manner. I'm not releasing the details pending my investigation, but I *can* say she was often seen here at Le Cirque Casini on the arm of SS officers.'

I feel my throat tightening. 'What was her name?'

'Sandrine Aubert.'

Why does that name sound familiar? Then I hear a girl scream.

Jeanne.

'*No, no, no!* It can't be... not Sandrine.'

I spin around to see her falling to her knees, her white satin cape spread around her like a holy shroud. I run to her, hold her in my arms, and she starts sobbing. I keep her tight to my chest, rock her back and forth for what seems like endless minutes. My little girl is hurting badly inside.

My baby needs me and I'm not leaving her.

Then when I've discovered such joy in finding her, fate whips a fierce wind in my face when Philippe sweeps back into my life minutes later after the detective leaves... Stops, stares, and pulls me into his arms.

I don't resist.

He grabs me with such passion, I cry out, then he kisses me with such tenderness, his lips commanding me to remember him. Remember us.

'Lia, Lia, is it really you?' he whispers.

'Yes, my love. I'm here. I'm home.'

I put my fingertips to my mouth. My lips sting from his kiss. I can't move. I just stand there, feeling my world spinning right again. He kisses me again and takes away every lonely moment I've had since I ran away...

And I don't want him to stop.

34

PARIS OUTSKIRTS—MAY 1943

Le Cirque Casini
Jeanne

Why is Papa kissing the new bareback rider?

Lia.

I mean, really *kissing* her. Long, hard, sucking the breath out of her, pulling her to her feet and grabbing her around the waist. And then she kissed him back. Wildly and with abandon, like two people filled with passion that goes far beyond kissing.

I hate her. My head is spinning with questions, emotions I don't understand. I'm so confused. I can't stay here another minute. I turn and run, leave them to their disgusting display of affection. I want to keep on crying, but I can't. I've run out of tears. This blasphemous display of intimacy between my papa and this woman has shocked me so much, I'm dried up.

How dare this woman set my nerves on fire with her wanton behavior? She acted so kind, so caring when we heard about Sandrine, I thought I'd found a friend even if she is so much older than me. For a moment, I saw myself in her face when I'm that age, but that was my imagination, *n'est-ce pas*? I'm so desperate to prove I'm grown up, but I'm not. I've never had to face anything on my own. Papa has always been there for me, but tonight he betrayed me and I shall never forgive him.

How am I going to fly on the trapeze? God, I want to, but he ruined my birthday by kissing Lia; no explanation, acting like I wasn't there. They were so wrapped up in each other, it was disgusting. And me? I'm still reeling from the news about Sandrine. Feeling responsible for Sandrine's death is the hardest thing I've ever had to face.

How can she be dead? She gave me this beautiful costume, she was going to see me wear it tonight, she was pretty and funny and I wanted to be just like her.

Do you also want to end up like her?

I keep hearing in my head what the detective said... about the mass murderer. I want to tell him what I know; that Sandrine was afraid of the SS after what they did to her, but she found a wonderful doctor to help her. But when I look around for him, he's gone.

I feel so abandoned. And here I thought Lia cared about me, speaking to me in quiet tones when the detective dropped the news about Sandrine, making me feel like I'm not alone. Then Papa shows up, looking for me, alerting me the ringmaster is about to announce The Flying Jouberts and this happens?

God, I want to die.

* * *

'And now, mesdames and messieurs, The Flying Jouberts!'

The spotlight hits me with a warm glow. I wave to the crowd below from the perch. Uncle Édouard is beside me, waving. Papa is the catcher. I've barely said a word to him. I merely smile, but I don't let on how much he upset me. We're at the end of our act and this is my big moment, but I feel dizzy and cold. *Cold like Sandrine lying dead?*

Yes, something died in me tonight when I realized I caused that girl's death. I never should have interfered. I knew she wanted revenge against the SS—it had to be them—but she never would have gone after it if I hadn't helped her regain her confidence.

The ringmaster calls out, 'And now Mademoiselle Jeanne Joubert will perform the two and a half somersault for the first time tonight, on her eighteenth birthday!'

I feel like retching; my knees wobble. I'm not ready. In rehearsal, yes, but that was before they betrayed me. Papa, Lia. I shake my head *no*.

'Come, Jeanne,' Papa says, swinging toward me in the catcher position 'You can do it.'

I can't. My world is all wrong. Sandrine is dead and Papa kissed that bareback rider. My eye twitches, my shoulder hurts, there's not enough resin on my hands. One little thing wrong and my timing's off.

You have to try, I hear in my head.

I grab the flybar and leave the perch. I ignore my internal clock that's jammed up with so much emotion, it's off by a second, maybe two. I keep swinging from the flybar higher and higher, but every muscle in my body freezes up. I'm hot up here, the air is stuffy, and for some reason I can't breathe. My chest hurts so bad it's like I slammed into a wall. Panic grips me. An attack on every muscle in my body. I can't hold on. My arms scream with pain, like they're ripping off my shoulders. Then I go numb. Everywhere. My God, now I can't feel *anything.* I have no control over my body and I let go of the flybar.

Down... down I go.

I fall into the net.

* * *

'Mesdames and messieurs, stay in your seats, *please!*' the ringmaster calls out, then blows his whistle. 'Mademoiselle Joubert is unhurt. Let's hear it for the clowns one more time!'

The funnymen race into the ring, but I pay no attention to their silly antics when I climb over the top of the net and flip my body over as I've done since I was a little girl. At the last second, my instincts kicked in and the panic that consumed me snapped and I broke free and landed safely in the net. But I'm done. I'm not going back up there. They send in the clowns as a diversion so the audience forgets I made a fool out of myself. I couldn't do the two and a half somersault. Damn, I couldn't even kick high enough to do a single. I completely froze.

Lia rushes over to me, still wearing her bareback rider costume. She looks ridiculous in that pink tutu and I tell her so. Her eyes darken. I've hurt her. *Bon.* I hate her. She kissed my father; she deserves it.

Lia takes my hand. 'Climb back up to the perch, Jeanne. Try again. You can do it. I have faith in you. So does your papa.'

That sets me off on a path I don't want to follow. As if she has the right to tell *me* what to do. She's not my mother, not that Maman cares. She didn't put in an appearance all evening. I pull my hand away abruptly. My words come out hot, but my eyes burn cold when I ask her, 'Why did you kiss my father?'

Her eyelids flutter. 'We were friends, good friends, Jeanne, before you were born.'

'Well, you're not *my* friend.'

'Jeanne, please... listen.'

'*Leave me alone!*'

I borrow a trick from this inglorious *artiste* and walk around the sawdust ring waving and blowing kisses to the crowd. The stalls are full, everyone waiting for me to go back up to the perch. Mox is holding the rope for me and his presence is strangely comforting, but I won't put myself through that humiliation again. I can't do it.

I turn and walk out of the ring. There's little applause. One, two people. I don't blame them. They know a coward when they see one.

So do I.

Me.

35

PARIS OUTSKIRTS—MAY 1943

Le Cirque Casini

Lia

'I'm going up, Socks. I'll do the two and a half somersault. Give them what they came for.'

Socks grabs me, cups my face in his hands. His eyes glow. He's scared for me, really scared. 'You *can't*, Lia. You're putting your life and your children's in jeopardy if anyone recognizes you.'

'What choice do I have? Jeanne needs me.'

'Have you told her?'

'No.'

'Then don't do this. She'll have another chance, you won't.'

'I've made up my mind, Socks, and you can't stop me.'

'*Please*, Lia.'

'I have to do this to save Jeanne and Le Cirque Casini. If we give the audience something special, they'll forget what happened.' I hug him, he feels my shaking. 'Watch my children for me, Socks. I can't explain, but their lives are in danger. Terrible danger.'

He nods. 'Of course, Lia.' I don't mention I saw the Gestapo man enter the tent with a woman wearing a wide brim chapeau pulled down low over her face. Herr Geller. I can't describe the horror that rages through me, turning my blood ice cold. Does he know I'm here? No, that's impossible, but what if he recognizes me? He knows me as a blonde, not a redhead. Still, I'm not safe. He's ruthless and enjoys torture. I swear he's half-demon and finds pleasure in pulling the wings off a butterfly while the tiny creature struggles to live.

I shudder, imagining what he'd do to the children.

And to me. He possesses a fierceness that consumes him with a red-hot flame that never ebbs. I can't fathom what pain inside him fuels his need to hunt... to kill. I'm deadly frightened of him, his power, his greed.

Yet I love my daughter more.

I won't let him stop me from doing what I must.

I look up at the perch. Philippe and Édouard are waiting for Jeanne to return, while I keep an eye on the Gestapo agent. He's all over this woman he brought, tipping his hat and finding her a seat. She must be from the Swope Circus in Berlin. She looks vaguely familiar, but I toss the insane idea I know her out of my mind. It's too outrageous. And dangerous for me. I can't think about that now, my daughter needs me. If only I could tell Jeanne I'm her mother. Not now. She's in danger... I must keep her safe. Circus Casini has a new owner. A Nazi. If the Gestapo finds out she's my daughter, that she's a quarter Roma, we will both risk being deported to a concentration camp. I will never let that happen. So I'll keep my secret. Now and in the future. *I* know she's my baby girl; that's good enough for me. And Philippe? The way he kissed me set my world on fire. I can't give him up again. I love him, but can I trust him?

'Are you sure you know what you're doing?' Socks asks.

I smile wide. 'No, but then, that's the magic.'

* * *

Jeanne

In the cool shadows outside the sawdust ring, I stare with envy at this circus queen. Lia. No one gets more applause than she does when she enters the ring in that pink leotard sans tutu. As if the audience senses something special is about to happen. Even without spangles and beads, she appears elegant, sophisticated, as she makes her ascent up the rope, stopping to blow a kiss to the crowd.

What's she doing? Who is she?

And why am I so drawn to her? Like there's a page missing in my life and her name is on it?

I hate her, but I also admire her. I watch in awe along with everyone else when Lia reaches the platform, grabs the flybar. She and Papa have words; hot, passionate words. I can't hear what they're saying, but he slides into the catcher position. Then a miracle happens. Lia swings on the flybar higher and higher and in a breathless moment that I will never forget, she executes a perfect two and a half somersault, bringing the house down.

I race out of the tent into the night with the applause still ringing in my ears. I've never seen such skill, such style and finesse on the trapeze, she flies through the air in an act of grace blessed by the gods. A winged creature without wings. While I am so utterly naïve and stupid and have no talent in comparison. Just stars in my eyes because my name is Joubert. I can *never* be like her. She's so pretty and wild and... *free.*

So what now? You flubbed your birthday. It was a bust.

No more excuses. No more tears.

I know what I have to do.

* * *

Lia

'Jeanne is missing, Lia... I can't find her anywhere.'

It's Socks. He found me in the dressing tent, sitting, wondering what my next move is. I'm fighting back tears I never shed, tears that welled up in me when my daughter panicked and lost her confidence. Not uncommon for a flyer to lose their focus after a major trauma. In Jeanne's case, hearing about the murdered girl, then seeing her papa kiss me, a stranger, when she's already hurting on her eighteenth birthday, not least because her mother ignores her.

Now she's missing?

I grab Socks by the shoulders. 'When did you see her last?'

'She was mesmerized watching you execute the two and a half somersault, but then she ran out of the tent.' Socks goes very quiet. 'I saw a well-dressed man go after her.'

'The police detective?'

I wish that Inspecteur Varon would stop warning me about a mass murderer targeting circus queens and displaying their dead bodies like pretty 'angel dolls'. That man looks at me in a way Philippe never did and it scares me. *And* intrigues me. Oh, God, what have I gotten myself into?

'No, it wasn't him,' Socks says, then, 'But I've seen this man hanging around here before. He has an odd way of staring at you, like he can see the bones under your skin.' He grits his teeth. 'Philippe mentioned he's a friend of Jeanne's, a physician willing to help out with serious falls and open wounds. I guess old Socks isn't good enough anymore to tend to our injured. Now we've got some fancy man poking around here.'

I can't let Socks see the terror in my eyes. What if the man is the murderer the detective is looking for? No, that's crazy. Why would he show himself here? That killer surely likes dark alleys in Montmartre. Still...

'We have to find Jeanne, Socks.' I race out of the dressing area, go back to the main tent, walk up and down the rows of seats, looking for a clue, check the menagerie tents, the cookhouse, with Socks right behind me. We head back to the main tent, praying she's there. She isn't.

'She's run away, Lia, just like you did.'

He's right. Why does that bother me so?

'Does Philippe know?'

Socks shakes his head. 'He'd already left by the time I found out.'

'Left? With whom?'

'I saw him getting into a Mercedes touring car with a woman.'

I nod. The new Nazi owner of Le Cirque Casini from the Swope Circus. After our kiss, I urged him to find Jeanne, explain to her, while I picked up Anna and Jakob and put them to bed in the wagon that we're sharing with the Rémon family. Now it seems he didn't. Why is this woman so important he can't find time to help out his daughter deal with what she saw?

Because she's a Nazi. And you don't say no to them.

'It's my fault,' I admit. 'I did this. If I hadn't come back...'

'Don't blame yourself, Lia. We live in troubled times. We don't know if we'll survive until tomorrow, but we keep going, put on the best show we can even if there's a war on.'

I look up at the trapeze, the idle swing still as death high up in the big top, my heart crying out for what I lost so many years ago taken from me again. It's springtime 1943 and the circus season is just beginning, and my child hates me.

I wonder what winter will bring. Will we still be here? Jeanne, Philippe, Socks... and me. I've saved the other children from the Nazis. Can I save my own child?

'What are you going to do?' Socks asks.

'I won't rest until I find Jeanne, Socks. I have to. She is my daughter.'

'I regret I have to break up your cozy family reunion, Fräulein Zollo—'

That voice. That horribly, grating raspy voice is in my ear, his hot breath blowing on the back of my neck. Herr Geller. I can't believe it. I want to run, but where? Socks is beside himself.

'Who *is* this man, Lia?' he says in a loud whisper.

'Go to the Rémon wagon... *save the children*,' I say in a voice too low for the Gestapo to hear when—

Herr Geller pushes Socks out of the way. He stumbles but keeps his balance. I grab the old clown's billowing sleeve, pulling him away from the Nazi, but he looks like he wants to land a punch on the Gestapo agent's fat face. I shake my head vigorously back and forth, my eyes pleading with him to do nothing.

'*Go, Socks, please!*'

'Not until you're safe.'

I close my eyes tight, every lovely moment I've had since I made it back to Cirque Casini breaking apart like dry straw. I know what's coming, and the Gestapo doesn't disappoint.

'You're under arrest, Fräulein, for aiding and abetting the escape of a Jewess and her two children.'

I spin around, keeping my head high. 'You're mistaken, monsieur. I'm Lia di Montieri, not the person you seek.'

'Your red hair didn't fool me.' He laughs. The sound reminds me of a hyena we once had in Circus Richter. 'No mistake, Fräulein. Not after I saw you do that two and a half somersault.' He gives the signal and two armed German soldiers run out of the shadows and grab me. I resist, and I feel the sharp edge of a bayonet rip my leotard. Is that a drop of blood I see on the tip of the sword?

'Take her away!' he orders. Socks blocks them with his balloon body suit. 'She said you made a mistake, monsieur.'

'No mistake, you silly clown. I followed her here from Roubaix and, oh, she's slippery, dragging those two Jewish brats with her, but no one escapes Avicus Geller.' He punches Socks in the stomach. 'Get out of my way or I'll arrest you, too.'

I'm done.

Just like Félix the Clown, the Nazi soldiers march me away from the world of circus that I love. The two children I saved. Socks. Philippe. And Jeanne, the daughter stolen from me now found. All gone in an instant. I'm reminded of the gold spangles sewn onto my costumes. They can withstand tugging and pulling high up under the big top, but once the delicate spangles are ripped from the silk, they flutter down to the earth and lie in the sawdust.

Useless and forgotten. No longer shiny and bright.

Like me.

PART V

WE'LL MEET AGAIN

36

PARIS—2007

Le Cirque Casini
Lia

'I have often imagined what would have happened to my circus family if I hadn't returned to Paris in 1943. Would anything have changed? I think not. The Nazis would still have taken over Le Cirque Casini, Jeanne would still have had that panic attack that made her lose her ability to fly... and The Magician would have gone on murdering girls.

'But I never would have seen Jeanne's eyes, wide and so blue, when I took her place that night on the trapeze, a spark in them like a diamond hitting the light just right for a moment and then it's gone. As if she knew I held the key to a mystery that's haunted her all her life, but couldn't believe it. She didn't want to. She hated me. I had kissed her papa and it hurt her. She didn't understand and she wouldn't listen. She pushed it to the back of her mind. She was still in shock over the murder of Sandrine Aubert. So I said nothing. But I could feel her body shaking, her whole world crashing in that instant. I knew then I must keep my secret for her safety... and mine.'

I slump down in the wingback chair, exhausted. I'm left with a surprising fatigue I hadn't expected, the adrenaline surging in me earlier waning, like the slow drip-drip of a leaky faucet. An *old* faucet. But I'm not giving up the spotlight. Not yet. There's more for me to confess. Like how I forced myself not to dwell on what happened that night and the devastating loss of my daughter all over again. Like how I was determined to get her back. Keep her safe. And, if I was lucky, be part of her life.

God, I'm done in. But I'm not done. Not by a long shot.

Funny, how ego plays a part in how you feel. I refuse to 'act my age' and give in to the old lady syndrome of how we're expected to shut up and disappear into the background. Instead, I dig deep down into myself to find that circus queen I was. I straighten up in the stuffed chair, suck in a deep breath and continue in a loud, clear voice, 'After Jeanne went missing, I concentrated on keeping my circus family together. I had to fight the Nazis to find her. A harrowing experience. In the end, I *did* make a difference and it's that part of the story I shall tell next.

'But not before I recollect myself, allow the trauma and pain I had buried for eighteen years to burst out of me. That night I let go with the pent-up emotions I'd kept under wraps for years. It all came rushing back and I couldn't stop it if I wanted to, the woozy moments of her birth in the convent, the nuns arguing among themselves, the Mother Superior demanding the child, my heart racing like I'm riding a tempest, the memory suddenly clear of what happened that night. I had a child. A daughter.'

I sigh.

'I need a moment. Please.

'So we're going to have an intermission. You know, like they do in the films... or used to. When everyone gets up and stretches their legs, grabs popcorn, heads off to the *toilette*—I intend to be first in line. I'll be back soon with the second half of my story in *Flight of the Stolen Children*. I assure you, the players haven't changed. We'll all be there... Jeanne, Philippe, Gisèle, my lovable clown Socks. Inspecteur Varon, the man I came to know as Berge, and Mox.

And of course, Josephine and Bébé. What's a circus story without the elephants?

Though also the Nazis. Damn them.

I shall also be introducing a player from Berlin: Margit Swope. The new owner of Le Cirque Casini you met briefly before I was arrested by the Gestapo. Yes, *that* Swope from the circus where I performed for the Führer so many years ago. A formidable character who throws the circus into an uproar we never saw coming.

And finally, I wish I didn't have to mention him, but I do. The Magician returns and he's more calculating and deplorable than ever. A plastic surgeon who oozed charm but had a warped sense of propriety and used his healing gift for evil.

'We shall return to 1943, fighting the Boches every inch of the way to liberation. An exciting journey with more twists and turns than I ever saw coming.

'Until we meet again, I shall leave you with this preview... In the next part of my story, my romance takes a strange turn, Socks risks everything to avenge a lost love, and Jeanne falls into the clutches of The Magician.

'And because of my work in the Resistance, I nearly lose my life... and my beautiful daughter.

'So please be patient with me. I won't let you down. I shall return soon.

'I promise.'

* * *

MORE FROM JINA BACARR

The next powerful and emotional historical novel from Jina Bacarr is available to order now here:

https://mybook.to/JinaBacarrNewBackAd

AUTHOR'S NOTE

Ever since I was a young girl and first walked the grand boulevards and narrow cobblestone streets of Paris, I've written about the City of Light. My first attempt was writing a novel à la Nancy Drew when I was thirteen. It was set in Paris and involved a wartime mystery my juvenile heroine was trying to solve while on summer holiday in France with her family. Since I teamed up with Boldwood Books, I've been fortunate to write several stories about the Occupation of Paris. And like most writers, my intrepid past finds its way into each story, like when I found a portrait of my glamorous grandmother who was a ballroom dancer, my encounter with the Roma at a campsite in Belgium, my stint as a perfume model, stories I heard about my socialite great-aunt from Philadelphia... to more serious and deeply personal topics like losing a baby and sexual violence against women.

And yes, there's a story here, too.

The Stolen Children of War takes us behind the scenes of the brave people who risked their lives to rescue Jewish and Roma children from certain death by the Nazis. Imagine you're a mother, knowing the Gestapo are coming for you... and your children. That you'll lose your babies forever, stolen from you by these heinous thieves. Panic doesn't begin to describe the unbelievable vacuum you find yourself in. I had something similar happen to me when I lost my little boy in a mall. Your entire body goes numb, your vision blurs, your eyes searching everything that moves, hoping to see that familiar head of blonde hair bobbing up and down in the crowd, those pudgy cheeks, big blue eyes. Then you ask yourself, what was he wearing today? His favorite coveralls or short pants? T-shirt? You drive yourself mad trying to remember every detail...

My story begins when my son was three years old on a hot Saturday afternoon in a crowded shopping mall. You don't forget these things. The day, the place, the weather. It all becomes critical to finding him. My little boy was a normal, precocious, gregarious little kid who loved baseball, learned to swim at seven months (float, actually, in a pool), and charmed everyone he met. Including me. I adored him.

I was a single mom working two jobs, so having a Saturday off to browse the sales at the local department store was a real treat. The mall overflowed with a frenetic crowd eager to save a few bucks at the weekend event which included a circus festival in full swing in the mall. I promised my little boy we'd go see the clowns after I checked out the sale. We went everywhere together, but boys will be boys and he didn't find costume jewelry shopping exciting, so when I let go of his hand for a few seconds to try on a pair of earrings with the usual 'Stay where I can see you' I should have known better. I turned my back to lay the earrings back down on the counter and when I turned around...

He was gone.

Vanished. Disappeared. My baby was nowhere to be seen.

At first, you can't believe it. This fabulous little kid who drives you crazy at times but always asks you to read to him after supper, who gives you the best hugs ever, was gone. It's a hole in your heart so big you can't fix it. Empty like a fat round balloon someone popped with a pin. It's that quick.

Then your mom superpower kicks in.

And nothing can stop you from finding him... You're racing around like a Marvel comic book heroine at super speed. You ask everyone if they've seen him, while holding back tears so you don't lose focus. You don't stop for a second. The more ground you cover, you tell yourself, the quicker you'll find him. I ran out of the store into the mall teeming with kids and their parents. Grabbing at the chance he was headed for the clowns at the other end, I went there, came back. Nope, didn't find him. Here's the really, really scary part... that little voice in your head that says, *What if he ran outside the mall and he gets hit by a car?*

I melted into a puddle of despair.

It gets worse.

Minutes go by. No one has seen him; the crowd is getting bigger, meaner looking in your eyes, and then you get hit in the pit of your stomach with the one scenario you can't, won't, believe.

What if my little boy was kidnapped? Stolen? Right here in the mall. What if?

It happens.

No, God, he's only three years old. He's my baby. My chest hurts so bad, I let the tears well up then overflow—I can't stop them—and head back to the department store. It seems like an eternity has passed, but it's only a few minutes. Time to bring in help. No cellphones then, so I jump onto the store escalator going up to the offices on the third floor where I could ask security for assistance.

Then I hear over the store loudspeaker—

'We have a little lost boy about three years old in the men's department...'

Little lost boy, I scream inside. Oh, my God, it's him! My baby.

Without thinking I could fall and get killed, I spin around on the escalator steps heading up at a fast pace to the next floor and start walking down the moving steps, muttering, 'Excuse me, excuse me.' I never realized how difficult it is to go down a moving escalator going up. I turned my ankle, nearly fell, but grabbed onto the handle rest and made it back down to the main floor.

I did it.

With my heart in my throat, I race to the men's department, praying it's him, that he's okay and he isn't terrified, crying his eyes out.

Did I say crying? Not my kid. The little charmer was sitting on the floor surrounded by a bevy of salesladies and female customers, laughing and having the time of his life, eating candy out of a white paper bag the clerk gave him, fawning over him like he was a little prince.

My heart burst with joy like a big yellow sunflower raising its face to the sky. My little boy was safe. I ran to him, crying, 'It's Mom, I'm here, baby, are you okay?'

'Here, Mom, candy!'

The ladies started clapping and crying at the same time while I hugged my little angel so tight I never wanted to let him go. My story has a happy ending, but for so many mothers, Jewish and Roma, their children were stolen from them. When I began putting together my circus novel during the Occupation of Paris, I was struck by the idea that many Jewish and Roma circus people hid in plain sight in the circus, but what happened to their children? And how many others sought refuge in the circus?

So I created the fabulous trapeze *artiste*, Lia di Montieri, and her quest to help these children escape the Nazis as well as find her own lost child stolen from her at birth.

ACKNOWLEDGMENTS

I can't thank enough the amazing team at Boldwood Books for making it happen. My fabulous editor, Isobel Akenhead, who always has my back. She's a good soul and has a wonderful sense of story that keeps the emotions high and the action coming at you. Isobel does a great job of bringing me back to earth when I get too carried away. She has a big heart and she brings that sensibility to her work, and I thank her for that. She also brings her editorial knowledge and expertise to every story and I shall be forever grateful to her for her belief in me.

I also want to thank Nia Beynon, Sales & Marketing Director, who brought me into the Boldwood Books family and is always there for us authors. The entire marketing team headed up by Claire Fenby. And CEO and Founder Amanda Ridout, who never fails to astonish me with her energy and innovation in publishing to make Boldwood Books an industry leader and winner of several major book awards, including the recent Independent Publisher of the Year at the British Book Awards 2025.

Thank you also to my copyeditor Jennifer Kay Davies and my proofreader Arbaiah Aird for their help in making the story the best it can be. And to you, my readers, the moms and moms-to-be, grandmothers and every woman who's ever held a baby in her arms and kissed their furry little heads and held them close to their breast and marveled at these astonishing little creatures. How they fill your heart and make it whole.

Let us never forget the brave mothers who gave up their children so they might live and have children of *their* own. Thank you... and though you may hear it many times, it's never enough, so I shall say it once again.

We must never forget.

ABOUT THE AUTHOR

Jina Bacarr is a US-based historical romance author of over 10 previous books. She has been a screenwriter, journalist and news reporter, but now writes full-time and lives in LA. Jina's novels have been sold in 9 territories.

Download your exclusive bonus content from Jina Bacarr here:

Visit Jina's website: www.jinabacarr.wordpress.com

Follow Jina on social media here:

facebook.com/JinaBacarr.author
x.com/JinaBacarr
instagram.com/jinabacarr
bookbub.com/authors/jina-bacarr
goodreads.com/jina_bacarr
tiktok.com/@jinabacarrauthor

ALSO BY JINA BACARR

Her Lost Love

The Runaway Girl

The Resistance Girl

The Lost Girl In Paris

The Orphans of Berlin

The Stolen Children of War

The Wartime Paris Sisters

Sisters at War

Sisters of the Resistance

Letters from
the past

Discover page-turning
historical novels from
your favourite authors
and be transported
back in time

Join our book club
Facebook group

https://bit.ly/SixpenceGroup

Sign up to our
newsletter

https://bit.ly/LettersFrom
PastNews

Boldwood

Boldwood Books is an award-winning fiction publishing company seeking out the best stories from around the world.

Find out more at www.boldwoodbooks.com

Join our reader community for brilliant books, competitions and offers!

Follow us
@BoldwoodBooks
@TheBoldBookClub

Sign up to our weekly deals newsletter

https://bit.ly/BoldwoodBNewsletter

www.ingramcontent.com/pod-product-compliance
Lightning Source LLC
Chambersburg PA
CBHW011759010726
47497CB00012B/3206